SO... IT'S DEFINITELY ALIENS

He fell from the stars. Now she's falling for him.

Raven did *not* sign up for this saving-the-world crap.

But after unlocking a galactic map, surviving an attack from the deadly robotic Enil, and kissing her alien coworker, she's officially on the run—with the fate of planets possibly lodged in her brain.

Now the Enil are hunting her. So is the government. And, because the universe has a sense of humor, Raven's stuck in close quarters with the undercover alien who's determined to keep things *strictly* professional.

Which would be fine…except, as Raven and Sky race to stay ahead of their enemies and track down his elusive partner, Bast, the unresolved tension between them crackles hotter than Sky's spark powers.

She's not sure what's more dangerous at this point: evil robots from outer space, the star map and what it's doing to her, or the feelings she's developing for Sky.

The bad news? It's definitely aliens.

The worse news? *She's falling for one of them.*

STARFALLING

It's Definitely Not Aliens
Book 2

ELLE DEYESSO

Published by Waking Dream LLC

PO Box 15065

Fort Wayne, IN, 46885, United States

Cover design by Danielle Shafer

Interior design and formatting by Vellum

Editing by Danielle Fine – Design by Definition

For more information, visit: www.elledeyesso.com

❀ Formatted with Vellum

This one is for the weirdos. The ones who got in trouble for reading books under desks, daydreamed about faraway worlds, and never quite felt like they fit in. You may still feel like that now.

But here we are. Sharing space. And aliens.

*Here's to being **weird** and **proud**.*

Also for my husband. You're the best co-pilot ever on this crazy spaceship ride. You are my everything.

Content Note

This book contains mentions of grief, particularly related to the loss of parental figures.

While grief is not a central focus of the story, it is a shared experience between both main characters and is discussed openly. If this is a tender subject for you, please take care while reading.

Other notes:
Seizures/seizure activity
Trauma- or PTSD-adjacent memories
Mention of near-drowning
Explicit, consensual sexual activity (on-page)

CODE GREEN
GRID D442: aerial contact lost.
No radar, no visuals.
(Lens caps were off this time. Dave triple-checked)
No confirmed Type 2 or Type 3 activity.

Possible explanations:
- Cloaking
- Dimensional hop
- A misidentified bird or frisbee
- They're gone

Visit www.fetr.net for updates
Join our Skywatch Spotters and get a free hat!

To unsubscribe, reply STOP
We are the Friends of the Extraterrestrial Races
Absence is still data. Keep your eyes on the sky.

Chapter 1

PANTSLESS PANIC WITH PLADIANS

I was about to get naked with an alien.

Not *totally* strip-to-your-skin, all-the-bits-out naked, but definitely at least partially naked. I was shedding clothing in his vicinity.

I would be *sans* pants.

Even if it wasn't full-on nakedness, it counted for something. Especially since I'd been fantasizing about getting *any* kind of naked with this particular alien since before I'd discovered he was from a planet called Pladia.

Unfortunately for me, the circumstances were all wrong. First and foremost: he wanted me to immediately put clothing back on.

"Just…change into *these*?" I whispered, shaking out the green T-shirt and holding it up. I wasn't sure why I was whispering. "What about paying?"

I wrinkled my nose at the clothing. Ridiculous, considering our predicament. But the shirt was at least four sizes too big, the same neon color as my terrible work uniform, and clashed with the traffic-cone orange basketball shorts.

The alien—who went by the name Sky Acosta—let out a huff that bordered on annoyed without looking away from the crack in the door of the shoebox-sized dressing room we'd crammed into. He didn't answer.

I arched an eyebrow and tried not to let my own irritation rise. A little shoplifting should've been the least of my worries, but intergalactic stakes or not, *stealing* wasn't my thing. He also hadn't exactly been communicative since he'd slammed the car into park, told me to grab my bag, and towed me into this tiny mall in the middle of Nowhereville, Kentucky.

And now, apparently, he was ordering me to steal clothes. Desperate times called for…illegal measures? Was that a saying?

I tried again, leaning a little closer and raising my voice to a normal volume. "Sky, are you *sure* that was License 16 out there or—"

I forgot what I was about to say when he straightened and turned, nearly knocking me over in the process. I stepped back instinctively—but there was nowhere to go, and I smacked my elbow on the scuffed cinderblock wall.

"Ow." Grimacing, I rubbed it.

"Sorry." He rocked onto his heels with a wince. "I'll just…"

He shuffled away half a step, but it wasn't like he had room to retreat. His broad shoulders took up more than half the teeny stall.

I tried not to notice.

"It's fine." Why did they call it a funny bone when it was decidedly *not* funny? "Are you sure it was them?"

It seemed…I don't know. I'd say hard to believe, but my suspension of disbelief had gotten tossed out the window around the time I'd landed myself in the middle of an intergalactic conspiracy.

Two days. It'd only been two days since I'd gotten handsy with the alien artifact and escaped the Enil. It'd been quiet, too. No glowing orbs in the sky. No evil robots. Not even the secret government task force Sky was certain were involved now that things had gotten messier.

Granted, the alien-metal cuff on my wrist was hopefully doing its job scrambling the signal I was emitting, which helped us dodge at least the Enil.

But not License 16. Clearly.

Sky sighed and pulled off his black ball cap, jammed a hand through his messy, mink-brown curls, and fixed me with the *Look*. A tight-lipped, exasperated one I'd become way too familiar with since we'd fled One Willow.

To be fair, we were both on edge. Lack of sleep and a spontaneous cross-country road trip after barely surviving those aforementioned robots would do that to a person.

At the thought, my palm itched. I curled my fingers around the strange white swirls and shapes barely visible on the skin there—the only outward evidence of this entire messed-up situation. Well, besides the alien crammed into this pseudo-closet with me.

"No, it might not have been them." Sky's low concession jerked me from my thoughts. His *Look* had faded, and he wore a faint frown instead, his twilight-blue eyes intent on mine. "But I think we should err on the side of caution, don't you?"

They were pretty eyes. Human eyes. You'd never guess he hailed from a whole other planet. His totally-not-freaky synthetic skin suit had given him a human form—a whole, bona fide human body, actually—and those ridiculous cheekbones and strong jaw were shadowed by day-old stubble and a few bruises from his battle with the Enil. He passed for a beaten-up Midwestern nice guy in his mid- to late-twenties.

Albeit a really hot, way-out-of-my-league Midwestern nice guy in his mid- to late-twenties, especially when he gave that charming half smile. It made that rogue dimple pop—

"Rae?" he asked. "Did you hear me?"

I jolted. Shit, I'd been staring dreamily up at him, and he'd been speaking. I cleared my throat, adjusting the pile of clothing.

He was giving me the Look again.

"Yeah, I heard you," I said. When he slowly raised his brows in disbelief, I relented. "Okay, no. Sorry. Zoned out. What'd you say?"

A tiny muscle in Sky's temple bounced, and his inhalation was slow and steady, as if he fought for patience. "I said, even if I'm wrong and that wasn't them tailing us off the highway, it doesn't hurt to be careful, right?"

"Right." I shifted, gathering the clothes to my chest. "I'm just not sure why I'm changing—"

"On the off chance they saw us coming in. I think we should split up. I'll create a diversion, too." He paused to swipe a hand over his mouth. "We probably should've ditched the SUV sooner."

We didn't know for *certain* they'd put two-and-two together yet, but I was sure being seen together and then vanishing into thin air after that attack on my university would have raised some eyebrows. Especially my friends and family's—

I forced the thought away. Now wasn't the time to think about that.

Sky seemed to sense he'd swayed me, turning back to peer through the crack in the door again. "You've got to trust me. This isn't my first run-in with License 16."

"Okay." Steeling my spine like I was facing a firing squad, I turned to the mirror. I really shouldn't have been worried about fashion choices, considering I'd been wearing the same jeans and long-sleeved shirt for over a day. They were covered in chalky dust, questionable smudges, soot, and lots of wrinkles. My hazel eyes were shadowed and bloodshot from lack of sleep, and the bruise on my forehead where I'd crashed headlong into a vending machine had turned an ugly purple-yellow. It was one of many. Including the six-fingered Enil handprint hidden beneath my blouse.

The changing room's stark, overhead bulbs weren't doing me any favors, either. Seriously, it was inhumane, putting that kind of lighting in changing rooms. I slumped in dejection.

Sky spoke over his shoulder. "I'm going to create a distraction, and you walk out of here. Get to the parking lot, and I'll meet you there. It'll be simple."

I tore my attention from my reflection—and the zit forming on my chin—and nodded at the back of his head. Throw on this crazy outfit and stroll past the government agents hunting us. Super simple.

I managed to keep my sarcasm to myself as I dumped the clothing at my feet, preparing to strip. "What kind of diversion?"

In response, he lifted a hand. A static charge raised the hair on my arms, and a second later, tiny blue sparks danced over his finger-tips—a brief crackle before disappearing.

"Of course. Your suit magic." Would it ever not be heart-stop-ping, watching him activate the synth-skin? Between that, and his ability to turn invisible…

"It's not magic. It's science." He twisted to slant me a faint, tight smile. "Hurry."

"Okay." I twirled my finger at him, biting my lip. A flush crept up my neck. "Can you turn around?"

He gave a start and whipped his head to face the wall. "Sorry. Um, go ahead."

Go ahead and get mostly naked. No big deal. Just take my clothes off around the man I'd been daydreaming about for the better part of a year.

Quit stalling. Rolling my lips together, I wrestled the shirt from my body and let it drop before looking down at my plain cotton bra. I couldn't remember the last time I'd washed it. When I got home, I'd be rethinking my laundering habits.

I smoothed my greasy blonde braid down before reaching for the button of my jeans, ready to shove my pants down. I couldn't help but glance Sky's way.

He waited with his head down, palm braced on the wall. The fingers of his free hand tapped against his thigh in a rhythmic motion that gave away his impatience. His white shirt—he seemed to have a perpetual supply of those stashed in his car—stretched taut over his tense back.

In another life, this would've been an answer to prayers, a changing room striptease with my hot bartender crush. But that was before. Now Sky was off-limits.

Friends, I reminded myself. *We are* friends.

The alien from outer space had firmly put my ass in the friend zone. And his own, too. I'd agreed because, after all, it'd be difficult to focus on escaping bad guys and saving my brain if we were constantly distracted by getting naked. Naked *together,* I mean.

Possibly kissing.

Like we'd already kissed.

I swallowed, forcing the memory away. Which was harder than it sounded since I was trying to figure out the best way to get my clothes off when this space was small enough that my elbow brushed Sky's side as I bent to grab the shirt. When I straightened hastily, he'd shifted forward until he was practically plastered against the wall.

Fine by me. For the record, having no deodorant while trapped in a confined space with the guy I wanted to climb like a tree was my personal version of hell. I'd been eyeing the perfume counter when we'd—

The overhead speaker squealed to life and an announcement spilled out: "*Attention, all customers and employees. The mall will be closing temporarily due to a reported gas leak. Please proceed to the nearest exit in a calm and orderly manner. Authorities are on site to assist with evacuation protocols. For your safety, exit the building immediately. Please refrain from panicking. The situation is under control. Thank you for your cooperation.*"

It began to repeat, but I'd heard enough. The blood drained from my face, and I inhaled sharply, clutching the baggy shirt to my front. Sky twisted to look up at the disembodied voice's origin. Shouts echoed from the department store beyond our changing room, and something crashed to the ground, shattering with a tinkle of breaking glass.

So much for staying calm. That sure sounded like panic to me.

"That's not good, is it?" I whispered. Gas leak, my skeptical backside.

"No," Sky said, eyeing the distant speaker. His mouth had hardened into a thin, somber line. "I'd say that just confirmed it. License 16 is here."

The warning repeated, followed by instructions for exiting the building. My heartbeat picked up until it felt like it was trying to punch its way out of my chest. Adrenaline tingled in my limbs.

Suddenly, my earlier issues with the clothing seemed ridiculous. We had to get out of here. I tightened my grip on the shirt.

"They're clearing this place out, which means it's going to be harder to blend in—" Sky turned his head…and only then seemed to realize I was half naked, hiding behind the bundle of glaringly green fabric.

The speaker buzzed as his eyes widened. I froze like a deer in headlights.

"Working on it," I muttered, blood rushing to my face. "If you could, um, give me a minute." I stared determinedly at the wall behind him. He couldn't see anything beyond my shoulders and bra straps, but it was that *awareness*…

That stupid, ever-present awareness that hadn't gotten the friend-zone message.

Recovering, Sky spun on his heel. "Sorry. I didn't mean…" He cleared his throat and waved a hand in my general direction. "Go ahead."

I swore I'd caught a faint redness staining his cheeks, but maybe I'd imagined it. Surely Sky wasn't blushing at my naked shoulders in the middle of running for our lives. That was my job. My cheeks blazed hot enough I was surprised my hair wasn't smoking.

Taking a deep breath, I got to work slipping the shirt over my head. I wrestled my stiff, dirty jeans off, too, kicking them aside and dragging on the silky basketball shorts instead. My fingers shook, pulse kicking.

"Are you done?" Sky asked.

It was as good as it was going to get. "Yeah."

I'd barely finished speaking before he'd turned again. I wasn't prepared for the way his dark eyes flitted down, taking in my attire. It didn't help my rapid heart rate. His expression gave nothing away.

Stepping close, he pulled off his hat and gestured for me to lift my head. "Put this on, too."

All too aware of my fiery blush, I took it from him, trapping my braid under it and pulling it tight. Tugging at my shirt, I glanced in the mirror again. At least the hat hid some of my fire engine-red complexion.

Sky took in my reflection until, apparently satisfied, he started to twist toward the door—only to pause and look back. His expression was serious. "When I say so, I want you to go straight for the exit, okay? Do you remember where we came in?" I nodded. "Good. Head that way. I'll make sure you're in the clear."

My stomach dipped. We were doing this. Making a run for it. For some reason, despite the fact that I'd spent the entire last *day* running, this felt more dangerous.

My mouth was desert-dry. "Okay. What about you?" I managed to turn in a tight circle, facing away from the mirror. It brought me up close to him in the itty-bitty changing room. Close enough that my borrowed hat's bill nearly bumped his chest. I tipped my head back to see his face.

"Me?" he repeated, angling his chin down.

"Yes, you. What if they catch you?" After all, he was the one more likely to end up in places run by people in lab coats.

"They won't." He tried for a smile that was too tight-lipped to be comforting. "Maybe we'll get lucky, and it actually *is* a gas leak."

An incredulous laugh slipped out of me. "I don't know whether that would be good luck or bad."

"A little of both." He glanced at the door, then me. "They're not going to catch me, Rae. I've made it this long without them getting their hands on me, and I've got the synth-skin's abilities. Just focus on getting out of here, okay? Blend in, keep a low profile, and wait for me in the parking lot. I'll be right behind you. You'll be safe."

Before I could formulate a response, he reached for me. I swayed in surprise as he adjusted the bill of the hat, pushing it back so I didn't have to crane my neck quite as much. Heart skipping, I slowly raised my eyes to his.

"Be careful," he murmured. His closeness coupled with his husky voice was enough to send butterflies the size of airplanes surging to life in my stomach. I'd gotten better at seeing through his calm façade, and that was worry softening the edges of his mouth, tipping it down. A mouth directly in my line of sight.

But then he pulled back as quickly as he'd leaned in. The airplanes nose-dived, and I wrenched my gaze from his lips. He was already turning away, putting space between us. As if the moment hadn't happened.

"Do I meet you at the SUV?" I asked to fill the sudden, tense silence.

In the distance, yelling rose above the repeated announcement. Somewhere closer, a door slammed. Bending, I snatched up my bag, shoving my discarded clothing into it.

I'd just straightened and shrugged the strap over my shoulder when Sky slid the lock on the door. He answered casually as he tugged it open.

"No, not the SUV. We're going to steal a car."

Chapter 2

BABY'S FIRST FELONY

We were going to *steal a car*.

I'd been worried about these clothes, and Sky's plan was to *steal a freaking car*?

Cold sweat pooled in my armpits and trailed down my spine beneath the baggy T-shirt. I did my best to slow my choppy breathing as I wound through the racks toward the department store's entrance, head down. My legs felt strange and tingly. Probably a result of the gallons of adrenaline dumping into my system.

We're going to steal a car.

I didn't think my life had gotten *felony* stressful.

What would my mom think about me now? My pulse skipped at the thought. Sky'd insisted we go radio silent, and I hadn't even been able to call anyone to explain. Not Mom, or work. Not even Amelia. They'd all be worried.

Of course, not as worried as they'd all be after seeing my mugshot on the news following my arrest for grand theft auto.

I shuddered, quickening my pace. I hated that it—stealing a *car* —made sense. Like I was slowly becoming someone who rationalized law-breaking. Wearing stolen clothing. Plotting *this*.

But it was an obvious solution. We'd been spotted in the SUV.

We had to ditch it. When Sky'd told me to grab my things when we parked, I hadn't thought much of it in our rush to lose ourselves in the mall's late-afternoon shopping crowd.

But now I knew. He'd had me do it because he'd already had a plan. One that involved possible jail time.

I gripped my book bag's straps tightly enough that my knuckles turned white. The speaker overhead repeated the evacuation instructions every couple of minutes. Around me, customers and employees shouted, scrambling for the exits. Nobody had tackled me yet. I was almost out of the store. Once free, it'd be easy enough to follow the shining tiled floor back to where we'd come in.

I could do this. My heart was beating so fast, I felt it in my eyeballs. I wiped my slick palms on the silky orange shorts and forced myself to keep moving. Why had Sky dressed me like a construction worker in high-vis? Not exactly inconspicuous. I ducked my head, tugging my ball cap down. Like it'd help hide the neon green billboard I was wearing.

I kept my face lowered as I waved away the cloying cloud of floral scents by the perfume counter. A few more steps, and I passed through the store's entrance. Everything echoed out here—the shouts, the commotion, the speaker's announcement. My knees wobbled, but I turned and started down the hallway.

All around me, people poured toward the mall's large, multi-doored entrance. The parking lot waited beyond.

A parking lot with a whole lot of cars ripe for the stealing.

My stomach plummeted straight past my dusty, dirty shoes. I shoved the swell of anxiety aside. First things first. I had to get out of here without being spotted.

If anyone was even after us. I didn't see any suspicious suits—or police—but that didn't mean they weren't here somewhere—

BOOM.

An explosion rocked the building. I staggered, catching myself on the nearest display rack. Packaged watches rained down, and lights flickered. Screams rang out, and the sound of pounding feet drummed as the crowd of mostly orderly people panicked. Disoriented, I clung to the watch display as the fire alarm's high-pitched sirens shrieked to life.

That sound. I flinched, chest tightening. Last time I'd heard that, it'd been…

The Enil. They'd been attacking the university.

But that couldn't be it. Surely, they hadn't…

No. I was wearing the bracelet. Clasping the shiny, purple cuff—the cuff that was *supposed* to be protecting me—I pushed off the display rack and spun in place.

I didn't see Sky or any sign of alien robots. No evidence of a gas leak, either. It had to just be License 16's excuse to empty the mall.

But then…what had that explosion been?

Screw it. I wasn't sticking around to find out. Everyone else was rushing, too, so I broke into a run. A frightened mother raced with a stroller in front of me, her toddler wailing as the wheels bumped over tile. The evacuees flowed around the corner leading to the mall's entrance.

I'd almost reached it when my instincts prickled. Slowing, I jogged to the walkway's side and paused in front of a shoe store.

Maybe the boom had been Sky.

The lone security guard I spotted was too busy huffing and puffing as he ran for the exit to notice me. He was getting the heck out of Dodge, too. No one paid me any mind.

Which also meant I'd worn this dumb disguise for nothing. Maybe it'd be helpful for the *car-stealing* I was about to participate in.

Guts roiling, I turned and headed for the corner and the doors beyond. I'd made it only three more steps before another rumble vibrated the floor, pitching it enough that I stumbled and flattened myself against the wall this time.

Dread spider-walked down my spine as I slowly straightened. Okay, *that* wasn't Sky. He could turn into a storm in a skin suit, but he didn't make whole buildings shudder.

The lights overhead flickered again, and I gasped as, with a crackling pop, they went out, plunging the corridor into blackness lit only by the white glow of emergency lighting. I couldn't hear anything through the rise and fall of the ear-splitting alarm.

But I didn't need to.

I knew this tingle in the air. I knew that strange hum vibrating deep in my bones. The sensation was like millions of crawling insects burrowing beneath my skin—and just as horrifying.

It meant this mall escape had suddenly gotten much more dangerous.

The Enil were here.

I *ran*. This time, I threw all I had into it. The corner drew nearer. A glance back showed a handful of dark forms sprinting toward me from past the department store, details lost to the darkness. It was impossible to tell whether they were fleeing like me or were *after* me, but suddenly it didn't matter as much. I darted around the curve.

Only to scream as something barreled right *through* the wall to my right.

Display-case glass shattered. Drywall cracked, dust rained down, and sparks sizzled as a panel of overhead lights crashed from the ceiling. I covered my head, cowering in place. Screams, alarms, and the rumble and boom of settling debris pounded my eardrums.

Chaos. This was chaos. The kind that had somehow become my life lately.

Trembling, my insides cramping with fear, I lifted my head, peering through the dust cloud. Pale light shone in rays through the grit settling around me.

Oh. Oh no. The light was coming from *me*.

I lifted my arm and spread my fingers. My hand—my marked palm, specifically—was glowing. Bright white shone from the glyphs like they were illuminated from the inside. Which I supposed they were. By alien tech I still didn't quite understand.

The garbled, mechanical howl split the air like Godzilla's signature roar filtered through a broken auto-tune.

I clutched my hand tight, fear chilling my insides. I knew that sound, too. I heard it in my nightmares, and now, it threatened to stop my heart. Panic jolted every nerve ending.

Somehow, the Enil had found us. I needed to get out of here *now*. How had they tracked us? Was it *me*—

A moving shadow materialized at my side. I opened my mouth to scream again—only to choke on it when a hand wrapped around my upper arm. A second later, a tense Sky materialized, shedding his suit's cloaking tech and melting into view.

I was too freaked out to even acknowledge that weirdness.

"The Enil—" I started, raising my voice over the panic and chaos.

"I know. You're going to have to go the other way." He pulled me in a circle, pushing me back in the direction I'd come. "Get to the other exit. I'm right behind you!"

I'd taken one step before another roar sounded, this one much closer. A sharp *pop-pop-pop* echoed—gunshots. Someone was fighting back.

I didn't stay to find out who. I took off, barely pausing to see if Sky was following. He was, of course, easily, his long legs far outpacing me, though he checked his stride to stay close. My heart drummed against my ribs. Rounding the corner, I chanced a glance back then gasped when Sky slammed to a halt and yanked me to his side, shielding my glowing, fisted hand with his body.

Then I saw why. A group of uniformed men and women in body armor formed a line in front of us, bristling with guns.

For a second, I gaped at them, and they stared at us. Then a woman stepped forward, gesturing sharply. "You need to evacuate! Get out of the mall!"

Oh—oh *shit*! If it weren't for Sky's grip, I'd have stumbled back a step. I knew her. I'd seen her before in the anthropology hall after the tablet explosion. She was one of the government suits who'd been there, looking on, while the police interviewed me. She wore the same tight bun as before, only she'd exchanged her black blazer and slacks for a dark uniform and bulletproof vest.

She either didn't recognize me or didn't care, because she shouted, "*Now*! For your own safety!"

Damn it. Had this stupid outfit and hat really worked?

Before I could process it, another garbled howl split the air, and I stopped breathing, clutching Sky's waist with my free hand. The sound was terrifyingly close.

Sky's hold on my arm tightened, and when I caught his eyes, there was a grim determination in them. He was readying himself for a fight. But against whom? The Enil or License 16?

An incredulous huff escaped me. If given the choice between the angry robotic alien or the armed humans, I knew which I'd prefer.

Well, *neither*, but—

"*Go!*" shouted one of the government agents as they rushed at us.

I tensed for an attack, and Sky shifted in front of me…but they only surged past us and toward the far corner. Toward the sound of heavy impacts thudding against tile. Each one shook the floor, a *thwump, whur, thwump, whur, thwump*. Gears whined and shrieked.

Those were footsteps.

Which meant it was too late. The Enil was coming.

No, not coming. *Already here.* Even Sky's broad shoulders didn't block what was lumbering around the bend.

A tiny sound escaped me, half whimper, half curse.

Sky had told me once that no two Enil looked exactly alike; they were built from whatever scrap happened to be lying around the planet they landed on. This one was no exception. The hulking suit in front of us wasn't the alien itself, just the vessel, a walking shell for the canned consciousness they launched across the stars.

Parts of this shell had clearly come from a washer and dryer. The Maytag label was still visible on one panel, and the whole thing had the bulky, boxy frame of an appliance graveyard escapee. I shrank back as it stomped forward, a seven-foot-tall horror on four thick, stumpy legs made of levers and gears.

The arms—what the hell was wrong with its arms? Three, writhing, tube-like appendages thrashed through the air like angry snakes. Its head was a mishmash of shiny blue plating, jagged metal fused with what looked like a television screen. When it swiveled toward us, two glowing green eyes fixed on where we stood. Their impact burrowed beneath my skin, stirring horror.

Because this wasn't some mindless monster. The Enil had wiped out entire *planets*. Looking like pure nightmare fuel was just an added bonus.

From somewhere deep inside that horrible trash heap of a body, a mechanical roar filtered out. It sounded like an angry train. Except this train had claws and wanted my brain.

And it was coming right for us.

Sky whirled, dislodging the death grip I had on his ribs. "Run!" he barked, shoving me. "Keep going for the other door. Don't look back!"

He didn't have to tell me twice. I forced my locked-up legs to move and sprinted with all I had. My ragged breathing echoed in my ears as I pumped my arms, moving faster, faster, pushed by the fire alarm, the shouting, and the sudden crack of gunfire as License 16 engaged the Enil.

They were indeed fighting back, but I knew it wouldn't do much. Nothing would.

The groan of shifting metal and its bone-rattling roar told me the Enil wasn't a fan, though. I disobeyed Sky's order and glanced over my shoulder just as I passed the department store entrance—

And skidded to a stop.

Sky wasn't behind me. He'd vanished, in fact. Had he activated his suit?

In the mall corridor, License 16 had the Enil surrounded, half-obscured by clouds of smoke. Muzzle flashes cut through the haze, brilliant white against the darkness. But the bullets pinged harmlessly off the Enil's thick metal armor, littering the floor in tiny piles.

The creature struck, sweeping out one snake-like arm. I bit the inside of my cheek, a shouted warning lodging in my chest. The first few agents were flung like rag dolls, slamming into the walls and sliding down. They didn't get back up.

Throat tight, I balled my hands into fists. Orange light leaked between the fingers of my right one. The Enil had only one real weakness: the power source embedded in the center of its body. Even that was nearly impossible to reach. Especially with human weapons.

They didn't stand a chance.

Only one person I knew did.

Or rather, one alien.

As if on cue, a blur of motion sliced through the smoky dark, darting behind the human agents. I sucked in a breath. *Sky*.

A second later, a bolt of blue lightning exploded from nowhere and struck the Enil dead center. Familiar *Pladian* lightning. With a mechanical groan, the creature staggered back, crashing into the wall hard enough to send cracks racing across the surface. Pieces broke off and collapsed into piles of drywall and mortar, and I threw up an arm as the ceiling shuddered ominously.

I should've been running, but watching Sky fight rooted me to the spot. The shimmer of masked movement. The sparks. The eerie blue glow.

It was like something out of a movie—a dream—only this was *real* and happening in front of me.

I snapped out of it when the Enil pushed itself upright with those writhing tentacle-arms, shaking off dust and debris like it barely noticed. The ground rumbled as it lumbered forward a step. Sucking in a breath, I staggered backward, prepared to run again.

As if he'd had the same thought, Sky's form rippled and vanished again. But the distraction had worked. License 16 had fallen back, dragging their downed agents with them. I'd been too mesmerized by the Pladian to notice.

Which left me. The Enil's glowing green gaze swept the room, searching…and I realized I was still standing there, gawking like an idiot, my balled-up hand a barely-there glow.

I spun and bolted, holding Sky's hat in place as I tore down the corridor. The soles of my worn-out shoes skidded on slick tile. Sunlight gleamed ahead, a glint of hope at the end of the chaos.

The entrance.

I could make it.

My lungs burned, and sweat cooled on my skin, but I didn't dare slow down. I tore down the walkway at full tilt, dodging a display of sunglasses and leaping over a pair of abandoned shopping bags.

Almost there. A dozen yards. Half that.

I had half a second to register dark forms on the other side of the glass, obscured by smoke, and then the doors I was aiming for burst open. I slid to a stop and whipped my arm behind my back as a group of armored soldiers poured in, toting heavy guns. They wore helmets and body armor—all in all, they looked way more prepared than the people in measly bulletproof vests. Even the way they moved was more precise as they flooded through the entrance and fanned out.

Were they part of License 16, or was this some new threat? Their uniforms weren't marked, and they weren't exactly carrying badges.

The question was: were they worse than the extraterrestrial monster rampaging behind me?

Before I could decide, a shrieking, metallic roar tore through the hall. Piercing and *loud.* I clamped my hands over my ears as the glass windows and displays exploded. Emergency lights sparked and burst. Smoke clogged my lungs, my nostrils. The floor bucked beneath my feet like something alive.

Nope. Not worse.

They also seemed not to care one iota about me. The new soldiers were already moving, assembling in formation. I flung myself against the wall as gunfire cracked the air in staccato flashes and ear-splitting reports. They were firing at the Enil.

It kept coming anyway. And meanwhile, the light coming from my squeezed-tight hand hadn't faded. I tucked it behind my back. Had the Enil spotted me through all this? Did it recognize the halix's signature, despite the cuff?

I was trapped. Trapped between the evil alien robot and armed humans who had no idea what they were up against.

But, for a moment, they were distracted. Gunfire rang out. Electricity sizzled and crackled. The Enil's screech pummeled my eardrums.

Taking advantage of the commotion, I pushed off the wall and vaulted over debris. No one tried to stop me. The ground trembled beneath heavy thuds, and more gunfire split the air.

I didn't look back as I hurled myself through the broken doorframes. Shards crunched under my feet as I spilled out onto the sidewalk. In the sun's glare, the light from my hand was barely detectable. I'd made it out.

The madness outside rivaled that within.

I slowed to catch my breath, taking it all in. Red and blue lights strobed across the pavement. Smoke hazed the air, blurring the scene, and firefighters, cops, and paramedics shouted over the rising din of honking horns and screeching tires. I spotted several blacked-out vehicles, but they were nearly lost in the flood of people surging through the parking lot, some screaming, some stumbling. In the middle of it all, a news van weaved through the madness, swerving to avoid fleeing pedestrians.

It was pandemonium. Flashbacks from TWU—the attack on the university—swam back. Water and flames, screaming. Sky's body tumbling through the air.

Destruction followed in my wake lately.

Squeezing my hands into fists, I picked up my pace again, rounding the corner until the doors were out of sight. Only then did I stagger to a halt by the curb, bracing my hands on my knees and doubling over, gasping for air, heart hammering. I flinched as muffled gunfire cracked behind me, followed by the garbled, mechanical roar of the Enil.

They were fighting it. Humans were fighting back.

It was a losing battle, though. I pinched my lips together, a knife of sickening guilt plunging deep. The Enil were relentless.

Sky was right: they were single-minded in their purpose. It *was* just like the university. Was it *my fault* that thing had shown up here, too? The cuff was supposed to prevent them from tracking me.

Nausea rose, but I swallowed all the turmoil for now, straightening. I couldn't afford to spiral. On the off chance it *was* here for me, I needed to put as much distance between me and the murdery spacebot as possible.

I scanned the parking lot. On to the next hurdle: the car. Sky had told me to meet him. I squinted against the dust and smoke clouding the air. I didn't see him anywhere. What if he hadn't made it out?

Before I could process my next move, tires shrieked and an

engine revved high. I turned just in time to see a small black sedan barreling along the sidewalk's edge. Dull sunlight glinted off the windshield, obscuring the driver, but it was coming right for me.

I grabbed my bag's straps, ready to bolt…but then it passed into the building's shadow, and I made him out through the glass.

Not License 16. *Sky*.

With what I assumed was a *stolen car*.

My heart gave a solid, hollow thump. Oh God. This was happening.

The sedan jerked to a stop at the curb, and the passenger window rolled down just enough for him to shout, "Get in!"

Screw it.

Desperate times called for illegal measures. Stealing a car sounded better than being caught by License 16—or worse, the Enil.

I lunged for the handle, my sweaty palm slipping before I managed to yank the door open with my still faintly glowing hand. I dove inside and barely got it shut before Sky hit the gas and spun the wheel, slamming me sideways against the door panel.

"Hold on," he said—belatedly.

I shot him a disbelieving look as I yanked my bag off my shoulder and flung it to the floorboards. I scrambled for the seatbelt with shaking fingers. It took two tries to get it buckled, but it clicked in place just in time for him to wrench the wheel the other way, sending us squealing around another bend. The engine whined as we tore toward the far exit.

I twisted in my seat. Smoke billowed from the small mall's broken doors. Lights flashed, sirens screamed, and emergency vehicles sped past us without slowing. A pair of unmarked black cars just like the ones Sky had seen following us earlier peeled into the lot, joining the handful already there.

In the distance, helicopters buzzed the horizon, too. If they planned to cover this up, they had their work cut out for them. No way they could pin this on a solar flare. Not with an Enil crashing through walls and flailing those horrifying tentacle arms in full view of swarms of people.

I fisted my hand and leaned forward, searching the rest of the sky I could see through the windshield. At least I didn't spot any UFOs—no glowing orbs up there. Not that it meant much. They could very well be floating out of view somewhere above us, watching humans scatter like panicked cockroaches.

"How'd the Enil find us?" I asked. My voice wasn't quite steady. "I thought you said the cuff blocked the signal."

"It does," Sky muttered, jaw tight. His eyes stayed fixed on the road as he swerved to dodge fleeing foot traffic and another news van. "I think they're following License 16, and they're the ones who found us."

"*What*? The Enil are following them? How?"

"The usual way." He aimed a brief frown my way before giving his focus to getaway driving. "The Enil may look like machines, Rae, but they're an alien race capable of space travel. They're not stupid. They'll be monitoring communications."

I knew that. Blood drained from my face, anyway, at the thought of them plugging into humanity's chatter. It somehow felt so much more...invasive. Eerie.

I stared at him, then yelped and smacked my hand against the dash when he swerved again, barely missing a crowd of people sprinting across the road.

Sky didn't even slow for the stop sign. He flew through the intersection, heading for the mall's main exit. A line of cars waited at the red light, while police vehicles sat at odd angles, trying to direct the exodus. An officer waved traffic through in a steady stream.

"Sky..." I clutched the seatbelt strap. My palm's glow had dimmed to almost nothing, but for all I knew, the police had our descriptions or something.

"I see them." He tightened both hands on the wheel and glanced in the rearview mirror. "Keep your head down."

I grabbed the bill of my hat and yanked it lower over my face, slouching in the seat.

Nothing to see here. Just a stolen car containing an alien and a human wanted by more people than I could count. When had this become my life?

Sky braked, easing us to the back of the line. My pulse hadn't come down from the sprint, and now it spiked again. My still-heavy breathing seemed loud in the tense quiet. I really needed to consider taking up a cardio regimen. *If* I survived.

The car's engine idled, and I spared a glance at Sky. He stared intently forward, face tight. From the speakers, a country song crooned about relaxing on a porch, something steel guitar-y and calm, like the universe's idea of a joke.

Then we were moving again, inching forward with the flow of traffic. The turn signal clicked. I held my breath as Sky pulled into the lane. We'd been waved through.

I risked a glance out from under the hat's brim and nearly collapsed with relief as we merged onto the main road. Beside me, Sky let out a long, slow breath and flexed his fingers on the wheel. We'd made it.

I slumped deeper into the seat, eyes closed, every muscle vibrating with exhaustion and adrenaline.

We'd escaped the Enil. Dodged License 16.

Successfully committed grand theft auto.

…I guessed that counted as a win?

Chapter 3

ROAD TRIPS, REVELATIONS, AND OTHER CRAZY THINGS THAT START WITH R

I OPENED my eyes. Perspiration cooled on the back of my neck. Shivering, I pushed my hat back far enough to see.

Traffic was jammed. Probably due, in part, to the mechanical death machine currently rampaging through the mall. But we were moving, crawling further away by the minute.

Distance was good. Distance was safe.

Or…saf*er*, especially considering the government had descended in full force, too. I shifted in my seat, anxiety rising at the thought.

That'd been a close call. Too close.

For both of us.

Sky navigated the gridlock with practiced ease, gaze flicking between the mirrors and the road ahead. Tense silence settled while he found an on-ramp and followed it onto the highway we'd fled after spotting our License 16 tail.

I gripped the seat as we took the curve. I didn't see anything suspicious behind us, but, considering I hadn't been the one to spot that car before… "Do you see anybody following?"

"No. I don't think so." Sky adjusted his grip on the wheel and glanced at the rearview mirror again. "Not yet, anyway."

That was something. The tiny ball of lingering panic in my chest dissipated. License 16 was a little preoccupied, and ironically, the Enil might've just saved our asses.

I never thought I'd be *thankful* for their appearance.

But then I thought of the humans still inside the mall, those limp agents flung like discarded socks, and the relief died. How many people had been hurt? Maybe the Enil had given up when we'd gotten away and beamed back up to their ship, leaving behind a pile of useless, broken parts and some undoubtedly confused mall workers. I clung to that hope.

I sat back into the seat, plucking at my sweaty shirt. Guilt slithered into my stomach, turning it. Until the incident at the university, I'd somehow convinced myself I was the only one in danger. The only one affected by this mess I'd stumbled into.

But the attack during midterms had shown me otherwise. It was a wake-up call. This wasn't just about me. It wasn't just about Earth.

No, it was even bigger than that.

It was about Sky's people, his home world…but yeah. Mine was getting caught in the crossfire.

I smoothed my damp palms over my silky shorts and took advantage of his distraction to study Sky. He was quiet, focused on the swelling river of cars around us. Nothing about him *seemed* rattled by what we'd just been through.

Must be nice.

The memory of sickly green eyes boring into my soul crept back, and I blinked hard, erasing the image. Taking a deliberate breath, I twisted the cuff around my wrist, taking comfort in its presence. Sunlight slanted through the windshield and lit up the strange metal in an amethyst shimmer. It gleamed like oil on water. Pretty, in an otherworldly kind of way.

I raked escaping strands of hair behind my ear. Goosebumps prickled to life as sweat dried on my skin. Reaching out, I closed the A/C vents on my side.

The A/C vents in this *stolen* car.

God. We'd stolen a car.

Unable to ignore it any longer, I scanned the interior. It was full of someone else's life: a foam coffee cup in the holder, receipts jammed under the radio, lip gloss, a gas card. The radio played soft music we hadn't bothered to turn off. Big sunglasses hung from the rearview mirror beside a grinning, vanilla-scented smiley air freshener.

The back seat held a crumpled takeout bag, a zip-up sweater, and an empty water bottle. Lived-in, but clean.

We'd stolen someone's ride—probably someone who'd been in that mall. Were they still trapped inside? No. Surely they'd evacuated and were safe with the responders now swarming the scene. I hoped.

"I can't believe we stole a car," I muttered.

I pulled off the hat and tossed it on the dash. My braid slid over my shoulder as I plucked the sunglasses from the mirror and slipped them on. There was another twinge of guilt at stealing someone's shades…but considering we'd already commandeered their car, it felt like a bit of a rounding error.

"I know. It's not my favorite thing, either." Sky hit cruise control and sat back with a heavy sigh, steering one-handed as he ran the other through his hair and jerked his chin at the hat. "Can I have that back?"

I handed it to him, and he pulled it on, adjusting the brim to block the sun.

Tucking my tongue into my cheek, I eyed him sidelong. "So…do you do this often?"

"What?" He raised a brow as he gripped the wheel again. "*Steal* cars?"

I sent a very pointed look at the illegally obtained ride we were currently cruising in. His lips pinched into a line before he concentrated once more on the road. He took a second to respond, as if he were choosing the words carefully.

"It's probably not a surprise," he said, his tone quiet. Subdued. "But I've had to do things I'm not particularly proud of since coming here. The mission… Well, I've done what I had to, Rae. I'm sure you can understand that."

I shifted in the seat, rolling his answer over in my mind. Sure. I did. I didn't have to like it—it didn't seem like *he* did—but I understood.

He was an undercover alien. I doubted there were a lot of resources for a stranded Pladian here to save his planet. At least he'd *tried* to blend in and do things the right way. *Human* things. Tending bar. Paying rent. Knowing him, he probably even paid taxes and gave to charity or something.

I caught myself staring and tore my gaze away, toying with the cuff again.

"They'd have found us sooner if that wasn't working," Sky said suddenly, and I looked up with a frown.

"What?"

"The band. The dampening field." He nodded at the cuff, splitting his attention between me and the highway. "If the inhibitor was weakening, the Enil would've found us much sooner."

I cupped the cool metal. I could only hope he was right. Because if *they* were on our trail…

I shivered and leaned forward to check the empty horizon again.

Sky caught it. "I think we're fine," he said, adjusting and bending one knee. I didn't miss his worried glance toward the clouds, though. "We just need to keep moving. Once we stop, I'll verify with Bast. He's been keeping an eye on his scanners." When I bit my lip, he did a double-take and sighed. "We're fine. You're *safe*, Raven. The cuff blocks the signal."

Despite the lingering anxiety, I forced myself to nod and relax back into my seat again. A moment later, out of the corner of my eye, I caught his very human-looking yawn only partially hidden behind his hand.

"You'll need sleep soon, right?" I asked, trying for nonchalant. "Do you want me to drive?"

His furrowing brow told me he didn't like the thought of that, but too bad. The synth-skin made Sky mostly human. He might be able to go invisible and shoot lightning from his fingers, but he also needed to eat. He needed water and had the same urges as a normal Earthling.

All the urges, if recent experiences were to be taken into account.

I battled back a flush while he shrugged. "No, that's okay. I'll stop soon."

That wasn't an answer. I opened my mouth to suggest that "soon" be sooner rather than later…before thinking better of it. Fine. He knew his limitations. I didn't exactly know where we were going, anyway, other than the state of Florida. Come to think of it, Sky wasn't using GPS. Did all Pladians have a built-in sense of direction, and if so, why did they need *me*—

"What about you?" Sky asked, cutting into my thoughts. I blinked when he glanced my way. "Are you okay?"

There was concern there, in the way his dark eyes swept over me, as if taking stock. Enough that I looked away, toward the windshield and the traffic outside, my belly fluttering.

It was silly to let myself be affected by it. He was just as worried about the map in my head, after all. The one that could save his people.

"I'm fine," I said, ignoring the twinge. Out the window, the trees blurring past were in the throes of autumn, painted in oranges, gold, and red. Tennessee was a pretty state in the fall. Or was this still Kentucky? I'd lost track. "How much longer do you think we have?"

"Did you just ask, 'Are we there yet?'"

His teasing tone caught me off guard enough that I turned my head. He wore a faint grin, clearly trying to break the strange tension that'd settled between us.

I latched onto the attempt, grateful. "Funny." I shot him a half-hearted scowl. "You know what I meant."

He huffed a laugh, his attention back on the road. "We'll be there in maybe a day or so. We're meeting Bast outside the town where he's been living. He'll lead us the rest of the way."

Bast. His mysterious alien partner. The other half of his *Pair,* which is what the Pladians called their undercover operatives sent to find the halix info caches. Probably an easier task when it hadn't been downloaded into an unsuspecting waitress's brain.

"You haven't been to his place?"

"No. Not this one. We try to stay mobile. Bast, especially. One Willow was the longest I've stayed put since we landed."

Landed.

Right. Landed. In a spaceship. Which, speaking of—

"Wait," I said, shooting up straight. It suddenly occurred to me I'd never asked him… "Where *is* your ship?"

Sky's faint smile faded, and his eyes darted my way before he focused once more on the road. Stilted silence fell, punctuated by twangy guitar. A muscle ticked in his jaw, like it did when he was upset, and for a second, I thought he wouldn't answer.

Which sometimes happened when my questions got a little too alien-y. His Creed, the Pladian intergalactic NDA, kept him from spilling *too* much.

But then he surprised me. "It's with Bast."

He'd *answered.* I leaned forward, eager. "Bast has your UFO?"

Sky shot me a look. *The* Look. "He has our *craft,* yes. It was easier to keep it hidden where he is. And he needed it for…his work."

Well, this was getting juicier. Sky was telling me things. *Alien* things.

"His work? What's he doing?" I asked, trying really hard to keep the excitement from my voice. "I thought you were both here for this." I waved my marked hand, the faint glyphs catching the light.

"We are. But…" He hesitated as he changed lanes to pass a slow-moving van. His tone turned clipped. "Bast's been looking for another ship."

"Wait—*what?*" Juicy was *right.* I couldn't tear my attention from his tightening face. I didn't miss the fact that his shoulders had drawn up a little, too. "There's *another* ship? Here? Like, one of yours or the Enil or…?"

Sky's jaw flexed again. The radio filled the silence with mournful lyrics about a lost truck. I tucked my tongue inside my cheek, swallowing the urge to press.

Finally, he spoke. "No. Not the Enil's. Our ship was damaged on entry. The comms array, specifically."

"Okaaay…"

I waited.

He aimed a sideways glance my way, clearly clocking the fact that I was hanging on every word. With a resigned huff, he loosened his tense grip on the wheel. "Once we have the map, we'll need to contact our main ship. But to do that, we need parts from the *first* ship to fix our comms."

"The first ship." I was parroting everything he said, but I couldn't stop. "There were others? Other Pladians here? Are you talking about the original ship that left the tablet?"

"No." He grimaced, then spoke haltingly, like I was yanking the words from him. "Bast and I…we weren't the first Pair dispatched to find the halix on Earth."

Shock zinged through me. My mouth opened, then shut again because I couldn't think of a single thing to say. Luckily, Sky didn't need me to urge him on.

"There was another team," he continued quietly. "But their ship didn't make it."

I found my voice. "It *crashed*?"

"Yeah." He turned his head, and those dark blue eyes locked onto mine, full of mysteries and a tiny bit of chagrin. "In Roswell, New Mexico."

Chapter 4

HI, WE'VE BEEN TRYING TO REACH YOU ABOUT YOUR MISSING SPACESHIP

AIR WHOOSHED out of my lungs like I'd been sucker-punched.

"Holy *crap*. Sky." I gaped. "You—Bast is looking for *the* Roswell ship? That was freaking *real?*"

He raised a brow slowly, eyes on the road. "You thought it wasn't?"

"Well, I…"

Of course I did.

I hadn't thought the Roswell crash was a real, *actual* UFO. I'd always figured it was a hoax. Just another conspiracy theory. Something to laugh off, like my coworker Kelly blaming the recent electrical glitches and weird lights on aliens.

Apparently, I'd been wrong about a few things. As evidenced by the alien currently driving this stolen car.

The Roswell UFO was *real*.

If this kept up, I'd start questioning everything. Bigfoot. The Loch Ness Monster.

That company trying to reach me about my vehicle's extended warranty.

I threw up my hands. "Why haven't you told me any of this?"

"It didn't really concern you, Rae," Sky said, sighing. "It didn't affect the map or your part in this—"

"Oh, my *part?*" It came out sharper than I'd intended, fueled by lack of sleep…and the tiny splinter of hurt wriggling its way into my chest. "In case you haven't noticed, I *am* a part of all this. I mean, come *on*. The *Roswell* ship? Besides." I shoved my marked palm toward him. "This should mean top-level clearance."

"Rae." His tone was soft but laced with exasperation. "I trust you completely, and we *are* in this together. But there are still things I haven't told you. Details about Pladia—"

"Details about Pladian physiology or whatever techno-babble, fine. I get that. But this?" I shook my head. "We've been stuck together for, like, *six days* and not once—*not once*—did you think to mention Pladians were responsible for the crashed alien spaceship smack dab in the center of Earth's science fiction genre?" It was three days, max, but still. I gawked at him. "Roswell, Sky. *Roswell.* Kind of a big deal."

Sky aimed a frown my way. "That's not fair. I've been open with you. You know I have." He scrubbed a hand over his hair. "I didn't think about it. In case you hadn't noticed, there've been more important things to worry about."

And just like that, his reasonable, *accurate* response took any misplaced wind right out of my sails. I tipped my head back against my seat. "You're right. Sorry. It's just a shock." I blinked at the traffic outside without really seeing it. "The Roswell ship is a Pladian UFO. Wow."

"Yeah. It was. Or is." He pursed his lips. "And technically, it'd be an IFO, right? Since it's identified?"

I snorted. Alien jokes for the win. I was a sucker for them.

Sky sobered, monitoring the semi-truck changing lanes in front of us. "Do you remember what I told you about Pairs?"

"Yeah, the Pladian teams searching for the halix?"

"Exactly. That program started over eighty Earth years ago now." He chewed the inside of his lower lip. "*Long* before I was born. No one had been successful in retrieving the halix data when Bast and I and the other second-wave trainees started the program."

I slowly leaned back against the door, staring at him. "So the first Pair sent here didn't…" It didn't feel right to finish. I kept my eyes on his profile and saw it tighten.

"Didn't make it, yeah. Their craft launched from the main ship just fine, but something went wrong. From what Bast and I have been able to piece together, it didn't handle the entry into your atmosphere." He flicked his eyes toward me then back to the traffic. "I assume you know the rest."

I could fill in the blanks: a crashed alien ship, a government cover-up. Kelly would have a freaking *field day* if she ever found out.

"When the mothership didn't hear back from Earth's Pair, they eventually dispatched another." Sky resituated his body in the seat, discomfort threading through the motion. "Bast and I were already in the program, so we were trained as replacements for Earth infiltration…"

I sat forward again, yanked by the invisible lure of that breadcrumb of info. He was so guarded, he rarely spoke of his life before this. When he did, it always threw me a little, imagining him somewhere else. Somewhere that made his shining, silver skin feel ordinary. Living aboard an alien ship, wearing a different face, learning about Earth and how to blend in.

It always made me wonder who he was before that. Before he'd grown used to this human suit. If that was the real Sky or if… *this* was.

After all, he'd been here on Earth for over a decade—longer than I'd been an adult. He'd landed as the Pladian equivalent of eighteen and been living among us ever since.

I guess not *totally* single-minded, either. He'd apparently been open to distractions since he'd confirmed he'd…you know, had *relations* with humans since landing. What had he called it? Right. *Immersing himself fully in the human experience.*

I imagined he'd immersed himself very skillfully, too—

"So, as I was saying," he went on, and I jolted guiltily at my train of thought. Thankfully, his attention was on the road, not my burning face. "When we finished the program, Bast and I were sent to Earth. Our ship landed fine, but the communications array didn't hold. The tech on the mothership is aging. It wasn't meant to function forever without returning to Pladia."

His knuckles paled around the wheel before he deliberately loosened them and rubbed his fingertips into the center of his forehead instead, like he was smoothing out the frown grooves there. "We've been lost out here for too long," he muttered. "We need to get home."

Home. Pladia. The place that, if we succeeded, if we somehow got this so-called map out of my head, he'd be heading to.

Tufts of dark hair poked out from under his faded black ball cap, and muscle shifted beneath his sweat-stained white shirt. The graceful line of his shadowed jaw, the angle of his dark brows pulled low over those impossibly deep blue eyes, the lingering bruise on his cheekbone—it all *looked* so human. But he wasn't.

A car changed lanes in front of us, forcing Sky to slow. On cue, he scowled at it and cursed under his breath. It was familiar enough that I had to hide my smile.

Okay. He may be a Pladian, but he had human mannerisms down pat.

"Is your name even Sky?" I asked before I could filter my thoughts.

"What?" He blinked once, twice, splitting his attention between me and the driver who'd cut us off. "Where did *that* come from?"

"Sorry." I winced. *Good question.* "I don't know. You don't have to answer that." He'd spilled a lot of information just now. It seemed like I'd found his limit.

But his shoulders relaxed, and the next glance he sent me was more bemused than annoyed. "It's fine." His voice was hoarse. Strained. "Um, it's sort of my name, yeah. Sky is…the humanized version."

I wrapped my arms around my middle, waiting for him to shut me down.

Somber, his gaze left the road for an instant and snagged on mine. Like he was considering me—it. The question. Golden sunlight bathed his face, and something passed between us. Coiled, charged, nearly making me shiver.

It wasn't just about the name. It was all of it. Everything we'd been through. Everything unspoken. The weight of all this.

An alien. From another world. And still…somehow, still Sky.

"Skaiven," he said, barely above a whisper. Clearing his throat, he faced forward again. "Close enough to Sky that it felt…right."

"*Skaiven*," I repeated, rolling it over my tongue. *Sky-vehn.* It was musical. Exotically beautiful in the same way the bracelet I wore was.

His lips tipped up at the edges, though he didn't pull his attention from the road.

"What?" I asked, with a self-conscious laugh. "Did I say it wrong?"

"No." He scraped his teeth over his bottom lip like he was trying to bite back the smile. "No, that was right. It's just…strange to hear someone else say it. Well, someone besides Bast when he's annoyed." His grin solidified, then softened toward wistful. "It's been a long time."

A decade. It was hard to fathom going that long lying to everyone you met. Without letting anybody in. No wonder he was so guarded. I took in his profile, the contemplative look he wore. "You've really never shared any of this with anyone before me? *Ever?*"

That hint of a smile vanished entirely. "No." His expression closed off. "I told you. I swore an oath to our Creed, Rae. We're not allowed to interfere with a planet's native culture. Revealing ourselves in any way…sharing real names?" He shook his head. "Telling a world that's still unsure aliens exist that we, in fact, *do?* That'd interfere in a big way."

Right. It'd certainly *interfered* with my life. I'd seen how seriously he took that Creed of his, too. I'd seen his conflict the day he'd told me his story.

Which made instances like this feel like a gift.

A warm, bubbly feeling built in my chest, threatening to settle into something gooey and dangerous before I caught myself, shaking it off.

The map. The mission. That needed to be our focus.

Sky adjusted his position, the seat groaning under his weight. "Anyway," he said, tone back to business, "we've been tracking what's left of the Roswell shuttle. Bast is hoping to salvage the onboard comm tech. Use it to repair ours." He cast a meaningful glance my way. "Either of the onboard computers might be able to interface with the halix."

I waited a beat. "Okay…and?"

He nodded toward my hand. "And there's a chance we can use it to extract the information from *you*."

"*What?*" Whoa, whoa, *whoa*. Nobody had said anything about *interfacing* with alien computers. Wasn't that what'd gotten me into this mess in the first place?

"It'll be fine," he said, as if picking up on my sudden surge of panic. He dismissed it with a flick of his fingers. "I told you—you're safe."

Easy for him to say. He wasn't going through any alien extractions anytime soon. I eyed him dubiously before twisting my palm up. The setting sun peeked through the trees lining the road, illuminating the alien markings—the writing—embedded there in yellow strobes. Faint, white curling lines and dots, a few shades lighter than my skin.

Sky had said the script was part of the ancient Pladian dialect. A message. A greeting. To me, it felt more like a warning.

But still, like his name, strangely beautiful.

I tilted my hand toward the light. The lines shimmered, pearlescent and eerie.

"So Bast hasn't found it?" I asked, eyes still on my palm.

"The other ship? No. Not yet. He has leads. But your government has moved it from location to location. From what we can tell, they've dismantled it, experimented on it, and hidden it away." He clicked his tongue in irritation. "Finding the mainframe unit we need for this has been like that game. The one with the upside-down cups and the ball."

Shell game, I translated, but I didn't interrupt.

"It doesn't help we're not the only ones looking for it. The whole world wants a piece of the technology your country's been hoarding for the last century." Sky's voice had an edge now. Judgment. I looked up, raising a brow. "You're all the same species, and yet you can't stop fighting each other. You could've achieved incredible things by now, you know. If you worked together instead of tearing yourselves apart."

"You're not telling me anything I don't know," I said, snorting. I clasped my marked hand in my unmarked one and rested them in my lap. "Humanity isn't up to par with the high and mighty Pladian saviors of the galaxy. I get it." Sky narrowed his eyes at me, like he was trying to decipher if I was being sarcastic, and I shrugged. "It's true. You should see my Facespace feed."

He slanted his lips as if to say *fair enough.*

"So how close is Bast to finding it? Any idea? You guys should really think about putting AirTags on your alien tech."

"I'll pass it on to our engineers next time I see them. Bast said he's close. He's doubled his efforts since finding out about you."

Finding out about me. I could only imagine what Sky had told him.

A waitress from work accidentally blasted herself with the halix before it blew up, and now I think there's a map in her brain. Also, she's way too curious for her own good, the Enil are hunting us, and I'm pretty sure she wants to jump my bones.

I nearly winced. That sounded about right.

However he'd explained my involvement, I really hoped "doubling his efforts" meant Bast would find that ship *soon.* I wanted my life back.

Before the Enil took it. And the map along with it.

Who'd have thought my continued existence would hinge on the *Roswell UFO,* of all things?

I leaned forward, turning on the heat before collapsing back into my seat. The late fall chill clung to the air, even inside the car. My temples had begun to throb again—stress headaches were becoming a constant companion—and the soreness from all the running, screaming, and battling evil robots from outer space had settled in.

I needed a hot meal, a soft bed, and about thirty hours of sleep.

I'd settle for a coffee with extra, *extra* cream, though, if we were going to keep driving through the night. Again.

In the contemplative silence, the radio switched to a commercial. Something about a local rodeo and a brand-new ring. The announcer sounded *way* too excited, but I didn't pay it much mind, too lost in my thoughts.

The sooner we made it to Bast, the sooner all this would be over. With Sky and everything else.

That *shouldn't* make me feel mixed emotions. I should feel only relief at the thought. Not this twisting in my stomach at the thought of him flying off into the stars.

Sky didn't say anything else. When I glanced at him, his face was unreadable, shadowed beneath his hat as we raced down the highway.

I gave up trying to decipher his expression and settled in for the ride.

Chapter 5

CHICKEN SANDWICHES
AND PLAYING CHICKEN

BY THE TIME Sky turned onto a narrow, rutted lane, night had fallen. We'd put hours between us and the mall—enough that I'd stopped constantly looking in the mirrors and started paying attention to the hunger pangs settling below my ribs instead. The scent of fried chicken wafting from our takeout bag wasn't helping. My stomach grumbled as we bumped along the sloping path. I had no idea where we were, but Sky seemed to know.

"You're sure we're safe here?" I asked, gazing out at the dark landscape. All I could see were shadowy pines and the bumpy dirt path illuminated by our headlights.

But then we broke free of the trees, and for a moment, I forgot all about secret agents and death machines. "Oh *wow*."

The stars had come out in full force, scattered across the velvet sky. The only manmade lights glittered far below, where a valley was speckled with gold—tiny homes and buildings nestled between mountain ridges. The peaks cradling the town were just a few shades lighter than the sky.

With the moon only a sliver, the stars were *alive*.

"We're safe," Sky said, killing the engine. He sat back and lifted his phone, most likely reading another text from Bast.

He got to stay in touch with people while my dead device was only taking up space in my book bag. *Radio silence*, he'd said. We didn't know who was watching who. Although…after that run-in with License 16, maybe he was onto something.

It still made my chest prickle as I side-eyed the device he typed away on—a specially-encrypted phone, courtesy of Bast's apparent tech know-how.

I wasn't stupid. I knew Sky was right to recommend we let things cool off and have a plan in place before I contact anyone. He had more experience with all this running, sneaking, and evading.

But the ever-present anxiety at the thought of my loved ones—my mom, especially—sometimes made that hard to remember.

I left him to his texting and climbed out. Groaning, I stretched until my spine popped, every joint kinked from sitting in a car for over a day straight. The cool mountain air filled my lungs and raised goosebumps on my bare arms as I rotated in place, neck craned. The sky was so close, it felt like I could reach up and rake my fingers through the Milky Way.

But the night was also chilly, even with the jeans I'd changed back into when we'd stopped for food. Reluctantly, I tore my eyes away and leaned back into the car, snatching the zip-up sweater from the car's backseat, silently apologizing to its owner. I slipped it on as Sky finished texting and climbed out, juggling both drinks and a plain paper bag. The scent of fried chicken sandwiches—not burgers, for once—drifted on the wind, settling in my empty stomach.

"What'd Bast say?" I asked as he pushed the door shut with his hip.

"Well," he circled to the front of the car, "the cuff didn't malfunction. Your signal is still obscured, based on the readings he's getting."

I slumped a little, relief chasing the lingering tension from my back. "That's good." The cone-shaped pines ringing the gravel patch swayed in the breeze. A single, mournful night bird crooned somewhere nearby. I hugged myself, grateful for the oversized, overly stolen sweater. "So the Enil really were…"

"Following License 16, yeah," Sky finished, his voice fading as he approached the car's hood.

When I turned from the trees to follow him, the view knocked the breath from my lungs, and I let out a low whistle. "This is a heck of a spot."

"I know. I've stopped here before. It was a…long time ago, but I was hoping it was still here."

I turned at the low, almost reverent sound of his voice. He'd paused closer to the ledge, our food in hand. I stared at him, just as taken aback by the sight of him as I was by the valley.

I wanted to ask why he'd been here, but I swallowed the urge. If I started asking questions about his life before, I'd never stop.

He looked, for once, unburdened. Tired, sure, but for the first time in days, he could almost pass for relaxed, lips soft and faintly curved, eyes heavy-lidded as he tipped his head and took in the vivid stars. He'd shed the hat when the sun set, and the wind teased loose strands of dark hair, tossing the curls over his forehead.

Silhouetted by the silver starlight, he stirred something in me I didn't want to dwell on. I made myself look away. Luckily, a second later, Sky gave a little shake of his head, like he was surfacing from somewhere deep, and turned from the postcard-perfect view. "Are you hungry?"

"I'm assuming that's rhetorical. My stomach's eating itself." I forced a smile and tugged my sweater tighter, meandering toward the car.

Then I stopped in my tracks when Sky set the food on the car's hood and, with effortless grace, hoisted himself up beside it. His shirt clung to his tapered upper body as he stretched out his long legs with a sexy little groan that slid straight along my spine. My mouth went dry.

He'd made that exact same sound when I'd kissed him.

Oblivious, he picked up the drinks and settled against the wind-shield. Catching myself before I started drooling, I pretended to study the wheel well so my face wouldn't catch fire. God, I had it bad.

Friends, Rae. Friends.

His easy, oblivious smile wasn't helpful. "Come on up. Hood's still warm."

The car wasn't large, but this wasn't going to be nearly as smooth as whatever the heck he'd just done. Here went nothing.

"Don't laugh," I said and planted one foot on the tire. It took two awkward tries, but I managed to haul myself up, landing with my butt in the air. I flopped sideways, more like a fish on dry land than anything, the side of my face mashing against the hood.

What do you know? He was right. It *was* still warm.

Muttering a curse, I pushed myself up, glaring at him in warning. Sky cleared his throat, expression carefully neutral as he held our drinks and waited for me to rearrange my limbs.

To his credit, he didn't laugh. Just handed me a Coke once I'd tucked myself against the glass beside him.

"Thanks." I took it, burrowing into my sweater. "You won't get cold?"

"Hm?" He glanced down at himself, at the thin, short-sleeved white tee that'd seen better days, before shaking his head. "I'm fine."

Just then, his phone buzzed, and he lifted his hips and slid it from his pocket, glancing at it.

"Bast again?" I asked, blinking fast in the screen's bright light.

"Yeah." He pocketed the device before I could make anything out. "He sent me the name of the motel he's going to meet us at. He's working on some tests to run, too."

He waved in the direction of my marked hand, the one not holding my drink, and I curled my fingers around the design. "Great. Tests. Can't wait."

"You'll be fine, Rae," he said, dipping his head to meet my eyes. "Trust me, okay?"

"I *do*." I reached for my drink, avoiding that galaxy-filled sapphire stare. "Jury's out on the other Pladians."

"That's fair." Sky leaned back and picked up his own soda, letting out a snort. "Knowing Bast, that's probably for the best."

Intrigued, I raised a brow. For some reason, a blend of nervous excitement bubbled up each time I thought about meeting his partner. Which was silly. It wasn't like I needed to worry about impressing Sky's friends. It wasn't like we were…*dating* or something.

Just…you know, on a life-or-death quest to save some planets.

When Sky didn't say anything else, I didn't press, and we lapsed into a comfortable quiet. Save for the sounds of Sky slurping his drink in his obnoxiously loud way. Clearly proper straw use hadn't been part of Earth-infiltration training.

To distract myself, I dug into the bag, taking out the pair of chicken sandwiches and boxes of fries. My stomach growled as I handed Sky's off, unwrapped mine, and peeled off the top bun so he could add the pickles he disliked from his sandwich onto mine. It'd become an unspoken ritual at some point in the last day.

I wolfed down three greasy bites before I even came up for air. When I did, Sky was watching me like I'd just unhinged my jaw and devoured it whole.

"You could've said something if you were that hungry," he said, smirking as he bit into his own sandwich.

I shook my head, talking around a handful of fries. "I didn't realize it. Something about being chased by the government and almost smashed by an alien mech-suit distracted me."

"Yeah. That." He leaned back against the glass, sobering again. "I was hoping we'd have more time. I figured License 16 would have their hands full with the Enil sightings."

"What *is* License 16?" I asked when I'd finished chewing. "I'd never heard of them before Kelly mentioned them. Her FETR group apparently has a source or something." It was still difficult to believe Kelly had been onto something with all her alien conspiracy talk.

Sky contemplated his sandwich. "From what Bast's dug up, seems like they're a special task force assigned by the last president to chase alien-related phenomena. Which," he made a face, "until recently would've probably been pretty boring."

It was anything but boring now. There were aliens galore to chase around. I reached for my soda. "Do they know about you guys?"

"The Pladians? Or me and Bast?"

"Either. Both."

"Not that we can tell." He shrugged. "Bast is good at burying any records or mentions of us as *humans*—the stuff we haven't specifically planted to give the appearance of normalcy. And of course, the synth-skin makes us hard to track otherwise." Blowing out a breath, he snagged a fry. "But with all the Enil activity lately, they're bound to be watching more closely."

The wind stirred the hair off my neck, and I shivered. That probably meant they were watching *me* more closely. Not that I hadn't known that. It was just strange. My entire life, I'd felt…not boring, exactly. Just *normal*. Steady.

Okay, maybe a little boring. I liked reading nonfiction, cardigans, cozy nights in, and volunteering in the archaeology lab. The most exciting thing in my life had been working at Oasis, really. And anything Amelia dragged me to.

Now I was the subject of a planetary (interplanetary?) search and on the run with an alien. Wearing a bracelet made of shining metal with ancient Pladian writing tattooed on my palm. Boring was a heck of a lot safer.

But that was exactly why my family and friends would be so worried. It wasn't like me to disappear. To run off without a word.

"When do you think I can call home?" I asked, hunger waning. I rested the hand holding the sandwich in my lap and turned toward him. "My mom, Sky. She's got to be so worried."

When he raised his head, the understanding and apology in his eyes answered my question. Not yet. He didn't even need to say it.

He did, anyway. "Soon. Once we get to Bast's, we can figure something out."

Soon. That could be tomorrow. Next week. Never, if the Enil succeeded in smashing me or the halix's information melted my brain.

I shuddered.

But because none of this was Sky's fault, I took a deep breath and pushed it aside for now. Despite my rapidly vanishing appetite, I finished my sandwich in a few bites and sipped my Coke, tipping my head back against the windshield behind me.

Boring may have been safer, but this entire whirlwind of an adventure had definitely changed my perspective. Particularly when it came to those stars blazing overhead. Bright and clear and endless.

They meant something different now. Starting with the not-a-man sitting next to me. They meant *Sky's home.*

"It's still hard to believe you're actually from up there," I murmured, tilting my face back until my neck ached. "You're a real, live alien."

Even now, it felt so overwhelming to say aloud. As if at any moment, he was going to laugh and say *gotcha.* Like this was all some elaborate joke. I'd almost believe it if I hadn't seen his sparkly silver skin and inverted black-on-blue eyes. If I hadn't watched him battle the Enil. If I hadn't nearly died.

"Real and live for *now,*" Sky said dryly. He shifted beside me, bending a knee and draping his forearm over it. Our shoulders brushed ever-so-slightly. I felt every atom of the contact.

"Which one is home?" I asked, partly to distract myself from his heat and partly because I wanted to know.

Out of the corner of my eye, I saw him glance my way. "Pladia, you mean?"

When I nodded, he turned his head, looking up. After a few long seconds, he pointed.

"There. See where the stars form kind of a… Well, here." He leaned in, close enough that I forgot how to breathe. Close enough that his hard chest pressed against the entire length of my arm. His face was tilted toward the sky, but his proximity lit every nerve.

"I don't—" I began, flustered, but he cut in.

"Do you know the constellation Equuleus?"

I blinked, stunned. "You're kidding."

"What?" He pulled away enough to twist toward me, clearly confused when I started laughing.

"Equuleus. As in equine. The horse-head constellation."

"Yes…" he said slowly, eyeing me like I'd lost my mind.

Honestly, he might not be wrong.

"After the incident at the university, after I got this," I flashed my palm, the marks barely visible in the dark, "I kept seeing Equuleus. I'd wake up with the shape burned into my eyesight before it faded. Like…" I cast around for the words. "The after-effect of staring at the sun."

Excitement flared in Sky's dark gaze. "The map," he whispered.

I grimaced. I didn't want to say it out loud. It made it too real, though all the evidence was pointing firmly in that direction.

Sky, however, was already on board. "It has to be your mind attempting to make sense of the info cache," he murmured, more to himself, turning his gaze back to the sky. "I'm beginning to think the ancient Pladians miscalculated how human biology would handle the halix."

No, really?

I kept the sarcasm inside. Along with the anxious leap in my gut at the thought. Instead, I followed his stare upward, thumbing the pale whorls on my skin. They were indiscernible to the touch, the skin smooth. Impossible to ignore, though.

"If you know where it is, why can't you just…you know, go there?" I asked, squinting at the stars Sky had indicated. I recognized the shape now. I wasn't sure which one was Pladia's sun, but a thrill tingled through me anyway. Aliens—*people*—lived on a planet orbiting around one of those sparkles.

Sky sighed, resting his head against the glass. "It sounds easy. But traveling vast distances in space is a lot more complex than that. It requires exact coordinates. Jumping without them is like…" He lifted a hand and let it fall. "Shooting an arrow at the sky and hoping to hit one of those tiny points of light." He exhaled a humorless laugh. "You could end up in the middle of the star or stranded in deep space or…anything, really." His eyes were distant, trained high. "But it may come down to that. We've only got enough fuel for one jump, and what little we have left is depleting quickly. Bast and I are one of the last Pairs, and if this doesn't work…"

His throat worked in a swallow. *This*, as in his mission. He tucked his lower lip between his teeth, and I watched the motion too closely before catching myself and following his gaze up, toward those stars.

Space *was* large. Unfathomable in the same way time was, once you stopped measuring it in days. Fossil records were logged in centuries. Millennia. Periods of time most people never had to think about—or didn't *want* to.

After all, the human mind preferred compressing things like years and distance. It made everything feel more manageable. Less overwhelming. Less *intimidating*. Which is exactly how looking up felt right now.

Or looking at the person next to me. Hell, this entire situation, when I thought about it too much.

If Sky failed—if *I* did—it affected so much more than just the two of us. His people were counting on him.

Sky's people.

Sky's person? Did he have someone up there worrying about him, like my family and friends were undoubtedly worrying about me?

Or…maybe something even *more* than that?

"Is somebody waiting for you?" It slipped out, and I immediately smashed my lips shut. Damn it. Too late to claw it back.

Even if the question was way too revealing. Probably too personal, too. Though…friends asked questions about each other's love lives, right?

…*right?*

Sky didn't answer at first. But his gaze shifted back to me, and he studied me for a heartbeat before finally: "Up there."

It wasn't a question, but I nodded anyway, focusing on the stars and hoping the darkness hid my warming face. "I mean—I know you said you were born on the ship. Not Pladia. So I know it wouldn't be up *there* up there…" I cleared my throat. "I was just curious."

I tried for a casual shrug, as if the question was *totally* no big deal. Not a nagging curiosity about his extraterrestrial dating history.

I took a drink to cover my cringe.

Sky stayed quiet long enough that I thought he might not answer. Then, like when I'd asked about his name, he surprised me by not dodging this, either. "My parents died during a skirmish with the Enil," he said without much inflection.

But even without it, I caught the undercurrent of emotion. My heart squeezed. Mostly because I *knew* that quiet ache that never quite faded. At the reminder, my own poignant grief uncurled from where it slumbered, and I searched the sky for the Big Dipper. My dad's favorite. The one he'd always pointed out. Something about the scoop shape always grounded me.

"I'm really sorry," I said, setting my drink aside and turning toward him.

He gave his head the smallest shake and adjusted his straw, rattling ice. "It happened a long time ago."

"Doesn't really matter though, does it?" He looked up from his drink, and I offered a small smile that felt a little sadder than I meant it to be. "Time changes it, but it doesn't make it go away."

He didn't smile back, but some of the tightness eased from his expression. He lowered the cup. "You lost somebody."

"My dad." This conversation had gotten deeper than I'd intended. I dropped my eyes, picking at a frayed stitch in the stolen sweater's hem. "Cancer when I was a teen. It dulls, but it's never really gone."

"I'm sorry, Rae. You're right. It's never really gone."

We were quiet for a moment, the undercurrent of shared loss heavy until Sky asked, "Is it just you? I thought you mentioned a brother the other day."

I latched onto the slight subject change. "Me and Dustin—the brother. He's older, but not by much. He hadn't moved out yet when Dad…" I tugged the unraveling piece of yarn, exhaling slowly. "It was just the three of us after Dad." I wiggled my shoulders to shrug off the melancholy and made a face. "Dustin somehow found someone to put up with him and got married last year, though. They're having their first baby soon. Any day now."

I felt Sky watching me, absorbing the words, and I wound the loose string around my fingertip. Hopefully Lisa hadn't gone into labor with my nephew yet. Because if I missed that—if I didn't get to share the moment with my family, after everything we'd been through…

My throat tightened, and I reached for my drink to ease the sting. Swallowing, I busied myself messing with the straw instead. "Anyway. And, of course, Amelia. She's basically a sister."

One who'd undoubtedly be *pissed* when I finally saw her again.

Talking about all of them had the urge to call home rising again, anxiety surging at the thought of how worried my mom had to be. And Dustin, Lisa, and Amelia. All of them. I fought it down.

We'd been over this, and I wouldn't have to wait much longer.

Besides, I didn't want to spoil the moment. Not with how close Sky and I were sitting and how warm his arm felt against mine.

When I turned my head, he was still watching me with a furrowed brow and a slight downward tilt to his mouth. I deliberately lightened my tone and summoned a smile.

"What about you? Do you have siblings?" I pretended to frown thoughtfully as I sucked down more Coke. "Do Pladians even *have* siblings? Do you, like, grow in test tubes or maybe like some weird cellular mitosis—"

I broke off with a giggle when he rolled his eyes and nudged me with his shoulder. "Mitosis? Really?" He aimed the Look my way, but this time it was feigned.

I lifted my free hand in a shrug. "I've seen the movies."

"I'm sure you have." He waited a beat, then slowly arched a brow. "I already told you we reproduce the same way as humans, remember?"

Mid-drink, I nearly choked on my soda. Forcing it down the correct pipe, I looked away. "Yeah. Right. I guess you, uh, did. Now I remember."

As if I could forget that particular conversation. He'd said *things* worked almost the exact same with humans and Pladians, too. Couldn't erase that tidbit of information if my life depended on it. It'd branded itself into my brain.

Like he knew exactly what he was doing, Sky let out a low chuckle. "Hmm. Ah, no, I don't have any siblings. Bast is…"

Another laugh, this one ending in a sigh. "Well, he's it. A pain in the ass, but the closest thing I've got to a brother. We were in the same…I guess you would call it an orphanage. We went into the Pairs program together and then trained to come here."

I cataloged that as I set the drink down and picked up another French fry. That made me even *more* curious about Bast, knowing their history. The idea of seeing Sky around someone he considered family, someone who knew him—*really* knew him—would be… interesting, to say the least.

Also interesting was the fact that he'd made no mention of anyone *else*. Nobody romantic, anyway. Not that it mattered, of course. It didn't. He could have a whole Pladian husband or wife, and it would make no difference.

The thought brought an irrational surge of jealousy with it. I chomped the fry.

"Or were you asking about something else?" Sky asked, not bothering to mask his amusement, and I froze before cramming a whole handful of fries into my mouth, chewing to buy myself time. They were getting cold.

Out of the corner of my eye, I caught his smirk, though he rubbed a hand over his mouth to hide it. By the time I forced myself to look his way, he'd wiped it away.

The breeze tugged his dark hair as he slowly shook his head. "No, I don't have a Pladian lover waiting up there for me. If that's what you're asking. Once I entered the Pairs program, I knew I was coming here for an undetermined amount of time, and it didn't make sense to start something." He lifted one shoulder, then narrowed his eyes. "Is that what you're wanting to know?"

Flustered by the direct question—and the equally direct stare, not to mention the confusing emotions his answer stirred (was that relief?)—I fumbled for my soda again and studied it intently. Somewhere nearby, the night bird squawked again, and the trees rustled. The light wind did nothing to cool my hot cheeks.

"Sure. I guess." The wad of potato I'd tried to swallow threatened to get stuck, and I gulped my Coke to wash it down. He was still looking at me. I could feel it. I sighed and rolled my head his way. "*What?* I was just curious…"

He gave a noncommittal hum, his shadowed eyes sweeping over my face, and I flushed harder. This time not from embarrassment but awareness. Awareness of the fact that we were lying side by side atop this stolen car, our backs to the windshield, our shoulders pressed together. Talking about the people we loved and life. While a spread of stars that rivaled any piece of art I'd ever seen sparkled overhead.

It was…well, it would've been insanely, cosmically romantic.

If he hadn't told me nothing could ever happen between us, either. For the exact same reason. If this were *any* other circumstance rather than an alien on a secret mission from the stars and the girl who had the key to saving his people stuck inside her brain.

If he hadn't kissed me until I couldn't breathe and then promptly apologized before depositing me firmly in the friend zone.

But that kiss… It'd been passionate, fiery, and exactly what I'd imagined for all those months I'd dreamed about it. About *him*.

"What are you thinking about?" Sky asked, cocking his head.

I nearly swallowed my tongue. The blush I'd been fighting roared back. "I, um…" I cast around for something—*anything*— other than *I was thinking about that time I made out with you in my stairwell.* But my traitorous eyes snagged on his mouth.

I knew from experience it was soft. Damn it, why did he have to be so perfect? Even the timbre of his voice—

"Rae…" he murmured, and only then did I realize I'd leaned closer. Just a fraction of an inch, but enough to be obvious.

"Oh. Oops. I…" I drew back fast, retreating, clutching my drink to my chest tightly enough that I nearly spilled it all over both of us. That *was* embarrassment scalding my face now—

All thought evaporated when he grasped my chin and gently tilted it, his mouth quirking at the corner in a wry smile. I almost dropped the drink a second time. His fingers were warm beneath my jaw, firm enough to hold me still, to anchor me in place.

When he spoke, it was quiet. Threaded with something deeper.

"You know that if things were different…if I could…" The hint of humor faded. He searched my gaze and sighed. I felt it on my lips. "If we'd met in different circumstances, this would be…"

"Um, different?" I breathed. He was close enough that if I leaned in again, our mouths would meet. It took all my willpower, but I didn't.

"Different. Yeah." His small smile came and went. He hadn't pulled away. Still hadn't let go of my chin.

My throat had gone dry. I sank my teeth into my bottom lip.

And then, almost like *he* couldn't help it, his attention dropped to it.

A flurry of wings erupted in my stomach. He was looking at my mouth. Tingles spread down my neck and into my chest. My heartbeat pounded in the base of my throat.

I didn't know if I could breathe. Didn't know if I wanted to.

His eyes drifted back to mine, and they were tight with frustration or maybe that was indecision and…and *desire*. Dark and gleaming with want.

Shock trickled through me. He did a great job of hiding it, but it *was* still there. He *wasn't* completely unaffected after all.

I had the ridiculous urge to laugh in triumph, but I stayed frozen in place, staring up at him. His fingertips were light pressure beneath my jaw. Flutters erupted in my belly.

This was it.

For one wild, radiant moment, I thought Sky Acosta was going to throw his reservations—his inhibitions—to the wind and kiss me. And I was *so* going to let him. Out here, on top of the world, suspended between the stars and the earth, it felt like nothing else mattered, anyway.

Not the Enil. Not the government. Not the invisible boundaries between us. Lines in the sand.

There was only the thud of my heart. His hand on my skin. That perfectly shaped mouth I could practically taste.

Screw it.

I watched his eyes as I leaned in. Watched his lids lower as he tilted his head ever so slightly, bringing our lips into alignment—

A horn blared, loud and jarring, and headlights speared through the night. I yelped and jerked back, sliding too far on the metal beneath me. *Shit.* I threw my hands out to catch myself…and my drink went flying.

Sky's eyes sprang wide, and he reached for me. But it was too late.

Off balance, I tipped backward. The lid flew off my cup. Soda exploded in a mushroom cloud of droplets that sparkled in the headlights as they pelted back down.

Covered in Coke, I tumbled right off the hood.

Chapter 6

AIN'T NO REST STOP FOR THE WICKED

I'D LEARNED rest stops in the middle of the night were pretty hit or miss. Either the night shift person swiped a few paper towels over the counter and called it good—or they had a meticulous, third-shift cleaner who took their job very seriously and blessed late travelers with sparkly clean commodes and sinks.

This one was stuck somewhere in the middle. Two stalls were out of toilet paper, and the trash can was overflowing, but the whole thing smelled vaguely like cheap lemon-scented cleaner. The sink I washed my hands in had only the faintest rust ring. The counter was clean enough, too, when I flattened both palms on it and leaned in, peering at my reflection in the smudged mirror.

The unfortunate yellow lighting wasn't much better than the dressing room's had been. Still bright enough to illuminate the red splotches of embarrassment riding high on my cheeks, though. Those wouldn't seem to fade.

When I inhaled, the scent of cleaner mingled with the whiff of sickly-sweet cola I was wearing like my least favorite perfume ever.

Unwanted images replayed in horrible detail, and I groaned and hung my head. Apparently, a full day couldn't pass without me embarrassing myself in front of Sky. That almost kiss. His sigh against my lips, the way he'd leaned in…

And then…

My tailbone still smarted from the impact with the ground. My pride even more.

I rubbed a palm over my face—then flinched as my fingers brushed the healing bruise on my forehead. Straightening, I let my arms dangle to my sides instead.

I'd fallen *right* off the car.

By the time I'd climbed back to my feet, a cola-covered Sky was in the middle of apologizing profusely to the angry driver and informing him we hadn't intended to trespass. Luckily, the driver—a farmer who owned the next lot over—had let us leave without calling the cops.

But the damage was done.

Biting my cheek, I plucked at the neon green shirt, now stained in spots. After ensuring I hadn't given myself a concussion diving off the vehicle, Sky had brushed off my soda fountain reenactment, too intent on driving.

I closed my eyes, tipping my head back. It was almost like being near him zapped all common sense from my brain.

Then there was the fact I'd almost kissed him. He hadn't exactly fought me on it, either. He'd been the one touching me, cupping my face and staring so intently. *He'd* leaned in—

"Get it together, Rae," I muttered, glaring at myself in the mirror.

It'd been a long couple of days, and I was tired and strung out. And judging by how slowly Sky had been moving when he slid out of the driver's seat at this rest stop, he was feeling it, too.

I leaned down and hefted my book bag. Between the books and clothing I'd shoved inside, it was bulging at the seams. If only I'd thought to stick some deodorant and a toothbrush in there, too. But I didn't typically pack for an impromptu road trip when heading to my midterms.

I'd had no idea how off the rails life was going to get.

With one last morose glance at my washed-out reflection, I

shouldered the bag and headed for the door. My head ached. I didn't know the exact time, but it was late. Bordering on early. Maybe I could convince Sky to sleep a little at this rest stop. Even a cramped car nap sounded good right about now.

I yawned into the back of my hand as I shuffled into the rest stop's lobby. It was empty, save for some vending machines, a wall of pamphlets, and a drinking fountain. I made a beeline for the snacks, digging in my bag's front pocket for change. My fingers brushed my dead phone.

The urge to draw it out was strong, but it wasn't like I could power it up. I didn't have a charger cord. I'd never realized how much I relied on it until I was cut off like this.

Pushing aside the discomfort, I zipped the compartment and shoved the change into the machine's slot, punching the button. The pack of gum clattered in the receptacle, and I bent to fish it out, sighing as I straightened.

The thought of calling Mom lingered. Something about a quiet, empty rest stop during these early abandoned hours drove home the loneliness. The disconnection. I frowned at the wintergreen-fresh stick I unwrapped. Maybe they had a payphone here. Did those things still exist? I shoved the gum in my mouth and resumed walking. If so, maybe I could sneak in a quick call, even if the idea of hiding it from Sky immediately dropped a heavy stone into the pit of my stomach—

"*Oof!*" I collided with a hard body and stumbled back a step. I'd have fallen if a pair of strong hands hadn't grasped my upper arms, dodging the Enil bruise on my left one. I gaped up at familiar twilight eyes, nearly swallowing my gum. "Sky! What—"

"We have to go *now*," he ground out, tension riding the words. I gawked at him. "Come on."

"What?" I stumbled a little when he propelled me forward by the arm. "What are you doing? What's going on?"

"License 16."

Shock rocketed through me, and I nearly tripped again. "*Already?* I thought we'd lost them!"

He yanked me along fast enough that I was almost forced to run to keep up. Pulse racing, I looked over my shoulder. The lobby was still empty. The bright interior lights had turned the two sets of glass doors into black mirrors on either side. I didn't see anybody else. In fact, I didn't spot *anything* I'd consider a threat. Certainly no government agents.

But apparently Sky had, because he was on a mission as he pulled me into an alcove past the bathroom.

"*Sky,*" I hissed. The slap of my shoes against the tile sounded too loud. "What about the car?"

"They were looking at it when I spotted them." Sky let go of me. His face was a hard mask, mouth tight. "We're going to have to leave it."

"Then what—"

He abruptly pulled me to one side. "In here," he ordered, and his fingers closed around my wrist, tugging. I had only a second to register a flare of blue sparks—summoned electricity—and the click of an electronic door lock. Then Sky pushed me, and I staggered into darkness, disoriented, hands outstretched.

They bumped into metal grating first, then cardboard. I couldn't see a thing.

"Sky—" I turned and, for the second time in the span of a minute, ran face-first into his sternum with a muffled yelp.

This time he caught me by the shoulders, and I hastily backed up, out of his grip. But there was nowhere to go. My bag thumped into a hard surface behind me, and something rattled. I craned my neck.

A closet. He'd shoved me into a closet. I was crammed in next to a broom, mop, and a bucket. The shelf I'd run into was lined with bottles of cleaning supplies, boxes, and packages of toilet paper. "What—"

"*Sh.*" Sky tapped his lips and, with his other hand, pulled the door closed. The latch gave a soft *snick*.

Damn it.

Here we go again.

This closet made the mall's changing room look like a penthouse suite. Was I going to spend the whole day packed into small spaces with Sky? The universe really had it out for me.

Blinking hard, I tried to force my eyes to adjust to the sudden lack of light. I lurched when blue sparks flared, but it was only a brief crackle before the pale glow died and the mechanical lock activated again. A card reader. Sky had just sealed us in here. How the heck did that work?

Not for the first time, I had a sneaking suspicion there was more to Sky's synth-skin powers than just the ability to manipulate electricity. But we had more pressing matters to deal with right now, and I kept the questions behind my compressed lips, breathing hard through my nose. Tension radiated from him. From us both. My muscles quivered with it.

I jumped when Sky shifted, brushing against me. A touch of claustrophobia tried to rise and something…else. Awareness.

I could feel his chest expanding with each breath.

We were pressed together thigh to shoulder. Any attempt to wiggle for more space only succeeded in somehow flattening my pelvis more tightly against his. He made a sound, a surprised puff of air, stiffening against me.

"What are you *doing*?" he asked, voice low and a little hoarse.

"Trying to get more room. I'll just…" Blood rushed into my cheeks as I crowded the shelf at my back again instead and held as still as possible.

License 16. License 16 was here, and we were in danger. I had much more important things to worry about than the fact that the seam of Sky's jeans dug into my lower belly.

"Sorry I hauled you in here like that," he whispered after a strained beat. "I didn't have time to explain."

I'd created a few inches of space between us, but his breath stirred the fine hairs near my temple, heightening the force of my blush. Somehow, he radiated the heat of a small sun.

I had no idea what to do with my hands, so I grasped the shelf behind me. The air smelled like my wintergreen gum, bleach, and that acidic lemon cleaner. And, of course, Sky. Night wind and sandalwood. That was clear as day since my nose was practically squashed against his collarbone.

The awkward angle I was holding myself at was beginning to make my back ache, but I didn't dare slump forward.

"It's okay." I silently reminded my nervous system of that fact and chomped my gum a little more violently. "What *happened*?"

Muffled voices drifted through the door. Sky went rigid again, and I gripped the shelf harder. After a second, the sound faded and a child's laughter echoed. No government agents. Not yet.

I tried again, barely a whisper. "Are you sure you saw License 16 or…?"

Maybe he'd just seen somebody loitering in the parking lot and jumped to conclusions. It made sense he'd be a bit paranoid. That was quickly becoming my middle name.

He didn't answer right away, instead leaning closer to the door, like he was listening for more sounds outside our cleaning closet. When none came, some of the tightness bled from the long line of him pressed against me, and he finally murmured, "I was on my way back to the car when a dark SUV pulled up. It wasn't marked, and I didn't get a good look, but they'd parked our car in and were checking out the plates and looking in the windows."

My pulse sped. Not *our* car, if we were getting technical. Which was probably part of the issue. "Maybe it's not License 16. Maybe somebody called in a stolen car or something and…and that was some undercover cop or…"

Not exactly a better alternative, but at least it took the extraterrestrial conspiracy out of the equation.

I felt Sky shrug. "It's not worth taking the chance. Who knows who's looking for us? We're better off lying low."

He was right. Seemed like the entire galaxy was chasing us at this point. "So what's the plan? We just spend the night in this closet?"

There wasn't even enough room to sit down unless I sat down on *top* of Sky. My belly flipped over itself. Though…spending the night in Sky's lap crammed inside a cleaning closet wasn't nearly as appealing as it might've sounded prior to it being an actual possibility. Something about being surrounded by toilet paper made it way less sexy.

"There's a roadside motel not far from here," Sky said. "Did you see it?"

"No." I tilted my head back. If I squinted really hard, I could sort of make out the outline of his head. I hadn't seen any motel, but I'd been half asleep when he pulled off the highway.

Then the full implications of that settled in. My mouth went dry. Now *that* felt a lot more dangerous than spending the night in this janitorial closet with him. So far, we'd spent this little road trip in the car.

A motel meant a bed. And a bed meant…

Nothing, Rae. A bed meant sleeping.

I was suddenly grateful for the darkness. At least he couldn't see the redness I felt warming my cheeks. "So, what, we hide in here until they're gone and then…? Make a run for it on foot?" I never thought I'd be sad to part with the car we'd stolen from a stranger. "How far are we talking?"

"Half a mile? Maybe?" Sky moved again, and this time his knee bumped mine. Immediately, he stilled, and the shape of his head tilted down. "Sorry. There's not much room in here."

Gee, I hadn't noticed. The laugh I attempted was more of a strangled wheeze. "My bag isn't helping, but I can't reach…"

"Here." I froze in place when his fingers brushed my arms, feeling their way up past my elbows to my shoulders. My heartbeat stuttered at the light touch, and then he was gripping my bag's straps. "Lean forward," he said quietly. "Slip the straps off. I'll help."

My throat worked in another saliva-less swallow as I did what I was told, rocking forward.

Right into him. Again. But this time was different.

My chest flattened against hard muscles beneath soft cotton. He adjusted his stance, and his thigh slipped to the outside of my leg. He was so warm. My breathing didn't feel quite steady when I extended my arms behind me—especially when the motion thrust my breasts harder into him.

And then Sky sucked in a near-soundless breath, and I stopped moving.

Everything seemed louder, more noticeable in the darkness. I could feel his heartbeat where we pressed together, the pound of it. Or maybe that was my own racing. It was hard to tell the difference.

Regardless, awareness crackled like the sparks he'd just produced, heating my blood.

License 16 was possibly searching for us in this very building. This was *not* the time to be focusing on how nicely we fit like this.

Then he slipped the straps down my arms, twisting, and the bag thudded softly at my feet.

"There," Sky whispered, easing back. Those few inches between us felt like a mile. "Better? We may be here a while."

Without the extra bulk behind me, I could finally lean against the shelf. Lemon cleaner-scented air rushed between us, and I filled my lungs, only then realizing I'd been holding my breath that entire time. I blamed my dizziness on that.

"Thanks," I managed. It still wasn't much space because when I reached up to shove hair off my face, my elbow scraped his stomach. I slapped my arms to my sides. "Sorry."

His laugh was forced. "It's okay."

Silence fell. Needing a distraction, I strained to hear beyond the closet, but nothing filtered through.

If what Sky had seen was just law enforcement responding to a stolen car, maybe they'd tow it and move on. People dumped stolen cars all the time, right? At least, that's how it worked on TV.

Maybe we'd get lucky.

Judging by how the evening—hell, the whole week—had gone so far, I wasn't counting it. Just today, we'd dealt with being followed to the mall, the Enil showing up, then that *fiasco* at the lookout…

I closed my eyes, mortification rising again. Might as well get it out of the way since there wasn't anything else to do in here.

"I'm sorry about earlier," I whispered, turning my face toward the door. Just in case he could see better than I could. Who knew with alien super-suits? "About the…the soda, I mean. And the…" *Almost kiss.* "Well, all of it."

When I opened my eyes again, they were starting to adjust. Enough that I caught the gleam of his in the dark. He was looking at me.

"You didn't mean to fall off the car, Rae," he said, a hint of humor in his voice. He'd leaned against the shelf at his back, arms braced behind him. "Speaking of. How are you? From the fall?"

I tucked my tongue in my cheek. God, how embarrassing. "I'm fine." I ignored the traitorous twinge my tailbone gave. "It wasn't *that* far." I'd also managed to tuck and roll, but I didn't mention that part. Might as well avoid admitting I'd gotten good at *falling* off things.

"That's good." It was carefully neutral. I could almost make out his expression now, though. It looked suspiciously like a smile. I narrowed my eyes.

Did I actually bring up the kiss part? Broach it? Maybe if I put it out there, it'd clear some of this weirdness between us—

Footsteps thudded right outside the closet, and I gasped, whirling as much as I could in the small space. In an instant, Sky was upright, too. He somehow succeeded in wedging himself between me and the closet entrance. A shadow blocked out the faint line of light below the door.

Someone was standing outside.

I didn't dare breathe. My pulse hammered in my throat.

Muffled voices trickled in. "What about in here?" The door handle jiggled, and I snatched handfuls of Sky's shirt.

This was it. They were going to find us. I waited for the door to wrench open, for light to spill in, for shouts, but…

But it didn't happen.

"It's locked," said the voice, and the handle stopped moving. "Card reader hasn't been damaged. The manager said the janitorial staff left hours ago."

Someone else answered, but it was too faint. The shadow moved away. Air rushed from my lungs, and I sagged.

That'd been close. Too close for comfort.

Realizing I was clinging to Sky, I unwound my fingers from his shirt's material and drew back as far as I could. He awkwardly shuffled and bumped his way across from me until he once again leaned on the other shelf.

In the dimness, I caught his gaze. We exchanged a look, though neither of us spoke. The time for whispered conversation was over. They were still out there. He'd been right. They *were* looking for us. Or at least for *someone*.

Which meant we were trapped in this stupid closet.

Thanks, universe.

But when the immediate danger didn't return, my lids grew heavy. It was warm and dare I say cozy, in an antiseptic, coffin sort of way. If I hadn't had to focus on staying upright, a nap would've sounded great. Even with Sky's proximity.

At first, more indistinct voices had carried through the walls. Those eventually faded, too. I didn't hear any movement—anything at all, actually, besides our combined breathing.

After somewhere between fifteen minutes and an hour had passed—hard to tell inside janitorial hell—I shot Sky a questioning look. Surely we could try our luck now.

He gazed back, impassive. Apparently not.

I alternated between battling to keep my lids open and my chin off my chest. The only thing that helped was the stinging, acrid citrus scent. It was so strong. I never wanted to smell lemon again.

I'd just begun to nod off again when pain jolted me awake—a stabbing ache deep in my calf. A cramp. Dehydration, I was sure, along with standing in this same position for who knew how long. Stifling a curse, I shifted from foot to foot, trying to alleviate it— until Sky stilled me by brushing his fingertips over my hip. I wrenched my eyes to his just in time to see him reach above me with his other hand. Why was he so close—

Oh. I'd nearly knocked off a bottle of toilet cleaner. Sky carefully set it back on the shelf.

"My bad," I whispered, biting the inside of my lip.

He gave me a long look as he lowered flat-footed again, and then he leaned in to whisper, "I think we can try slipping out now. I'm going to trigger the lock again. I'll go first, okay?"

His breath grazed my ear, warm enough it almost distracted me from the fact that he'd said we were finally getting out of this damn closet. Adrenaline shot through my tired body and awakened nerves. "You think it's safe?"

"Only one way to find out. Hang on. I'll just…" He tried to turn, but that brought us bumping into each other, shoulder to hip. I rocked back—and banged my head against the metal shelf.

"Shit," I hissed, rubbing it. Then I forgot I had a head when his hands closed on my waist, steadying me.

Slowly, I raised my eyes. I could see him clearly now, the glitter of his gaze, the fact that he'd bitten his lip and a dark curl had fallen over his forehead.

"You okay?" he asked, the timbre of his voice low and intimate in the small space.

"Fine. Just…" I dropped my hand. Heat crept up my neck. "Bumped my head."

His fingers tightened the barest bit before slipping away.

"Okay. I'll slide past you." His words vibrating from his chest into mine. He turned his head toward the door, and I stared at his Adam's apple, inches from my face. It moved when he added, "Stay here, okay?"

I gave a nonchalant shrug to hide an overwhelming amount of chalant. "Sure."

A few seconds later, he shorted the lock, the scent of ozone lingering in the air. He eased the door open, and I peered around his broad shoulders. I couldn't see much, but the coast must've been clear because he nudged the door further and slipped out.

Then his form rippled as he activated his synth-skin's cloaking mechanism. I watched him melt from view and shook my head slowly. So strange.

I used the opportunity—and the fact that I could move again—to bend and shrug on my bag. Every muscle felt stiff and creaky. Situating the straps, I eased forward a step to peek around the alcove's edge, back into the lobby. An instrumental rendition of a popular pop song echoed eerily, and the windows reflected the empty space with its vending machines, bathrooms, and wall of pamphlets.

I didn't see anyone. I didn't hear anything, either. Maybe we really were in the clear.

A heartbeat later, when Sky melted back into view and I bleated in surprise, I really hoped we were. I slapped a hand over my chest. "Jeez. You scared me. Are we good?"

"Yeah." He slanted his mouth apologetically, glancing over his shoulder before facing me again. In the bright light, his face looked even more drawn and weary. "I don't see anybody. They're gone." He jammed his hand through his hair. "Come on. They towed the car, so we'll have to walk to the motel."

I stifled my groan. "You're sure you saw one?"

"A motel?" He raised a brow at me and, at my nod, sent a ghost of a wan smile. "Yeah. Come on. It's not far."

At least a motel meant a shower, right? I could walk half a mile if it meant getting to be clean again. Sighing, I hefted the bag and followed Sky through the empty space, to the doors. He pushed one open, holding it wide for me.

I slipped past him and into the night.

Neither of us spoke. I focused on putting one tired leg in front of the other as we followed the winding sidewalk along the parking lot, to where it ended and gravel ran between the highway's shoulder and ditch beyond. Our shoes crunched over stone in haphazard, off-beat rhythms. The interstate on one side was quiet save for the occasional semi-trailer and lone car, and the sloping, barren field looked desolate in the sliver of a moon's light.

I could see the glow of a building in the direction Sky had pointed us. The motel. Was that half a mile? A mile? It was hard to tell. The chilly night breeze was cool enough to make me shiver, and I was just considering digging out my stolen sweater again when a light swept over us.

Sky was on me before I could make a sound, dragging me into the ditch.

The world spun in a blur of whirling dark sky and tall grass. The air rushed from me in a grunt as I landed on my back in the underbrush, Sky's palm cushioning my head. My bag slipped from my shoulder and tumbled to the ground beside us.

And Sky came down on top of me, a solid wall of heat trapping me against the dirt.

A gasp got stuck in my throat as my eyes found his against the backdrop of the stars. A dark curl fell over his forehead. He'd caught himself on his elbows, his chest flattening mine.

Before I could recover, light swept the grass around us again, and I went rigid. Headlights? A searchlight?

I didn't have a chance to ask.

"Stay very still," Sky murmured, barely louder than the wind.

Then he began to fade from view. Just like before.

"Are you…" I started, but then I couldn't find my voice at all.

A tickling sensation poured over my skin, like the brush of staticky fingers all over. I stopped breathing.

I'd never been this close to him when he'd cloaked. I could *see* him and yet I *couldn't*. I'd always thought he'd disappeared entirely, but that wasn't the case. The faint outline of Sky remained visible against the stars. *Or a version of Sky.* The shape of him was sharper, leaner, smoother. Not human.

A shape I recognized.

I'd only seen it once, but it was burned into my memory.

His *alien* form was visible with the cloaking tech activated like this.

My pulse gave an extra hard thump. I was vaguely aware my mouth was hanging open, but I couldn't seem to close it.

He'd curved the hard length of his body over mine, tucking me under him. His leg was wedged between my knees, his forearms bracketing my head. His heart pounded. I could feel each beat against my sternum. His body heat chased away my earlier chill.

His breath feathered my lips.

I could almost make out his eyes, but when I tipped my chin and looked down…I couldn't see *either of us.*

I was invisible, too.

"Holy shit," I choked out. This was *insane.*

"*Shhh,*" came Sky's disembodied whisper. "*Easy.*"

Right. *Easy.* Because being chased by the government, hiding in a janitor's closet, and getting *vanished by alien tech* was just part of a normal day.

The bubble of hysterical laughter lodged in my throat. I raised my eyes to the vicinity of his. A faint blue shine met mine. *Alien eyes.* Goosebumps swept along my arms for a wholly different reason than the cold.

The light combed past us again. I could see it through him, but his outline was even more visible when backlit. A shadowy shape.

Steps scuffed somewhere on the shoulder of the highway, out of sight, and voices drifted on the night air. Casual. No shouting. It didn't *sound* like a threat. My breaths came fast anyway, forcing my invisible torso against Sky's with each pant.

A car engine revved. Tires crunched gravel, and the beam drifted away.

I stared up at the faint blue gleam of Sky's eyes, the stars sparkling *through* him, until the shape of his head tilted. He raised himself a fraction. Just enough to look over the ditch's edge. Whatever he saw had him exhaling heavily.

His silhouette shifted, then shimmered before finally snapping back into view.

Just like that, he was human again. Visible.

"Oh my God," I wheezed, air rushing back into my tight chest. "Holy *shit,* Sky!"

"It was just a car." His shoulders lowered. "Just someone pulling over for a second. They're gone now."

Only then did he seem to realize he was still on top of me, caging me in.

He blinked down. I blinked back.

"I'm so sorry," he said, a pink tinge darkening his cheeks. He heaved himself to the side in a smooth roll, sitting up and shoving his fingers through his messy hair. He extended his other hand. "Here. Are you all right?"

"I'm fine." I waved his help away and pushed into a seated position on my own, brushing off dry dirt and grass. My face burned. I wasn't sure what was more disconcerting: the fact that I found being tackled into a ditch by Invisible Sky hot or the whole *Invisible* Sky part. "That was *crazy*. How was I invisible, too? And did you know you can see your…your…" I flapped a hand at him, struggling.

He stared at me and ever-so-slowly raised a brow. I blanched. "Your Pladian form! God, I mean you can see your Pladian form. Sort of." I stopped, gathered my flustered thoughts, and then tilted my head his way, narrowing my eyes. "How exactly does the invisibility thing work?"

"Ah. Well." He let out a puff of air. "It's hard to explain the synth-skin's light refraction tech."

"Right," I mumbled, eyeing him. "I'm sure."

He avoided my gaze as he stood and scooped my bag up, brushing it off while he scanned the highway, like he was double-checking we were in the clear. I climbed to my feet and reached for the strap, but he was already slinging it over his shoulder.

I opened my mouth to protest, and he shook his head. "I've got it. Are you sure you're good? I didn't hurt you?"

"I can…" I sighed, knowing better than to argue with *that* stubborn set of his mouth. "I'm okay. You didn't hurt me."

I'd felt a lot of things while trapped under him. Pain wasn't one of them.

God, I definitely needed sleep.

"Okay. Come on," Sky said, gripping the bag's strap and turning. "We should keep moving."

That little incident had at least given me the rush I needed to keep going. My legs felt a little steadier as I followed him into the night, trying very, very hard not to replay the feeling of him pressed against me. Of that faint blue shine of alien eyes and the illicit thrill it gave me.

And failing spectacularly.

This was going to be one awkward motel stay.

Chapter 7

DO YOU NEED SOME ALOE
FOR THAT SLOW BURN?

THERE WAS good news and bad news.

Good news: the motel was even closer than Sky had thought.

Bad news: I was experiencing the saddest, most disappointing shower of my life.

I stared up at the slow, weak trickle of rusty water leaking from the nozzle above my head. It came out in spurts. Rust clogged half the holes, which could've been part of the problem.

Not that I was surprised. The dingy bathroom wasn't much bigger than that cleaning closet, and I'd been excited it *had* a shower in the first place. That excitement had tanked fast. Running water wasn't going to do me much good if I couldn't wash with it.

The nozzle sputtered and spat a blast of droplets into my face. I flinched back, cursing, but then the flow increased. Not by much, but enough to work up a lather with the cheap shampoo/conditioner combo the motel had provided.

I'd take what I could get.

Sighing, I turned my back and slicked my hair, wetting the greasy strands. The bar of soap wasn't much better. I could already feel it drying out my face.

Skin care wasn't high on the list of priorities when you were running for your life. Sleep wasn't either. My eyes felt like they were full of sand.

Like the shower, it didn't matter how shitty the bed was. I'd be passing out in it as soon as possible.

I ran my fingers through my tangled hair and tilted my face under the spray, spitting out the rusty, sulfur-tasting water.

I would be waiting a bit longer before collapsing, though. There was a 24-hour gas station across the road. Once I was clean, I'd head over there for food and supplies. Maybe a toothbrush.

The water pressure spluttered, and I tensed.

Please let it hold until I get the soap out of my hair.

When it recovered and started flowing again, I speed-rinsed, glancing at the locked door through the crack in the yellowed curtain.

Sky was waiting in line for the next shower, in our tiny room with its pair of double beds. He'd barely been on his feet. Which was why I was making the gas-station run.

Hair as clean as it was going to get in water that smelled faintly of rotten eggs, I turned off the wimpy flow and stepped out of the bathtub, wrapping myself in the sandpaper-textured towel provided.

Visible in the smudged mirror, the shine of the purple bracelet on my wrist caught the light. It matched the faded edges of my fore-head bruise and the ones under my eyes. I looked almost as exhausted as Sky. I'd have to be, considering spending the night in a motel room with him didn't even seem nerve-racking anymore.

I dressed quickly in the same wrinkled, smelly jeans and shirt and twisted my hair into a loose braid while it dried. It'd have to do. I hoped like hell the gas station had deodorant. And that toothbrush.

Shouldering on the stolen sweater, I opened the bathroom door. Musty steam rolled out with me. I waved it away, vision adjusting to the dull orange light cast by the single lamp between the beds.

The place was a dump. It smelled like mothballs and stale cigarette smoke, despite the no-smoking signs posted everywhere. The peeling wallpaper had seen better decades, and more than one suspicious-looking stain darkened the yellow and pink floral motif. I wasn't entirely convinced there weren't bedbugs lurking beneath the hideous pink comforters.

Sky stood near the window, peering out through the crooked blinds. He turned as I stepped out of the bathroom. Even rumpled, wiped out, and disheveled, he was gorgeous. It wasn't fair.

"Finished?" he rasped, fatigue weighing down the words.

"It's all yours," I said, moving aside. I gathered the shoes I'd kicked off. The battered knock-off Chucks had seen better days, too, charred and dusty from the fight at TWU and the mall. "I'm going to make that run to the gas station."

Sky's murmured assent as he crossed the room was barely a grunt.

"About that, though. How do I go about buying anything?" I asked, wincing as I perched on the bed's edge. My tailbone smarted from being in the car for so long—and from the tumble I'd taken off the hood. I forced the thought away before a blush could rise. "I didn't exactly grab cash on our way out of town."

I hadn't thought to run by the ATM. I must've missed that in the *How to Flee Evil Agents and Eviler Aliens* manual.

"You can use this card," Sky said, pausing in front of me and reaching into his pocket.

I finished tying my second shoe and sat up as he extended a black credit card with a logo I didn't recognize. "What is this?" I stared at it, then him. "I didn't realize Pladia Credit Union had a branch this far south of the Milky Way."

"You come up with that right off the top of your head?"

I couldn't bite back my grin. "Yeah."

"Hilarious." He shot me a deadpan look, though the corner of his mouth twitched. "Bast made it. He's got a program that skims money off…" He pushed the card at me again. "You know what? I'm too tired to explain it. Swipe the card. Help yourself."

"Sorry," I said, stifling the smile. Maybe I was slap-happy. I took it from him, standing and slipping it into my back pocket.

He was studying me somberly enough that I frowned.

"What?"

His jaw jutted to the side, a line appearing between his brows. "You sure you're okay going alone?"

"To the gas station? It's, like, thirty seconds from the front door, Sky. I don't think the Enil are going to swoop down in the time it takes me to grab a toothbrush and go."

…would they? I bit the inside of my cheek, glancing uneasily toward the window. When I looked back, Sky's scowl had deepened. He didn't appear convinced, either. That didn't exactly help matters.

He didn't push the issue, though. Tired Sky had less of a protective, control-everything streak. Noted.

"Grab me a toothbrush too. If you don't mind," he said instead, stepping back.

"Yeah." I rocked onto my toes and stuck my hands into my sweater pockets. "Anything else?"

"That should be good." He squeezed his nape, exhaling heavily through his nostrils. "I'm going to shower. I'll make it quick."

A flash of him naked and soapy hit me, and my brain stuttered. With effort, I blinked it away as he turned.

"Sure. Same. Well, not, like, the shower, but you know." I jerked a thumb toward the door. "Gas station. Quick run."

He hesitated with his hand on the bathroom handle. "Uh huh. Be careful."

"You too," I said then immediately winced. What'd he have to be careful of besides really shitty water pressure?

He just shook his head and disappeared into the bathroom, shutting the door behind him with a decisive *click*.

"'Be careful'? Really?" I muttered, whirling. "God."

What *was* it about his presence? Falling off cars and tripping over my words…no wonder he was nervous that the fate of his world was lodged somewhere in my brain.

I blew out a sharp breath and moved to the door.

Spending some mysterious alien money would make me feel better. So would finally brushing my teeth. Deodorant, toothpaste, and emotional support snacks were in order.

With one last glance at the bathroom, I grabbed the room key and left Sky to his very naked shower.

The gas station was a whole twenty-five seconds away, not thirty, and if I hadn't seen an actual UFO in action, I would've said it was lit up like a crash site. Its outdoor speaker played classic rock, and squealing guitars echoed against the motel's façade, creating a strange doubling effect. Insects trilled and thrummed in the tall grass pushing in along the edges of the cracked asphalt parking lot. This far south, the night air was balmy, and I pushed up my sweater's sleeves, regretting the extra layer.

The place was also surprisingly busy for three a.m., both inside and out. I wove through a few vehicles sitting at pumps and parking spots. The door chimed as I entered, and I hesitated in the entrance, squinting under the assault of fluorescent lighting. The interior was somehow even brighter than outside. Half-blind, I shuffled toward the nearest aisle.

With Sky's intergalactic credit card burning a hole in my pocket, I got to work.

They did indeed have toothbrushes. Deodorant, too. Even a razor, which nearly made me cry. A T-shirt wedged between the Slim Jims and motor oil caught my eye. The front read *Mind Your Biscuits*. It seemed weirdly fitting, so I snatched it up, too. Who'd have thought a little retail therapy would do the trick during an alien infiltration?

Five minutes later, I plopped a bag of steaming gas station taquitos on top of the excessive mound of items I'd stacked by the register.

"There," I told the cashier, beaming. "That should be it."

The woman behind the counter, round, middle-aged, and exactly the type to run a tight ship, eyed my pile, then me, then the pile again. "You need a bag?"

I imagined myself trying to carry everything across the gravel strip in front of the motel and stifled a laugh. "That'd be great."

As she rang me up, I glanced around. The place doubled as a truck stop, I realized. Hence the twenty-four-hour glow and the people tucked into booths near the coffee machines and rotating hot dogs.

Most of them looked like they'd been on the road a while. I recognized the vibe. I, too, had seen some things—

I stiffened.

There was a police officer sitting in the nearest booth.

My stomach lurched, and a phantom fist squeezed the air from my lungs. The loud music and lights seemed to fade, and my vision narrowed to the uniformed man hunched over his coffee at the nearby table.

Could he have come from the rest stop we'd just fled? Sky hadn't gotten a good look at whoever was in that dark SUV, but we'd heard those voices.

I tried to tamp down the rising panic.

The cop didn't look like he was working a grand theft auto case. He looked…bored. Unless he was staking the place out. Or waiting. Or—

Get it together.

It was fine. He was just grabbing a cup of coffee. And I was just buying junk. He had no reason to suspect me of anything.

I dragged my gaze away. And it got stuck.

No reason at all—unless, of course, he'd seen *that.*

Unless he happened to be watching the TV mounted above the cigarettes and lotto tickets.

The one currently showing my face. Grainy, grayscale, and deeply unfortunate.

Oh no.

No no no.

I stared in horror, ice running through my veins. Was that my *driver's license* picture? How the hell had they gotten that? And why?

And while we were at it, why was it always the *worst picture ever?*

Numbness spread through my chest. A ticker at the bottom of the screen helpfully explained that authorities were "seeking information from Raven Barrister regarding an incident at Willow University." I tried to read the rest, but it scrolled too quickly, the lines blurring together.

I'd seen enough. Information. They wanted information from me. My name and face were on the television screen.

I was wanted *for questioning*.

My pulse kicked into a full sprint. I fought the urge to glance at the cop again and instead tried to look as relaxed as humanly possible while the cashier continued her very slow, very thorough scan of my pile.

Oh God. I was *wanted*. By the *authorities*.

The bright lights seemed to narrow in, like a spotlight. I was caught out in the open. Sweat prickled my upper lip.

Would they *arrest* me? Would they confiscate the band on my wrist? My protection would be gone. The Enil would find me. I'd watched the last one swat away human soldiers like they were *gnats*—

"Forty-four ninety-two," the cashier said.

I jumped, and my tiny gasp slipped out before I could bite it back. The woman raised one penciled brow.

Gathering the remnants of my shredded nerves, I offered a shaky smile. "Sorry. Too much caffeine."

Hopefully that explained why it took me three tries to insert Sky's sketchy alien credit card. My fingers weren't exactly cooperating.

While the card processed, I transferred my weight from foot to foot, heart hammering. What if it didn't go through? What if Sky, or Bast, had made some mistake and their woo-woo charge limit was maxed out, and it caused a scene? Surely the officer would notice me then.

I caved and darted another look at the cop. He was glued to his phone, coffee untouched.

Which was great, because my face was *still* on the screen behind him. I was staring back at me. Looking haggard and, frankly, unamused.

Why hadn't I worn makeup the day I'd gotten that photo taken? I would have had I known it would eventually be blasted to the entire country on the late-night news. My knees wobbled.

The card reader was taking forever. Years. My lungs were slowly constricting. Cold perspiration stuck my shirt to my spine.

The display flashed *accepted* before the device screamed at me to remove the card. My hand shook like a leaf in a thunderstorm as I yanked the plastic out and shoved it in my pocket. The cashier was staring at me. I forced a bright smile that stretched my cheeks too far. Because surely that would help. She probably thought I was on drugs.

"Thanks!" I said too loudly. Snatching up the pair of bags, I whirled in place.

I couldn't help but look again.

The TV picture had finally changed to something else. A story about local politics. I wheezed a relieved breath. The police officer at the booth still hadn't torn his eyes from his phone. He hadn't noticed.

But I still hightailed it out of there like my ass was on fire. The bell jangled in protest as I shouldered the door open and rushed into the night, gulping the humid air down. I forced myself to walk instead of sprint across the parking lot. Gravel crunched beneath my shoes and the packed-full plastic bags bumped my thighs with every stride. Heat lightning flashed in the distance of an otherwise clear, star-dusted sky.

Twenty feet.

A glance back showed the gas station lights bathing the small building in a pool of white. The cop was a mere silhouette in the window. He hadn't moved.

I sped up anyway. Just a little. Fifteen feet. The one-story motel with cracked, faded siding dominated my view. Our door was close.

A car rolled past in the street beyond, its bass thumping in time with my pumping heart. I forced myself to keep breathing. The officer hadn't followed me.

Ten feet. Five.

I broke and ran the last few steps, shuffling the bags to one hand and wrenching out the room key. My fingers shook as I jammed it into the lock. I barely got it turned before I shoved my shoulder into the door. It burst open, and I stumbled in.

Once it was closed, I collapsed back against it, eyes squeezing shut.

Holy shit.

Groaning, I slid down until I sat on the dirty carpet, my back pressed to the door. The bags flopped to either side of me. I buried my head in my hands.

I was wanted by the police.

Somehow, that felt more messed up than being wanted by the Enil.

Chapter 8

GALAXY'S MOST
WANTON—ER, WANTED

I LEANED my head back against the door, staring at the stained ceiling with unseeing eyes. My stomach pitched.

That had been *my* face on that television. Not Sky's, of course. He had a freaking cloaking suit, so maybe they didn't even *have* a picture of him. Meanwhile, they had the most heinous photo of me in existence. And now everyone was seeing it.

Everyone.

My poor mother. This was even worse than I could've imagined. If the police were actively looking for me, she had to be so worried. Had she reported me missing? I tried to remember all those true crime shows. How long did you have to disappear before someone took it seriously?

But that hadn't just been a missing poster. They'd tied me to the incident at the university.

Which wasn't entirely wrong, but...not like they were implying! What questions could they possibly have for me? What would my job think? My professors? Another tidal wave of nausea rose at the thought. My friends. My *family.*

I was strait-laced, normal, kind of boring Raven Barrister. I wasn't the kind of person who'd be wanted for questioning.

I needed Sky to let me call home. So I could fix this. There had to be a way to fix this.

Everything was spiraling so far out of my control.

I cupped my bent knees, digging my fingers in like I could stabilize this tumble into insanity. The shower was still running. Through the door, I could hear the creaky pipes and the patter of water. I'd only been gone ten minutes, max.

Restlessness drove me to my feet, and I smoothed back my drying braid. Sky and I needed to have a conversation *now*. There had to be a compromise. My legs trembled as I paced the length of the room, tearing off the stolen sweater and tossing it across the bed I'd claimed.

I'd been content to let him drive—literally and figuratively—but this…seeing my face up there was *too* much. It felt a bit like I was on a sinking ship. Or maybe a crashing spaceship, since there were too many freaking *aliens* in my life to count.

Uttering a frustrated groan, I strode back to the door and snatched up the bags. Sky was taking too long, and I needed to channel this frantic energy into something. I yanked my purchases out, slamming them none-too-gently on the top of the dresser situated at the foot of our beds. I'd gotten enough toiletries to last us at least a week…but I hoped like hell I'd be home and back to normal life way before that.

Was normal a thing now? Probably not. God, I didn't even know.

I'd made it halfway through unpacking when the water stopped, and I paused with the deodorant in my hand. When Sky didn't immediately appear, I ripped off the packaging and applied the aloe-scented antiperspirant. I was sweating enough to need it. Funny how being plastered all over the twenty-four-hour news would do that to a person. My throat tightened, and I forced down the lump.

Sky would see reason. He'd understand my family needed to know I wasn't an actual *fugitive*. Well… I grimaced. I mean, sure, I'd helped steal a car. And a sweater. And I think I still had those sunglasses, but—

Hinges creaked behind me—the bathroom door opening. I launched into it without turning around. "You won't believe what I just saw, Sky. I'm wanted." Clutching the deodorant, I whirled. "*My face*. I saw my face on the—Oh."

Words died. I died a little, too.

A very shirtless Sky stood in the bathroom doorway, framed by steam. He'd paused in drying his hair, towel in hand, water glistening on his skin. His slicked-down curls dripped at the ends, and his surprised gaze was locked on me.

"Um…" My tongue felt thick. I forgot how to breathe.

He was all lean, carved muscle, barefoot, and his jeans sat low. *Criminally* low. They exposed the entire, slicing shape of his hipbones. The flat expanse of his ridged stomach, the tiny trail of hair leading into his waistband—

All rational thought—and my saliva—fled the scene.

"I…" I barely caught myself before dropping the deodorant on the floor. I was gaping. I knew it, but I couldn't seem to close my mouth.

"I thought you'd still be…" Sky slowly resumed towel-drying his hair, narrowing his eyes. "What do you mean you saw your face?"

My throat worked. His abs had abs. I'd forgotten. How was it even possible to be that…that *hot*? Sky could've moonlighted as an underwear model…you know, in between slinging drinks and saving worlds. He'd sell *so many* boxer briefs.

Now I was thinking about him in his underwear, which was *not* helpful. Blinking, I wrenched my gaze away and gave him my back, tossing the deodorant down. My whole body felt hot and tingly.

Holy topless alien, Batman.

Somehow, I scrounged up my voice. "There was a, uh…news story on the TV. In the gas station." I grabbed a toothbrush, looked at it like it was the most fascinating object in the room—not the half-naked fantasy behind me—and furrowed my brow. "It said I was wanted for questioning by the, um…" *What was the word?* What were words? "Authorities."

Saying it aloud chased away the fluster and brought the anxiety surging back. I tipped my head up, though I didn't turn away from the *incredibly* interesting wall as I added, "There wasn't anything about you, though. Just me. *'Wanted for questioning about the university incident,'* apparently." My guts roiled at the memory. "That means I'm wanted by the police now, Sky. My family will have seen that. And if they catch me, this thing's gone." I held up the wrist with the alien bracelet attached to it. "And there'll be nothing to stop the Enil from finding me and…and…"

I lowered my arm to my side again, unable to finish. The image of those soldiers being tossed by the washing-machine Enil at the mall drifted back. I didn't stand a chance.

"They're not going to catch you," Sky murmured, almost absently. Like he was lost in thought. He sounded closer, and it was enough to gird my loins. I turned toward him. He'd moved to stand by the end of my bed, and as his eyes found mine, he said it again, more firmly. "They *won't* catch you."

"Okay." I kept my gaze firmly on his face—somehow—and took a deep breath. It was time to try again. "But you've got to let me call home. I need to contact my mom. She'll be worried. Confused." Frustrated, I tossed the toothbrush over my shoulder and took a step forward. "They aren't looking for *you*. Just me."

Sky blew out a heavy breath and twisted, flinging the towel. The motion flexed the slanted muscles along his ribcage. My mouth somehow went even drier.

I focused on his face the second he swiveled back.

"It's a stab in the dark," he said, swiping his damp hair back from his forehead. "This is a tactic to flush you out. License 16 is *trying* to get you to do this. Get you to panic. Tip your hand. I'm sure they suspect we're together—they *were* after my SUV, but they won't have surveillance of either of us to prove anything. If you recall, the synth-skin prevents footage of me, just like your cuff does for you."

"Well, it's working! I'm panicking, okay? And—" I reared back. "Wait, what? My what does *what?*"

"The cuff." He jerked his chin at the shiny metal encircling my arm. "It creates a distortion field like my synth-skin does."

"I didn't…" Had he told me that? I blinked rapidly, then shook my head. I couldn't keep track of all this alien tech and what it was capable of.

But it didn't matter. That wasn't the point. He might be able to stay off-grid—to be invisible, both literally and figuratively—but I had a whole *life*. My very human, formerly *normal* life that was being systematically dismantled by this mess. Ruined.

It didn't matter if this was just for show. I was *wanted*, for God's sake.

I slammed my lids closed and pressed my thumb and pointer into them, gesturing vaguely in his direction with my other hand. "This is easier for you, Sky. I'm not like you. It's easier when all this isn't…*real.*"

When I opened my eyes again, he wore a frown. And still no shirt.

"What's not *real?*" he asked, an edge to the question. His mouth pressed into an annoyed line. "Me?"

"You know what I mean." I tried not to look at his naked shoulders. The words had come out wrong. Of course that wasn't what I'd meant. Infuriating man. Infuriating *alien*. "I meant that this is… it's just my *real* life. My friends. My family. Maybe even my *career* at this point, if the professors think *I* had something to do with…" I faltered, cringing at the thought. "If they think I have something to do with the stuff at the school."

He studied me, seeming to absorb that. He was standing awfully close, and he smelled like cheap motel soap and that fresh night-air scent I'd always associated with him. There was a droplet clinging to his shoulder.

I forced myself to look away from it in time to see him cast a glance toward the locked door, jaw tight. When he turned back, it was with a sigh.

"The police looking for you doesn't change the fact that we have to stay under the radar. In fact, it should be a reminder to be even more careful." He set his hands on his hips, like he was digging in. Or bracing. "I'm sorry, Rae. You can't call them. Not yet. Just give it one more day. Let's get to Bast's, and—"

"Well, maybe we could—"

"No. I'm *sorry.* I am. For now, you can't."

I snapped my mouth shut, temper flaring like a breathed-on ember. *Can't.* He was telling me I *couldn't.* I'd been chased by aliens. I was wearing alien marks and being dragged around the whole damn country by an alien. It didn't matter if he happened to be a ridiculously attractive alien. This was so far outside my normal, it wasn't even funny.

And...frankly, it wasn't fair. I hadn't asked for *any* of this.

I shoved my braid over my shoulder, unwilling to give up. "This is *my* life we're talking about. My family. My friends. My everything's been upended by this...intergalactic mess I've been dragged into. What harm could a quick—"

"*Galactic.*"

I squinted at him, momentarily sidetracked. "What?"

"It's galactic." He raised a brow. "If it was intergalactic, it'd involve multiple galaxies, and we're from the same—"

I cut him off with a disgusted click of my tongue. "You know what I mean." I looked around at the peeling wallpaper and stained carpet. "This might be your brand of normal, all this running and hiding and shitty roadside motels, cut off from the world, but I have a life. And this is...this is really messing things up for me. My mom —" My voice broke, and for some reason, that pissed me off even more. "My mom is probably freaking out right now!" I faced him. Let him see the plea.

He did, judging by the way his face tightened. Grooves bracketed his mouth. It didn't matter, though.

"I understand. I do." He took a slow breath. "Rae, I know it's hard, but I told you when we started this."

I didn't want to hear him say no again. I pressed a little closer. Close enough to touch, though I kept my hands to myself. "This is real *for me*, Sky. That's what I meant by what I said earlier. It has *real-world consequences.* Ones I don't get to just..." I threw up my arm. "Fly away and leave behind! Not all of us can hide behind fake credit cards and...and fake skin that scrambles cameras!" My voice was louder than I'd meant it to be, but these emotions...they were flowing now.

This was just the icing on top of this really shitty sci-fi cookie my life had become. I deserved to call home. To let someone—*anyone*—know I was still here.

Still me.

Because I *was*...wasn't I?

There it was. The crux of it. I wasn't even sure who I was right now. Stealing cars. Blowing off tests and work and...*laws*. Leaving the people who mattered most in the dark. I was careful and—

I jolted when, with a muttered curse, Sky snatched up my wrist.

"What—" I broke off when he grabbed the other one, and my heart stopped as he *planted my hands on him.*

Directly on his chest. His very bare, very warm chest.

The metal cuff slid down to my forearm as shock arrowed through me. Before I could even move, before I could even think, he'd angled so he could meet my eyes. His were bright with emotion. Temper. Shadowed with something deeper.

"Does this feel real to you?" he asked, low and silky and... angry? Was that anger?

Too late, I realized I'd dug at a sore spot. Maybe I shouldn't have rubbed it in his face that he was alone here and on a strange planet and...

I knew he was real. I did. Guilt welled up. I hadn't meant to imply otherwise. My emotions just felt heavy and—

"I'm *real*, Raven," he said in that same quiet, husky voice. "I am just as real as you are. All of this is. This situation is *real* for me."

I gazed back at him in the sudden, weighty silence, overflowing with a scrambled mess of feelings. Something about the heat of him, the strength of his grip—the conviction in the words—scrambled it all up even more.

"This is life or death for me," he murmured as he searched my eyes. "This isn't just you versus the Enil. Or the police. Or the government. We are in this together. *Whole worlds* hang in the balance."

"I-I know," I whispered. It was all I could manage past my tight throat. I *knew* that. I *knew* there was so much at stake and yet...

Sky's heartbeat thudded beneath my palm. His *very real* heart. My own sprinted like it was trying to outrun the churning emotions.

As if he could see them, his frown melted into something softer. "I know this all probably feels like it's spinning out of control."

It was so in line with my earlier thoughts, my lips parted in surprise. That wound-up, seething knot in my chest loosened a fraction, dissolving some of my earlier panic along with it.

Sky sighed, and his fingers relaxed on my wrists, but he didn't release me yet. I didn't try to pull from his grasp, either. Maybe it was his touch calming the anxiety. Or maybe it was the fact that, with the flash of irritation he'd shown a second ago fading just as rapidly as it'd appeared, he was looking at me now with…understanding.

He shifted his weight without breaking eye contact. "I understand that it's damn near impossible to find your footing right now. I get it. I understand why you feel what you feel and why you want to call your family."

I…I was feeling things, all right. Mostly how hot his skin was. Lean muscle contracted beneath my palms when he squeezed my wrists gently. It felt…strangely vulnerable. Being *seen* like this. Warmth crept into my cheeks, and I was the one to drop my eyes. Hopefully the lighting was too dim for him to notice the blush.

How had he managed to turn this around? I'd gone from feeling angry to…to whatever this was. Off-kilter.

"But you can't call anyone yet. I need you to stick with me," he said, bending his knees until I was forced to look at him instead of his clavicle. Even that was nicely shaped. "I have a plan, and I told you I would keep you safe. You have to let me do that." His brows gathered, tugging at the healing scrape on his forehead. "You said you were going to try to trust me. So try. Okay?"

I wet my lips and nodded. "I do. Will, I mean." Breathing out, I settled on, "Okay."

I didn't know what else to say. He was right. About all of it. I did feel out of control. Was I really that transparent? Or was he just observant? Watching me and learning. *Paying attention.*

Something about that made me feel shaky inside. Shakier, even, than the prospect of being hunted by my own government and the Enil.

His midnight eyes were so close to mine. I could see shards of silver and lighter blue in his irises. And truth. His words, his gaze, held so much *realness* that shame settled in my gut.

I shouldn't have said he wasn't real. My temper—the shock at seeing myself on that stupid TV screen—had made me spew things I didn't totally mean. I scraped my teeth over my bottom lip and tried to gather my scattered thoughts. To apologize.

After all, Sky's stakes in this were just as high, if not higher, than mine. He was a soldier who'd lost people in this war. A fighter who, even now, battled for the survival of his whole race. All while trying his best to protect me.

Even if it was just for the map's sake.

Except right now, with the way he was gazing down at me, his calm mask gone, his mouth tight, and his tired eyes shadowed in the orange-tinted lamp's lighting, a part of me thought maybe—just maybe—it wasn't *only* about the map.

I dropped my attention to my hands. Against the tapered expanse of his upper body, they seemed small. Pale. His grip was a hint of pressure, and the shining metal cuff on my right arm gleamed dully. God, being this near him made it hard to think straight.

So when my words came, they slipped out in a jumble. "You always feel so…human."

His shoulders jerked with his quick inhalation, and he went still. I did, too, because I wasn't sure where that'd come from. Why *that*. I sensed his gaze on me, but I couldn't seem to look away from the way his long fingers encircled my wrists. Could he feel my pulse racing there?

His answer, when he gave it, was throaty with emotion.

"I *feel* human."

That wasn't what I'd expected him to say. The profoundness of it drew my eyes up to his. There was something heavy in their endless blue. Weariness, but also a disconnect, like he was seeing something not there.

I stared at him, barely daring to breathe.

"I feel more human than Pladian these days," he said, and the raw words were so full of feeling that my mouth fell open before I caught myself and closed it. He let out a quiet breath and looked away. "Honestly, I've spent so much time here—and so much of my life immersed in humanity to prepare for it—it's hard to even remember who I was before this." His throat worked in a swallow. "Humans are…" He gave his head the smallest shake, darting a quick glance at me. His lips twisted into something almost sardonic.

"Messy," I filled in for him, a puff of laughter escaping as my attention drifted back to my hands pressed to his chest. "We're messy sometimes. And a little selfish. I'm sorry I said you weren't real. I didn't mean it. At all."

"I knew what you meant, Raven." A pause, and he tipped his chin down to study my hands, too. "Pladians aren't messy. They're —we're—controlled. Rational. *Logical.*"

"Logical," I repeated. There was nothing logical about the riot of emotion in my belly.

His battle wounds were on display, the injuries from the last fight with the Enil. The cut was almost invisible now, a slashing scab across the center of his chest. I could feel it under my palms, but only barely. He really did heal faster than normal. What had he called it? An optimized immune system.

Really, an optimized everything. I tried very hard not to look at his stomach muscles.

Which was difficult, because he was close, and I was touching him—really touching him—for the first time since that stairwell incident. Since I'd *kissed* him.

My heart rate sped at the memory. His fingers tightened on my wrists, like he *could* feel the sudden rush of blood beneath the delicate skin.

Slowly, I raised my face to his.

He was watching me, and something had shifted. He looked wary now. Guarded. The energy between us had changed.

Or had it? Maybe it was just always like this, and we were both pretending it wasn't.

I didn't think. Didn't pause.

It was part exhaustion, part high-strung emotion from what he'd just bared, and a large part the undeniable fact that I'd been stuck in close quarters with Sky Acosta for the past two days. Fighting him, fighting me. Fighting everybody.

And, damn it, I was *tired* of fighting.

"You know what all that sounds like?" I murmured, smoothing my hands up along his chest, following their path with my eyes.

His grasp loosened as I bumped into his collarbone, and he inhaled sharply through his teeth. Goosebumps rippled to life beneath my palms. I didn't look up, too mesmerized. My fingers trembled a little as they moved over his skin.

He did feel human. Still warm from the shower. Damp in places where droplets clung. His pectorals were firm and sculpted, and the muscles twitched in the wake of my light touch.

Mouth dry, I traced higher, skimming along his taut shoulders. The slope of sinew connecting to his neck. He was corded strength and restrained power. My heartbeat kicked up another notch.

"What does what sound like?" he whispered, low and a little breathless.

I feel human, he'd said. Blood thumped in my ears. This was all synth-skin, a suit. But merged with him on a DNA level. It *was* him. *Sky.* Alien and yet not.

Even though thinking about all this—these truths, this chaos—sometimes threatened to break my brain, he was real. Solid. Grounding me.

He was right. We *were* in this together.

"What being controlled and rational all the time sounds like to me?" My body was humming, tiredness slipping away to make room for a heady, molten energy.

His shoulders lifted and fell under my hands. Sky was breathing hard. So was I when I finally settled my gaze back on his.

The *heat* in his eyes hit me hard.

"Boring?" he whispered, the hint of a crooked smile touching his mouth before he became deadly serious again. Intent.

A sizzle shot through me. Landed low in my belly and erased all shreds of rational thought.

"I…was going to say exhausting, but boring's one word for it, yeah," I answered.

Safe was another.

Neither of which I felt when I rose onto my tiptoes.

Chapter 9

WE HAVE LIFT-OFF

SKY WATCHED ME the whole way, tracking my movement with hooded eyes. I tightened my hold on his shoulders and leaned in. Tilted up.

He didn't even try to stop me.

Instead, as soon as I touched my mouth to his, his lids squeezed shut. Like he was in pain. A soft sound rumbled from his throat. Half a sigh, half a quiet, *broken* groan that might've been a protest—

But he wasn't protesting.

That was the sound of Sky's control snapping. Something I'd been sure would never happen.

But, oh boy, was it *happening*.

His hands slid from my arms and hooked around my waist. In one swift motion, he pulled me against him. I gasped as he flattened a palm to my lower back, the other cupping my nape, drawing us together.

Our lips bumped once, then he slanted his head and…

I hung on for dear life.

Apparently, I wasn't the only one who'd been fighting this. I could feel that in the biting, restless way he kissed me, in the way his tongue slipped in and claimed. The way he gripped me like a life-line, like he was trying to drag me inside him.

The interlude in the stairwell had been tentative. A slow smolder that had grown.

This *flash-burned*. Like somebody had set a match to a fuse and that fuse was raw, visceral need. His. Mine. *Ours*.

I grasped his shoulders, his neck, his hair, throwing myself into the kiss as he backed me up. His hands roamed my sides, my hips. We collided with the dresser, and something clattered to the floor. Maybe the supplies from the gas station. Maybe the television. Who really cared?

I sure didn't as I wound my arms around Sky's neck. His teeth scraped my bottom lip, and he pinned me between his warm body and the piece of furniture. Engulfing me.

This was what I'd wanted. I wanted to feel something other than this spiraling, out-of-control free-fall.

I plunged my fingers into his damp hair, dragging through the silky strands, hiking my leg up along his. He murmured a sound of approval and tunneled both hands into the base of my drying braid, using it to tip my head back, deepening the kiss.

I waited for alarm bells. For him to pump the brakes like he always did because this was rapidly approaching nuclear levels. The release of all this impossible, burning tension. Like a rocket ignition.

Maybe because it was way past late at night—or maybe because this was a hot mess and we'd been stuck together for a week now—he didn't show any signs of slowing. And I sure as hell wasn't going to stop us. Why would I when he kissed like this and I could feel him hard already against my lower belly?

Stopping was the last thing I wanted.

Desire speared through me, settling between my legs, and I rolled my hips against his. Swallowed the tiny, ragged sound he breathed into my mouth. This was how I happily died. I knew it.

Sky was everywhere, crowding me back until my spine bowed over the dresser's top. I was forced to break the kiss to keep from toppling over.

"Shit," he muttered, wrenching his lips from mine.

"It's fine. I—" I broke off with a squeak when he scooped me up and set me on the dresser's edge instead. Bringing us face-to-face. My hands came up automatically to brace on his broad chest.

In the moment's pause, Sky drew back enough to look at me. His grip flexed on my thighs. He looked as undone as I felt, his hair a damp mess, lips swollen, eyes dark. Lust pounded an insistent throb like a second heartbeat.

"We shouldn't be doing this," he whispered—predictably.

I somehow found enough air to laugh. "I *knew* you'd say that."

"Yeah?" He raised a brow. His fingers spasmed again, and I waited for him to back away. Those eyes, midnight blue and on fire, took a leisurely path over my face, lingering on my mouth.

But then he shocked me by raising his gaze back to mine and stepping *closer* instead. His hands cupped my knees, nudging them wider so he could slip his hips between them. My heart stopped beating. His palms burned through my jeans as he smoothed them up my legs, coming to rest on my hips.

"Funny thing, though." He exhaled through his nose, long and slow. I nearly melted off the dresser when he sank his teeth into his bottom lip, his voice dropping to a rasp. There was something reckless in his eyes when they found their way to mine. Something not very Sky-like. "I don't think I really care about my rules right now."

That made two of us. My body was buzzing, skin humming and—

Oh. That's why.

The marked hand I'd pressed to his chest had begun to softly glow, spilling the palest white light over us both. Growing brighter. And beneath it…

"Holy crap," I whispered, splaying my fingers. Silver rippled out, and the flesh of his chest flickered between tan and the glittering shimmer of his Pladian form. Like thousands of sand-grain diamonds. The fine texture shifted beneath my palm. Soft and coarse, somehow, at once.

Alien skin.

My marked hand had disrupted the alien tech merged with his body. *Again.*

He looked down as I pulled my arm away and formed a fist around the shining glyphs, stifling the glow. The handprint-shaped silver smudge left behind on his chest rippled and faded, shrinking in on itself. Human-looking skin smoothed back out.

Blinking, I gaped up at him. "Why does that keep *happening*?"

"I don't know." He shook his head, another heavy breath escaping him, not quite steady. "But I really don't care about that right now, either."

Then he kissed me again, and I decided he had a great point. I tightened my knees, shifting restlessly on the dresser, trying to edge closer. He cupped my face and changed the angle, taking it deeper instantly.

Because *this* was what I needed. Screw silver skin and glowing body parts. I needed something real in the middle of all this insanity. I needed to feel something. *Anything.*

I needed…shit, I needed *Sky.*

The errant thought threatened to send me spiraling, so I refused to let myself absorb it. Which was easy enough because Sky's mouth had left mine and was trailing soft, nipping kisses beneath my jaw, the kind that had a whimper catching in my throat. His palms found my waist and slipped under my shirt, stroking fire up my sides. I shivered, bowing my spine.

Who needed thoughts? I wanted his hands everywhere. All over. And I was wearing far too much clothing for that.

Before I could question anything, I tore my mouth from his, reared back, and yanked my oversized tee over my head.

Only when the cold air rushed over me did I hesitate, clutching the rumpled fabric.

Sky had stopped moving, eyes wide and on mine. His hands hovered without touching. I'd caught him off guard.

Understandably. I'd just ripped my shirt off with no preamble.

For a moment, we stared at each other.

Maybe I'd miscalculated.

"I… Should I not have…?" It was too late, though, because the shirt slid from my tingling fingers to plop onto the floor. The pale glow from my palm was slowly fading, and the shadows crept back in, cocooning us. The clicking radiator under the window was the only sound until I added, "Sorry."

The chillier air nipped at me, and I crossed my arm over my bra. Stark bruises marred my pale skin, interspersed with still-healing scrapes. I was a mess. A self-conscious blush warmed my neck.

Sky wasn't looking at any of it, though. His gaze held mine. After a heartbeat, he licked his lips and said, "Don't be sorry." His jaw tightened, like he was fighting it—but then he seemed to lose the battle. He dropped his eyes. My belly heated as they darkened, and his soft, "*Fuck*, Rae," chased away any uncertainty.

And if that wasn't enough, between one breath and another, he tugged my arm away from my front, pulled me in by the nape, and kissed me.

Rougher this time. *Hungrier.*

My hands found his abs. His mouth slid along my jaw again and didn't stop this time. He nuzzled at the junction of my neck and shoulder. Teeth scraped skin, and I shuddered, biting the inside of my cheek against a high-pitched, pleading sound. His lips were soft and hot on the side of my neck, a contrast to the rough drag of his stubble. His fingertips glided along my ribcage, then smoothed over my arms, to my shoulders.

Perfect.

The Enil could've descended in that moment, and I wouldn't have cared.

All I cared about were Sky's searing, mind-destroying kisses along my collarbone. The heat of his breath, his palms. The fact that for the first time in days, I felt something other than exhaustion, sheer panic, or dread.

I needed more. Apparently, he did, too, because he curled his fingers around my upper arms and urged me back until I caught myself on the dresser and my head bumped the wall. I barely noticed with his mouth dipping lower and his tug on the edge of my bra strap.

Yes. I may have whispered it aloud. I didn't care. All I cared about was the fact that this was happening. *Finally.* I tunneled my fingers into his curls, and my lungs threatened to quit working when he braced his forehead on the center of my chest, exhaling a quiet curse while he tugged the fabric down—

A loud knock shattered the silence.

Sky jerked back so fast I nearly pitched right off the dresser's edge. Gasping, I thumped against the wall instead, instinctively crossing an arm over my chest again as my gaze snapped to the door. My palm's glow had died completely, and suddenly, the gathering dark seemed sinister.

Thud-thud-thud.

There it was again. More knocking. Loud. Incessant.

But not on our door. It was coming from the room beside us. I slumped against the grimy wallpaper.

It didn't matter. The moment was shattered like a fist through glass. The spell was broken. I could feel it in the sudden tension radiating from Sky.

Swallowing hard, I peeked up at him. He threw me a look, tight and warning-filled, and raised a finger to his lips. I nodded jerkily, gulping air. The abruptness of this shift in mood left me reeling.

Or maybe it was the fact that two seconds ago, I was ready to get him naked.

Sky didn't seem to be thinking about any of that as he turned and stalked silently toward the door. I tried really hard not to notice the shift and play of muscles in his broad back. It didn't go well.

Ugh.

Forcing my attention away from him, I hopped off the dresser and staggered a little when my knees tried to give out. My legs weren't quite steady yet.

For obvious reasons.

Bending, I snatched up my shirt and managed to find the right hole to shove my flaming head out of. My lips felt swollen and tingly.

How had *that* happened? One moment, we'd been talking and then…

We'd obliterated any of Sky's lines in the sand. One moment of insanity, and I'd definitely crossed out of the friend zone. And he'd been *right there* with me.

His voice echoed back, that weary, hoarse confession: *I feel human.*

Lingering lust beat like a battle drum low in my body. With effort, I ignored it, patting down my hair. My heart rate still hadn't returned to normal.

I'd wanted to feel something, and I was feeling things, all right. All sorts of confusing, throbbing, needy things. Things I shouldn't have been feeling, considering we'd agreed to be *friends.*

But none of that mattered right now. I focused instead on Sky, who now stood by the door, head tilted, listening to whatever was happening outside.

He'd flipped the switch. A flush rode high on his cheekbones and his curls were mussed from my fingers, but his eyes were sharp and alert. A far cry from the desire-blurred look he'd given me not a moment before.

Heat tried to coil in my belly at the memory of his hands, his mouth. Crossing my arms over my middle to contain it, I padded closer. Not too close, though. Touching him right now, after all that, might've made me erupt into a thousand glittering pieces of hormonal angst.

All that drained away as shouting filtered through the flimsy door panel.

"John? *John,* I know you're in there! Betsy at the diner told me! Get your ass out here!" Another round of solid, rapid pounding. "Don't make me bust this door down!"

My pent-up breath slid out, and my shoulders caved.

Just a late-night argument. Not the government. Not the police. Not a wandering Enil dropping by.

No danger.

But it *could've* been. Easily. It could've been the police or License 16 or… Well, I didn't know who else, but we weren't safe here. Not really.

And just like that, the motel snapped back into focus. Reality.

This wasn't the place for any of this. Not when we were

exhausted and drained, and I felt barely one step above a wet, shredded pile of wrung-out waitress. This was what Sky had meant by things getting complicated.

Even if it had felt so right—

I turned away from his stare, giving him my shoulder as I dragged both hands down my face. I needed sleep and maybe an ice-cold shower—even if it was with sulfur-scented water. I nearly stepped on the toothbrush I'd tossed earlier. I bent down and snatched it up.

Maybe just a good toothbrushing. I could wash Sky's taste out of my mouth.

As if on cue, his quiet voice broke through the whirlpool of my thoughts. "Raven."

That tone. I closed my eyes. I knew that tone. And because I did, I already knew what he was going to say.

Rotating in place, I sighed and held up my unmarked hand. "Yes, I know. That shouldn't have happened."

He didn't deny it. When I looked up, I found him still near the door, half in shadow. I could see enough to read the flat line he'd pressed his mouth into. His hands twitched at his sides. "Look, we're both beyond tired. I…"

He didn't finish. The distance between us felt a hell of a lot greater than three feet. When another long moment passed and he said nothing else, I let out a sharp breath, bent to gather a few toiletries, and turned on my heel, headed for the bathroom.

"I got you a toothbrush and some other things," I said over my shoulder. I paused at the door. "Let's just get some sleep."

His shoulders drew up and his mouth opened, and for a second, I thought he'd argue. I thought he'd say something—*anything*—to refute my dismissal of what had nearly been the culmination of every Raven fantasy, weeks of exquisite sexual tension, and a whole hell of a lot of emotion I still had no clue what to do with.

I thought wrong.

"Okay," he said, in that quiet, even tone I was starting to hate. His calm mask was in place again, hiding everything as successfully as the shadows. His Pladian composure, maybe. Logical. Rational. *Frustrating.* "Thank you. For getting the supplies."

I nodded once, stepped into the bathroom, and closed the door behind me, leaning against it.

The interruption had been a cold, hard slap back to what was really going on here. A reminder. And a realization, too. Sky wasn't just dangerous because he could shoot lightning, vanish, and take on angry robotic bad guys.

He was dangerous because I *saw* him now. That rare glimpse just now of vulnerability. Sky without that composure, the mask. The unbearably sexy way he moved, that lopsided, dimpled smile, or the fall of his silky hair.

Then there was the quiet, ironic sense of humor. The way he was protective without being overbearing.

No, I didn't have a crush on Sky anymore. I *liked* him. I admired him. I was a little in awe of him.

I knew him—the real him—and I genuinely enjoyed being around him. I felt safe with him. And sure, all right. Kissing him was awfully nice, too.

I closed my eyes and thumped my head against the door, suppressing a groan. No sounds filtered through the flimsy barrier, but I could almost sense him through it. That *awareness.* He'd been right, days ago, when he'd said crossing the line between us would complicate things. Confuse things.

I'd already been head over heels for Sky back when I was just a waitress and he was just a bartender. Now that I knew he was a strong, silent, deadly alien warrior with a tumultuous past and the weight of a world resting on those ridiculous shoulders? I was inches from being a goner. I mean, come on. Who wouldn't be?

Giving in to this, this pull between us, wouldn't just complicate things. It could ruin them.

Ruin *me*.

Letting out a shaky breath, I left the door and stepped to the sink. As I tore open the toothbrush and toothpaste, my hands trembled.

Fatigue, I told myself. Just fatigue. I just needed sleep.

Nothing like a good night's sleep to rid yourself of intergalactic —sorry, *galactic*—heartache.

Chapter 10

HOUSTON, WE HAVE A PROBLEM

THE STARS were endless.

Endless in a way that shattered every thought of individuality I'd ever had. Every sense of time and space and depth. Distances.

But one point, one place, pulled me toward it.

Purple-pink light shone from everywhere and nowhere, spearing through me, shifting toward white.

Stars. Stars and words.

A call. I'd felt this before, once. In a lab.

We are out here. Come to us. Reach for us.

The stars... No, that was a planet.

It was next to impossible to focus on it. Shape, light, color. Everything swirled and collided, a vicious growing pressure. A growing weight. A growing, gnawing urge—

The cry was wrenched from my middle, ripping me violently from sleep and into a storm of pain. Throbbing temples. Burning eyes. Everything hurt. What the *hell?*

I pried my lids apart, disoriented. For a moment, I was blind to everything but glowing symbols, dots, shapes. Copper coated my tongue. My body jerked. No, it was shaken. Somebody was shaking me.

Through the haze, deep-ocean eyes seized mine. I knew those eyes. Sky leaned over me. He was shaking me by the shoulders.

"Raven!" Another gentle jolt. "Raven. Come on. Come back." A pause while I tried to focus, and then he murmured, "That's it."

I blinked slowly, gasping. Sweat slicked my skin, and I was quaking so hard my teeth clacked. Sky's fingers dug into my upper arms, into the bruises there, though for once I didn't even feel it. His face was drawn, taut, and his lips pressed into thin, white lines.

If I didn't know better, I'd think he looked…worried. About what? It was hard to think past the blinding white light scorching my retinas. Where was it coming from? It was everywhere. I winced, throwing up a hand.

Oh. It *was* my hand.

"Yikes," I mumbled, staring at it. The cuff around my wrist burned way hotter than normal. That couldn't be a good thing.

Sky bent close, filling my blurry vision.

"Are you with me?" he asked, eyes roving my face. His skin was a shade paler than normal.

God, he looked *really* worried. About what? I'd been having a dream. The strangest dream…

Why was it so hard to form thoughts? "I…I think so."

He frowned, like he was trying to read something deeper in the answer. Like he wasn't entirely sure I was telling the truth. When I stared up at him in confusion, he released me and stepped back. Half turning, he planted his hands on his hips and unleashed a string of sharp, vicious words.

That sounded like a different language. One I'd never heard. Oh my God. Was he swearing in *Pladian*?

Head swimming, I squinted at him. The room was a little fuzzy around the edges, and my tongue felt like sandpaper. "What…?"

I bobbled slightly as he pivoted and dropped suddenly onto the edge of the mattress beside me. The way he stared at me, like he was trying to peer into my skull, made me straighten a little against the pillow. Immediately, my temples squeezed, and I winced, grabbing the sides of my head. "Ow."

"Are you okay?" he asked in that same, tight tone. He wasn't touching me, but when I peeled one lid open, the razor-sharp look in his eyes hadn't faded.

The pain ebbed enough for me to raise my face cautiously. Sensation slowly trickled back into my limbs, and I shook out my tingling hands. "What's wrong? What happened?"

I remembered a bit now. I'd been having one of *those* dreams again. The ones that seemed so important and weighty, but damn it, I couldn't remember.

And, *God*, my head hurt. I pressed the heels of my hands into my temples, trying to ease the throbbing behind my eyes. So much for sleep helping anything.

"What time is it?" I muttered, slamming my lids shut. The stupid glow from my palm was really getting annoying. Would it have killed the halix to give me an off switch?

"What time is it?" Sky echoed, his voice rising into an incredulous pitch. I opened my eyes as he jammed his hand through his hair, then pinned me with a hard look. "Rae, you just had a seizure."

That snapped me straight back to clarity, and I dropped my arms. That word—it brought to mind a rush of ugly memories. Old fear. "*What?* I had a *what?*"

"A seizure," he repeated flatly, nostrils flaring.

I stared at him. His chest heaved beneath his shirt. That tiny muscle ticked in his jaw, but there was a look in his eyes... That wasn't just worry. That was *fear*.

For me?

I mean, I supposed it was understandable. I'd been there. Fear- and grief-soaked memories tried to float up again, and with effort, I blinked them away.

"A *seizure?*" I whispered hoarsely, a strange disconnect settling over me. "Are you sure?"

"Yes." He rose, strode to the bathroom, where I heard him running the water. He returned with a hand towel and thrust it at me, jaw tight. "You remember anything?"

It came out grudgingly. Like he didn't want to ask. Or didn't want to hear the answer.

Right. Because this wasn't just a random seizure. It had to be related to the map, the halix's info cache. This had happened before —or sort of—when he'd tried to hypnotize me. Except there'd been a nosebleed that time, too, and I didn't think it'd been a full-blown *seizure*. Not that time.

Hopefully not this time. Although…

I touched my nostrils and felt moisture. Drawing my fingertips away, I wasn't surprised to find a smear of red. Sky's frown darkened, and he pushed the towel at me again. This time, I took it, and, while I cleaned myself up, I tried to recall what I'd dreamed of.

I really tried. I picked at the edges of the memory, but…nothing. Just that same irritating, I-forgot-something-important sensation. Like a word stuck on the tip of my tongue.

Giving up, I shook my head, glancing down at the shitty motel linen. I winced. That wasn't coming out.

"No," I told Sky, wadding the towel up and setting it aside. "Sorry. I can't remember it." Despite the selective memory loss, the more seconds ticked by, the clearer my head became. Enough that I tried to sit up, weaving a little. Sky reached for me but stopped short of touching me. Cradling my forehead in my unmarked palm, I balled up my still-glowing hand. "Are you sure it was a seizure?"

Sky met my eyes, something complicated flashing through his. Too fast for me to make sense of.

"If it wasn't a seizure, it was too damn close." He stood abruptly, shoulders stiff. "Can you stand?"

"I…I think so," I said, dragging my focus inward and doing a quick internal systems rundown.

The check engine light had definitely lit up like a Christmas tree. My head hurt like hell, like my brain had been diced in a blender, spat back out, and stomped on by an angry Enil. My stomach churned, too. But aside from that, and the fact that my hand was doing its thing, I felt…functional.

Damn, though. That cuff was getting warmer by the second. I clamped my palm over it. "Why is this thing so hot?"

"It's hot?" Frowning, Sky leaned in, brushing his fingers over the metal before drawing them away and rubbing them together. His mouth flattened into that grim line again. "I don't know. Between that seizure and this," he nodded at my wildly pulsing palm, "I think we need to move. As soon as you can. In case the containment field is failing."

"Move?" I gaped at the cuff. "In case the *field* is failing? You said Bast said it was fine."

"It was fine yesterday," Sky said, scanning the room, like he was preparing to gather our things. "The cuff wasn't meant to last forever, Rae. It was just meant to get us to Bast. He's our tech specialist."

"What does that even mean?" A tingle of apprehension tap-danced down my spine. The alien metal burned against my skin.

Sky opened his mouth to answer—

Shouting erupted outside.

In a few quick strides, he was at the window, pulling back the blinds. He swore again under his breath, shooting me a glance over his shoulder. "Can you move?"

My heart skipped. That tone was enough to make me try. I shoved off the covers, my body sticky with sweat. I'd slept in jeans and my new *Mind Your Biscuits* shirt, and now everything clung to me. I could've used another trickle-shower, but something told me that wasn't on the agenda. At least I had deodorant now.

I raked a hand through my hair and got stuck in my frizzy braid. "What is it? What's happening out there?"

I stood with the help of the stained wall. The room wobbled before evening out. Outside, the shouting grew louder. Was that a scream?

"It's time to go," Sky bit out, spinning from the window.

He was already moving, scooping things up, tension rolling off him in waves. His urgency kicked me into motion. Despite the shakiness, I found my shoes and shoved my feet into them, not bothering with the laces. I shrugged on the stolen sweater and swept all our purchases into my bag before slinging it over one shoulder and joining him at the door.

I tucked my glowing hand into my sweater pocket just as Sky pulled it open.

My mouth dropped open.

Outside, the world had descended into chaos.

Mainly because there were hovering lights in the sky.

A UFO.

Panic surged, slicing through the last vestiges of disorientation like a carving blade.

Enil. The Enil were here.

I wasn't the only one panicking. Clusters of people raced in all directions. Some stood frozen, hands shielding their eyes, faces slack with awe or fear or total disbelief. A baby squalled nearby, the unnerving sound echoing back against the motel's crumbling façade.

Cars sat at haphazard angles across parking spaces, doors flung open, drivers gone. Tires chirped and metal crunched, the unmistakable sound of a fender bender. No one even looked. Somewhere out of view, a woman was shouting something frantic, unintelligible.

But otherwise…the morning had gone eerily quiet.

And above it all, the UFO pulsed and glowed.

I couldn't tell how far away it was. It could've been directly over the gas station or two miles off. Depth perception was useless at this angle.

The ball of light cycled through a series of colors—blue, coral, green, pink. It was strangely beautiful, like a colorful snake. Or a mushroom cloud. Probably more apt for the Enil scout ship.

It'd come for us. For *me.*

Sky had to be right. The containment field generated by the band on my wrist must've failed. Maybe the dream had triggered it?

Didn't matter now. What mattered was getting the hell out of here.

My gaze snagged on a police officer not three feet away, speaking into his radio. I stiffened and looked away, but it was too late. He glanced up and saw me.

Not breathing, I watched his brow furrow. Like he was trying to place me.

Like he'd seen my face all over a wanted bulletin or something.

Great. Why settle for one threat when you could have two?

"Sky," I whispered, reaching for his arm with my free hand.

He was already moving. His fingers laced with mine, and he pulled me after him, fast, boots hitting the fractured sidewalk in rapid succession. His legs were longer, but I double-timed to keep up, glancing over my shoulder.

The cop was watching us. Eyes narrowed. His posture shifted.

I stumbled over a chunk of broken concrete. Sky's grip tightened, keeping me upright, but he didn't slow down. He was already veering toward the far edge of the motel, where the parking lot spilled into the wide-open sprawl of the truck stop.

Groups of drivers stood outside their cabs, heads tipped back, staring upward.

Catching my breath, I tried again. "Sky, I think he recognized me."

"I know," he said tightly. "Just keep moving."

Moving toward what? I rolled my lips inward, breathing hard. My skin was tingling, like a breath of static was dancing along it. Familiar. A sign the Enil were close. I didn't dare look back—at the UFO *or* the cop.

We reached the corner and rounded it fast. The fissured asphalt dotted with struggling plants was shadowed here by an overhang. A dumpster, scattered trash, and a half-collapsed fence blocked the truck stop from view.

"Hey!"

At the shout, I twisted around.

Just our luck. The officer had followed us.

If we had any luck at all, it'd just run out.

Chapter 11

GRAND THEFT AUTO II

WE PASSED into the shadow of the building at the same time the officer caught up with us. His second command rang out. "Stop!"

Sky shocked me by actually listening. He dropped my hand and turned slowly. Startled, I stumbled a little before following suit, the morning air harsh in my constricted chest. Sinking dread weighed down my gut.

Did I raise my hands? If I did, there'd be no hiding the glow.

We were so, *so* screwed.

Somewhere in the distance, sirens wailed, growing closer. Just beyond the motel roof's peak, the bright, multicolored glow of the Enil ship pulsed like a second, less stable sun. Just seeing it there, a ghostly orb gently radiating light, raised the hair on my arms. The urge to run, to flee, pounded in time with my headache.

I didn't hear any mechanical groans or distorted robot roars. That ship wasn't moving, either. So what were they doing? What were they waiting for?

...me?

If that was the case, why hadn't they attacked?

I looked down at the cuff. With my *still-glowing* hand buried in my pocket, it was barely visible. Maybe the device's containment field hadn't completely failed yet. The metal burned hot, just shy of painful, and I curled my fingers tight inside my sweater.

Right now, there was a more immediate threat: the police officer, approaching cautiously, one hand hovering near his gun.

"Both of you," he called out, voice echoing in the alcove. "Hold on a second."

He was middle-aged, dark-eyed, with a neatly trimmed mustache that didn't hide the hard set of his mouth. He eased closer, assessing. His walkie-talkie squawked, but static obscured all the words save for *UAP*.

Swallowing hard, I started to look toward the ominously silent Enil ship again before catching myself. My eyes met Sky's instead. He stood beside me, posture relaxed, but I knew him well enough to sense his coiled readiness. To recognize his stance.

He was preparing for a fight.

My pulse thudded in my ears, stomach hollowing. I squeezed my fist tighter, hoping the morning sunshine masked any otherworldly light leaking through.

Meanwhile, the cop came to a stop a few feet away. "Mind telling me your names?"

Neither of us answered. I wasn't sure I could even speak. My throat was too tight. And if I opened my mouth, there was a good chance I would vomit.

As if he sensed it, the officer turned his attention to me, zeroing in. "Miss? What's your name?"

Sweat broke out across my forehead. It was way too hot for this damn sweater. But it was hiding my glowstick of a hand

"My…" I started, rifling through lies. "Me. My name. Oh, I'm, uh…" *On the run from murderous alien robots and about to steal a car for the second time in a day.* "My name is—"

Sky cut in before I confessed to every crime I'd ever thought about committing. "We're just trying to get out of the area, officer. You saw…that." He gestured skyward. "Didn't seem like a time to hang around."

"Right," the officer said, looking over his shoulder before returning his assessment to Sky. "You got some ID?"

You'd think the UFO would be enough of a distraction, but this guy seemed to beg to differ. We'd caught his attention. Did we look that suspicious?

I looked down at myself. I looked like I needed a shower and a lesson in fashion, and Sky's exhaustion was more than apparent. But other than that, I didn't think anything about us screamed *Fugitives from the Law*.

Then again, I'd always been a terrible liar.

I raised my head, and the breeze tossed a strand of hair into my face. I caught myself a second before drawing my hand out of my sweater to tuck it behind my ear. A bead of sweat trailed down my spine. In the distance, the Enil craft pulsed gently between pink, coral, and green.

"What's this about?" Sky asked as he reached for his back pocket. The officer stiffened, fingers hovering over his gun. Taking the hint, Sky slowed his movement, extending his free hand as he slowly pulled out a wallet and held it up.

I eyed it, and despite my hammering heart, I couldn't help arching a brow. Did he actually have ID? He had to, right? He had a whole, secret identity to go with that face. I swallowed hard, looking between him and the police officer.

"Well," the cop said, relaxing a little when both Sky's hands were visible, "your friend there matches a BOLO I happened to see this morning. One that mentioned she may be in the company of a male about your height and description."

"A BOLO," I whispered, voice cracking. A *be-on-the-lookout*. For my face. With a male that looked like Sky?

My knees trembled, and my ears rang. It was somehow even *worse* to hear it confirmed. Sky and I were out here like some kind of extraterrestrial Bonnie and Clyde. Except not dating. And Bonnie and Clyde robbed banks.

And they'd died.

I was *really* trying to survive all this.

Sky's laugh was too light. Too easy. "A BOLO? Wow, that's pretty crazy." He pulled a card—apparently an actual ID—from his wallet and leaned forward to hand it over. "We're just on a cross-country road trip—"

Too many things happened at once.

The officer leaned in.

Sky lunged.

Static ripped the air in half.

A flash of blue-white light exploded between them. I gasped and staggered back, throwing up my arm to shield my eyes. My shoulder clipped the dumpster. Spots danced in my vision, and the alien bracelet on my wrist seemed to thrum.

All in the span of a single heartbeat.

When my sight cleared, Sky was crouched beside the cop, gently lowering him to the ground. He checked for a pulse, exhaled slowly, and balanced his elbows on his knees, glancing up toward the Enil ship. He spat a curse and swiped a hand down his face.

I stared, mouth agape. It had all happened *so fast*. The biting scent of ozone and burnt hair curled into my nose and sent my stomach into a slow roll.

"What the hell, Sky?" I wheezed. "Is he…?"

My question seemed to pull Sky back to reality. He swiped his ID from the ground and stood in a smooth motion, tucking the card away, expression shuttering as he turned toward me. "He'll be fine," he said, brushing off his palms. A muscle flickered in his temple, the only outward sign of emotion. "He's unconscious, that's all. He won't remember a thing. Low-level synaptic disruptor. The surveillance will be scrambled, too. Come on."

"Low-level *what?*" I choked out.

"The synth-skin…it doesn't matter. We've got to go." He extended a hand, motioning me forward. "Come on."

My body wouldn't move. My feet felt frozen to the asphalt. The officer was breathing. He was still breathing. I could see the movement of his chest beneath the vest. At least there was that.

When I didn't budge, Sky grabbed my hand again. I was too numb to resist as he tugged me after him. I barely noticed he led me off the cracked pavement and across the strip of grass between the motel and the truck stop, only vaguely registering the transition from scuffed asphalt to a soft, dew-covered field.

He'd just knocked out a police officer and *wiped his memories?* I'd known he was capable of that—he'd admitted as much and I'd seen the evidence with my own eyes—but there was a difference between talking about it and seeing it in action. The sneaking suspicion he wasn't telling me the whole truth about the synth-skin's abilities was getting stronger and stronger.

My toe caught on a rock, and I barely righted myself in time with the help of Sky's tight grip on my arm. He paused long enough for me to gain my footing, and then he was off again, towing me gently but firmly in his wake.

Paranoia rippling along my nape, I scanned our surroundings. People were still standing around, staring at the sky. At least they weren't looking at us.

Or that little nook around the building's corner.

Where we'd just…alien-tased a cop.

God, I really was going to be sick. I clamped my glowing hand over my mouth before remembering how bright it was. My shuddery exhale escaped as I crammed my fist back into my pocket to hide it and focused on deep breathing instead. In through my nose and out through my mouth.

I was so focused, it took me a few seconds to realize where Sky was heading. Toward a rusty red pickup truck on the far side of the lot. One that'd been parked there for a while if the fogged windows were any indication.

That sinking feeling settled in my stomach again. "Is that the one we're going to…?"

Sky shot me a sidelong glance and a tense nod, the grim set of his mouth telling me he wasn't happy about it, either.

Starting off the day with another round of car theft. *Great.* This just kept getting better.

We reached the vehicle far too quickly. Sky let go of me, abandoning me by the passenger-side door as he rounded the hood. A breath of wind stirred tangled strands of my hair against my neck, and I automatically grabbed the handle, tugging.

Locked. Of course it was.

People usually locked their cars so they wouldn't get stolen.

Like we were doing right now.

I pulled my hand back and glanced around. My heart was a trapped hummingbird in my chest. We were too exposed here, too obvious at the edge of the lot.

Not that anyone was looking. The crowd had thickened around the motel and gas station. The sky was growing lighter, streaked orange and pink with sunrise. The Enil ship still hovered there, silently glowing. A motionless threat.

My palm itched. "Why aren't they coming down?" I mused aloud, rubbing the markings.

"They probably can't get a read yet," Sky answered, voice carrying in the eerie quiet.

Then out of nowhere, that static charge burst into being again. So sudden and stinging, I jerked and gasped, slapping my marked hand to my chest. I caught a flash of light from the truck's other side, a brief flare that went out just as quickly.

A second later, door hinges groaned as Sky opened the driver's door.

The locks clicked. Swallowing hard, I tried my handle again. This time, it opened. He'd done it.

Like with that officer, he'd made it look easy. He was making *all* of this look easy. Like Sky might be a bit more dangerous than I'd realized. And that said a lot since I'd seen him take down several killer robots.

And now he was waiting for me to get into the truck. All my instincts screamed that this was insane, but my feet didn't care. The door gave a loud squeal, like it was trying to call attention to us as I yanked it the rest of the way open. With a deep breath, I tossed my bag in and climbed inside, hauling it shut after me.

The hollow *thunk* of it closing reminded me of a jail cell door.

Shoulders hunched, I looked around. Stolen Car 2.0 was way dirtier than the last one. Wrappers and empty cans crackled under my feet. It smelled like old cigarettes and engine oil. A dull, sticky residue coated everything.

Car thieves couldn't be choosy, though. Especially ones who'd just incapacitated an officer of the law and left him lying on the asphalt.

I suppressed a shudder, throat closing. Tightening my fingers into a ball to hide my glowing palm, I glanced at Sky. He was engrossed in examining the steering column, eyebrows pinched together beneath a tumble of messy dark hair. The white glow from my hand illuminated him in stark relief. His hat was gone—lost, I was sure, in our hustle to leave the motel. Stray curls brushed his ears and fell over his forehead, partially hiding the healing scrape there.

His eyes were still shadowed. Like he hadn't been able to get much sleep. Understandable, since he'd probably been rudely awakened by my...well, seizure.

The memory clogged my chest. Everything was happening so fast. Meanwhile, it was difficult to concentrate on anything with a hovering murderous robot ship looming overhead. One that was probably here for me.

Speaking of. I craned my neck. I could just make it out through the smudged back window. When I turned back around, Sky still hadn't moved. I opened my mouth to ask what the hold-up was—

He lifted his hand, splaying it on the dash. My teeth snapped together as sparks crackled at his fingertips, painting the inside of the cab blue. The familiar, static buzz nipped my skin. I couldn't look away, though, too mesmerized by the play of pale color emanating from beneath his skin. The eerie way it seemed to seep from inside him.

A single bolt jumped from his fingers, breaking the spell. I flinched back. With a sharp *snap*, the engine coughed, the gauges flickered—

The truck started.

Just like that. That was all it took to hot-wire a truck, Pladian-style?

"Okay." Sky blew out a breath and turned his head, attention dropping to my hand. I followed his gaze. The metal band was still hot but not *burning* anymore. At least there was that.

"Here. Let me see it," he said, reaching for me. "The cuff."

Too overwhelmed to ask questions, I twisted in the seat and held out my arm. Orange light leaked through the cracks between my fisted fingers. I looked away, taking the moment to peer through the windshield. No one seemed to be paying us any mind. The ship still had everyone's attention. The crowd at the gas station was growing, and I spotted more red and blue flashing lights. Police.

Sooner or later, somebody was going to find the cop we'd knocked out. A surge of panic stung my fried nerves.

Sky cupped my wrist, distracting me enough that I wrenched my attention from the growing mass of people here to gawk at the UFO. His fingers were warm as he angled my arm, studying my glowing fist for a second before shaking his head. "I still don't understand why it's doing this."

My laugh came out tremulous. "Just so you know, that's not really comforting, Sky."

"Sorry." His eyes flicked to mine. His mouth quirked briefly before settling back into seriousness. Concentration. I licked my lips nervously as he lifted his other hand and held it over the cuff, fingertips poised. "Hold really still."

I barely dared to breathe.

He touched the metal, and a tingling, prickling sensation spread up my arm. The scent of an oncoming storm filled the truck cab, raising the hair on my nape. A faint blue glow shimmered beneath his skin, mingling with the bright white leaking from mine.

We were a regular alien light show.

I cringed, gaze flying to the windshield, half expecting to see faces turning our way. But no one was looking.

When I turned back, the bracelet's appearance was *changing*, like something was shifting beneath its surface. I caught my breath, leaning closer before I remembered he'd told me to hold still.

"What's it doing?" I asked, glancing up at Sky. I couldn't seem to summon more than a whisper.

He didn't answer. His expression was pinched in focus, eyes narrowed. Beneath his light touch, the metal rippled—and I gasped. Those were *shapes and symbols* moving inside it. I hadn't imagined them. They were there, fading in and out of focus. Like letters inside that old toy, the Magic 8 Ball. The bracelet itself had begun to give off a faint purple light, too.

Dazed, I looked up at Sky. The brilliance caught on all those facets of blue inside his irises. As if he felt my stare, his attention drifted to me before he tilted his head back down to the cuff, brow furrowing. Energy flowed from his fingertips and into the device. The buzz increased until it tickled my forearm, and I tried not to squirm.

A second later, the sensation—and the glow—vanished. The synth-skin's electricity winked out, and the bracelet's surface stilled again, going inert and dead. Smooth and solid. Like it'd never happened.

I raised my wrist, twisting it. *Wild.* I was wearing *alien technology.* "What did you do to it?"

"Recharged it." Sky eased back into his seat, blowing out a long, slow breath. "It should get us by until we get to Bast's."

He let go of my hand. I'd been so transfixed that my arm flopped onto the console, knocking against the scuffed armrest. I pulled it back, wiggling my fingers and rotating my wrist. The metal was cool again. Back to normal. The light pouring from my palm was as strong as ever, though.

Urgency rushed back.

Sky reached for his seatbelt. "Ready?"

"Yes. So it's working now?" My fingers shook a little as I fastened mine. Even the belt was sticky. Ew. I wiped my hand on my jeans.

"The signal blocker?" He glanced at me, reaching for the shifter. "It should be, yeah, but we still need to move. Fast. Before the Enil send something down for a closer look."

That was enough to chill my insides. I twisted in my seat. The orb was still there, hovering. "Let's *go*, then."

"Working on it. One thing at a time," Sky muttered as he put the truck in drive.

The brakes squealed before we rolled from the parking spot. I held my breath as Sky headed for the road. Leaving the crappy motel behind.

In a stolen vehicle.

Stolen Vehicle #2.

God, I hoped the truck's owner wasn't part of that crowd of onlookers—and if so, that they wouldn't notice their ride cruising away without them. I couldn't help but turn back again.

The Enil ship shone over the chaos, pulsing like a fallen star. A media van had arrived. More police, too. The crowd spilled out into the streets and lawns. People had even come with posters, though they were too far away for me to read.

Their motions were impossible to mistake, though. They were waving their makeshift signs like they were *excited*. A derisive sniff slipped from me as I wrapped my arms around myself.

They should've been running and screaming instead of holding up messages like this was some celebrity meet-and-greet.

I wished we could warn them, on the off chance the Enil did send one of those mechanical monsters down.

But we had to get out of here.

I clutched my seat, watching the crowd growing smaller and smaller out the back window. A knife of guilt stabbed deep again. More innocent bystanders. More people caught in this crossfire.

I was the common denominator here, too.

Heart heavy, I turned back around, glancing at Sky. His jaw was set, his eyes trained on the road ahead, hands at ten and two. His sole focus was on getting us out of here. Probably where mine should be if I was going to survive this thing with my sanity intact.

Not on my guilt. About the officer. Those people.

We reached the parking lot exit. Sky stopped long enough to check for cars before making the turn. When he pressed the accelerator, the engine revved and kicked into gear, propelling us further away. The scent of burning oil filled the cab.

We left it all behind.

A regular extraterrestrial Bonnie and Clyde. If Bonnie had a flashlight hand and Clyde drove a getaway spaceship.

Hopefully, we would fare a lot better than they had.

Chapter 12

ALIEN ACTS OF SERVICE

THE SUN warmed my face when I swam back to consciousness. It took me a second to realize we weren't moving, and I jerked my head up. It gave a dull throb at the sudden movement.

Shit. I'd been sleeping so hard that I'd drooled. I grimaced and swiped the back of my hand over my mouth. My neck ached from the strange angle it'd been resting against the door.

I'd slept for a while, apparently. We were parked at a gas station, a tiny, Podunk one with a hand-painted sign in the window advertising worms and cheap cigarettes. The trees crowded close, gnarled, spindly things draped in thick curtains of dangling moss. Only one other vehicle sat at the pumps: a hatchback with a bumper sticker that read *I Brake for Gators.*

Sky was nowhere in sight, but the engine was still humming and the A/C was cranked.

Then again, it was probably easier to leave it running than to alien-zap it back to life every time.

I rubbed my eyes, forcing away the bleariness. I didn't recognize any of our surroundings. The last thing I remembered was Sky brooding and the dull roar of the truck's engine along an endless stretch of highway lined with spiky-looking pine trees, the morning light spilling in…

He was probably in that rickety gas station now. I raked my bangs out of my face and tugged down the sun visor. Faded receipts and a pen spilled out and clattered to the floor. I toed them aside and peered into the mirror.

My hair was a mess, and a car nap hadn't done much for the smudges under my eyes. Squinting, I leaned closer. My stomach dropped. Was that…?

It was. A tiny crust of blood clung to my left nostril. Leftover from the nosebleed during my alien-induced seizure.

Seizure.

A frisson of fear sliced through me. For a second, I smelled antiseptic and heard the beeping of monitors. Shuddering, I tugged down my sweater sleeve and scrubbed at my nose until it turned pink and the telltale traces of blood were gone. My head still hurt, but the pain had subsided a little. It was reminder enough, though.

A *seizure.* I'd never had one in my life. I rarely even got sick. And if I did, it was a runny nose or a cough, and I fought my way through it.

I'd been that way as long as I could remember. Admitting I was sick meant the hospital, and hospitals were where you went to die.

My throat constricted. I shook my head, lifting my gaze to my reflection. The bruise above my eyebrow was turning a lovely shadow of olive green.

It was a stupid thought. This, whatever was wrong with me, wasn't the same thing. I knew that. Logically.

After all, you could die anywhere. As evidenced by the *copious* near-death experiences I'd racked up in the last week. My university. The mall. Hell, my drive home from work. If I had a bingo card of "Places you can die by evil robot," I'd be close to yelling bingo.

I slapped the visor closed and leaned back, blowing out a puff of air. Then I glanced at the dashboard clock and froze, eyes bulging.

Somehow, I'd slept for *four* hours.

I swiped my marked palm down my face before shoving open

the squeaky passenger door and hauling myself out using the oh-shit handle. The humid air wrapped me like a sodden towel.

We were definitely in swamp country. I could almost taste the sour tang of stagnant water. The smell mingled with acrid gasoline and loamy, rotting leaves. Insects buzzed from the underbrush, a wall of droning song.

This had to be Marrow Bay. Where Bast lived. Or at least close enough.

Which meant I was about to meet another Pladian.

The ridiculous nerves slithered back in. This morning had been full of narrow escapes, and the last thing I should've cared about was what some alien stranger thought of me. Only whether he could safely remove these marks and the halix's energy signature.

I uncurled my fingers, studying my palm in the sunlight. The shapes and lines gleamed like inlaid pearl. The glow radiating from it had died as soon as we'd put some distance between us and the Enil. The UFO hadn't followed, which led me to believe whatever Sky had done to the cuff had worked. But for how long?

Footsteps scuffed over the asphalt. Heart stuttering, I tucked my hand behind my back and looked up.

It was just Sky striding from the dinky gas station's front. His shirt clung in sweaty patches, hair plastered to his temples, and when his head turned my way, the mirrored sunglasses he wore caught a glint of sunlight, flaring bright white.

I stared at him. Maybe it was the lingering grogginess or maybe the way the heat shimmered around him, but my mouth went dry.

There was something about his long legs encased in those jeans, the lean, rangy shape of him. He moved with a kind of innate grace, a confident stride that I'd always admired—even back when I thought he was just a broody bartender with the deadliest dimple known to man.

That admiration had morphed into something…weightier now. Even now, I felt his approach on a visceral level. Like a tug in my midsection.

The still-fresh, way-too-vivid memory of last night's kiss was also there. Lurking.

It took me far longer than it should have to notice the Styrofoam cups he carried in each hand.

"Hey," he said, reaching me. I reined in my thoughts before I started drooling again, and this time for very different reasons. If he saw my flush, hopefully he mistook it for a reaction to this heat. "I didn't mean to wake you up. Figured you could use the sleep." He held out one of the cups. His expression was serious, but the corner of his mouth lifted. "Here. Coffee. Like you like it. Too much cream, no sugar."

I paused in reaching for it, slowly dragging my attention from the drink to him. His face. My mouth opened, but the words got stuck.

How...? He knew how I liked my coffee?

For some reason, my swallow proved to be difficult. It was such a small thing. Insignificant. And yet, it said everything.

We hadn't spoken much this morning yet. It'd been a whirlwind, and we clearly had more important things to worry about than rehashing our let's-be-friends pact. But the heavy emotions from the night before were still there, simmering below the surface. At least for me.

I hadn't sorted through any of it. Not the Enil appearance, the police officer Sky had technically assaulted with alien tech, my apparent seizure.

Everything we'd said to one another.

Definitely not that kiss.

And now, here we were, standing in the swampy heat, with him holding coffee he'd picked up that just happened to be exactly how I liked it...

Friends. He'd said we were friends and there would be nothing between us. I couldn't read anything into that kiss. The almost... well, what *could* have happened if we hadn't been interrupted.

I couldn't read anything into a cup of coffee.

It was just exhaustion and tension and the fact that there was *so much* wrapped into this little road trip. Sky was clearly attracted to me—and by now, it was *very* obvious I wanted him, planet of origin notwithstanding. But he'd set boundaries for a reason.

One lapse in judgment didn't mean he'd changed his mind.

I couldn't forget: the *map* was why I was here. Why we were on this wild adventure together.

Nothing else.

I peered up at him. I couldn't read his expression behind the glasses, but he was looking at me with a slightly pinched, tentative curve to his lips. Like he was picking up on the confusing rush of thoughts.

Maybe having an alien badass as my friend wasn't all bad. Even if that small, tucked-away part of me longed for a version of this where we were something more, I could've picked a worse friend than a super soldier here to save his world. One who could shoot lightning from his fingers and brought me coffee without being asked.

So I took the cup and summoned a smile that felt a little too bright. I masked it with a nudge of my elbow when he slid past. "Anyone ever tell you you're an angel?"

Sky leaned his shoulder against the truck's dusty side panel and shoved his sunglasses atop his head. Tucking his free hand into his pocket, he sent me a more solid, lopsided grin. "Actually, yes. Mrs. Dailey, every time she comes in with her friends and orders my Cosmopolitans."

It startled a laugh out of me. Feeling a little less emotionally shaky, I braced my back on the truck and tried a sip of the coffee. Way too hot. I settled for blowing on it.

Sky's faint smile lingered as he sipped from his own cup and watched me over the rim. The golden sunlight lightened the color of his eyes to a deep blue, like his namesake.

There was something about that look that flustered me again, so I scanned our surroundings instead. "So is this it? The place?"

"Marrow Bay? Yeah." Sky eyed the graveyard of tires half-hidden behind the building. "Not exactly a tourist destination."

"But an extraterrestrial one?" I arched a brow and tested my still-scalding coffee again.

Sky sniffed dryly. "That would be Planet Earth in general at the moment."

I hated how true that was. "Is Bast meeting us here?"

"No. We've got a little bit to go. Our new ride guzzles gas, and I figured we could both use coffee."

I shifted uncomfortably, glancing at the stolen beast of a truck we were both leaning on. When I turned back around, Sky had lifted his face to the sun, eyes closed. His mouth curved faintly, and his long lashes cast crescent shadows across his cheeks.

He was absorbing the light. It was strangely familiar. I didn't realize I'd smiled until he cracked one eyelid and frowned at me. "What?"

"Nothing," I said, biting my inner lip. Then I decided *what the hell* and explained, "You reminded me of a sunflower. They shift to follow the sun, you know."

They also happened to be my favorite flower. I kept that part to myself, though, as Sky made a thoughtful noise and closed his eyes again. A moment passed, slow and syrupy in the thick heat. I blew on my coffee and listened to the sound of bluegrass music filtering from the gas station shack.

"There's no sun in space," Sky said suddenly, in a quiet, wistful voice.

It surprised me enough that I lowered the cup, looking over at him. "What?"

"Obviously, I mean. Plenty of stars, but…you know." He breathed a laugh and let his head fall a little further back. That contemplative softness lingered around his mouth. "Not like this. And because I was born on the ship, sunlight wasn't something I really understood until I got here. That's when I figured out how much I like it."

Coffee forgotten, I watched him bask, something soft catching in my chest.

He looked so…*human* right now, enjoying the warm light, his dark hair in messy waves, stubble softening the angles of his face—that cowlick at his left temple refusing to be tamed.

I feel *human*, he'd said last night.

And yet that offhand remark was a reminder that he'd been

born on a *spaceship*. In space. A spaceship that, if we succeeded, if we really survived all this, he'd be leaving on.

I tore my attention from the pretty starboy haloed in gold light and frowned down at my coffee instead. My pulse felt a little unsteady. My next sip was tolerable, so I took a gulp, needing the burn. Maybe the caffeine would level me back out.

When I raised my head again, Sky had opened his eyes, and they were on me. His mouth was in a somber line now, like he, too, was twisted up in his thoughts.

But before I could decipher that contemplative look, a high-pitched squeal jolted me out of the spiral. I tensed, nearly spilling my coffee.

It was just a child. No evil robots. A van had pulled into the tiny gas station. Its side doors flung open, and a herd of small kids tumbled out, running in haphazard, cooped-up circles. Their parents trailed after them, trying—and failing—to corral them.

It reminded me so strongly of road trips with my family, of Dustin and me fighting over the back seat of Dad's Land Rover, that I nearly smiled. But thinking of my mother reminded me she'd have heard her only daughter was now a wanted fugitive, and that urge shriveled, along with my nostalgic smile.

Gripping my cup, I turned away from the family and found Sky's expression solemn enough for me to brace myself.

I wasn't disappointed.

"We should talk about what happened last night," he said, angling so that he faced me, his grip flexing on his Styrofoam cup.

My heart gave a nervous thump. I knew without asking he meant the kiss, and my shoulder blades pinched together. *Oh, here we go.*

Sighing, he raked a hand through his hair and tucked his fingers back into his pocket, glancing around us. "We probably should've talked about this already, but with everything—"

"Sky," I interrupted, resisting the urge to curse. The rising gooey emotion was effectively stomped dead. I examined the Spanish moss dangling from the nearest tree to avoid looking his way. Was it actually moss? A vine? Some other kind of plant? "We don't need to go over it again. It was just…" I waved a limp hand, then batted at a dive-bombing fly. "Urges. Tension. It's been…a crazy few days."

"Urges," he murmured, a touch of humor creeping in. "Sure."

I couldn't help it. I slid my eyes his way, biting my lip against a completely untimely snicker. *Urges* was one way to describe the fact that I would pay money to lick his biceps.

The way he was looking at me, though, with a fond kind of exasperation, wasn't helping. "You said just friends," I blurted.

He blinked a few times. That glimpse of humor winked out. "Yes. I did. *Do*, I mean. I do want to be, uh, friends." He took a breath and seemed to gather himself. "I don't want there to be any awkwardness or confusion. I do think giving in to the…" He gestured at the space between our bodies. "We're both adults, and we're, uh…" His throat worked in a swallow as his gaze slid to mine then away. "We're clearly attracted to each other, but… I still think giving in to the urges would complicate things."

Too late for that. I forced an airy laugh, anyway. It sounded more strangled than anything. "It doesn't have to be a big deal. We're friends. It was just a…a kiss. Nothing…"

I took my shirt off and was ready to strip naked on a nasty motel room dresser.

A whisper of heat coiled low at the memory. He'd been just as into it as I'd been. Which didn't help a damn thing.

Self-preservation loosened my tongue, and words poured out. "It was just a kiss. Seriously, I kiss my friends *all* the time—" I clamped my mouth shut.

What?

Sky's brows formed a V, and he tilted his head to the side. "You…do?"

I *so* didn't. Helpless, I gave a shrug that I hoped looked more convincing than it felt. The way he was eyeing me skeptically said it wasn't.

Awkward silence settled.

That awareness was back, weighing down the moment. He was looking at me like he was trying to decipher my thoughts. That made two of us. I had the strongest urge to glance at his mouth, but I rolled my lips together and forced myself to maintain eye contact.

The longer the strained pause lasted, the more his stare softened until he finally asked, "Are you okay?" He switched the coffee to his other hand and inched closer.

"I'm fine," I lied. The sunlight flared behind him. I raised a hand to shield my eyes. "Why?"

"Well, we're on the run and you haven't slept in a few days. Then there's the seizure. And the part where we just narrowly escaped the Enil," he said, dry as dust, but then he pitched his voice lower. "And you seemed really upset last night. About the news story. Before…well, before."

Before we nearly tore each other's clothes off. Right.

It was all blurring together. The hottest makeout session of my life. The evil robots from outer space. Cops. Alien map complications…that was just a regular old Wednesday at this point. Thursday? Whatever day it was. I'd lost track.

I lifted a shoulder again. There were no words for the tangled, growing mess of feelings at this point. About any of this.

Sky didn't press, thankfully. "Okay. How's your head?"

"I'm *fine*," I muttered, lowering my arm and taking a sip of the coffee. The Spanish moss swayed in the breeze. It had to be moss. Why else would they call it that? "It's just a headache."

Sky stepped into my space, prompting me to look up at him in surprise.

"You had a *seizure* this morning, Raven," he said with the emphasis that sentence deserved. "If you're feeling off at all, I want you to tell me, okay?"

I wasn't into alpha males. However, there was something about the gentle, calm way he asserted himself that did it for me. "Okay," I whispered.

He didn't back up. "And you don't recall the dream at all?"

"No." I nibbled at my bottom lip. Not being able to remember felt oddly like letting him down. A stupid reaction. It wasn't like I could help it. "Sorry. I don't. No map epiphany."

There it was, the real reason for his concern. I took another sip of the coffee to wash down the bitterness and pushed off the truck. "Are we going to get going or…?"

Sky reached for my shoulder this time, tugging me back toward him. "I'm serious. If you're feeling anything—"

Because I had trouble thinking clearly with him touching me, I pulled out of reach. "Will you stop manhandling—*alien*-handling me? I told you I'm fine."

"*Alien*-handling? Really?"

I flushed and glared at him.

He held up both hands. "Okay. Sorry. But we don't know what we're dealing with, here. I really need you to be honest about how you feel—"

Something in me cracked a little. "You think I don't know that, Sky? That there's something going on in my brain that we don't understand? As you so helpfully pointed out, I had a *seizure* this morning. I've seen someone have a seizure, you know." The thought that'd been lurking, that deep, dark stain spreading inside, finally spilled out before I could bite it back. "My dad had them. Before he died. I saw it firsthand…"

My voice broke. *Damn it.* I drew back, exhaling shakily. I hadn't meant to say all that. To tell him. But it was too late now.

"Raven." Sky's arm twitched like he was about to reach for me again before he'd thought better of it. "I'm sorry. I had no idea—"

"I *know*. I know you didn't know. You couldn't have." I swallowed hard like it'd help the ache in my throat. Something about him made me speak without thinking, and I hated it. Hated how stretched thin I felt right now. Emotionally and physically drained. This stupid headache wasn't helping anything. Nor was the fact that I couldn't seem to shake it—and that I'd just slept for hours and felt like I could sleep another day at least. "I'm not saying that to make you feel bad. I get it. I know the map is the important thing here. I know that's why you're protecting me and why I'm here." I made it a point to look around us, at the dingy gas station and stooped, crowded trees. "Wherever here even is."

"What?"

I rolled my eyes, then squinted up at him. It was difficult to see his face with the sun's glare.

"It's okay," I said, attempting a stiff smile. "But I can't tell you what I'm feeling because I *don't know.* I don't even know what day it is." A snort slipped out. "So I'm really sorry I don't know what I was dreaming about at the motel and—"

"You think I'm keeping you safe just because of the map? Because of the halix?"

I blinked, caught off guard. He shifted and blocked some of the sun then, and now I could see his expression. There was tension around his mouth, a sharp glint in his eyes.

Anger? Why would he be mad about that?

"It's okay, Sky," I muttered, looking away. "I don't..."

I barely bit back a frustrated groan. This wasn't helping anything. I was being snippy. Taking it out on him. The throbbing in my temples was getting worse.

"Sorry. I'm sorry. I woke up crabby," I muttered, blowing out a breath. "Can we just get going?"

Sky was quiet long enough that I looked up at him, gripping my cooling coffee tighter. He'd pressed his lips together, and he watched me for a long beat, face set in that unreadable mask again.

For a second, we simply stared at each other in the hazy heat.

Sky looked away first, jaw working in a quick clench and release. Something swam in his dark blue eyes as he gazed into the distance, toward the swaying Spanish moss. Something that could've been regret.

A car door slammed nearby. I jumped, glancing over. It was just the van's passengers piling back in, but it was enough to break the spell. Jolt me free of the chokehold the moment had on me.

And when I turned my attention back to Sky, whatever emotion I'd glimpsed had vanished from him, too.

"All right," he said, straightening his shoulders. It was the calm, polite tone he'd always used at work. Pleasant enough but guarded. That stupid bartender voice. His *Pladian* voice, I suddenly realized. Logical. Reserved. *Rational.* "We can get going. But please let me know if anything feels off, okay? If your headache gets worse, or if you get dizzy."

If anything felt *off?* I almost laughed. That summed up my entire life right now. "Sure," I said instead, cupping my coffee in both hands. I managed a tight-lipped smile. "I will."

"Good." He took a drink and scanned our surroundings. "We're almost to the motel Bast is going to meet us at. We'll regroup. He'll be able to help with everything."

With everything, huh? I *highly* doubted that.

We didn't talk as we climbed into the truck. Sky's phone dinged after he'd settled into the driver's seat. He glanced at it, then slid the sunglasses back down, setting the device on the console. Neither of us spoke as he shifted to drive, and I watched the little family in the van disappear in the rearview mirror, the ache of nostalgia, of lone-liness, settling somewhere deep.

Like a festering wound.

Chapter 13

WARNING: HEAT
SIGNATURES DETECTED

"He's late," Sky muttered as he paced the motel room's length, spun on his heel, and started back the way he'd come. At the window, he cracked the blinds with two fingers, peering out into the parking lot.

From my spot in the middle of the queen-sized bed, the slant of golden Florida sunlight made my eyes water. I turned my head, burying a yawn in my shoulder as the TV screamed about bathroom cleaner.

"Is this normal?" I asked. Keeping my eyes open was a losing battle. Four hours ago, that gas-station coffee had felt like a lifeline. Now the lumpy mattress was dragging me under.

"Him being late?" Sky asked without turning. His hair was a mess from all the times he'd shoved his fingers through it. "I'm sure he's got a good reason."

The TV blared again, and I mashed the volume button until it was a low murmur. Meanwhile, Sky resumed stalking the length of the small room. He paused near the door to put his hands on his hips and tip his head back, sighing heavily.

"Are you worried about him?" I asked, pushing up onto an

128

elbow. I couldn't get a read on his emotions. He was more guarded than usual.

His movements, when he turned back around and passed a hand down his face, were slow, though. He was tired, too.

"Bast can take care of himself," he said. But his tight mouth told me I'd hit the nail on the head.

"You can…" I glanced around. The options were the dangerously wobbly wooden chair by the window or the bed, so I patted the mattress beside me. "You can sit down, Sky. Pacing isn't going to make him get here faster. You'll just wear yourself out more."

"I'm fine." He didn't look fine. He looked haggard and dead on his feet. Come to think of it, short of whatever nap he'd managed this morning before my seizure had woken him, he hadn't slept in days.

I stared him down long enough that he relented, looking out the window one more time before finally crossing to the bed. When he sat, though, he left plenty of space between us.

Which was fine. I was too tired to throw myself at him, anyway. My headache thudded in time with my pulse.

I set the television remote on the nightstand and rolled onto my side, watching him toe off his shoes with my temple cushioned on my arm. He checked his phone again before thumbing the screen off. He glanced up to find me watching him and lowered the device.

I must've looked as bad as I felt because he frowned and said, "You can close your eyes, Rae. Sleep if you need to. Might as well get some rest while we wait. I'll be right here."

"No, it's okay," I said around another yawn, tucking my face into my bent elbow. "I'll just…"

I didn't manage to get anything else out before my eyelids slid shut.

I AWOKE WITH A START. For a second, I saw *shapes*. A dream clung to my mind. A memory. Something important, but it slipped away faster and faster as I swam toward awareness and…

I was even cozier than before. My headache had dulled, and I was comfortable. Warm.

Huh. Very warm. I frowned and cracked my eyelids.

I was on my side with a heavy weight pressed to my back and a steel band around my waist.

No, an arm. That was an arm. A bare, tanned forearm with a light dusting of dark hair, attached to a long-fingered hand splayed over my stomach—

I was wide awake in a single heartbeat.

How had I ended up cuddling with *Sky*?

He'd fallen asleep. We both had, and maybe I was still dreaming because this was too perfect, the way his body curved along mine, his chest rising and falling gently against my spine.

Sky Acosta was a cuddler. I never would've pictured it, but now? Somehow, it fit.

Hell, *we* fit.

It wasn't the first time I'd had that thought, nor was it the first time this warm, mushy emotion threatened to spread in my chest. I focused *instead* on my immediate problem.

I was stuck.

The arm he'd slung over me tucked me against his front, and Sky was…well, not quite spooning me, but our knees were bent at the same angle. He was curled protectively around me. And for some reason, it made a feminine thrill ignite.

Oh no.

My pulse fluttered in the base of my throat.

If I knew Sky—and I liked to think I'd gotten to know him *pretty* well—I'd bet he hadn't intended to do this. This had probably been a subconscious, instinctual…*thing.* He'd be embarrassed when he awoke.

Which begged the question: did I spare him—and me—that moment and extricate myself, or did I pretend to stay sleeping and let it play out? I could, for as long as it lasted, let myself enjoy real, actual cuddling with Sky Acosta. It was the kind of thing I'd always dreamed about, after all.

He'd turned out to be just as fantastic a cuddler as I'd thought he'd be.

I was surprised his partner hadn't shown up yet and woken us. Careful not to move too quickly, I lifted my head. The television's mutters were inaudible, and the light filtering through the blinds was still that burnished yellow of golden hour. We hadn't been asleep long, then.

Just long enough for…*this* to happen.

As I lowered my head to the pillow again, Sky groaned, a faint sound of protest that rumbled from deep in his chest. I felt it vibrate against my back. Every hormone I owned perked up. The arm around my waist constricted, dragging me tighter against him. I couldn't help my breathless squeak. He was warm and hard, and—

And *hard*.

A flush rocketed through me, settling low. *It's just a natural reaction.* I knew that. I shouldn't read into anything—but neither my pulse nor my body got the message. My heartbeat took off at an uneven gallop.

His hand flattening on my belly did nothing to slow it, either. His palm was hot through my *Mind Your Biscuits* shirt.

I needed to wake him up. Before this got even more out of control. But what if he thought *I'd* initiated this? We'd *just* had a conversation about boundaries. About being friends.

He shifted a little behind me, pressing harder into my backside, and panic surged.

I licked my dry lips and whispered, "Sky? Are you awake?"

"Mmhm," came the gravelly response. Not convincing. Especially because his hips tilted forward again, and oh *God*—I hadn't imagined it.

He *was* hard.

"Sky?" I whispered hoarsely, body lighting up. Every cell of my being wanted to wiggle back and return that pressure.

Somehow, I stayed still.

I knew the second he woke up because he stiffened, fingers digging into my belly. I bit my lip to stop a grimace. His shocked inhale was loud in my ear.

"I... Did I fall asleep?" he rasped, recoiling so suddenly that I had to work not to be offended. His arm disappeared.

But because I was cool, calm, and collected, I forced a laugh I really hoped sounded light and carefree and twisted to look back at him. "It's fine. We were both..."

My attempt at composure failed.

Because now I was experiencing what it was like to wake up next to Sky.

He'd pushed up onto one elbow. Those twilight-blue eyes were heavy-lidded when they found mine, curls a rumpled mess over his forehead. He blinked rapidly, like he was trying to find his bearings.

It was...endearing. Cute.

I wanted to tackle him.

I watched alertness—*awareness*—bleed into his gaze as he ran his fingers through his hair slowly, his gaze sliding away from mine.

Probably because we were close enough to kiss again. And he had to know *I* knew it'd affected him. Sheer willpower kept me from glancing at his mouth. Or lower.

"Sorry," he whispered, giving me a semblance of a smile that was almost embarrassed. I tried not to gawk when a hint of redness tinged his cheekbones. "I don't know how I drifted off and..." He studied the worn comforter underneath us.

I could finish that sentence. *I don't know how I drifted off and ended up plastered against you.*

I took a deep breath. Held it. *Do not kiss the hot alien, Rae.*

"It's *totally* fine," I said, waving a hand. This was *all so fine.* "You were tired. And it was...um." I couldn't find a word. He was biting his lip. That wasn't fair at all. "Warmer."

"Warmer. Yeah." He huffed a laugh and shot me a look from beneath his lashes. "That's one way to put it."

Okay. *Hotter.* This time, I barely stopped myself from looking down, where I'd felt his cock through his blue jeans. That seemed like a really bad idea right now.

I froze when he reached between us.

"You have a..." He brushed my temple and tucked an escaping

strand of hair behind my ear. He pulled his hand back quickly. "Hair."

"Oh. Thanks." I self-consciously smoothed my palm over my head. "I probably look terrible."

Exhausted, running on no sleep, adrenaline, and barely contained sexual frustration. I could only imagine. I probably looked like I'd been through the ringer—

"No, Rae," he said quietly. "Not even slightly."

My heart skipped like a stone over water at the murmured words. I lifted my head just in time to watch him glance at my mouth. Linger there.

The TV's muttering was loud in the sudden quiet.

Sky seemed to catch himself, and he looked away first, patting his pockets. "I should…check the phone. For Bast. He probably called. I didn't mean to fall asleep."

"Yes. Phone." I tried to swallow, couldn't, and nodded instead. "Bast."

Solemn, more awake than he'd been a second ago, Sky stilled and raised his face. Contemplated me. I waited. I wasn't sure for what.

A line formed between his brows. "This is a bad idea," he said, almost to himself. His phone hadn't made an appearance.

"It is," I murmured, then caught up and frowned. "Wait, what is?"

He didn't laugh. Didn't even smile. A muscle in his temple bunched like he was clenching his molars. "What you said at the gas station earlier…" His eyes roved between mine. "About me just keeping you safe because of the map?"

It was enough to pull me from my stupor, and I winced. *Ugh.* Why had I blurted that out? I shook my head and tried to do damage control. "I shouldn't have said that. It was dumb. I don't know why I did. I'm just tired and cranky because of these headaches. And I—"

"It isn't true," he interrupted. His voice was frayed, like the confession had been torn from somewhere deep.

"I… what?" I reared back to get a better look at his face. "No, Sky, I don't need…"

I wasn't sure what I was trying to say. It was hard to think when he was looking at me like that.

"It's not just about the mission." His stare was hypnotic in the gold light. More like a night's expanse than ever. The silver specks looked like stars. "I know that makes everything more complicated —because it *can't* change anything. But you deserve to know that I care about what happens to you, too. As a person."

"Right." All the moisture had fled my mouth, but I tried to lick my lips anyway. "That's…you know…that's what friends do."

He exhaled through his nose, a dry snort, brows flicking up, though he didn't refute it.

"I'm glad we're, um, friends." My heart had lodged itself in my throat. "Since we're confessing things." He was watching me carefully, but his pupils had dilated. This pull was a living, writhing thing beneath my skin. I lowered my voice to a conspiratorial whisper. "I don't *actually* kiss my friends like that."

He stared for a heartbeat before his mouth twitched. "Oh yeah? How *do* you kiss your friends, then?"

"Usually with my shirt on," I said, fighting a grin. Relief fluttered in my chest at the crack in the strange tension. "Definitely not with tongue."

Sky laughed then—a genuine, surprised chuckle that made his dimple appear. "Well, that's a damn shame for your friends then."

I blinked, caught off guard, before a ridiculous giggle slipped out, one I tried to smother by slapping my hand over my mouth. It was too late.

At the sound, Sky's grin widened, and he bent his elbow, resting his temple on his fist.

"While we're doing this," he flicked a finger between us, humor lingering in the crooked curve of his lips, "and sharing things, I feel some non-friend things for you, too, Raven. It's not that I don't. You're not just some means to an end, okay?"

My heart skipped a beat, and I lowered my hand from my mouth. The urge to laugh at all died, and my stomach flipped over itself. This was dangerous territory. Even more dangerous than waking up snuggling with the way-too-attractive undercover alien. This was *feelings* territory.

"I…"

Dangerous for *so* many reasons.

"Okay?" He studied me, cataloging my reaction. The shock I was sure was written all over my expression. "I want to make that clear."

I finally extracted my voice from where it'd vanished into the void. "You don't need to tell me things just because it's what you think I want to hear. I'm going to help you save your planet regardless."

"I know," he said, smiling a little. Softer this time. "That's part of the appeal."

He was so close. How did I keep ending up so close to him? Had I scooted closer or had he?

It was like he was a magnet—or better yet, we were planets, stars, stuck in each other's inexorable gravity. He was impossible to escape. And his lips looked so soft, kicked up at the corner like he was hiding some sort of private amusement—

"Speaking of not making things easier, it's really hard not to kiss you when you're staring at my mouth like that, you know," he murmured huskily.

"Oh. God. I—" Blood roared into my face as I tried to scramble back.

Only I'd slid too near the edge. My back met air. Not again. I flailed and would've fallen right onto the floor, but Sky uttered an oath and snatched me by the belt loop of my jeans, hauling me back onto the bed.

A little too forcefully.

The mattress squeaked, and the air rushed from my lungs as he overcorrected.

One second, I was tipping backward; the next, I was sprawled over him, staring down into his wide eyes, my hands flat on his chest.

He was warm and solid beneath me, his mouth parted. His

hands rested beneath either side of my ribcage, and his pinky touched bare skin beneath the rucked-up hem of my shirt. Our lips were only inches apart.

"T-thanks," I stammered, gaping. He'd reacted *so quickly*.

"Yeah." His throat bobbed. "Don't mention it. Didn't want you to…fall. Again."

Because all I did lately was fall around him.

The air conditioner clunked along, and canned laughter spilled out of the television. In the lazy, afternoon sunshine leaking through the blinds, Sky's eyes seemed to glow with an inner light. His fingers tightened on my sides.

I had no idea who moved first, but one moment we were staring at each other, and the next, his mouth was on mine. One of his hands lifted and tangled in my hair—and all I could taste, breathe, feel was *Sky*.

But it was over as quickly as it started. He didn't draw away, but he did end the kiss and rest his forehead against mine. "I'm sorry. I shouldn't have done that."

"I thought I did it." I couldn't catch my breath. My lungs were filled with his scent.

His laugh was barely a huff of air. He pulled back, smoothing stray strands away from my face with both hands. The casual gesture knotted me up almost as much as his kiss.

His sliver of a grin was rueful. "Maybe it was both of us."

I steadied myself on his chest. His pulse thumped under my hands, keeping time with mine. Because it was either make a joke or attack his mouth again, I managed a smirk. "A girl could get a complex with how often you apologize after kissing."

"Well." The curl to his mouth deepened. "I'm sorry for that, too?" That stupid dimple peeked through.

It was almost hard to look directly at him when he smiled like that.

I also couldn't seem to look away.

"I'm not really sorry about any of it," I said, voice catching. I made myself meet his eyes. "Since we're being honest and all. And I wish you weren't sorry, either."

His smile faded slowly, and he started to speak, only to stop and press his lips together. He'd made no move to slide out from under me, and he felt...good there. Lean and strong, the hard planes of his body molding to the soft parts of mine. My thigh had somehow found its way between his, and I could feel the length of him straining through his jeans. Proof he was affected by this, too, by our proximity. It wasn't just me.

Something about that made me feel bolder. Silenced any lingering self-preservation.

Was this a mistake? Probably. Had we just finished sort of covering that? Definitely. Did I care? Not even a little.

And it seemed Sky finally didn't, either. At least, if he did, it wasn't enough to stop this inescapable pull.

Because he muttered something that sounded like a curse again before angling his head, leaning up, and sliding his mouth over mine.

That was gravity, all right. I was sucked right in.

He tasted like Sky, like mysteries and the unknown and yet somehow so familiar. Somehow, he'd become *familiar*.

Which didn't bode well for me at all, but I wasn't going to pay any attention to that right now. My entire brain was occupied with the way his tongue brushed mine. The slow, languid warmth that'd started to simmer the moment I'd woken up boiled over. Sky's arm wound around my waist. I could've drowned in the feel of his lips moving, the softness of his hair when I slipped my fingers into his curls. His other palm curved around my nape.

"Raven," Sky muttered, tugging my lower lip between his. He made a sound, a strangled moan, as his mouth sketched a line up my cheekbone to my ear. "We really shouldn't...Bast—any minute—"

"Uh huh." Who was Bast again? I tipped my head back as he kissed his way down the side of my throat.

With a rough sound, he hooked under my knee and yanked me the rest of the way over the top of him, my thighs falling to either side of his hips. I gasped. The sudden shift had me catching myself on his chest, and the new position ignited fire in my belly.

I stared down at him in surprise.

Breathing hard, Sky eased flat onto his back beneath me. His gaze stayed on mine as his hands settled on my legs. Neither of us said anything.

There were too many emotions to decipher in his dark eyes. Like he was torn in two.

There was a part of me that knew I should have the same reservations. I *should*.

I didn't. At least not right now. Maybe I would later. When I'd overthink this. Or maybe see reason. But right now…

Right now, I just wanted him to kiss me again.

Sky didn't say anything. I waited for him to start in with the *we-shouldn't-do-this*. To pull away. Beneath the thin layer of his tee shirt, his heart raced.

So when his mouth twitched at the edges, it threw me. I drew back and frowned. "What? What is it?"

"To be crystal-clear," he murmured, with a hint of a smile, "this isn't intended to feel *friend-like* at all."

Before I could ask what he meant, he grasped me by the nape again, pulled me down, and kissed me.

Chapter 14

BEAMING UP THAT ONE-BED TROPE

THAT WAS the best news I'd gotten all week.

And he was right. It really, really *didn't* feel friend-like in any way, shape, or form. Not when he was kissing me like that. Like he couldn't get enough.

Neither did the way his hips rolled beneath mine. He kissed with his whole body, hands roaming, like he couldn't decide where to grip, to touch, to pull. My blood had taken up a pound, settling between my legs.

He molded my waist, then settled far enough back to be just shy of cupping my ass. I clung to his tense shoulders, his tight jaw. I couldn't seem to get enough air, but air was overrated.

"We really should stop," he told the side of my neck. Instead of doing just that, he tightened his hold and dragged me deliberately over the hardness straining through his jeans. Fire raced up my spine.

That…that wasn't going to help matters. In fact, that seemed *incredibly* counterintuitive to what he was saying. But because consent went both ways—and I wasn't about to try to cajole somebody into heavy petting, even if that somebody *was* Sky—I opened my eyes and forced myself to form words. "We can…stop. Sky. If you don't want this. I'm not—"

I broke off with a squeak when he sat up without warning, catching my weight with a palm between my shoulder blades before I could tip backward.

"Trust me." His other hand stayed firm on my waist. Our uneven breathing mingled, and I tangled my fingers in the material stretching over his chest, watching the sapphire of his eyes shrink to a ring. His voice was strained, lower than I'd ever heard it. "It has nothing to do with not *wanting*. Nothing, Rae. Don't think that for a second."

I believed him. I could read it all over his face. Desire. The same thing churning in my veins. In all the sensitive needy parts. This was part torture, part heaven.

I released his shirt, and my fingers crept up to the back of his neck, into his soft hair. Toying with the curls there. His lids lowered, and his sigh feathered my lips. The sound of the television mingled with the clank of the struggling air conditioner. A distant car horn from a world outside that I barely remembered existed.

The hand he'd planted between my shoulder blades slid down the knobs of my spine in a soft caress until he reached the sliver of bare skin beneath the hem of my shirt.

"It'd be a hell of a lot easier if I *didn't* want you," he whispered, opening his eyes again. He swept them over my face. Something like resignation pinched his brows together, though he gave me the smallest smile. His wandering fingers traced shapes on my lower back. Glyphs, maybe. "I tried."

I licked my lips. "Yeah… I know that feeling."

"I'm not sure whether that makes it better or worse," he murmured, leaning in, and then that was it. I lost track of time.

His mouth was everywhere. Sky was everywhere. Possibly everything. We rolled on the bed until the soft mattress cushioned my back and my thighs cradled his hips.

My palms found their way under his shirt. To his abs, all eighty-seven of them. His skin was scorching. Burning away every lingering thought that this might be a bad idea.

As if he agreed, he groaned into my mouth and grasped my knee, wrapping my leg around his waist. Fitting us together more tightly. His weight pressed me down, and I tugged at his shirt, needing more skin. More Sky.

But then he broke the kiss and shifted suddenly to kneeling, still tangled in my legs.

Stifling a protest, I pushed up onto my elbows. This was it, apparently. Where he decided this was far enough.

"What…" I started, but then he reached behind himself, and my teeth clicked shut. In one smooth motion, he jerked his shirt off and tossed it aside.

Oh. Okay. That, I was fine with.

Expression serious, Sky swept a hand through his hair and lowered himself back down to his elbows slowly enough that I felt every inch of him coming to rest over me.

But he didn't kiss me. Not yet. Instead, he braced himself on his forearms, somber despite his flushed face and mouth swollen from kissing. "Are you sure about this? Because it doesn't change the mission, and the map…"

"What map?" I said, going for his lips again.

His hoarse laugh brushed my cheek as he tilted his head and evaded me, instead angling to meet my eyes.

"I mean it," he said. I could feel his heart pounding, but his expression was calm. "I want to know this is really what you want…"

He didn't finish, but he didn't have to.

I'd already made up my mind, though. This was the first time in days I hadn't had to *think*. If I was going to die tomorrow, crushed by the Enil or killed by the alien map embedded in my brain, I wanted to experience this.

With Sky.

I wiggled until my hands were free, reached behind me to unclasp my bra, and then grabbed it and my shirt, yanking the whole thing over my head. Refusing to quail, I threw the bundle aside. It landed somewhere beside the bed. I'd worry about it later.

Sky stopped moving. His gaze crashed back into mine and held. His lips were parted like he'd forgotten how to breathe.

"Does that answer your question?" I was trying for aloof confidence, but I fought a blush as I settled back on the pillows.

"I'd say so, yeah." His throat worked as his eyes finally swept downward.

My skin prickled. Self-consciousness wormed its way in, and I started to bend my arm over my chest. After all, I wasn't exactly built like a model, and it was bright in here—

"No," Sky whispered, catching my wrist and pinning it gently to the pillow. He rose over me and gave a slow shake of his head. "I want to see all of you."

My throat tightened, but thankfully, his lips found mine again, distracting me from the overwhelming swell of emotion those deceptively simple words wrung out of me. His mouth trailed over my jaw, my neck, down over my collarbone. He'd let some of his weight settle in.

Truthfully, this had been building since that kiss in the stairwell.

Since that very first moment we'd touched, when I'd realized there was a hell of a lot more here than just a little crush on the cute bartender.

Despite the fact that he was an alien. Despite the reasons we'd tried to set boundaries in the first place—

Sky's mouth closed on my breast, and I stopped thinking. His hand found the other, kneading soft skin, rolling the sensitive peak between his fingers. I tightened my grip on his hair as my spine bowed off the mattress. I couldn't help the small moan that slipped out. He murmured something—encouragement, maybe, or it could've been the alphabet—against my skin before his mouth trailed lower.

Lower still.

My heart thudded hard against my ribs. Desire, thick and hot and pulsing, twisted deep, and I forced my eyes open, not wanting to miss one second of this. Sky was watching me through his lashes as he kissed his way past my navel. Goosebumps and twitching skin followed in his wake. Unable to stay still, I lifted my hips.

As if he liked that, liked that I couldn't help but writhe under him, his mouth curled into a small grin, something that straddled the line between shy and carnal, a lock of hair falling into his eyes. That smile was devastating. It would live rent-free in my brain for the foreseeable future.

I stopped breathing entirely when he reached my waistband and nipped at the soft skin of my lower belly. I sank my teeth into my lip when he rose to his knees again and reached for the button. Only to pause and lift his eyes to mine, a question there.

He was double-checking. Of course he was. A consent king. I should've known. God, why did he have to be so perfect?

"Is this okay?" he asked, right on cue, and the rasp in his voice made my insides flip.

He was breathing hard, disheveled, flushed…and still steady. Like Sky always was. And now he was waiting. No, *asking*. Because we'd gone from an exploratory, sleepy kiss to both of us shirtless in the bed.

But I trusted him. And I needed this. *Wanted* it.

So I nodded, reaching for the button myself, but he'd already eased it open. I tensed, nerves skittering, but Sky was moving again, stretching his long body out alongside mine and cupping my face, turning it toward his. Kissing me until I'd forgotten all about nerves and melted back onto the bed. Only then did his free hand trace down the center of my throat. Between my breasts. Past my sternum. He flattened his palm on my belly again before easing beneath *my* waistband and angling to get past the zipper.

I didn't have time to tense again before he found me clearly drenched. No hiding how much I was into this now. A flash of embarrassment hit until he groaned and leaned his forehead against mine. "*God*, Raven." He brushed a kiss over my lips, eyes heavy-lidded. "I've been *dying* to touch you like this. You have no idea. Since that day in the stairwell."

"What a…" I gasped, and my knees fell open at the first slow glide of his fingers over hot, hypersensitive skin. "What a coincidence because I've also…been dying for you to…"

I forgot what I was saying when he dipped those fingers inside me, and a throaty sound I'd never made before slipped free. Sky's mouth found mine as he tested the barest curl.

I gasped, body surging from the mattress in response. Every nerve stretched taut. I clutched at his forearm, and tendons and sleek muscles flexed beneath my grip. "*Sky.*"

"There?" he whispered, drawing back enough to see my face.

"*Yes.*" I tightened my hold on him until it had to hurt. I forced myself to loosen my grip and mumbled curses instead and a few yeses —a combination of both. Tension coiled in my belly, constricting as he added pressure from his thumb, taking up a steady rhythm.

He watched me with his lip between his teeth and his brow furrowed like he was *learning* me. Cataloging every expression and sound. Like I was the only thing that existed in his world at that moment. It undid me even faster than his touch.

The orgasm hit in a sizzle of cascading sparks, and my strangled cry got stuck. The relief of finally letting go sapped every ounce of strength from my muscles, and I collapsed back with a shudder.

When I returned to reality, Sky had buried his face in my neck, gulping air like he was drowning. The word he uttered didn't sound quite human, and he mouthed a kiss into the side of my throat before his fingers wrapped the waistband of my jeans in a white-knuckled grip. Fighting for *control.*

It was unbearably sexy. He was always so reserved. So composed. My body heated all over again as another wave of lust built. I wanted to watch that control shatter. I needed all of it.

All of him.

So I rolled to the side, reaching for him. My fingers found the hard length beneath his jeans, and he let out a strangled sound, jerking, when I cupped him through the material. His head came up.

That was what I needed.

But then his hand covered mine instead. Stilling it before I could find his zipper. I froze, looking up at him in confusion.

His chest heaved. His gaze was dark and wide. I could see his pulse pounding in his neck as he swallowed hard.

But he was still holding my hand in a loose grip. Stopping me.

"I'm on birth control," I blurted, in case he was concerned about accidentally creating a hybrid species.

He blinked—twice—then looked away with a choked laugh. I frowned as he gently pulled my hand away. Disappointment stabbed deep. Doused the fire in my blood like a bucket of ice.

Rejection bloomed right after, and shit, it stung.

"Sorry," I whispered, sitting up. My cheeks blazed, and I wrapped my arm around myself, hiding. My body still purred from the orgasm he'd just given me. With his hand. Had that ever happened before? Not that quickly without battery-operated help. "I'm sorry," I said again, wincing and looking away. "I didn't mean to push."

"It's not that." Sky rose onto his elbow, his expression pained. He ran a hand through his hair. "The synth-skin—I can't carry any diseases or anything, and I can't…" He waved that same hand. "I can't get you pregnant. We're not…compatible. Like *that*, I mean. Genetically."

"Oh." I stared at him. "Then…?"

The golden light fell over his face as his eyes found mine. There was something like disbelief in his eyes.

"You really are okay with," he gestured at himself, "all this?"

I slowly followed the motion down his ridiculously hot self and back to his face. "Um… I'd have to be insane not to be."

He smiled a little, the barest twitch of his lips, but his eyes were completely serious. "I'm an *alien*, Rae."

"You said it works the same, right?" My face was on fire. So was the rest of me.

He let out an incredulous burst of air. Did he not see himself the way I did? Because now that I'd gotten to know him—the real him—Sky was even *more* appealing…

I didn't get a chance to analyze any of that before he shook his head and said, "Well, yeah, it does, but I'm… When the mission's done, I'm…"

Ah. That. He was leaving. He didn't need to finish that sentence. I already knew, just like I knew it brought up a whole mass of complicated feelings. I didn't know where to start voicing any of them or if I should even try.

So I showed him instead. I grasped either side of his face and drew him in for a kiss.

Slower this time, but just as full of want and the consent he was looking for and a whole lot of hell to the yes. Because I didn't know much about anything right now, but I knew I didn't care about any of that. Maybe it meant I was insane, but...

I just wanted Sky.

And he seemed to sense it. Or maybe it was the enthusiastic French kiss and the fact that I was trying to throw my leg over his. With a stifled moan, he rolled back onto me. The length of his body pressed me into the bed again, and I finally got my knee up and wrapped around his waist. Like he couldn't help himself, he rolled his hips in a slow, gentle grind that lit me up like a solar storm.

His hands wandered as the kiss turned into something hotter, something with intent behind it.

Finally.

This was happening. I'd made up my mind.

I hooked my fingers into the edge of my still-unbuttoned jeans, trying to slide the material down. I hoped like hell it was dark enough to hide the sorry state of the panties I'd hand-washed in the sink—

Something was knocking.

Sky stiffened, head lifting. His attention cut toward the door, and he frowned. At the same time, his phone buzzed. I watched understanding dawn in his eyes, followed by shame as he realized the exact same thing I just had.

Somehow, we'd *completely* forgotten we were waiting on Bast.

It felt like surfacing from a dream. And tumbling right into a nightmare.

Sky's partner was finally here and he'd just interrupted what was most likely about to be the hottest sex I'd ever had—with a human *or* alien.

Sky looked back down at me, brows pinching together. Regret.

Maybe something else. Something more complex. I had a sinking feeling that was guilt.

The buzzing went off again, and there was no mistaking the three thuds on the door.

"Sky?" a muffled, masculine voice called. "You in there?"

I dropped my head back with a sigh.

Forget the Enil. Forget License 16. The real villain here was terrible cosmic timing.

Chapter 15

IS BAST SHORT FOR BASTARD?

MY FACE flamed as I fought my way into my bra and tee shirt once more. I didn't feel quite steady on my feet, and I kept my back to the room. My heartbeat hadn't settled. The rustling as Sky tried to put himself back in order wasn't helping.

We'd almost…

Finally.

And then we hadn't.

Was it for the best? Would it have been a mistake? It didn't *feel* like one. I felt nothing but crushing disappointment and a massive amount of unresolved lust.

God. I tried to pat down my braid. It was a tangled mess from rolling around on the bed.

With Sky.

The pleasant ache between my thighs from the orgasm I'd just had hadn't quite faded, either. I bit my lip against a shiver.

Damn it.

"Rae," Sky started, voice rough enough to send another curl of lust through me, but I flapped a hand at him behind my back.

"It's fine. Don't…" *Don't make it weird.* Don't mention the fact that we'd just nearly *had sex* in a seedy motel room.

Don't mention the fact that we'd just talked about feelings.

I straightened my clothing and whirled in time to watch him yank his shirt over his head. His expression, when it emerged, was tight, and he dragged both hands through his disheveled hair.

"We need to talk about this," he said, taking half a step toward me.

I flinched when another round of knocks came.

"I can hear you in there," said the muffled voice, the dry note clear as day.

I gestured with both hands at the door. "*Later.*"

Sky's mouth thinned, and I tried not to flinch at his bitten-off curse. What a mess. *I* was a mess. He pivoted on his heel and, in socks, strode to the door, and I wrung my hands while he turned the lock and wrenched it open. Late afternoon sunlight streamed in, haloing him in gold.

"Where have you been?" he demanded.

"Well, hello to you, too," drawled a raspy male voice. "Why the hell did it take you so long to answer the door?" A pause, and then a sardonic, "Do I *want* to know?"

I flushed, rolling my lips inward. Despite myself, I inched forward and tried to peer past Sky's shoulders.

"Seriously?" Sky jammed his arms across his chest. "You were supposed to be here hours ago."

"So sorry I couldn't text and drive. I'm good but I'm not that good. I was too busy making sure you weren't followed. You're welcome?"

I finally sidled enough to the side to see around Sky's frame and out the door.

That was Bast?

A man stood a few feet away, leaning back against a motorcycle parked halfway on the sidewalk, one battered boot braced on the pavement. At my movement, the stranger's mirrored aviators tipped my way. A strong, square jaw worked a wad of gum, though he paused as soon as I inched into view.

That was…not what I'd expected.

He was built like a boxer in a cut-off black shirt, his thick arms tanned, shoulders broader than Sky's. Ripped black jeans encased long legs. Despite the bike at his back, he wore no helmet, no gloves. No sleeves, even.

It was giving Sons of Anarchy, swamp-flavored.

I still hadn't found my bearings when the rider turned his head back to Sky and said, "You look like hell." He jerked his chin my way. "And that must be your Google Maps."

Mouth open, I blinked. "You really *are* Bast."

The shock was *real.* I didn't know what I'd expected. Maybe another reserved, controlled, charming Pladian like Sky. Somebody quiet and calm.

Not…*this.* This guy looked like he wrestled alligators for fun.

"Glad to know my reputation precedes me." The motorcycle rider—Bast, apparently—shoved his aviators atop his head. His hair was cropped too close to his head to determine the color, but it appeared several shades lighter than Sky's. Eyes the same rich emerald as the dense trees around us traced over me, lingering on my *Mind Your Biscuits* shirt before his mouth slanted derisively. "And you must be the waitress who convinced my saint of a brother to break the Creed."

I stiffened, jaw unhinging even further.

Beside me, Sky sighed and braced a shoulder against the door-frame. "I told you it wasn't like that. This is Raven Barrister. Rae, this is Bast." He waved in Bast's direction. "I'd say it's short for Sebastian, but Bastard is more fitting."

Bast sent me a smile that didn't reach his eyes, leaning back on his bike again and crossing his arms. "I'd shake your hand, Raven Barrister, but I don't want to show all these nice people my shiny bits." He winked. "I prefer to do that in private."

Flushing, I managed to shut my mouth.

Sky was right. Bastard *was* a lot more fitting.

And Bast was *nothing* like what I'd imagined.

THE STOLEN truck jolted and jerked over ruts hard enough that I was pretty sure I'd broken a rib. I clung to the handle above the door like my life depended on it. And it might, the way this was going.

We hit another hole, bounced up, and came back to Earth with a bone-rattling crash. One more of those, and the entire rusted truck might come apart.

"Damn," Sky muttered, white-knuckling the wheel. He glanced my way. "You okay?"

"Peachy," I said through tight lips.

We hadn't spoken much. Bast's interruption—and his insistence we get on the road the second he'd declared it safe—had made it impossible to talk about what had almost happened. That meant the lingering tension was thick enough to feel heavy, though.

I glanced Sky's way. Now wasn't the time for it, either. I was afraid to unclench my teeth. I might bite my tongue off.

How the hell Bast was navigating this sorry excuse for a road on a motorcycle, I had no idea. Maybe it was easier that way.

I distracted myself by peering through the front window. Bug splats and humidity streaked the already smudged glass, but I could still make out lichen- and moss-draped branches, tangled clusters of spindly limbs and winding trunks. The sunlight had dulled to murky gray as the trees thickened, and I could already smell the sickly-sweet swamp water.

Another clang, and we went airborne again, sailing several feet before we landed with a shock-destroying thump.

Sky bit out a curse.

I was still not opening my mouth for anything.

"I don't know how much longer this thing's going to last," Sky said with a hoarse laugh. "Leave it to Bast to pick a place on a road completely impassable to anyone sane."

Another jolt rattled my skull. I gripped the handle harder, silently praying it wouldn't snap off. "He seems…um, nice," I forced out through my teeth.

"Bast?" Sky risked a sideways glance, one brow raised. "He sure as hell does not. He's an asshole." But the corner of his mouth tipped up, and there was something like quiet happiness in his eyes as he refocused on the road and the friend currently leading us deeper into the swampy depths of nowhere.

I followed his gaze. Bast was the closest thing Sky had to family. Too bad the guy seemed like a total prick.

I immediately felt guilty and, uncomfortable, adjusted my grip on the handle. Maybe I could try harder. Be nicer…

Wait. No. I nearly rolled my eyes. Why was I worrying about it? That wasn't why I was here. I was here to get these symbols off me and find my way back to something resembling normalcy. Not to placate Pladians with obnoxiously loud motorcycles and even more obnoxious mouths.

Abruptly, the trees cleared, and the dimming daylight poured back into the cab.

"Finally," Sky grumbled, maneuvering the truck around a dip in the road.

Loosening my death grip on the handle, I leaned forward to peer through the windshield.

It was…a trailer?

Bast had led us to a rundown, beaten-up gray trailer that'd been plopped in the middle of nowhere. A small shed peeked out from behind it, but that was it. Just trees, a trailer, and the shed.

I raised both brows as the other Pladian steered his bike toward the tarp-covered awning built onto one side. Sky parked the truck at an angle in the flatter part of the yard and exhaled heavily. I was too busy gaping at our surroundings to even be relieved the ride was over.

Junk was strewn all over. Old tires, car parts, a pile of what looked like flat-screen TVs, and a tangled spool of copper wire. A line of rusted burn barrels stood in a neat row along a square of gravel, and a single plastic chair sat beside a blue and white cooler like it was holding court.

Well. Today was just chock-full of surprises. Not exactly what I'd expected from a secret alien base. In fact, it looked like a place I was way more likely to get murdered in than saved.

I peeled my fingers from the handle, the joints aching from

being clamped so tight. Shaking them out, I grabbed my bag and hesitated, glancing at Sky.

"Ready?" he asked, looking between me and where Bast was now ambling toward the trailer's door.

Ready to venture inside the sketchy-looking trailer where the sketchier-looking alien lived? No. Absolutely not.

"Sure?"

It was more of a question than an answer, but it must've been convincing enough because Sky opened his door. I forced myself to leave behind the truck I was suddenly much fonder of.

Here went nothing.

My shoes squelched on the springy ground, and I killed three mosquitoes in the time it took us to reach the rickety stairs and the waiting Bast.

He still wore his aviators, despite the sun being filtered beneath the trees, but I could tell he was sizing me up as we approached. He gestured us inside with an exaggerated sweep of one muscular arm. "Welcome to my humble abode. Wipe your feet at the door."

He pushed open the screen door. Sky followed. After a quick glance back at the rusted truck and the overgrown lane disappearing behind it, I swallowed the lump in my throat and stepped into the ultra-secret alien trailer in the middle of BFE.

I started to wipe my shoes and Bast snorted. "Don't bother, MapQuest. I was just fucking with you."

Of course he was. I set my teeth at the nickname and, with effort, turned my attention to the space. The living room was a cluttered mess. Maps, sketches, clippings, and faded printouts completely covered the far wall, windows included. Several rickety tables lined one side of the room, all buried under a mess of parts, wires, and tools. Loose sheets of paper formed ankle-deep drifts beneath them, like the floor of some chaotic, techno-woods.

I thought I spotted the gleam of something iridescent in that nest of equipment. Something that looked a lot like the material I wore on my wrist. I did a double take and—sure enough, it *was*. Pladian metal shone purple-pink from beneath a stack of gears.

Alien technology.

I tore my gaze from it. This trailer read like a hideout for a hoarding conspiracy theorist who had a thing for leather furniture and mosquitoes.

It was a little terrifying.

I eyed Bast sidelong. *This* was the super advanced alien Sky referred to as a technology god? He was supposedly my only hope. The one person Sky thought could fix everything.

Right now, I wouldn't trust him to make me a sandwich. Especially considering the state of his kitchen counters. Was that *mold?*

I tightened my grip on my book bag's strap. Next to me, Sky turned in place, taking it all in with a small tilt to his lips. As if, unlike me, this was exactly what he'd expected. "I like what you've done with the place," he said, smirking at Bast.

"Right?" Bast gave a shit-eating grin, all white teeth and crinkled eyes.

I looked past him. A beat-up leather couch and two matching, sagging chairs filled the rest of the room, all facing a flat-screen TV currently paused on… Top Gun?

Bast must've followed my look, because he said, "I feel the need for speed." With full, young-Tom Cruise confidence.

I had no idea what to say to that. To any of this, really. This was not at all what I'd expected. I tried not to gawk, stepping aside as he circled us.

Bast bumped shoulders with Sky. "Isn't that right, Goose?"

"Whatever you say." Sky shook his head. "Pretty sure you have those backwards, though."

"Sure." Bast laughed, a carefree sound that made me jump. He spread his arms dramatically as he made his way into the cramped kitchen full of take-out boxes, crumpled paper plates, and an impressive collection of crushed beer cans. "Anyway. Here it is. The Fortress of Solitude, except with way better company. Three bedrooms, two baths, and it's even on a septic. Classy, I know." He yanked the fridge open and grimaced. "I've got beer, MREs, and some canned shit."

Then, for the first time since we walked in, he looked directly at me. "No gourmet for you, Starmap. Sorry to disappoint."

I narrowed my eyes. MapQuest. Starmap. Google Maps. I was racking up sarcastic nicknames like frequent flyer miles. Still, I remembered my plan to *try* to be civil, so I offered a smile that felt more a baring of teeth. "I'm not picky."

Sky shot me a sideways look, like he'd picked up on a tone I'd tried to hide. I puffed out my cheeks, ready to apologize, but he'd already turned to Bast. "You got somewhere we can sleep? Maybe shower?"

At the thought of beds and showers, what'd nearly happened in the motel room rushed back. I snapped my mouth shut and instead battled a rush of redness trying to creep its way up my neck.

"Sure," Bast said, nudging the fridge closed. "Two bedrooms down the hall."

Two. That meant Sky and I wouldn't have to share.

Which was good…

Right?

My cheeks grew warmer.

"There's a shared bathroom," Bast was saying when I was able to tune back in. "One of the bedroom's got a futon and a bunch of crap in it. The other one's fancy. My room's full of alien tech, so I save the guest room for company." He flashed me a grin that was positively salacious. "If you know what I mean."

I pressed my mouth into a line. God, I really wished I didn't.

Sky sighed, setting a hand on my shoulder. I jumped at the contact, but he didn't seem to notice. "All right, Bast. Stop trying to get under Raven's skin. She's had a rough few days."

Bast feigned a *what, me?* expression of innocence that looked almost believable.

"I don't care which room I take," I told Sky, ignoring Bast. I managed something like a smile. "But a shower does sound good." A real one, since the shitty one at the rundown motel had barely counted.

"All right." Sky scanned my upturned face, something flickering in his eyes before his expression smoothed. "C'mon. Let's get settled. Bast, you wait here."

"In my *own house?*"

"Out of the way for two seconds," Sky called back as he led me down the small hallway.

As soon as we reached the pair of bedrooms across from each other, he ushered me inside the larger of the two. I pivoted to face him where he lingered in the hallway.

"Are you alright?" he asked, leaning closer. "You look over-whelmed."

An understatement. I exhaled a laugh and scratched at my eyebrow. Damn it. One of those mosquitoes had gotten through my defenses. "Your friend's…a lot," I admitted.

Sky shot an exasperated look over his shoulder before gripping the door frame over his head. "He's trying to get to you. Don't let him. It's his way of testing boundaries."

Right. I adjusted my hold on my bag. Not letting Bast get to me was easier said than done when everyone, from government agents to cops to angry mech-suits, had been trying all freaking week.

"I'll work on that," I said anyway, for Sky's benefit.

I scuffed my toe on the worn beige carpet. Like the trailer, it'd seen better days. Awkward silence settled between us, and after a heartbeat, I peeked up at Sky.

He let go of the door frame and lowered his arms. When he spoke, it was in that careful, guarded tone. The one I hated. "Do you want to…talk or anything?"

The leap in my pulse, the surge of fight-or-flight adrenaline told me talking was the last thing I needed right now. I shook my head, dropping my eyes to my dirty shoes again. "No. No, I'm okay. I think I… I just need a second to decompress."

I didn't look at him, but I could see him out of my periphery when he shifted his weight and jammed his hands into his pockets, the motion agitated. When he spoke, though, his voice was neutral. "Okay. That's fine. Why don't you settle into this room? No rush. I'll be out here."

"Sure," I murmured. I made myself look up in time to see him turning. His shoulders were tight. Guilt stirred as I watched him disappear back down the hallway without another glance.

It wasn't like I didn't *want* to talk about what'd just happened between us. I just didn't know what to say. Not yet. Besides, what would it accomplish? Nothing had *really* changed. Not really.

Right?

I sighed. When I heard low murmurs coming from the living room, I let out a long breath and turned to inspect the space.

I'd never tell Bast this, but the "fancy" room wasn't half bad. The double bed was clean, as were the comforter and sheets. Shockingly. The very basic nightstand was chipped, but it held up a lamp and tiny alarm clock. It was sparse with a typical bachelor's palette. Comfortable, though.

I slowly lowered myself onto the mattress's edge and scrubbed my palms on my stained jeans, looking around. We'd made it. This was Bast's. The next part of this crazy alien story started here.

Which meant, like it or not, I had to play nice with the guy who lived in a mold-infested tech cave.

Hopefully, he also had mosquito repellent.

I snorted. That was something I hadn't thought to toss into my bag. Yet another entry I'd need to add to the *Fleeing Evil Agents and Eviler Aliens* survival guide. Working title. I should've been taking notes about all the things I should and shouldn't have been doing on this wild journey.

One of which was sleeping with one of the good aliens.

My insides lurched at the thought, and I sighed and dropped my head into my hands.

Sky had been worried it'd complicate things, and apparently, he hadn't been wrong. Because this was the beginning of the end, wasn't it? Now that we'd found Bast, we could get this map out of my brain, and all this would be done.

And the fact that I wasn't feeling strictly happy about that was a problem.

Another one to add to the list:

Do not get emotionally entangled with the alien who was days away from leaving the planet for good.

Groaning, I let myself flop back onto the bed.

Chapter 16

IT'S NOT THE SPACESHIP; IT'S THE PILOT

I'D JUST FINISHED re-braiding my hair when knuckles rapped my door jamb. "Knock knock."

I whirled. "Sky."

"Hey." He slid his hands into his pockets and gave me a small, close-lipped smile. Whatever frustration he'd felt when we'd last spoken was gone. He looked relaxed. Calm, even. He'd changed, too, into a black tee shirt—Bast's, I assumed—and a pair of black joggers.

Which, coincidentally, were nearly as dangerous as gray sweat-pants. They hugged his lean thighs and slim hips—

I hastily returned my attention to his face. He'd been talking that whole time. I hadn't caught any of it.

"Sorry." I blinked rapidly. "What?"

He raised his brows, that quirk to his lips deepening, but he repeated, "Are you hungry? Bast made some…well, it's not really food, but it's edible."

"Hey! I heard that!" Bast yelled from deeper in the trailer.

Sky glanced over his shoulder before sending me a wry look. It made me smile a little.

It felt stilted, though. Their camaraderie was obvious. *Brothers,*

Sky had said, and I could tell. Such a strange feeling, being the odd one out.

Especially considering, out of the three of us, *I* was the only one who belonged on this planet.

I scrubbed my palms on my jeans, forcing myself to focus once more on Sky. He was here, offering me food.

I wasn't hungry. That ever-present headache was still thumping away at my temples, twisting my stomach into knots.

But because I was a people-pleaser, I lifted a shoulder. "I could eat."

With one last glance toward the bedroom and the bag I'd left atop the bed, I followed Sky down the short hall, through the cluttered living room. On the TV, an action sequence punctuated the silence. Three bowls of brown sludge waited on the counter. One remained untouched. Waiting, it seemed, for me.

"It's chili," Sky said when I stared a beat too long. His eyes twinkled, though his mouth stayed set in a sober line.

I darted a glance at Bast, who was watching me with a narrowed stare. I crossed the rest of the way to the waiting bowl. "Cool. Uh… thanks." I picked up the spoon.

"Beer?" Bast asked suddenly.

I paused mid-scoop and looked up. He held out a knockoff brand in a bottle. If I hadn't known better, I would've said this had the distinct feel of an olive branch. If an olive branch came with shitty carbonation and less than four percent alcohol content.

I looked from the bottle to him. "Oh, I only drink craft."

His eyes flared. Straightening, he opened his mouth—

"I'm kidding," I said, biting my lip against a smile. I swiped the beer from him. "That's payback for that joke you made about me being picky. Thank you."

Bast stared in shock as I cracked the top with a waitress's ease and took a long pull. Yep, it was shitty swamp beer, but it scratched an itch I hadn't known I had.

Beside me, Sky chuckled. I didn't miss his approving glance, nor the way his shoulder brushed mine as he rested his elbows on the counter. My stomach fluttered.

I told myself it was my hunger finally making an appearance.

"Well played, Biscuit," Bast said, crossing his arms over his broad chest. His slow grin was the first genuine one I'd seen all afternoon. "Well played."

The real smile made him look slightly *less* like a prick. He was attractive in his own right. Not my type, but I could see the appeal. When he wasn't being a jerk.

"What's with all the nicknames?" I took a bite of the chili. It was warm and…goodish.

"Well, Biscuit's because of the shirt." He nodded at my graphic tee. "Sure is something."

"For the record," Sky chimed in, "we haven't exactly had access to a full closet since we've been on the run."

"Speaking of." Bast set his beer down.

I chewed my sludge-chili as he strolled to one of the white tables along the wall. He rummaged through a pile and pulled out a tiny black box. From my perch at the counter, it looked like part iPad, part Geiger counter, part something I couldn't even name.

He muttered to himself, nodding, and I frowned warily as he strode back to the kitchen. At my side, Sky made short work of his chili, seeming unconcerned.

That made one of us.

"I got this thing ready for a scan," Bast said, lifting the device and waving it. A series of tiny green lights flashed at its base. "I've been working on some things I want to try."

When he brought it near me, I leaned away before I could catch myself. To be fair, I didn't have the best track record with random alien tech.

He didn't notice, judging by the way he continued without a pause, attention on the touchscreen he tapped. "I'm going to try a recalibration later—with the recent broken containments in mind. After you get settled. But for now…"

He tilted it closer. This time, I held still, and it only took a second for him to draw back.

"There." I couldn't make out the display from this angle, but after a second, he appeared satisfied, the creases in his forehead smoothing out. "No signal. That cuff's definitely working." For once, he looked completely serious when he raised his moss-green eyes. "I'm real interested in what shorted it out in the first place."

My appetite waned when his attention dropped to my marked palm. I balled it into a fist, but Sky nudged me with his elbow.

"It's okay. You can show him."

"Yeah." Bast flashed me a coy smile as he rounded the counter to stand on its other side, setting the strange alien device between us. Its surface was dark now. "I'll show you mine if you show me yours."

This time, I registered the weaponized, flippant flirtation for what it was. The aim to disarm. Distract. I cocked my head, eyeing him. Maybe he was more calculating than I'd realized.

"You have a halix signature on your hand?" I said lightly, feigning surprise. "I thought I was special."

"That's what Sky tells all the girls," Bast drawled, then lowered his voice to a stage whisper. "But don't worry. I think you're special, too."

I blushed at that, eyes on my food. Beside me, Sky set his spoon down with a clatter, shoved his bowl away, and released an annoyed huff of air. "Bast. Cut it out. I told you to stop messing with her."

"What? I can't call her special now? It's not every day an Earthling gets to wear Pladian writing."

Their banter barely registered. I was still clutching my own utensil, so I made myself relinquish my grip on it. It felt oddly vulnerable to uncurl my fingers and stretch my hand across the counter. The shiny scrawls gleamed under Bast's yellow panel light.

His eyes dropped, and any hint of teasing vanished from his expression. He didn't touch me, but he leaned closer and let out a low whistle. "Well, damn, Sky. You were right. That's the halix greeting all right. Interesting."

"That's one word for it," I muttered, drawing my hand back and picking up my beer for a long drink. Like our host, it was growing on me.

"And the dreams…" he started, only to trail off when Sky shot him another look.

I swallowed, grateful. I wasn't ready to talk about that yet. Not when I couldn't remember them. Not when the only thing I *could* recall was what came after.

Like seizures.

Chills raced down my arms, pebbling the skin.

I pushed the thought aside, and the glass clinked when I set the beer down.

"So." I spun the bottle on the counter, watching the condensation drip down. "Are we going to get started?"

"On?" Bast leaned on his elbows, cocking a brow.

I glanced between him and Sky. "Extracting the…" I swirled my finger by my temple. "The whatever's up here. The calibration or whatever you said you wanted to do."

He opened his mouth, but Sky interrupted. "We still don't have the working interface."

"Right, but…" Bast lifted a shoulder, crossing his arms. "We could try to figure something out with the tech we do have. Probably have to jury-rig some stuff."

I gaped at him. "You want to jury-rig some stuff to interface with my *brain?*"

Bast's slow, evil smile reminded me of the Cheshire cat, but Sky cut him off with a raised hand. "Why don't we get some rest first? Rae and I have had a rough couple of days."

I nodded, rubbing my marked palm. That was an understatement and a half.

Sky looked between Bast and me. "Rae should recover her strength before we try anything. Besides, you said the cuff's working, right?" At Bast's lazy shrug, Sky turned my way. "We're safe here. For now. Let's catch our breath before we start trying to figure out the halix. It'll give Bast time to tweak a few more things, too."

"Sure," I said slowly, still struggling with the idea of Bast throwing together some Frankenstein machine to hook me up to. As much as I wanted to return to normal life, I wasn't exactly chomping at the bit to have them rummaging around inside my head.

I looked between the two aliens. "So what? What do we do in the meantime?"

"Whatever it is waitresses who are way too fucking curious for their own good do with their free time," Bast said, snorting.

"Well…" I pushed aside my half-eaten bowl of chili-sludge with my fingertips and worried my lower lip. "There's something else you can show me. Something I've been afraid to ask for."

In my periphery, I saw Sky's head slowly turn my way.

Bast's brows rose, and he smirked. "I'm listening. You should know, though. Blondes aren't usually my type."

He *definitely* wasn't mine. I somehow refrained from saying it aloud. *My* tastes ran more along the lines of lean, broody bartenders anyway. A prime example of which was currently staring at me.

"Since we have time to kill…" I glanced at Sky, then back at Bast, lifting my chin. "I want to see the ship."

Silence fell. The sink dripped. From the living room, jet planes screamed through the sky.

Bast blinked.

Then he shoved off the counter and threw his hands up. "Jesus, Skaiven! Is there anything you *didn't* tell her?"

"Yeah," Sky said with a long sigh. He snatched his beer up by the neck. "I didn't warn her about you."

That couldn't have been truer.

TEN MINUTES LATER, I stood in Bast's backyard flanked by aliens. The sun had sunk well below the tree line, and night was falling in a cacophony of insect song and the cries of other, larger creatures. Eyeing the increasingly dark foliage, I resisted the urge to shudder and swatted mosquitoes while Bast unlocked the shed.

"I'm still shocked as hell he told you about this," he called over his shoulder. "And the Roswell ship?" He glanced back. When I shrugged and nodded, he shook his head. "I don't know what you did to him, Biscuit, but you should do it more often. My boy Sky here is usually a stickler for the rules. The Creed, especially."

"Don't I know it," I muttered.

A brief flashback of kissing him while we rolled over the mattress tried to rise. I ignored it.

Sky's arm bumped mine. I was suddenly very aware of how close we stood. He was looking at me, too, as if trying to decipher what my passing comment had meant.

I was both relieved and disappointed when he stepped forward to help Bast pry open the heavy door, revealing a…

Completely empty shed, save for a falling-apart lawn mower and a box of—Well. Those were old porn magazines. I cocked my head.

So he hadn't been lying. Blondes *weren't* his type.

"They were here when I moved here," Bast said, holding up his hands. "I swear."

"Uh huh." I pursed my lips. "This is some ship."

"For fuck's sake. I'm not gonna just leave it lying around. It's not show and tell." He nudged the box of Playboys aside with his toe and kicked at a patch of dirt underneath. "Stay back."

A few more scuffs of his boot revealed a button embedded in the floor. He pressed it, and a panel on the wall slid open, revealing a softly glowing pad. He walked over and placed his palm on it. A beam of light shot from the ceiling and scanned his entire body.

My eyebrows climbed. Okay, *now* I was impressed.

Finally, with a metallic groan, the floor began to split. Sky's fingertips grazed my lower back, steadying me when I instinctively stepped back. I glanced at him, gaping, and his answering grin was lopsided. "Just wait."

I turned back as the opening yawned wide to reveal a set of corrugated metal stairs leading down. Soft blue light filtered up from below.

"Happy?" Bast asked, brushing his hands off. "This Area 51 enough?"

"It's getting there." Licking my lips, I inched forward and peered down the stairs. They descended into murky dark.

"After you, Scully," Bast said, gesturing at the mysterious opening in the shitty shed floor. "Boldly go and all that shit."

After me. To go see the alien craft underground.

Heart in my throat, I peeked back at Sky. He tilted his head, as if to urge me on. That smile had turned into something…charmed. By me? By my excitement?

Well, I refused to be embarrassed. After all, alien spaceships might be part of his everyday life, but this was *kind of* a big deal for me.

I started down the stairs.

Turned out Bast had an entire bunker down there.

And inside, a UFO awaited.

Chapter 17

DOWN TO ORGANIC INTERFACE

I was standing inside a freaking UFO.

"Holy shit," I whispered, for the six-hundredth time since Sky had placed his palm on the rocket-shaped craft's side and an opening had simply...appeared in the smooth, purple-pink metal. "This is insane. Like something out of a movie." I pivoted slowly to face him. "There aren't even buttons."

Sky's soft laugh echoed in the domed room. Bridge? Was that what this was? "It's just science. Pladian tech operates on organic interfaces," he said, trailing his fingertips over a Y-shaped contraption in front of him. He turned toward where I stood behind the row of scoop-shaped, waist-high seats. "Like the navigational mechanism here. The part doing the actual steering interfaces directly with your brain, through touch." He tapped his forehead. "Most of our technology works that way." He brushed a hand down his chest and gave me a self-deprecating smile. "The synth-skin is the same way."

"Right. Synth-skin. Organic interface," I whispered, turning in a circle.

I tried not to think of how close I'd been to organically interfacing with his synth-skin and the Pladian in it.

Luckily, I had plenty of distractions.

More of the joystick-looking things jutted from the shining purple floor at random intervals—steering or controls, I assumed. Past Sky was a blank wall. Bast said it became translucent when in flight, but now the effect was slightly claustrophobic. The entire oval room—ceiling, floors, and walls—was constructed of the same featureless metal, unmarred except for the open doorways, one of which Bast had disappeared into.

I couldn't stop staring at the seats, though. They were eerily human-shaped. Which made sense. When I'd gotten a glimpse of Sky's true form, it'd been shockingly familiar. Two legs, two arms, two five-fingered hands. Eyes, nose, mouth. All the important bits.

Well, I *assumed*, anyway. Flushing, I slid a quick glance his way.

He *had* told me our evolutions had taken similar paths. That reproduction worked in a similar way. The anthropologist in me badly wanted to beg for more information, but I knew better. So did my self-preservation. The less I thought about Sky's mating habits, in alien form or otherwise, the better off I'd be.

Plus, Sky had willingly shared so much about his mission already. He drew the line at details about his people.

Not, I guessed, his ship since I was *standing in it.*

"Pladian technology just bypasses the clunkiness of physical manipulation," he was saying when I stopped fixating on his anatomy and tuned back in. "Interfacing directly is quicker, easier, and a lot more effective." *Interfacing.* There was that word again. I rolled my lower lip into my mouth. "You can travel, navigate, fight —whatever without worrying about mechanics. It's at the speed of thought."

"It does make sense." I turned in a slow circle. "Except the synth-skin syncs with you on a DNA level. This ship doesn't, right? Your...um," *if you can't beat them, join them,* "interface is just temporary?"

"Exactly," Sky said, sounding pleased. Like he was happy I was following along.

Barely. It was hard to wrap my brain around any of this.

I was inside a motherfreaking UFO.

The ship wasn't big. Maybe the size of two school buses plastered together and shaped oblong.

According to Sky, this craft was built for small jumps, surface landings, and, in a pinch, close-range battles. Close-range *space* battles.

I was standing in a motherfreaking UFO designed for *space battles*.

I forced myself to keep breathing. Anything to calm the part of my brain wanting to jump up and down and scream in excitement.

"Okay," I said, clearing my throat. I channeled cool, calm, collected Raven. Following the example of the Pladians who'd built this thing. "So this ship is like a, what…a drop ship?" At Sky's nod, I poked the sloping panel-stand in front of me. Nothing happened. Most likely because I had the wrong DNA. "Which means you don't have to go into…like, cryo-sleep or anything?" I peered at him over my shoulder. "Unlike your bigger ships, which I assume—"

"Rae." Sky clicked his tongue and dragged a hand through his hair. "You know I'm not going into details."

"Yeah." I bit back a grin and ran my fingers along the curved backrest of a nearby seat. At least, I assumed it was the backrest. Everything was so smooth and sleek. I couldn't *not* touch it. "I know. It was worth a shot."

He leveled me the Look and opened his mouth, but a voice interjected.

"So he doesn't tell you *everything*." Bast ducked in through the rounded doorway, thumbs tucked into his belt loops. "Just the stuff that might end up getting him experimented on. Noted."

I didn't bother with a reply. It was hard to care about Bast's smart mouth when I was looking at all…*this*.

The ship itself was beautiful. Almost fluid, with no sharp edges or hard lines. Just graceful curves and sloping surfaces. Really, it looked like it'd been sculpted rather than built. Like art.

All the systems were dark, every pink-purple panel glossy and unmarked. It had been since we'd climbed a set of steps and entered a short, rounded hallway. The only exception was an open section of the floor near Sky. Wires spilled out, trailing across the metal like entrails. Boot prints and grease smears marred the pristine surface. I was willing to bet they were Bast-sized marks.

I meandered over to it, frowning down. "What's this? The…" I tried to recall what Sky had said was wrong with this ship. "The communications issue?"

"That's the comm unit control panel. Yep," Bast said, popping the P. He crouched beside the open hole in the floor and picked up one of the shining silver wires, twirling it between his fingers. "It's fucked. But I'm close."

Sky leaned both his palms on one of the chair-backs beside me. "You're close? To fixing it?"

"Nah. Finding the replacement." Bast stood and let the cord drop. "The Roswell ship's mainframe."

There it was again. A casual Roswell reference. Would that ever stop making my stomach lurch?

"Since when?" Sky asked as I eyed them both and digested the fact that my life now consisted of discussing UFOs in serious, concerned tones.

Bast nudged a wire back into place with his boot. "I think I've narrowed down the energy signature, and I've been tracking a few different possibilities. Once I pin down the right one and verify it, we're golden." He jutted his chin toward my hand. "And then we can definitely dig that map out of you, Biscuit."

Dig the map out of me? I'd take *extract* over *dig*. I recoiled. "You really couldn't find a better way to phrase that?"

"Nope," he said, his smile widening. "Not going to sugarcoat it, sugar."

I glared at him. "Don't call me that."

"It'll be a simple process," Sky told me. He sent Bast an irritated look before turning an apologetic smile on me. "I told you I won't let anything happen to you. Anything we do to retrieve the halix data will be safe."

Right. Because he'd clearly done this before. I kept the words to myself, but I couldn't help my raised brows. He seemed to pick up on the fact that I was unconvinced because he erased some of the distance between us. Coming closer, but not too close.

"You'll be okay," he said, dipping his head and lowering his voice. "I promised you, didn't I?"

Before I could answer, Bast scoffed. "Neither of you can take a joke. Fine." He spread his arms. "We will endeavor to determine how to safely remove the halix data from your brain, O Human Liaison." He sneered. "Better?"

"I'm surprised you know those big words," I muttered, and he snorted.

"Brains *and* beauty, babe."

Sky sighed, and shaking my head, I turned back to the console. I forgot some of my nerves when my attention fell on the symbols etched across it.

They looked familiar. Squinting in the murky darkness, I leaned in. Flowing Pladian writing covered the surface. Like the ones decorating my palm and what I'd drawn all over my midterm. The same ones I'd sometimes seen shifting in the strange metal signal-blocking cuff I wore.

Maybe even the ones I'd seen in *dreams.*

Something I'd seen…recently. Maybe even this morning. I frowned down at the controls, barely registering them. The memory was hazy. The more I chased it, the blurrier it got.

I hugged myself against a shudder. Like I could anchor against the surge of surrealism.

Pladian writing. The markings in front of me, at least, were real. Tangible. Because I was standing in a spaceship. With two aliens.

I couldn't hide from it anymore. There was no coming back from something like this. From an experience like this.

I wanted so badly to return to my "normal" life, but truthfully, what was waiting there? That normalcy I was chasing—*craving*—was going to look a lot different after all this. *I* would be different.

Nothing would ever be the same. From a micro-level: missing midterms and work, rent—God knows what else—to a much larger scale understanding of how very *un-alone* humanity was out there in the sea of stars. How very small our tiny rock was when measured against the vastness of space.

How fragile we were against things like…killer robots and aliens like Sky and Bast. Beings who could travel solar systems, change skins, and melt away memories with touch.

It may *feel* surreal, but it was all *very* real.

I ran my marked palm over the console. I could've sworn the surface warmed beneath my hand, but everything remained dark. Nothing moved. No glowing lights from my end, either, though I thought I caught movement in my cuff. I twirled it around my wrist, eyeing it. It gleamed innocently back at me.

Sky murmured something to Bast that made the other Pladian bark a laugh. The unapologetic sound drew my attention away from the panel and back to them. Bast was shaking his head with another of his shit-eating smirks, and Sky was grinning in response. It flashed that killer dimple in his cheek. I hadn't seen it enough in the last few days.

He hadn't been smiling a whole lot, which checked out. There hadn't been much to smile about while running for our lives.

But now, standing with the alien he referred to as a brother, Sky looked as close to relaxed as he could get, given the circumstances. That stubborn curl tumbled over his forehead, and he tossed his head to dislodge it from his eyes. The gentle purple glow emanating from everywhere and nowhere highlighted his high cheekbones and cast shadows beneath his graceful jaw.

He also looked like art. Carved and chiseled. Sculpted. Like this craft.

Running my opposite thumb over the Pladian writing on my hand, I looked away, battling a pang in the center of my chest.

It was impossible to ignore the fact that I was as out of place as that grease stain Bast had smudged on the floor. Maybe even more, considering the boot had been attached to an extraterrestrial when it'd left the mark.

And Sky would be leaving soon.

In the very ship I was standing inside.

I tucked a strand of hair behind my ear and swallowed hard, looking around.

It wasn't one-sided, the attraction. At least there was that. Sky had even come close to admitting…*feelings*. But did any of it matter?

There wasn't a future here. He was part of something much bigger than any childish crushes or daydreams.

Why did that sting so much?

Complicated, indeed.

When I turned back to the Pladians, Sky's grin had faded, but his lips were still curved, his head tilted down as Bast rambled on, gesturing animatedly. I recognized that soft emotion. Affection shone in Sky's gaze as he arched a brow at his friend.

It was easier to tell myself he was off limits. Easier than considering how attractive he looked right now in the dim, otherworldly lighting. Than acknowledging how I'd begun to find his presence soothing. Grounding, even.

Whether it was some kind of extraterrestrial Stockholm syndrome or that I was just a sucker for the broody protector vibes, I didn't know. But I did know Sky'd begun to feel…a little like home.

Where had that come from? I scoffed quietly at myself and studied my feet instead of the pretty alien boy, dragging my toes over the slick metal. My dirty shoes glowed faintly blue in the ethereal lighting.

I was going to get hurt if I let myself fall into *that* sort of dangerous sentiment. We were stuck together on this wild, life-threatening adventure. I should be focused on trying to stay *alive*.

Friends, Sky had said. He'd set that boundary. And he was right that it *was* for the best. It didn't matter how cute that dimple was or how vividly I could still feel the phantom press of his body against mine, his lips on my neck, the way he'd watched me come apart on his hand—

I shook off the memory, cheeks heating. I had a life outside all this craziness. Outside all these confusing feelings. One I wanted to return to as soon as humanly possible.

Emphasis on human.

But I still didn't see a way out.

When I turned my back to the console, Bast was rambling on about energy converting and signal vectors. But Sky's eyes found mine across the space. He sent me a faint, close-lipped smile. Beyond that, he was difficult to read in the gloom.

Not that I would've been able to even under a spotlight. Not with that mask in place. He was too good at hiding in plain sight. But then…he'd had to be.

I didn't think I ever would be.

For some reason, that made me feel even colder, hollower. Rubbing my arms, I turned my attention to the ship.

And felt Sky studying me all the while.

HE WAS STILL EYEING me carefully when we returned to the trailer. I avoided looking his way, still too tangled in the convoluted mess of my emotions. As if he sensed it, he was silent as he followed me to the guest room I'd been given for the evening. We reached it, and stepping through the doorway, I blew out a heavy breath and pivoted to face him.

He'd halted just outside the room. Bast had made himself scarce, mumbling something about readings. The trailer was quiet, save for the muffled insects outside and explosions from the living room television.

I needed sleep. The exhaustion had settled in my bones. I was certain it'd be easier to sort through what I was feeling when I wasn't dead on my feet.

Sky tucked his hands into the pockets of his joggers, leaning his shoulder on the doorjamb. "You look tired."

"I am." I rubbed my temple. My headache was worsening again, turning into tiny spikes that whittled their way in behind my eyes.

"You want to shower?"

I whipped my gaze back to Sky's. "What?"

"Not with *me*." That adorable pink tinge kissed his cheeks. I couldn't get enough of the fact that he blushed. How had I never noticed it before? "I meant, do you want to take the first shower?"

I had no room to judge him with the way my face caught fire, too. "I didn't think you… I mean, that's not—" I stopped myself. God, could this get any more awkward? "In *Bast's* bathroom? I'm almost scared to see the state of his shower."

Sky smiled a little. "It's better than that first motel. And don't faint, but he picked us up toiletries. He figured we'd be staying for a bit."

If I was the fainting type, I would have. I gaped at him instead. "Bast went *toiletry* shopping?"

"He did. The asshole act is mostly just that: an act," Sky said. His grin dawned the rest of the way as he took his hands from his pockets and crossed his arms. I tried not to notice how it bunched up his chest muscles. "Mostly an act, anyway."

Right. *Sure.* I bit my lip to hide a smile, but I couldn't fight my arching brow.

Sky's grin slid crooked. "Okay, *most* of the time," he added wryly.

I snickered. "You two are very different," I said on a sigh.

"In some ways."

When that was all he offered, I glanced past him to the darkened doorway across the hall. "Are you staying in there?"

He followed my gaze, then nodded. "I'd planned to." When he turned back, his expression was serious again. "Will you be okay?"

"Okay? Sleeping?" I frowned at him. "Why wouldn't I be?"

He didn't say anything, but he gave me a significant look. Right. Of course. The seizure.

I'd almost forgotten about it with everything else that'd happened. The memory sent a chill sliding down my spine like an ice floe. I wrapped my arms around my middle and shrugged. "I'm sure I'll be fine. It's not like you won't be across the hall…"

Sky's expression was unreadable.

I busied myself studying the light switch beside the door. The moment stretched out. He made no move to leave.

It suddenly occurred to me… was he waiting for me to ask him to *sleep in there with me?*

Surely not. The idea made my belly drop out and my palms grow damp. My pulse kicked up a notch, and I swallowed hard.

Did I want him to?

After my spiral in the ship, that shaky, unsure feeling was back. I didn't know what to make of it. What the hell I was feeling when it came to Sky.

About anything, really.

I made myself look up. At him.

The sun had set, and the room's shadows crept in, painting hollows in his striking face. He was impossible to read, and his composure was annoying.

"Do you want to talk about it yet?" Sky asked, the words softer than they'd been a moment before. The way he was looking at me now, a bit warily, I didn't have to ask what he was talking about.

My tongue got stuck on the roof of my mouth. The humming awareness between us kicked up another notch, stirring heat in my lower belly. For a split second, I recalled his eyes in the golden light, the shards of blue glazed with desire as he kissed his way down my stomach—

I jolted as he tossed his head to dislodge a curl from his forehead. When I didn't answer, he tucked his tongue into his cheek and looked away. "We don't have to, Rae."

Giving me an out. And I, being the coward I was, gladly snatched it up.

"I think I just need some sleep. If that's okay?" I jabbed a thumb toward the bed. "It's hard to think straight. Been a really… long day."

I held my breath and waited for Sky to argue. To frown. To do something.

Instead, he only studied me for one more, long beat before he pushed off the doorframe, tucking his hands back into his pockets. Shut down. That polite mask was back in place. "Sure. Sleep well then."

"Okay. Thanks. You, too." I didn't move as he turned and disappeared back down the hallway. I heard Bast call out, but I couldn't make out the words from here.

I frowned at the empty doorway.

Should I have asked him to stay with me? Or would that have made everything worse?

Did I *want* to talk?

God, I didn't know.

I swiped both hands over my cheeks. I really did need sleep. That would help.

And let's face it: I highly doubted I'd have gotten *any* sleep if Sky was in my bed.

Chapter 18

BLACK COFFEE AND
OTHER BITTER THINGS

DESPITE THE CIRCUMSTANCES, I slept like an exhausted log in Bast's guest bed.

No nightmares, no seizures, and no nosebleeds. Just sleep so deep I woke up face down, confused and disoriented in an impersonal room.

Memory swam back.

Right. The extraterrestrial secret base disguised as a Florida marshland trailer.

Sighing, I flopped onto my back and blinked blearily at the ceiling. Sweat had matted my bangs to the side of my face and my eyes felt crusted over. God, it was a good thing Sky *hadn't* slept in here. Having him see me in this state would've been less than ideal.

The memory of our awkward last encounter woke me the rest of the way, and I squinted at the window. Murky sunlight filtered through the pulled blinds, bright enough to tell me it was late. Well into the afternoon, in fact, if that clock on the nightstand was any indication.

"Shit," I muttered, swiping the back of my hand over my mouth. The scent of coffee hovered in the air. Someone else was already awake out there. Sky or Bast? Or both? It'd be a little embarrassing if I'd been the only one to sleep away half the day.

I sat up slowly, clutching the sheet and comforter to my chest and attempting to run my fingers through my hair. It got stuck on the tangles. I gave up and looked around instead.

I didn't have a change of clothes. The idea of putting dirty ones back on for the third day in a row made my skin crawl. Did Bast have a washer and dryer in this place? It was hard to imagine him doing laundry…but he *had* shopped for toiletries.

Then my eyes fell to my very dead cell phone on the bedside table. *Shit.* I stiffened at the stinging rush of hot guilt. I hadn't pressed Sky *or* Bast last night about calling home. Somehow, I'd been too caught up in the whirlwind of what'd happened between Sky and me at the motel, our arrival here, the ship—my own exhaustion. It'd fallen by the wayside.

What'd that say about me? As a daughter? A friend? Especially after how hard I'd pushed Sky for it before. My stomach rolled over itself.

I'd do that today. First thing. Sky had said I only needed to wait until we reached Bast. And we had. It was time to see if his faith in Bast was misplaced or if he really was the alien tech god Sky seemed to believe him to be.

I pushed off the bed, wobbling briefly before I found my balance. My head still ached, but it was tolerable. Yawning wide enough to crack my jaw, I shuffled toward the door, lured by the scent of roasted, caffeinated beans. I could use a pot. Maybe two. Creamer seemed like wishful thinking, considering where we were and who our host was.

I opened the door and stopped short. There was a pile on the threshold. Clothes and…a note. Brow furrowing, I looked around.

The hallway was empty, and the trailer was quiet. Eerily so. The door across from me, Sky's room, was closed tight and dark beneath. Was he still sleeping? That'd make me feel a little better, at least.

Bending, I picked up the pile. Black sweatpants and a black tee shirt. Bast couture, if I had to guess. They smelled clean enough. Maybe he *did* know how to do laundry, after all.

I lifted the note. The scribbling was a little tricky to make out.

Figured you'd want to change. Shower's good if you want it. Went out. Don't touch the alien shit in the living room. In case you didn't learn last time. – B

I curled my lip. Charming. Even if I was loath to accept his help, a shower *and* clean clothes were impossible to resist. I'd been too wiped out to take one last night. With a final peek at Sky's door, I grabbed my bag and left for the bathroom.

Bast really *had* picked up toiletries, too. They were still in packages. Tiny, travel-sized ones, the kind you'd get at a motel.

In fact, the whole room had that impersonal feel. Same as the kitchen with its paper plates, bare countertops, and equally bare cupboards. The only lived-in part of this place was the…well, living room. The TV and shitty furniture, and that table full of alien junk.

It made sense, given how often Sky'd said they moved. It made me wonder what his apartment above Oasis looked like. Did he have a home up there, or was it just a…landing pad? I grimaced at my own joke then sobered.

Fitting, though. After all, their presence on the whole planet was temporary.

That thought brought with it that tangle of emotions, and I pushed them aside.

BAST STILL WASN'T BACK when I finished and ventured into the living area. The trailer was steeped in stillness. Taking advantage of the opportunity, I padded to the table piled high with junk, trying to discern what he could possibly be working on.

It was a lost cause. The only thing I recognized was Sky's phone plugged into a stack of blinking, unmarked black boxes. I knew it was his from the generic blue-sky background glowing on the screen. Charging or syncing or whatever it was that alien-hacked cellular devices did when not in use by said aliens.

The rest of the pile looked like an electronics section had thrown up on a landfill. Half the items were rusted or cracked, picked apart and pieced together in some kind of messy, hodgepodge tech-nest.

Computer parts like memory and circuit boards, LCD screens, and some of the cords looked like what I'd used to hook up my TV to my soundbar. Others, I didn't have a clue about.

Earth items melded with alien tech. All of it had seen better days.

Oddly enough, it was also a metaphor for my life right now.

I itched to poke around, but I didn't touch any of the "alien shit," and not just because of Bast's dumb note. The bits of pink-purple were clearly visible through the mess, though. Pladian metal. The very same on my wrist.

I leaned in, peering at it. Like the ship's building materials had been, there were no angles, just sweeping, artistic, flowing curves. These pieces ranged in shape and size, some no bigger than my hand or fist, and others larger. Like the tablet I'd once touched. The one that'd changed everything.

My marked palm gave a tingle, and I curled my fingers into it.

Shivering, I rotated the cuff and straightened, tugging the neckline of my borrowed shirt back into place as I turned my back on the table. Bast's clothes were way too big, but at least they were clean. I had to admit, having shaved legs and truly washed hair for the first time in the better part of a week made me feel like a new woman. Even if it had been a shampoo-conditioner combo, because come on. This was Bast we were talking about.

Leaving the table, I wandered into the kitchen in search of coffee. To absolutely no one's surprise, I couldn't find creamer in his fridge, but beggars couldn't be choosers and I was too groggy—even after a shower—to forego caffeine. Still, I grimaced and shuddered as I gulped down a lukewarm, bitter mouthful. I didn't know how Sky did it. Drinking black coffee was the worst.

At the thought, I eyed the hallway in the direction of his bedroom. He'd pushed himself too far. I was glad he was sleeping in. Even if it was strange to be alone—truly alone—for the first time in who knew how long.

I settled into the sagging chair nearest the smudged window, beside the table full of junk. The glass was mostly covered by print-outs of what appeared to be lines of code, but I could see out through a tiny sliver. The sun tried to sneak through the tangled canopy outside, golden orange and watery.

Truthfully, it was kind of nice to finally have some silence—

The front door burst open, and Bast barreled in, pausing in the entry when he caught sight of me.

Never mind.

"Well, well. She lives," he said, smirking as he kicked the door shut after him. He wore black on black again, and these jeans looked like they'd lost a fight with an army of scissors. He was carrying an unmarked box and a plastic bag, and he carted both to the table. As he passed, he jerked his chin at the chipped coffee mug I held. "Sorry, Biscuit. Starbucks doesn't deliver to the swamp."

I deliberately forced down a sip, somehow battling off another shiver. "It's fine."

His skeptically slanted brow showed he didn't believe me, but then he busied himself pulling objects from the bags, and I forgot about it.

Frowning, I sat forward. "What is all this?"

"This, Starmap, is what we're going to use to dig into your brain."

I aimed a dirty look his way. "You can stop with the weird nick-names at any time," I grumbled, even as I scooted the chair to get a better look.

"It's how I show affection," Bast shot back, lifting a handheld gaming console to the light. An orange *Used* sticker had been slapped on the screen, and he ripped it off, flicking it off somewhere into the tangled mess.

I set the coffee down on the rickety table, ignoring his muttered, "Careful," and stood, slinking over to peer past him. In addition to the gaming system, he'd dumped out several packs of coin batteries from the unmarked box. How did all this junk fit together and become something useful?

"Well, I appreciate that crappy nicknames are your twisted form of affection," I told him, wrinkling my nose, "but you can probably keep that to yourself, too."

"Aw, what's wrong? Not into Pladians?" He turned to face me.

He was so tall, my nose barely reached his shoulder. "That's not the vibe I got after interrupting you and my brother at the love shack hotel."

I jerked back, a blush crawling up my neck. "*What?* You didn't interrupt anything."

"Sure I didn't." He snorted. "Anybody ever tell you you're a terrible liar?"

Yes. I set my teeth, glaring.

His smirk sharpened into something a little less friendly. "I'm not an idiot, ya know. Well, not a *total* idiot, anyway. I get there's something going on with you and Sky." He crossed his arms and looked me up and down. "So let's get some things straight, sweetheart. Sky can do what he wants. Me?" He jabbed a thumb at his chest. "I'm not on Earth to make friends with the locals. I'm here to accomplish our mission and maybe have some fun on the side. And as for my job, there are *much* easier ways to go about this whole map-extraction thing. Not as pleasant for you, but it'd get it done."

For the first time since stepping foot in the trailer, a bolt of unease shot through me. I'd taken a step back before I realized I'd moved.

He caught it. Bast's eyes narrowed a little, and when he turned to toss down the gaming device, his jaw tightened. "But," he said, facing me again and spreading his hands, his wide smile just this side of forced, "Sky seems to care about keeping your sanity intact. And because I care about *him,* we're going to figure this out in a non-brain-melting way. Did he tell you what's riding on this? I'm sure he did since he spilled everything except his fucking shoe size."

"Thirteen," I whispered then stammered, "B-but I only know that because I had to order nonstick shoes for everyone at work!"

And remembered Sky's vividly. For reasons.

"Uh huh. Right." Bast eyed me like he was wondering about that whole sanity intact thing. "Anyway, you know why this mission is so important."

A statement, not a question, but I nodded anyway. "He told me. That's why I'm here." Gathering myself, I lifted my chin. "I don't need threats, either. I came with him by choice, you know. He didn't drag me."

"I wasn't trying to *threaten* you." That emerald gaze was assessing. "Just making sure we're on the same page. We've got some work to do to figure all this shit out. Are you sure you're in? Because it'll be a lot easier if you are."

He looked serious. Somber, even. It made me wonder which was the more real version of him: the space-himbo or this gritty alien techie trying to summon his race's salvation from the brain of a waitress with really shitty luck.

Or maybe it was some annoying combination of both. Maybe I'd judged him too harshly and there really was more to him than I'd thought. These Pladians and their layers.

"I'm in," I said, yanking the loose collar of the shirt back up my shoulder before folding my arms over my chest. "Of course I'm in. In case you haven't noticed, I put my *life* on hold to come here. The sooner we can figure this out, the sooner I can go back to it."

He sniffed at that, his disbelieving look telling me what he thought about *those* chances. But to his credit, he didn't voice his opinion. He only said, "Well, good. I'm glad we're on the same page. Because I didn't want to bust out the probes."

I rolled my eyes. "Don't start with that. Sky already—"

A low, amused voice cut in. "She already turned down the probes, Bast."

I forgot all about Bast and spun on my heel as Sky emerged from the hallway. I forgot all about probes, too. Mostly, anyway.

Because he was shirtless again, dressed in nothing but those joggers from last night, the waistband clinging to his hips. All sleepy and rumpled, and so much rippling muscle. His feet were bare and his hair a mess.

"Um." I blinked rapidly, trying not to stare and failing miserably. "Hi."

He scrubbed a hand over his face and the stubble there before fixing a bleary frown on Bast and me. "Sorry. I don't know how I slept so late. What's going on?"

I yanked my eyes from his abs and reached for my coffee, needing to hide my burning cheeks.

I'd had all…*that* on top of me less than a day ago. He'd been ready to get naked, too. He'd given me an *orgasm*.

My pulse took off as I raised the mug. Like he felt me think the word *orgasm*, Sky's gaze zeroed in. I nearly bobbled the cup.

Out of the corner of my eye, I caught Bast's smirk. Like he was finding all this awkwardness entertaining. The prick. To think he'd been growing on me. Maybe he had been, in the same way that mold was in his gross kitchen. I ignored him and gulped coffee.

"I was wondering when you were going to show," he said to Sky, turning back to the table and the trash heap on top of it. "I already made a run into town and came back. I left some shit for you if you want to shower and a shave and all that. You could use it."

"Gee, thanks," Sky said dryly, ambling closer. When I risked glancing his way again, I found his eyes still on me. "Did you get some rest, Rae?"

I heard the unanswered questions. *Did you have any dreams? Any seizures? Do you suddenly have possession of an interstellar map to another world that I could, by chance, have back?*

I swallowed a mouthful of cold, way-too-bitter coffee. "I slept great, actually. Nothing out of the ordinary." Besides everything, of course.

"Good." Sky stopped an arm's length away, studying my face as if he were trying to decide if I was telling him the truth.

I returned the favor. He looked better. The circles beneath his eyes had vanished and the scrape on his chest and the gash on his forehead had almost completely healed. His beard was scruffier than I'd ever seen it, and his hair was an endearingly curly mess, but all in all, he looked a lot more like the hot bartender I'd swooned over for all these months than he had in days.

Except everything had changed, hadn't it?

"You good if I go shower?" he asked me. He flicked a glance at Bast before meeting my eyes again and lowering his voice. "Everything's okay out here?"

"Yeah, yeah. I'm behaving," Bast drawled without turning away from the equipment pile and the batteries he was pulling out of their packages.

I couldn't help my incredulous scoff. *That* was behaving?

Bast caught it and rolled his eyes. "I was *joking* about the probes. I usually save those for at least the second date. Ladies love a good probe, you know."

"You are so gross," I muttered, turning to Sky. "It's fine. I can handle it. Go shower."

"Okay. I'll make it quick."

I settled back into my chair as he grabbed himself a cup of coffee, and Bast busied himself with whatever it was he was doing. Sky cast one, final glance over his shoulder before disappearing down the hallway, presumably to shower.

Which left me alone once again with the much less appealing of the two undercover aliens in my life. Luckily, Bast's focus had turned to taking the gaming device apart with a small screwdriver, the snark replaced by concentration. I watched him work as I forced down more coffee.

The pipes creaked in the walls when Sky turned on the water. I tried not to think about what it'd be like to join him. I somewhat succeeded.

After a moment of silence Bast seemed unconcerned about filling, I sighed and spoke up. "Sky said you could do alien stuff and make my phone safe." I pulled my knees up and looped my arms around them, coffee cup dangling from my fingertips. "To call home, I mean."

"Did he? Alien stuff, huh?" Bast stuck the screwdriver in his mouth and talked around it as he pulled apart the game console's pieces. "He mentioned that. We'll get to it. First things first: I want to calibrate the containment device." When he caught my blank look, he jerked his chin at my cuff. "That stylish bracelet you're wearing. I'm building a resonance amplification circuit…" He didn't bother to hide his patronizing eye roll. "Never mind. We're going to take a look at your cuff. Make sure the crystal is still resonating how it's supposed to. You know, so the Enil don't pop in to say hello after we trigger the halix—*before* we can dig out the map."

"Will you *stop* saying dig?" Over his antics, I twisted in my chair and, unable to stomach any more bitter coffee, set my mug on the wobbly TV tray nearby. I spotted the television remote atop it and picked it up. Only to hesitate, shooting Bast a questioning look.

He clocked it and lifted a shoulder. "Go ahead. Entertain yourself. I have to go to the ship for some salvage, anyway." He tossed down the gaming device. "I'll be back in a bit. Again: don't touch anything over here." He waved his hand in the table's vague direction. "Got it?"

I didn't dignify that with a response, flipping through television channels. His boots clomped over the trailer floor, and the walls rattled when he slammed the door after him with an inconsiderate amount of force. Which seemed to be the way he did most things. I clicked my tongue and shook my head, turning my attention back to the television.

And that was when I saw it.

Suddenly nothing else mattered.

Chapter 19

PHONING HOME

DAZED, I pushed out of the chair and moved closer to the big screen. The remote's plastic edges bit into my palm. I couldn't seem to loosen my grip, though. I couldn't look away from the images on display, either.

Because I knew that courthouse. That single, old white tree sculpture standing proudly at its front. The plaque that'd been replaced a few years ago when kids vandalized it.

That was *home*.

One Willow was on TV. On *national* television.

Numb, I pressed the volume up button with a trembling thumb in time to catch, "…tracking developing reports out of One Willow, a small Midwestern community that's seen an unexpected influx of National Guard personnel and unmarked federal vehicles over the last twenty-four hours. State officials are calling the deployment 'a pre-scheduled training exercise,' but local authorities say they were given no warning…"

My knees wobbled, and the room tilted. I leaned heavily on the back of Bast's crappy couch. Unmarked federal vehicles? Was that *License 16?*

What was going on?

My heartbeat drummed in my ears, and I swayed. The air I sucked in didn't feel like it was reaching my lungs. More words poured out in surround sound.

"The move comes on the heels of last week's unexplained closure of The Willow University after an event initially described as a minor equipment failure resulting from the solar storm caused chaos at the small local college. Eyewitness accounts of hazmat teams, an emergency campus evacuation, and alleged explosions have sparked widespread online speculation. Some commentators are linking the military presence to the region's recent surge in supposed *UFO* sightings, a claim federal agencies have declined to address."

The camera panned over the university campus's entrance and the caution tape and military members blocking passage. Soldiers with guns. Flashing lights. Barricades. This couldn't be *real*.

"However, recent anonymous sources have come forward to shed light on what some are now claiming was an *attack.*"

Attack.

And there it was.

My license picture.

Again.

The edges of my vision went fuzzy and darkened at the corners. My pulse skidded wildly, tripping over itself.

"Oh my God," I whispered, but the words barely made it past my lips. Adrenaline rocketed through me in a violent rush, leaving me queasy and shaking. My skin felt too tight. Too hot. For a long second, I thought the coffee was going to come back up. I slapped my free hand over my mouth.

The newscaster was talking, but it sounded like she was underwater. Or maybe I was, because I was having trouble breathing.

This was bad. So much worse than I'd realized.

"…local student Raven Barrister is still missing and, while authorities are not officially naming Barrister as a person of interest in the attack, they have gone as far as stating a possible connection between the TWU student and the incident…"

My legs buckled, and I sagged harder against the couch. I was going to throw up. Or faint. Or both.

"…possibly in the company of a dark-haired white male believed to…"

My mom. She'd be seeing this.

"…anyone with information regarding her whereabouts is encouraged to contact…"

The remote slipped from my hand. I heard the distant thump when it hit the floor before the ringing in my ears intensified.

Attack. Person of interest.

My face on national news and tied to what the news was calling an attack on the school. A freaking *government takeover* of One Willow.

The images on the screen flashed between dark, armored trucks and residents standing on familiar sidewalks looking on, their expressions ranging from disbelief to fear. A scribbled *Closed* sign hung in a local café window, the very same one Bob went to regularly for pancakes. Ominous black, unmarked cars rolled through a suburban neighborhood. I'd driven down that street dozens of times on my way to the bank from work.

The panic reached a fever pitch.

My mom. I had to call my mom.

The singular urge rolled through me like a tolling bell. My breath rushed out in a shaky sob, and I shot upright, driving my fingers into my hair.

My phone was dead. Useless. Bast had just told me he didn't have it figured out yet. I fisted my hands in the strands, drawing in a trembling inhale. God, if it was so serious that the government was taking over One Willow, maybe Sky was right and going radio silent was the smartest—

I froze.

Except he hadn't been. He'd been contacting Bast this entire time. Using a phone.

His safe, *alien-magicked* phone. The one they couldn't track.

My pulse skipped several beats before picking up to a rapid pound. The patter of water down the hall was loud in the heavy silence. Sky was still in the shower.

And Bast had stepped out.

An idea formed, one wrapped in guilt and misgivings, but I spun in place.

The image of the campus entrance swam back, those guns and masks. My *freaking picture* coupled with a story that implied I was somehow connected to a conspiracy that went deeper than anyone knew.

There it was. Right there on the table. Sky's phone.

My chest caved. Was I really going to do this?

"Shit," I breathed, squeezing my eyes shut. The television droned, already having moved on to a local story, something about a neighborhood initiative. The muffled sound of shower splashing drew my shoulders up tight enough to ache.

Then I blinked, and I saw my mom's face, pale and lined as we sat with my brother in a hospital waiting room. I couldn't recall the day, the visit. Just the feeling. So many, the memories ran together, both sharpened and dulled, somehow, by grief. Some of them were clear, though, like the moment she'd held Dustin and me and told us it was the three of us now against the world. That we'd be okay.

I'd abandoned them both without a word. And now…*this*.

I gulped air, clenching and unclenching my hands.

I *couldn't* let Mom keep worrying. Wondering. I couldn't *vanish*.

I was going to do this. Nausea rose, and I swallowed hard against it. At least, I was going to try.

My heartbeat slammed into overdrive. Adrenaline dumped into my veins as I crossed the room and picked up the phone with cold fingers. They shook so hard that I almost dropped it.

As soon as I lifted it, the screen came to life, that generic blue sky with a sun shining bright. It wasn't password protected—maybe because it was plugged in? I didn't know how this alien tech worked. A misstep, maybe, because he always kept it close every other time.

Except now.

Because he assumed it was okay to let down his guard. God. I gnawed on the inside of my cheek at the swoop of shame and swiped the phone open.

Normal icons. Nothing outwardly extraterrestrial. No smiling silver selfie or "I Miss Pladia" banner.

He'd been using it this entire time. He'd said it was safe. Mine wasn't.

But, fuck, this *felt* wrong. I'd never once gone through a significant other's phone. Not that he was…not that this was *that*. Not that I was going through it, either.

But I would've been lying if I said I wasn't curious. I'd gotten to know Sky, but he was still an enigma in so many ways. How did an undercover Pladian use a phone? What would I find if I *did* look through it?

I wasn't going to, so it didn't matter.

Focus.

Finding the text icon, I tapped it. A bunch of numbers were listed—no names. That was more like the Sky I knew. With willpower fueled by the sickening twisting in my stomach, I forced myself not to scan the messages themselves.

I couldn't risk a phone call. I didn't have time to explain everything, and I had no idea where to even start. Truthfully, I wasn't sure I could hold it together long enough to try. My mother might hate text messages, but it was the best I could do right now.

I pulled up a new thread and quickly typed her number from memory.

Then I paused, thumbs hovering.

The shower ran down the hall, and Bast still wasn't back from his trip to the bunker. But he probably would be soon. I didn't have time to hesitate.

But what did I say to her? *How* did I say it? There were so many words jammed inside me. My eyes prickled, and I swallowed past the lump in my throat, blinking away the blur.

I went with instinct, typing: *This is Rae. Don't answer this, but I'm safe. It's not what it looks like. I'll be home soon. I love you.*

I hit send and waited. The seconds seemed to slow. Clammy sweat beaded on my forehead.

The checkmarks popped up. Message delivered.

Chest tight, I deleted the text thread. The act somehow felt even worse than sending the message. My insides twisted in on themselves as I carefully set the phone where it'd been on the table and backed up on weak legs. I flattened my palm over my mouth.

It was *done*.

A rush sluiced through me, like someone had poured iced water down my body. Was it relief? Dread? I couldn't tell. My gut still pitched and thrashed like a dinghy in a hurricane.

I'd done it. I'd texted my mom.

I'd broken Sky's rules.

Everything was a fractured kaleidoscope of emotion. Too many shards to sort. The guilt was sharpest, but I shoved it aside.

I'd been smart about it. His phone was safe. I hadn't used *mine*. We were fine, right?

Except…wouldn't Sky have offered already if his phone was fine to use like that?

Doubt crowded in, and the floor seemed to undulate beneath me.

"*Damn it,*" I muttered, tunneling both hands through my damp waves again. Some of the panic had dissipated, and cold reality settled in. Too clear.

With a sharp breath, I spun on my heel, putting my back to my crime scene. I fled into my guest room, closing the door and leaning on the wooden panel.

Should I tell someone? Bast? Sky? My knees felt strange. Like jelly.

I'd done it. There was no taking it back.

And nothing had happened. There was no sudden burst of coral, orange, and green light through the blinds. No UFOs descending from the heavens. No Enil. No government agents in black kicking down the doors.

Just…silence. Even the shower had gone quiet. Sky was done.

My heavy conscience was a two-ton weight, and I tipped my head back, squeezing my eyelids shut and my hands into fists at my sides.

My mom…she deserved to know I was okay. With One Willow under government lockdown, with my *actual face* being tied to the university incident, she needed to be reassured. I'd *tried* to ask. I'd practically begged after I'd seen that first wanted bulletin.

And it wasn't like I hadn't thought it through. I hadn't endangered us. I'd used Sky's phone.

I pushed off the door, pacing the room, well-aware I was attempting to convince *myself*. The buzz of insects was barely audible outside. Or maybe that was my brain.

Had that text helped her feel better or had I made things worse? There was no way of knowing. Maybe I should've messaged Amelia instead. Let her convey it with a little more finesse. Mom wore her emotions on her sleeve; I'd inherited Dad's steadier temperament. There was a chance that short text would make her worry even more.

God. *Amelia.* Was *she* okay? She had to be worried out of her mind, too. Was she safe?

With a groan, I stopped in front of the bed and spun, falling onto the mattress. The daylight crept through the blinds in slices of pale yellow, illuminating the popcorn ceiling. I thought I heard a door open and close, either Bast returning or Sky moving around. I sat up straight, my senses on high alert, straining to listen.

Sweat slicked my palms at the thought of Sky strolling into the front room and picking up his phone. Would he know? Would he somehow be able to tell I'd used it? What if my mom didn't listen and answered my text anyway?

I should just tell him. I owed him that much. I'd tell him the first chance I got.

I hung my head, the guilt opening up into a yawning pit. There was a chance he'd understand. After all, I'd freaked out when I'd seen that news story. I'd been seconds from a full-blown panic attack. I screwed up my mouth, a weak sniff escaping. It wouldn't be the first time I'd acted without thinking.

Hell, it wouldn't even be the first time I'd gone and touched extraterrestrial technology without really considering the fallout.

Damn it. Bast's stupid note. I winced, scrubbing my damp palms on my sweatpants. I *had* touched the alien shit.

Well, it was done now. If it turned out to be a mistake, I'd deal with the consequences, for better or for worse.

As it turned out, it was, way, *way* worse.

Chapter 20

WELL, WELL, WELL. IF IT ISN'T THE CONSEQUENCES OF MY ACTIONS

THE LIGHT TAPPING on my door made me jump out of my skin. I lurched upright with a gasp. "*What?*"

Sky spoke from the other side. "Um, can I come in?"

Immediately, the guilt slammed back, slicing deep enough that I flinched and twisted my hands together in my lap. "Y-yeah, I'm here. Why? What is it? Did something happen? Because I've just been here…" Shit. I was rambling. I snapped my mouth closed to stop it, but judging by his pause, not soon enough.

I fisted my hands in the fabric of my borrowed sweatpants. The urge to hide under the bed was strong, but I'd put off facing him long enough. Queasiness settled in the pit of my stomach. "Sure. Yeah. Come in."

The door cracked open, and Sky peeked in, wearing a faint frown. He'd shaved. His curls hadn't quite dried yet, and they fell in damp tumbles around his ears when he turned his head, looking around the room. His midnight eyes found me and his frown deepened. "Everything okay?"

"Yes!" I rubbed my palms on my thighs and forced a smile. God, I didn't even know how to start this. "Fine. Why?"

"Well, for one, you're sitting in the dark by yourself."

Oh. That. I flushed as Sky nudged the door open with his shoulder.

"I'm just thinking," I said with a weak shrug. All the words jumbled together. I fought to put them in order, but it was hard with him standing there. His presence. The way my body seemed so aware of every tiny movement of his.

"I see." Sky stepped the rest of the way inside. He was carrying two paper plates, one of which he extended in my direction. "I figured you hadn't eaten yet. It's not much, but…"

He took a step toward me, and I tore my wide eyes from his face. Each plate held a neatly made sandwich. I tipped my head back to give him a questioning look.

"Peanut butter," he murmured, mouth kicking up at the side. "It's all Bast had."

I blinked slowly.

Sky had made me a peanut butter sandwich.

After I'd used his phone to contact my mother against his wishes.

The shame welled up, thick and hot enough to scald my throat. "Thank you," I said quietly, avoiding his eyes. "You didn't have to do that."

"It's either this or MRE bars, so…" He lifted the plate a little. "I figured you'd prefer this."

"That's nice of you," I whispered, taking it from him. My stomach turned when I looked down at the seemingly innocent bread.

"Bast's gone." Sky tucked his free hand into his pocket. He'd donned a shirt since showering, something I both appreciated and resented. The soft gray material clung to his shoulders and chest.

"Again? Where'd he go this time?" I scooted to the side and patted the mattress. I was stalling. I knew it. I did it, anyway, because he was wearing comfortable clothing and carrying a sandwich, and he looked refreshed—almost *happy*—for the first time in days.

I was about to ruin that. It was like kicking a puppy. A ridiculously attractive, far-too-good-for-me puppy. I shouldn't have used his damn phone. What had I been thinking?

"More supplies," he was saying when I focused on his words. "He said something about a converter. He gets in the zone when he's working like this. Hard to tell." Sky hesitated, then closed the distance between us, settling at my side and placing the paper plate in his lap before turning to me. "You sure you're okay? No…dreams or anything last night?"

I puffed out my cheeks. "Actually, no. I slept hard. This bed is surprisingly comfortable."

Sky glanced at it, then quickly back to me, and it only then occurred to me that we were alone and sitting on a bed. The last time this had happened, we'd ended up almost naked. The sudden rush of heat the memory sent through me caught me off guard.

Sky cleared his throat, picking up his sandwich. "Well, that's good. We both needed the rest."

I watched him take a bite. *Say it.* I just needed to say it.

Sky, I used your phone to text my mom because I freaked out over a news story about One Willow. I took a deep breath and squared my shoulders.

I waited too long. Swallowing, Sky spoke first, his attention on his sandwich. "So since we have a moment, we should probably talk about what happened at the motel. If you're up to it, I mean. I know this has been a lot, and I know you'd…probably prefer not to. And that's okay if you'd rather avoid discussing it. I get that it's awkward. But we're stuck together, and I think we should clear the air. The last thing we need is to be distracted." He paused, eyes on his plate, mouth tight. "That was what I meant by things becoming complicated. For the record."

I stiffened, blood creeping into my cheeks. Was that what he thought I'd been doing? Avoiding it?

Was that what I'd been doing?

For an alien from another planet, he was shockingly into communication.

I bit the inside of my cheek. He turned his head, and his sapphire eyes shone with sincerity and maybe a little wariness. A crease formed between his dark brows as he held my eyes.

"Okay," I said, setting aside my plate. "Sure. We should talk."

His frown smoothed out to surprise, like he hadn't expected me to agree. But it *did* need to happen. Maybe we'd start with this. Talk about what he wanted to talk about and *then* I'd tell him. Just get it out of the way, all at once.

Look at us. An alien and a human, doing *all* the communicating. Dozens of movies had been made about this, and none of them had involved peanut butter sandwiches.

Or aliens that looked like Sky.

Nerves jumped in my belly. Despite having not eaten, I wasn't the least bit hungry. The headache was creeping back. In fact, I wasn't sure it'd ever completely left. I folded my hands in my lap, rubbing my thumb over the near-invisible marks on my right hand.

Taking a deep breath, I dove right in. "I told you…before, that it didn't have to…to *mean* anything. I mean, I know that this," I flicked my fingers between us, "is complicated, but the mission—"

"Rae," Sky cut me off before I could spiral any harder, twisting on the bed to face me. His expression was so serious, his mouth turned down at the corners. "I get things have changed between us in the last few days, but that doesn't mean—"

In the front room, the door burst open hard enough that it slammed into the bedroom's wall, rattling objects. I gasped and lurched, nearly smashing my sandwich. Bast shouted for Sky, who was on his feet and out of the room, disappearing into the hallway before I could recover.

"What…" I started, leaping up and chasing after him. I rounded the corner just in time to see Bast tearing into the living room. I stopped short, but Sky kept going. Bast made a beeline for the table full of equipment.

"*Sky*! Shit! We've got to go, man. There's an alert out! Scanner picked it up." Bast yanked a duffel from under the table and began shoving things into it, too fast for me to follow. He rambled over his shoulder. "We need to go. *Now.* Grab everything we can. Food. Supplies. You know the drill. It should take them some time to get to us, but…" He pivoted to face Sky and gave him a grim nod. "We have to do the thing."

"The thing? What is the thing? What's going on?" I whipped my attention back and forth between them. Was he saying we needed to leave? Now?

"Damn it," Sky muttered. He turned on his heel and headed toward the hallway once again. "How the hell did they find us?"

Wait. *What?*

"Who's *they*?" I asked, my voice sounding strangled even to my own ears. "Will somebody explain—"

"License 16," Bast barked, glancing my way as he spun from the table and ran for the far door, the one leading into his bedroom. "The government goon squad. No clue how they tracked us down, but we need to move. Now. They're heading this way. And if they are, there's a chance the Enil aren't far behind them."

No.

Oh no.

My blood turned to ice. Guilt drove a battering ram *right* into my stomach, hard enough that bile rose. I planted my palms behind me on the wall to hold myself up.

It couldn't be a coincidence. I knew exactly how License 16 had found us.

"Skaiven," Bast said, coming to a stop in the middle of the room.

There was a note in Bast's voice that thickened the sick feeling pooling in my belly. Sky hesitated near where I stood in the hallway's entrance and turned back. I followed his gaze slowly, chest too tight to breathe.

My heart thudded once before it stopped completely as Bast looked Sky straight in the eye and said, "We don't have time to move the ship. I'm going to have to destroy it. Blow it. Charges are already rigged."

"Blow it?" I whispered, stunned. The *spaceship?* The one that was supposed to be the answer to all our problems? The one they were supposed to use to get off this planet?

My insides crumbled away, leaving nothing but ashes and twisting nausea.

What have I done?

I didn't have a single second to process, to wrap my head around *any* of it. Bast and Sky slipped into something like a choreographed dance, gathering and bagging things, barely exchanging a word. Like they were used to this. Fleeing. Running. Hiding.

And I'd just made it so they had to do it again.

And this time…I'd cost them their ship.

I fought the urge to vomit as I found my shoes, grabbed my bag and shoved clothing and toiletries inside, then returned to hover helplessly in the living room. In that time, Sky had thrown on a black hoodie and shoes. The equipment table was much emptier. The shiny alien metal disappeared into the bulky bags Sky and Bast hefted. Sky sent me a wordless look, scanning me as if to be sure I was ready to go.

"This place is rigged to blow, too. I'll wait 'til we're far enough away," Bast said, rugged features drawn as he shrugged on his leather jacket. Two duffels sat at his feet. "I've got bikes in the lean-to. One for each of us. Raven, you'll have to ride on the back and carry something."

"I can do that," I said quietly, unable to meet his eyes. I gripped the strap of my backpack tightly enough that my fingers ached.

This was all my fault.

"She'll ride with me." Sky swept up one of the duffels, handed the other to me, then paused, cupping the side of my neck, thumb tipping my face up toward him. "You good?"

A brief pause, a beat in the chaos. That casual touch because he was thinking of me even as the threat bore down on us and he prepared to blow up his only definitive way home.

God, I'd messed up. I choked down a swell of sickness, nodding, averting my gaze and slipping out of his grasp. He frowned, but this was clearly not the time for this, and he didn't press. He lowered his hand.

"Come on," Bast said, whirling for the door.

With one more glance cast my way, Sky followed.

Body heavy, I trailed them outside.

The thick humidity didn't chase away my chill. I barely summoned a few flicks at the mosquitoes that descended as I hurried after Bast. My heart's muted thud echoed in my ears.

I needed to tell them, but now wasn't the time. Bast's movements were edged with tension as he ripped the blue tarp off the lean-to. A pair of dirt bikes waited inside. Twisting, he tossed a pair of keys to Sky, who snatched them out of the air.

"Red one's yours," Bast said over his shoulder as he hefted his bags and faced forward.

"I've got a back-up place deeper in the woods. Just in case. It's a few miles away, but there's no way in hell they're gonna be able to get to it—"

He stopped talking abruptly, and a second later, I heard why. A new sound broke through the eerily quiet woods.

The whirl of blades.

Helicopter blades.

"*Shit,*" Bast swore, flinging his leg over the white dirt bike. He shoved his arms through the duffel's straps. "Time to go!"

Face tight, Sky handed me his other bag before yanking the red bike around. He straddled it, then jerked his head at me to jump on. His mouth formed a tight, hard line as he scanned the trees.

The choppers were growing louder by the second. My knees trembled as I hurried to him, shifting the pair of duffels to one arm. Or trying. They were too heavy.

"Give me one," Sky said, tense, his attention on the ridge line.

Avoiding looking at him, I did. He set it in his lap and threaded his arms through the straps before gripping the bike's handles, glancing my way. "You got the rest?"

"Yeah," I croaked. Taking a deep breath, I settled awkwardly behind him, my own pack secured to my shoulders. With my free hand, I steadied myself on his side.

Another time, I would've plastered myself to him, savored the feel of his back against my chest. The flex of his abs. The thrill of the ride.

But not today.

Today I was drowning in a pool of misery. Of shame.

Bast waited, bike rumbling, shoulders tight. The helicopters sounded like they were right on top of us. I swallowed hard.

"Hold tight," Sky said, patting my hand below his ribs, and then we were off.

Our tires jolted over a massive root, and it was enough to snap me out of my haze. My bag's weight threw me off, and I slid sideways. Gasping, I flung my arm around Sky's waist more securely and buried my face between his shoulder blades, hanging on for dear life.

Branches whipped by. We jerked and surged over the rotting, gnarled undergrowth. Sky handled the bike with expert precision, but even with it, the ride rattled my bones. This was worse than the truck. With effort, I raised my head and peered over his shoulder.

Ahead, Bast zipped and zagged through the trees, moving fast. His body flowed like he was a part of the bike itself. Our engines whined and revved. Leaves and branches slapped at us, leaving behind slimy trails.

"Hang on!" Sky shouted barely half a second before we hit a bump. The bike soared. My butt left the seat for a heart-stopping beat, and I swallowed a shriek.

We hit the ground again. I crashed back down with a tailbone-jolting *thump*. Pain speared up my spine, and I winced, squeezing Sky's waist.

"You okay?" he shouted at me.

I nodded, then remembered he couldn't see me. "Yes," I forced out instead, chancing a glance back.

Something was moving in the treetops. My stomach rolled. Those weren't Enil ships; they were human. I could just make out shining black through the branches and tangled growth.

Bast made a loop and came up beside us, slowing. "We're far enough away," he shouted over the grumbling engines. He held a small, rectangular device in one hand, and his eyes gleamed like chips of glass. "Brace yourselves."

He pushed the button.

Silence.

Against me, I felt Sky's flinch, and it drove a stake through my heart.

The blinding flare of light registered first. So vivid it lit the swamp far brighter than the afternoon sunlight.

Then the impact.

A hot blast of air shoved my hair back, stole my breath. The trees swayed, branches bent and cracked. A wall of dust engulfed us, gritty and tangy. I pushed my face into Sky's back, coughing.

The roar followed a split second later, a deafening, rolling boom that sounded like the world had broken.

Like I had broken it.

Chapter 21

THE FALLOUT

"**Leave the bikes here**," Bast said an hour later, dismounting with the smooth grace of someone who lived on the road.

I, on the other hand, peeled myself stiffly from Sky's back like a rusty puppet with broken strings. I'd thought that trailer was the middle of nowhere, but this...this felt like an entirely different world.

We'd navigated sketchy, narrow paths over rivers I couldn't see the bottom of and through trees so dense their branches clawed at me, trying to rip me from the seat. Vines and grasses had wrapped the trail thick with mist and webs of undergrowth that left ropy, sticky tendrils clinging to the bike and my legs. Somewhere along the way, I'd lost all sense of direction.

Sweat coated my skin, mixed with bug guts, mud, and the sulfur bite of swamp water. My shoulders ached under the weight of the bags. Every joint throbbed in protest at the movement as I stepped back on the spongy ground, away from the bike.

My heart hurt more.

Enough that I didn't look at Sky as he climbed off the bike. I couldn't.

Instead, I turned to take in the tiny shack Bast had led us to.

The A-frame, perched at the edge of a stagnant, green-tinged pond choked with cattails and algae, was about half the size Bast's trailer had been and pieced together with weathered wood. Someone had started painting it pale yellow but stopped halfway. The sagging steps leading to the porch were rotted or missing completely in places. No lights glowed inside, and the dark windows stared out at me like eyes. Accusing ones. The sun was still up there somewhere, but the dense trees choked the light, and the long shadows felt ominous and creeping.

Sky wiped the back of his hand over his forehead and squinted up at it. "What is this place?"

"It's a hunting shack. Bought it from this old crazy guy who used to come here to get off-grid," Bast explained, weariness dulling the words. He slung a duffel bag over one shoulder and, carting the other at his side, headed up the broken steps. "No electricity, but there's a generator. I'm gonna make a supply run. I've got a stash nearby. Skaiven, you'll need to check the cuff. Make sure it's still working."

Beside me, Sky glanced down at the metal bracelet on my wrist. He didn't say anything. I tried not to shrink.

The blocker wasn't the problem. I was.

Astute as ever, Bast paused with one foot on a mostly intact step. His head turned toward me. "Though if it wasn't working," he added, "I'd expect the Enil. Not the government."

I said nothing. My throat was too dry, and if I opened my mouth, I might throw up. I could feel Sky watching me. Despite the muggy heat, coldness encased my skin.

I didn't speak as Bast jimmied the front door open and lit a lantern inside. It cast a flickering glow across the small room. A wood-burning stove, a drooping couch, and a kitchenette. Two doors sat along the far wall; one looked like it led to a bathroom, the other to a bedroom. A ladder led up to a half-loft. It was surprisingly clean inside, if cramped, free of clutter besides some stacked paint cans near the door, evidence of the half-finished project.

I cataloged it all dully.

"There's a well, so the water works," Bast said, setting the lantern on a low table in front of the couch. It sent silhouettes crawling along the wood-paneled walls. "Run it first. Drink it at your own risk. I'll be back with bottled stuff." He turned toward us, wearing a faint smile that didn't quite make it to his eyes. "I want the loft bed. You know, in case I need to listen to you two…baking Biscuits or whatever. That way it's more effective when I throw myself out the window."

Normally, that would've activated something in me. Maybe made me scoff or quip back. But now, my stomach just sank.

Because I didn't deserve to do any baking with Sky.

When I didn't react, Bast's eyes narrowed a little. Then he gave a visible shrug and headed for the door, pausing briefly beside Sky. "You good?"

"We'll be here," Sky said. Low and quiet.

He knew.

My shoulders rounded, and I let my bag slide down one arm, all the way to the floor, setting the duffel down on my other side. The impacts sent up puffs of dust. I didn't bother to wave them away, just let them engulf me.

"Right." Bast opened the door. "Be back soon."

And just like that, he was gone.

Leaving me alone with Sky.

A bike started up with a whine. Its rumble faded. Sky waited a full heartbeat after the sound died off before he turned to face me. "Raven," he said, and that was all it took.

I forced a deep breath in and out. It took so much effort to lift my gaze to his.

"I did it." My voice cracked, and I licked my lips. They tasted like swamp water and dust.

The dust of *Sky's ship*.

My chest ached like something had been torn right out of it.

"What do you mean?" Sky asked. Carefully. Not much sunlight made it through the smudged, dirty windows, and the lantern's glow shadowed his expression. But his eyes were on me. Focused. Sharper than normal.

We hadn't even made it all the way inside and stood facing each other in the entryway. But I couldn't hold the words back anymore.

"I texted my mom," I whispered. "Back at Bast's. I-I used your phone. I thought it'd be good. Safe. Because you've been…you know. Using it…"

I couldn't finish, but it was done. Enough. It was out there.

I didn't feel better, though, having spoken the words. It somehow felt even worse. *So* much worse, especially as I watched Sky's reaction.

The shock, followed by disbelief. Then the blaze of understanding in his eyes, the hardness that came to them. The way his back stiffened, and his mouth flattened into a line so tight his lips went white.

His hands flexed at his sides and, like he wanted to have misheard me, he murmured, "You did *what?*"

I nearly shrank away at the cold tone. I'd never heard him speak like that. *Ever.* Even when dealing with shitty customers at work. My stomach knotted even tighter.

"There was a news story," I said hoarsely, clasping my marked palm in my other hand. "About One Willow. The government… They said *I* was…" I closed my eyes briefly, both to block out the images and to hide from Sky's accusing stare. "It doesn't matter. Your phone—it was sitting there on Bast's junk table, and I…I don't know. I panicked and I grabbed it, and I used it to text my mom. I'm sorry. I guess I'd…I'd convinced myself it would be *fine* because you've been using it this whole time, and…"

My throat was too tight for my voice to work anymore. I couldn't seem to find enough air, either.

He was gazing at me like he'd never seen me before. "It doesn't work that way, Rae. I'd have told you if you'd asked." His voice was utterly devoid of emotion. It was that bartender voice, but somehow worse. Empty and flat. "Bast and I have an end-to-end encryption that he set up specifically to allow for communication. Your mom's phone did not have that. And they were waiting for you to contact her like I'd suspected. *Obviously.*"

The guilt formed a vicious, spiky ball in my middle. "I…I get that now. I'm sorry. *So, so sorry.* I just assumed… I panicked…"

There wasn't an excuse for violating his trust. I knew that. My insides slithered, and my face burned with shame.

He gazed at me, face blank for a solid, hollow heartbeat before he seemed to break. I flinched when he shoved his hand through his hair. "*Fuck*, Rae! *Damn it.*"

He lurched away in the other direction. Biting my cheek so hard it hurt, I squeezed my hands together until my knuckles turned white.

Sky's harsh breathing was loud in the quiet, undercut only by the drone of insects outside the shack. He'd turned his back, and his shoulders were rigid, tight beneath his borrowed hoodie.

He was furious. It occurred to me fleetingly that, short of the interlude in the motel when I'd said that stupid thing about him not being real, I'd never seen Sky angry. And that mild irritation was *nothing* compared to this.

Guilt threatened to swallow me whole. I wrapped my arms around myself as he stalked to the single-paned window, braced his forearm against it, and hung his head. His free hand clenched and unclenched at his side, and he breathed slowly. Deliberately. Like he was trying to find his center. Trying not to lose it.

I'd really, really messed up. And there wasn't a damn thing I could do to fix it. My eyes burned, and I pressed a fist to my mouth. I wanted to explain, to justify, but what could I possibly say to make this better?

"I need some space," he muttered, low and tight. He didn't look at me. Didn't even raise his head. "You need to give me some space."

"Okay." I could make out a shadowy bedroom through a partially open door. I pointed at it. "I'll just…"

He nodded without even turning away from the window. Like he didn't care where I went as long as it was *away*.

I grabbed my bag. My legs felt like lead when I trudged toward the door, pushing it open. It was a simple bedroom with a twin bed and a tiny nightstand. Dusty and dark enough that I had a fleeting hesitation about spiders.

But it was hard to care.

Nudging the door shut with my foot, I let the pack fall to the floor with a *thunk*. The springs shrieked when I sank onto the bed's edge, and I dropped my head into my hands and let out a shaky breath. Another cloud of musty dust rose around me, and my sinuses tingled.

Even through the haze of panic and overwhelming anxiety that news story had ignited, I'd sent that text with good intentions. Because I had people out there who loved me. I'd thought it was safe and I'd just needed…

A tether.

Because my life was spiraling, and that one tie, that thin thread of a future, was all I had left to hold onto.

I rubbed the heels of my hands into my eyes. Those people would still be there when this mess was done. I couldn't just forget them. Couldn't set aside every connection, everything that kept me human in this wildly inhuman chaos. What was the point of surviving any of this if the people who made life worth living became the casualties instead?

My mother deserved to know her daughter was alive. Amelia deserved to know I hadn't just skipped town without saying anything.

But at what cost? At the cost of *Sky*?

The way he'd just looked at me… I sank my teeth into my cheek. There was no other way to describe it other than *betrayal*. I'd just hurt Sky.

My throat burned.

I'd give anything to be able to talk to Amelia right now. About all this. This mess I'd made of this situation. About Sky. About the freaking aliens and my hand and the entire *shit show* my life had become.

I'd thought it was too dangerous, too risky to tell her—but she'd *want* to know. Maybe it would've helped, sharing the burden with her.

Not that it would help anything right now. It was way past that. Nothing mattered now.

I tipped back until I lay flat on the mattress. A single tear leaked out, sliding down my temple into my hair, and I dashed it away with a disgusted scoff. I hated crying. I didn't cry. Even when Dad died, I'd barely shed a tear. I'd wondered then if something was wrong with me.

Clearly there was. I'd just destroyed Sky's chance at getting home, his entire mission, *his people's salvation*—my own chance at getting this map out of my brain.

I'd possibly just made the biggest mistake of my life.

Had License 16 showing up meant they were monitoring my mom and had texting her somehow put *her* in their crosshairs?

Had I just ruined *everything* by not listening?

Oh my God.

Too much. This was too much. The room's darkness seemed to close in. My next breath came out in a choked sob. I curled up on my side on the dusty, creaky bed, winding my arms around my waist. My eyes were dry, but my throat ached fiercely.

That weight increased until it threatened to crush my chest in an iron vice made of remorse and stupid, dumbass decisions.

Why couldn't I just stop and *think?*

Chasing professors into anthropology labs. Asking questions. Touching artifacts.

Now this.

I screwed my lids shut and buried my face in a blanket that smelled like stale swamp water, rotting wood, and mothballs. I didn't even care. Maybe if I tried hard enough, I could wake up from this nightmare.

But I knew better than to wish for good luck at this point.

There was no such thing for me anymore.

Chapter 22

SPACE, THE EMOTIONALLY
PAINFUL FRONTIER

I HAD NO IDEA how long I lay there. I hadn't quite fallen asleep, but I'd descended into something resembling it. An exhausted stupor. When I roused, my bladder was screaming at me.

I raised my head from my bent arms and rubbed my eyes, blinking slowly. At one point, I heard movement through the closed door, followed by raised voices, but it was quiet now. No one had come in. I wasn't sure if that would've made it better or worse.

The idea of leaving the room made my empty, queasy stomach roll over itself. Every time I closed my eyes, I saw that shock on Sky's face, followed by sinking disappointment. Hurting him cut me more deeply than I'd thought possible.

I didn't know what to do with that.

I forced my body upright and distracted myself by changing back into the baggy, glaringly green shirt from the mall escape. I couldn't put off using the bathroom any longer, and the sunlight creeping through the mold-covered window had deepened to dull gold by the time I gathered my nerves enough to shuffle to the door, wiping my sweaty palms on my borrowed sweatpants.

Here went nothing.

I eased it open—only to have the hinges shriek melodramatically. Wincing, I froze, waiting a full beat before peeking through the opening.

Bast glanced up from where he stood at the scuffed kitchen table. He'd already made himself at home, judging by the mound of electronics, cords, and alien metal taking up its top. He swept an unreadable gaze over me before turning his attention to the equipment again.

Jabbing a thumb over his shoulder at the window behind him, he spoke without raising his head. "He's outside."

That was it. Two words. His tone was nonchalant. He wasn't screaming, and he didn't look like he was going to blast me with Pladian electricity anytime soon. Even if I deserved it.

I didn't know what to do with that, either.

I hesitated in the bedroom entrance for another heartbeat before pushing the door open. Cleaner air rushed in. It was a little less stuffy in the living space. "I was just…using the bathroom."

"Go for it," Bast said dismissively, picking up one of the flatter pieces of Pladian metal and turning it over in his hands. "Generator's still out, but water's working."

"Thanks." I took a deep breath and headed to the bathroom.

It was cramped and dirty, and not one, not two, but *three* spiders kept me company. But there was a small shower in addition to the sink, and the toilet flushed. Finished, I washed my hands in the murky water and studied myself critically in the dusty mirror, taking in the healing bruise and circles beneath my bloodshot eyes. I did my best to smooth down my hair, but there wasn't much to be done. Giving up, I straightened my baggy T-shirt and made myself leave the bathroom.

In the main area, I hesitated again. Did I go back into that quiet bedroom, alone with my thoughts? Where *did* we go from here? Was there even a plan now or had I just—

"He's going to be out there a while, so you may as well hang out here," Bast said, interrupting my spiral—like he'd somehow read the direction it was heading.

I blinked. "What?"

"Sky." He snipped something with wire cutters and set them

aside, lifting the severed end and squinting at it. "If I know him, he'll be out there for a while longer. May as well emerge from hiding or whatever the hell you were doing in there. Probably not good for your human lungs to breathe all the asbestos and swamp mold in a confined space for too long, anyway."

I huffed a weak laugh, frowning in confusion. Was he not *angry*? "Um, okay."

Twining my arms around my waist, I padded across the small living room area and approached the table and the Pladian leaning over it. The lantern from earlier hung nearby on a hook in the wall, casting flickering light over the pile of junk and reflecting on the rough-hewn cupboards in the kitchenette behind him.

"So…what are you doing?" I asked tentatively.

"Oh, you know." Bast blew out a breath and set down the small device he'd been holding. Lights blinked on the screen, and he wiggled a tiny control stick haphazardly stuck to its bottom by electrical tape. "Trying to salvage something from this mess. Good news is the Enil don't seem to be following License 16 this time."

A tiny bit of the lingering tension bled from my shoulders in a rush. A part of me had been waiting for that. It would've been the rotten cherry on top if I'd brought the Enil down on top of our heads, too.

Bast didn't seem to notice me slump in relief, adding, "But I need to rework the power circuit on this thing to increase range." He twisted his mouth, pushing away the device. "I'd explain it, but you probably wouldn't understand. No offense, Biscuit, but you don't strike me as someone who'd be into alternative conductors."

I couldn't take it anymore. The words burst out. "Isn't this… kind of pointless?"

Bast raised his face slowly, a single brow angling upward. "Pardon?"

"All this." I let out a shaky breath and swept a hand at the junk. "After what I…" I compressed my trembling lips into a line. "Since I ruined everything."

Bast didn't say anything, and I didn't blame him. I wasn't sure what I was looking for. Absolution? An explanation? I felt as off-balance as the wobbly table stacked high with all his junk.

Rubbing my arms, I glanced at the window over the sink. Sky's lean silhouette was barely visible through the murky glass, a tall shadow against the gloomy swamp beyond.

Bast twisted to follow my gaze. Then, like I'd sufficiently distracted him, he let out a disgusted sigh and pushed from the table, sauntering to a dusty, beaten-up cooler. I hadn't noticed it before, but I was zero percent shocked when he produced a beer from it. He raised his brows and held the generic can in my direction, a wordless offer I shook my head at. With a suit-yourself shrug, he cracked it, the hiss of carbonation loud in the quiet. His boots clomped over the groaning wooden flooring as he headed back toward me.

The stone in my gut grew heavier. "I'm guessing he told you," I said as he reached the table, set the can down, and began to unspool more wires.

Bast snorted. "Well, yeah. What'd you think he'd do, hide it? Hate to break it to you, but it kind of concerns us both. What you did is a pretty big fucking deal."

"I wasn't implying…" My throat threatened to close, and I took a deep breath. "I know. I know I screwed up. I wasn't implying he shouldn't have told you."

"Good. So." He dropped the wires and leaned both fists on the table. His emerald eyes were bright and sharp when they snared mine. "First things first. Yeah, you messed up big time, Starmap. Not sure what the hell you were thinking. If I had to guess, I'd say you probably *weren't*." My shoulders curled inward because he was right. His smile was a little mean, like he'd meant it to hurt. "Second thing, though. You *didn't* ruin 'everything.'" He made air-quotes that had me frowning. "Close, but not *quite*. There's another ship on this piece of shit rock. At least, parts of one." He angled his chin down, giving me a patronizing look. "Or did that already slip your mind? Seems odd, considering the hard-on you seem to have for Pladian spaceships."

I gasped, clutching the base of my throat. Of *course*. "The *Roswell ship.*"

Bast nodded slowly. "Exactly. So we still have a way to dig…" He rolled his eyes. "Sorry. We have a way to *delicately and oh-so-carefully remove* the map from your brain. We also happen to have an alien tech god named Bast to rig a transmitter to talk to the mothership and let them know we need a ride home…" He spread his hands. "So yeah. You fucked things up. Definitely made it harder. But no. It's not impossible."

I stared at him, breathing faster. Could this be true? For the first time since he'd come crashing into the trailer and delivered the news that License 16 was coming and I'd realized what I'd done, a kernel of hope flared. Was there a chance I *hadn't* doomed us all?

I balled up my hands and tucked them back into my armpits. It felt too much to even hope, but… "So…you think we can *fix* this?"

"You do know I'm the tech specialist in our little Pladian Pair, right?" Smirking, he straightened and grabbed his beer, pausing with it raised. "I specialize in fixing shit. That's why I'm here. I like a good challenge. Makes life interesting."

I watched with wide eyes as he drank deeply. He swallowed and wiped his mouth with the back of his hand, put the can aside, and shrugged, picking up the wires once more. "Won't be easy, but I just need to recalibrate."

"And…" I swallowed hard, eyes darting to the window. "What's Sky think?"

"Ah." His long fingers plucked the thin silver threads apart with surprising dexterity. "See, me? I'm somebody who needs to talk shit out right away. I get angrier the longer I let it stew." He flicked a glance toward the window. "But Sky broods. It's how he works things through. Gains control, in his very Pladian way. He's out there getting swamp air and logicking his way into being reasonable." He waited a beat, then sent me a self-deprecating grin. "One of us has to be the respectable Pladian, right? I was born to rebel."

I didn't return his smile, looking Sky's way again instead. Bast wasn't telling me anything I didn't know. I'd watched Sky brood for days now. I hoped he wasn't getting eaten alive by mosquitoes this time around. "So you're saying I shouldn't go out there?"

Bast *tsk*ed, lowering the nearly untangled nest of wires. "I'm *so* flattered you're coming to me for romantic advice, but I'm not your guy for that. I'm a love 'em and leave 'em kind of Pladian."

That broke through the haze of guilt. "I'm not—I was *not* asking for romantic advice." I might not know him well, but Bast would be the *last* person I'd come to for that. I leaned on one of the carved chairs. "I just meant, you know him. You guys are…"

"Brothers? Aliens? Extremely handsome?" His snarky smile was all teeth.

God, he was so…*human.*

Bast smirked at me one last time before bending to dig through a pile of computer equipment. It was alarmingly easy to forget what he really was. What *they* were. Not that, in the scheme of things, it mattered here.

I feel *human,* Sky had said.

He might not actually *be* human, but he had emotions, just like I did.

And I'd hurt him. Even if there was a way we *could* pull this off, it didn't change the fact I'd violated his trust.

That was something, alien tech god or not, Bast *couldn't* fix. Broken trust.

Some of the cautious excitement I'd begun to feel faded. I tucked my hair behind my ear, focusing on Bast. And because I knew in his own, weird way—and for whatever reason—he'd just tried to make me feel better, I pursed my lips and asked, "Has anybody ever told you you're kind of a dichotomy?"

"Biscuit." He tucked his chin and gave me exaggerated doe eyes. "You shouldn't talk so dirty to me with Sky right outside."

I tried to bite back my smile and failed. His answering grin, swift and crooked, was genuine as he turned his attention back to his work.

"Seriously, though." I pulled out the chair I was leaning on and settled into it, pulling my knees up. I balanced my chin on them. "Even if you really do think you can figure this out…" I picked at a splinter coming free from the table's edge. "Why aren't *you* mad at me, too? Because of…well, what I did."

"Why?" He grunted, unspooling some of the untangled wire. "Because you made me blow up the spaceship I've spent the last decade trying to repair, which could, if I can't track and locate the Roswell ship, negate my ability to save my race from certain doom at the hands of a murderous race of planet-killers?"

I sighed, slumping in the chair until I was staring at the loft overhead. "Yeah, Bast. That."

"I mean, I'm not happy with you. I was *real* pissed earlier. But you didn't betray *me* in quite the same way you betrayed Sky. And I'm shocked we got away with lugging that damn ship around for as long as we did, honestly."

It wasn't anything I didn't know, but I nearly winced anyway. I felt Bast looking at me, and after a beat, I made myself straighten and meet his eyes. He fixed me with an intent stare, steady and frank. "That being said," he said, his rasping voice quiet, "I think if anybody understands the need to call home, it's us. After all, it's been what, a few weeks for you? Try a decade, babe."

I blinked slowly, taken aback.

But then Bast let out a chuckle, picking up his beer. "Get it? *Phoning* home?"

"Uh huh. *ET.*" I leaned back. My attention drifted past him, to Sky. He was pacing now, footsteps thudding softly with each pass. A board creaked on the rickety porch, the sound muffled through the wall.

"You could give it a shot," Bast said.

With effort, I dragged my focus from the shadowy figure drifting by the window. "Give what a shot?"

He lifted a shoulder. "Talking to him. He's a talker when he's ready. Annoyingly so. Guy's all about talking, you know."

"I know," I murmured, twirling the alien bracelet around my forearm.

"Don't know if he's ready. I'd wait personally, but if you're wanting to push…be my guest. Like I said, I'm not fucking Dr. Phil."

I watched him for another moment, as he arranged bits and pieces into piles. "Bast?"

He rolled his head my way with an exasperated, "Yes?"

I bit my cheek. "Thanks."

"Whatever." He scowled and took a swig from his can. "I just don't like drinking alone."

And that was that. He set the beer aside and bent to his work, and I tucked my lips between my teeth to hide a smile. Because he could spout off all he wanted, but I was beginning to see his true colors.

And he was right. Humor fading, I eyed the window. If he said Sky needed space, I'd give him space. As much as I hated to trust *any* kind of advice from Bast—let alone anything resembling romantic —he wasn't wrong about Sky. He clearly knew him well.

He'd talk when he was ready.

Even if this distance between us felt like a canyon.

That pit in my stomach remained, as did the dull throbbing in my temples. I pressed my fingers into both sides, massaging. I was so sick of these headaches.

"There's food," Bast said suddenly. He jerked his head in the direction of the kitchen behind him. "Some in the cabinets and that cooler." His attention was on the device he was currently wiring into a car battery. "In case you want something to do that isn't watching me. I'm usually into being watched," he looked up long enough to aim a lazy, suggestive grin my way, "but your moping is the wrong vibe."

I curled my lip and stood, pushing off the table. "There's something wrong with you."

"What'd I say about flirting with me?"

I rolled my eyes, giving him my back. The kitchen, if it could be called that, consisted of an L-shaped corner with a sink, cabinets, and a rusty-looking set of knives that screamed tetanus. No refrigerator, and the woodstove near the couch seemed to be the only place for cooking.

I opened the first set of cabinets just to keep my hands busy. Mostly empty. Nothing but dusty dishes and a bottle of rum I considered before deciding that probably wasn't the best idea on an empty stomach. The second contained ramen. I pulled a packet out and idly scanned the label. Anything to avoid looking at Sky outside. I lowered it with a sigh and spotted a newish-looking can near the top. Much more appealing.

I'd just stretched onto my toes, reaching for it, when the front door opened.

I thumped back down, whirling, pulse skipping.

Sky paused halfway in, and his attention flitted my way for the briefest second, his hand tightening on the handle. Something tumultuous flickered over his expression before it closed up. Head down, he eased the door shut after him, cutting off the cacophony of insects. The latch's click sounded like a gunshot.

"Finally. Jesus," Bast said loudly in the sudden, awkward silence. "I could use a second set of hands not covered in sketchy Pladian writing."

I clenched my molars, shooting him a tight look. He really couldn't help himself, could he?

Sky glanced at me again before leaving the entryway. "What are you working on?"

Bast started in with an explanation I wasn't even sure was in English. Tuning it out, stomach sinking at Sky's obvious dismissal, though understandable, I turned back around and put the ramen away. I stretched for the can again, fingers straining. I couldn't quite reach—

A shadow fell over me. This time when I turned, Sky was *right* there. Reaching over my head. My surprised inhale was full of his scent, sweat, the sticky humidity from outside clinging to him. His heat enveloped me.

He plucked the can from the top shelf and stepped back. My throat felt tighter than it had a second ago.

His twilight-blue eyes traced from the can to mine as he extended the soup between us. "Here you go."

I took it from him and curled both hands around it. "Thank you."

He studied me. A faint furrow marred his forehead. All those feelings, the guilt, the shame, the loneliness I couldn't seem to shake, welled back up in a tangle of words I opened my mouth to spew—

But then he was turning and rejoining Bast at the table. I didn't miss the pointed eye roll the latter gave before bending back to his work. Like he was so over all this tension.

I swallowed down all the things I wanted to say and gave them both my back.

Because he may be feigning annoyance now, but what Bast had said before was right. I knew better than to push Sky. He'd talk when he was ready.

So after locating a spoon, a rusted but usable can opener, and a bottle of water from Bast's cooler, I left the aliens to their muttering and took Sky's place on the old porch.

Space, I told myself. I could give him space.

Just me, the mosquitoes, and way too much time to think.

Chapter 23

AHOY, CAPTAIN OBVIOUS

THE CHICKEN AND NOODLES tasted metallic and a little questionable, but I still polished the can off in record time while sitting cross-legged on the weathered, moss-covered slat boards pretending to be a porch. Sunlight streaked through the leaves and branches in spears of light, dappling the spongy ground and fallen trunks. It decorated the stagnant pond with patches of gold. I eyed the ripples in the algae-streaked expanse from the porch's safety.

Were there alligators in there? I'd never spent much time in this part of the country. It was its own kind of beautiful in a drowsy, mushy way. Or would be if it weren't for the threat of creatures who'd perfected hunting before humanity had figured out how to build wheels. I thought I saw movement and peered closer, scooting my feet away from the porch's edge. We didn't have anything like *that* to worry about back home.

Then again, I was far, far from home.

I sipped my water and side-eyed the murky depths, glancing away only when a pair of bright green dragonflies flitted past. They dipped and twirled in the air before vanishing into the swaying grasses. The drone of insects and the raucous call of birds had become white noise.

Sighing, I eased back onto one arm, waving away a buzzing mosquito with the water bottle. The warped wood groaned beneath me.

I supposed I should be used to being hunted at this point. Was License 16 still out there, combing the swampy woods for us? Or had we escaped their clutches yet again? That had been a close call. All my fault, too. One of these times, we wouldn't slip away and then…

I shivered and sat up, spinning my cuff. All this running and hiding would be for nothing then. God, I hoped Bast was right. That we really could salvage this and there *was* a way to fix everything. My head gave a twinge. I set down my water and rubbed my temples with both hands.

The restlessness wasn't helping anything. These past two days had felt very much hurry up and wait. And here we were again.

I hated feeling useless like this. Worse. Like *I* was the problem.

Sighing, I drew my legs up and laid my cheek on my bent knees. I'd give anything to talk to Mom or Amelia right now. My best friend had been on my mind so much today. After all, she was my person, the one I'd turn to with heavy emotions like this. And the emotions today had been some of the heaviest—

Hinges squeaked behind me. Pulse leaping, I twisted just as Sky slipped through the opening, a tin mug in each hand.

I blinked in surprise, sitting up straight suddenly enough that I almost knocked over my water. My heart leapt into my throat.

Was this it? Was he ready to talk?

I couldn't decipher his expression as he turned, juggling the cups and pulling the door shut after him. He said nothing as he crossed to my side and sank to the worn wood.

My mind was blank, buzzing like the bugs around us. I'd spent the last half hour rehearsing what I'd say in *extreme* detail. I couldn't remember a single word of it.

Instead, I simply stared at him like a moron.

He studied me as he settled in, those dark, beautiful eyes sweeping over my face. I still couldn't quite gauge his emotions. If anything, he looked introspective.

He held out one of the cups. "It's rum and some of the soda from Bast's cooler. Not my finest work, but it's all I had." He said it with a tentative lift to the corner of his mouth. Not quite a smile but heading in that direction.

A full five seconds passed before I realized I was still staring. I lunged forward, fumbling for the mug. "W-wow. No, that's great. Um, thanks."

He nodded and stretched out his legs, reclining on one hand. Eyes on the pond, he lifted his cup to his mouth with the other.

Cradling my drink, I watched his throat constrict in a swallow. Clouds obscured the murky sun, casting thicker shadows, and the faint breeze tugged at his curls. A lock of hair tumbled over his forehead, and I wrenched my attention away, focusing instead on the cocktail he'd handed me.

He didn't *look* angry anymore, at least. Just…contemplative. My pulse sped. He'd shed the hoodie, and he wore only a black T-shirt, his shoulders relaxed beneath it.

The tension between us was still there.

Sky didn't say anything as he lowered his drink to his lap. A long moment passed, during which I wet my dry mouth with a swig of my own. Not half bad, considering there was no telling how long that alcohol had lived here.

"I had a whole thing rehearsed," I blurted, staring down at the cup I squeezed in both hands. "Just so you know."

Out of my peripheral vision, I saw his head swivel my way. "Did you?"

I grimaced. "I can't remember any of it."

"I think I like it better when you speak off the cuff."

That brought my head up. "Oh, I don't know about that. I end up sounding like a baby chicken."

He frowned. "A what?"

"Never mind." I turned to face him, nearly spilling my drink, urgency welling up along with a whole mess of disjointed words. "*Sky*—"

Like he could sense the swell of panic, he held up the hand not wrapped around his cup. "We can just sit for a second, Rae. Or better yet—how about we talk about something else and then we'll…" He glanced away and ran his palm over his mouth. "We'll get to the other stuff."

"Okay," I said slowly. The panic ebbed. My eyes fell to the drinks we both held. I lifted mine. "Okay. Then why bartending? Seems like an odd choice of profession for somebody with your particular…ah, skill set."

"My skill set?" he repeated, amusement coloring the words.

Right. I supposed I did need to specify. He *was* a Pladian of many talents. Some of which I was working hard not to think about at this moment.

"You know." I gestured upward with the cup, at the tree canopy and the patches of deepening blue beyond. "The *extraterrestrial* skill set."

He sniffed a laugh. "*That* skill set. Well." He tipped his head to the side and leaned back on one arm again. "It's an easy job for transient lifestyles. Someone's always hiring a bartender." He sipped his drink before lowering his eyes to it, swirling the contents. "Plus, it's an easy way to get information. If you're good at listening." His mouth twisted into a wry half-smile. "Alcohol tends to loosen lips."

All that made a shocking amount of sense. "Even for you? Have you ever even been drunk?" I'd never seen him tipsy. At work functions or otherwise—though his appearances at those had always been few and far between. I would know. I'd always watched for him.

He slid me a sideways look. "I'd make a pretty shitty bartender if I hadn't been." His lips twitched again. "I can get drunk if I try hard enough. Human in all the ways that matter, remember?"

I nearly choked on my rum, catching myself in time to force down the mouthful. *That* was a reminder I didn't need right now. Not when I was hyper-aware of his long, lean body stretched out next to me.

Not with all these unaddressed emotions thrumming between us thicker than the humidity and clouds of pesky mosquitoes.

"Right." I cleared my throat and changed the subject out of self-preservation. "Are you guys finished with whatever you were doing in there?"

"Mostly." Sky glanced over his shoulder, at the window glowing with faint lantern light. "Bast's got a few things to do still. I was just in the way now."

"I know the feeling," I muttered into my drink as I drained the last few drops.

Just then, the sun broke past the cloud cover in a stream of gold. Sky turned toward it and raised his face.

It was almost as if it were subconscious, the motion, the way his lids closed and his head fell back. I paused in the middle of setting aside my empty cup, something tightening in my chest at the sight of him bathed in warm light. Of him pausing for the shortest moment in this chaos to soak in a second of peace.

I'd *hurt* him.

Throat aching, I slowly lowered the mug the rest of the way to the porch slats.

"I'm really sorry, Sky," I rasped. There was no holding it in anymore. This flood of emotion. "I wasn't thinking. I panicked. Seeing One Willow on TV, seeing *me*, and what they were saying was…" I shook my head. "It hit hard, and all I could think of was my mom and how upset she'd be and how we've been through so much. It's just been us, and she *worries*—" I caught myself. Took a steadying breath. "But it was wrong."

Sky had opened his eyes. They were on me. "Since your dad, you mean," he said, something flickering in their depths. "It's been you guys since your dad." He shifted his body ever-so-slightly to face me. Like he was open to hearing what I had to say.

I tried not to let that hope kindle in my chest, but it did.

I managed to nod. "Still not an excuse. And I'm so, *so* sorry. I can't…" The words grew too thick for a moment, and I had to pause. When I trusted my voice, I tried again. "I can't tell you how sorry. That doesn't take back that it's done and what it means—and what it cost you. I know that."

He searched my face, brows tented. "One Willow was on TV. You said that before. What do you mean by that?"

I dragged my teeth over my bottom lip. "There was a news story about how the military had moved into town. They showed footage, and they were talking about TWU and how people were calling it an attack now or something." Anxiety surged, and I sucked down a deep breath to quell it. "But like I said, that's *not* an excuse. I shouldn't have used your phone like that. I convinced myself it was fine because you'd been using it..." My swallow got stuck, and I whispered hoarsely, "But it wasn't okay. It was a breach of trust."

His midnight eyes roved back and forth between mine for a second before his expression softened. A fraction, but I saw it. "Rae..."

Something about that tone, the weary resignation, hit me straight in the gut. I sank my teeth into the inside of my cheek.

Shoulders slumping, Sky sighed and ran a hand down his face. "I'm not saying it was right, but I understand why you did it." I stopped breathing. *He did?* He looked away, scanning the alligator pond. "I should've explained how our phones worked in more detail, for one—and I did tell you we'd figure out a way for you to call home when we got to Bast's. I wish you'd trusted me enough to talk to me first, but—"

"It wasn't *that*, Sky." My heart sped up. I couldn't help myself. I reached out and wrapped my fingers around his forearm. That brought his attention back to me, and he tensed beneath my touch, which didn't feel great, but I kept my eyes on his. "I do. Trust you. And to be fair, I *did* try to talk to you about it. I just..." I stopped, fighting to put the overwhelming flood of thoughts in order. It was hard with him looking at me like that, with a guarded, direct stare. Like he *was* really listening but with a wall still up. The truth came tumbling out. "I don't know what I'm doing. I feel like a human wrecking ball right now. Everything around me is just...falling down. Like this path of destruction is following me, and now One Willow—my family—is involved, too. I know that sounds selfish. After what I just cost you." I swept my free hand in his direction. "I guess case in point? I'm sorry. I'm sorry I'm making this about me right now." My bitter laugh scraped my throat.

"I get it, Rae," Sky murmured, barely louder than the buzzing insects. "And I'm sorry, too."

It surprised me enough that I snapped my head up, frowning at him. "For what? What do you have to be sorry about? You didn't do anything."

He raised his brows. "I'm sorry you're involved in any of this in the first place. If we weren't here, you wouldn't have gotten dragged into it."

I stared at him. Something cracked behind my ribs at the thought because that wasn't even something I could *fathom*. Not at this point.

But he wasn't done. His mouth tightened, nostrils flaring. "And...I shouldn't have reacted like I did. I don't lose my temper often. I don't like it."

Now *that* was too much. I rolled my eyes. "Come on, Sky. No. That was understandable." My pulse felt a little off-beat. Like it was a step behind and couldn't quite catch up. "You had every right to be angry with me. You *have* every right to be angry."

He looked away again. With his profile to me, I watched a muscle in his temple bunch and release. "I don't like losing control like that."

"Right. That's...um, very Pladian of you." I was still touching him, and his forearm was warm beneath my fingertips.

He turned his face my way again. Something passed through his dark eyes, humor maybe, but also sadness. "I think it's safe to say I'm not a very good Pladian." His half-hearted smile came and went, fading to introspection again.

Interesting that Bast saw it differently. He'd know, too. I kept that to myself. Sky was still gazing at me with too many emotions crowding that single look.

"I *am* sorry, Sky. That I cost you your ship," I whispered, because for some reason, it felt like I shouldn't speak louder than the wind stirring the curls over his forehead.

Only an arm's length separated us. The one I'd stretched between us like a test. The fading sunlight bathed him in soft yellow and caught on the shards of silver in his irises, limning the angles and planes of his handsome face. There were auburn highlights in his messy, dark hair I'd never noticed before.

"I know," he murmured. "I really do understand why you did what you did. Like I told you in the motel room, Rae, I know that this must feel so out of control. Isolating." He searched my eyes. "We're going to figure this out, okay? Bast and I are going to figure out what we need to do to get you back to normal life."

Here I was, apologizing for destroying his ticket home, and he was worried about getting *me* back to *my* life? My mess of a life that probably wouldn't be anything resembling normal ever again?

My heart was slowly dissolving into a puddle. All this. Him. The heaviness of this entire thing.

"You shouldn't say stuff like that. One, I don't deserve it after what I just pulled. And two, everything feels so impossible right now." There was a telltale prickle behind my eyes, blurring his face. I blinked hard. Not again. I was *not* doing this. I was not tearing up in front of Sky Acosta, even if this self-pity was stronger than ever—

Then he moved, startling me enough I gasped.

He draped his arm over my shoulders and tugged me close to his side.

Hugging me. Sky was hugging me.

A one-armed, partial hug, but it still counted.

It wasn't even a *sexy* hug. It was a sideways embrace, the sort you'd offer a good friend in need of comfort.

But it was a hug, nonetheless.

I hadn't realized how much I needed one.

Maybe I should've been, but I wasn't even *remotely* ashamed of the way I melted into it. Into him. He tilted toward me, too, so my head could rest in the curve of his shoulder. I took a deep breath to chase away the lingering tightness in my chest and got a lungful of his scent in the process. Soap—the same cheap travel stuff I'd used this morning in Bast's shower—sweat, a little stale swamp. Mostly male, that night air scent. Familiar now. The weight of his arm anchored me.

He rested his chin on the top of my head. "It'll be okay," he said, and I felt the words rumble where we pressed together. "Bast said you guys talked. He told you—this isn't the end. We've got other options. We're going to figure this out. I told you to trust me."

And I did. For some crazy reason, I trusted the broody, protective bartender from another world. Who was—*even now*—being my friend when I probably didn't deserve it.

The thought formed as I leaned into the hard line of him, let him hold me in front of our little murder hut in a backwater swamp with only the lurking alligators watching...

It wasn't *just* that I trusted him, either.

No, that wasn't even it.

It wasn't even that I was falling for him anymore.

I'd *fallen*.

Somewhere along the way, I'd lost track of everything at stake here and done the one thing I'd sworn I wouldn't do.

I'd fallen for the undercover alien who was never meant to stay.

I stopped breathing.

The realization hit me like a solid wallop right upside the head. Far stronger than it should have, all things considered. After all, it'd been staring me in the face for days now. Probably since that moment we'd sat in his SUV on the side of a rainy highway, and he'd told me about the world he was here to save and bared all his truths. Since I'd seen raw emotion and determination and realized he was far, far more complicated and fascinating than he had any right to be with a face and body like that.

A part of me had known then.

But it'd taken his cold shoulder, the visceral stabbing feeling in my middle when I'd watched the betrayal dawn in his eyes, to drive the point home.

I was in way too deep with a guy who'd be flying off into the stars when this was all said and done.

Damn it. I was so, *so* screwed.

Before I could process just *how* screwed, the door burst open.

Sky and I sprang apart like we'd been doing something wrong. My gaze flew to his, registering his faint frown. A flash of panic burned through me like a falling star as I imagined the emotions written over my face. A neon sign that said: *I have it bad for the hot undercover alien bartender.*

Could he *tell?*

But then he looked away and, luckily, there was another Pladian here to distract.

"Oh, good," Bast drawled as he leaned his shoulder on the doorjamb. "You two made up. Just in time. I got it working, so let's do this shit."

I pounced on the distraction. "Got what working?"

Bast waved a hand and turned his back, speaking over his shoulder. "Grab your phone, Biscuit."

"My phone?" I glanced at Sky as he stood in a fluid movement and extended his free hand, the other hooking our empty tin cups by the handles. I hesitated only a second before gathering my trash and placing my marked palm in his. He pulled me easily to my feet. Heat crept into my cheeks as he eyed me, like he was trying to read my expression. I hoped like hell he couldn't and brushed past, heading toward the door. "Why do you need my phone?"

Bast snorted and shoved the door wider so we could slip in after him. "Nothing says normal like Facespace and cat memes."

Facespace, cat memes, and epiphanies regarding feelings for my alien protector. No big deal.

I'd take whatever I could get at this point.

I followed the Pladians inside, murmuring a thank you when Sky stepped to the side and held the door open for me. I passed close enough my shoulder grazed his chest and sparks cascaded down my arm.

I was so, so screwed.

Chapter 24

SIGNAL RESTORED.
REGRET IMMINENT.

"**WHO IS AMELIA**, and why the hell did she send you fifty-seven text messages?" Bast asked, scowling down at my device. A cord connected it to a gently glowing piece of purple-pink metal powering it. I wasn't sure I wanted to know what the oblong piece of alien technology was doing to my phone.

Then what he'd said registered. I gasped, leaping to my toes and trying to snatch it from him. "*Fifty-seven* texts?"

He angled his body and held it out of my reach. "Hey! Careful."

"Don't read her text messages," Sky cut in, shifting closer to Bast's side and peering at the screen.

"You shouldn't be either!" I reached for the phone again. Panic ratcheted up a notch. Amelia had already humiliated me once in Sky's presence in a spectacular display of word-vomit I'd never forget. The last thing I needed was a repeat.

"I'm not. It's not quite done calibrating," Sky told me, tucking his hand in his pocket. "Give it another few minutes."

With one last suspicious look at Bast, I sighed and went back to eyeing the Pladian tech instead. Those wires he'd been separating earlier ran from it to a dozen other bits and pieces arranged in organized chaos atop the table.

If I looked closely enough, I'd swear strange shapes and bits of light floated beneath the alien metal's surface. The air around it seemed to hum. Fascinating. "What is this doing? Is this a piece of your ship?"

"Hm?" Bast looked up, then waved a hand dismissively, like I'd just asked about the weather. Not the glowing extraterrestrial technology within arm's reach. "Oh. Yeah. Think of it like an adapter. Helps us utilize Earth technology."

I leaned near enough my nose almost touched it. Almost. I knew better than to get too close. "How?"

"It's similar to our synth-skin tech. It's redesigning your device's circuitry right now using…" He frowned down at the touchscreen lying on the table. Strange writing like the stuff on my palm scrolled over the repurposed LCD surface. When he spoke again, it was distracted. "The easiest way to explain it in terms you'd understand is nanotech."

Aha. I knew it. I straightened and slowly raised my brows at Sky. "I thought you said your synth-skin just generated *electricity*. And the invisibility thing."

Sky opened his mouth, then closed it and rubbed his neck. His loose shrug made my stomach drop.

Bast's shocked laugh drew my eyes back to him. He was gawking at Sky. "Is that seriously how you explained it? I knew you were technologically deficient, Skaiven, but come *on*…"

"That's *not* what your suit does?" My eyes bulged. "Sky, you used that on my *brain!* You said it was harmless!"

"Neural manipulations *are* harmless, Raven," Sky said, his tone that placating, calm one I hated. "Pladian explorers have used them for as long as we've been mapping planets. They don't do any long-term harm—"

"Totally harmless," Bast interjected with a smirk. "I mean, look at you now, Biscuit. Your brain's in tip-top shape."

Sky shot him a flat look. "You're not helping."

My mouth fell open, and I rounded on *both* the infuriating aliens, but then my phone vibrated again in Bast's hand. This time when I tried to snatch it from him, he let me.

"Don't unplug it from the modulator," was all he said.

I sent him a glare but listened, stepping closer instead. Snickering, he raised both hands, palms out, leaning a hip on the table. I ignored him, too intent on lifting my screen to my face.

Holy *crap*. He was right.

So. Many. Notifications.

That was an overwhelming number of texts from Amelia. And so many more. Work. Kelly. My mom. Dustin. Numbers I didn't recognize. I had the strongest urge to turn the device back off. It was *too much.*

So many people. So many missed calls. My throat constricted.

My thumb hovered over the icons. God, I didn't even want to do it. To open any of them.

I squeezed my eyes shut. Took a deep breath in. Exhaled slowly. Yoga breathing.

Avoiding it all wouldn't solve anything. I had to see. Mouth dry, I began flicking through the messages. They ranged from angry to scared to pleading, and each word drove a sliver into my heart. My stomach tied itself into knots the deeper I dug.

Work. Bob. Kelly. Amelia. Dustin. Lisa. Jackie. Landon. Everyone I knew. Some people I hadn't even realized had my number.

My mom's calls and messages, at least, had stopped after yesterday. Did that mean she'd gotten the text I'd sent? Or had License 16 intercepted it? Did it work that way? That fear that I'd dragged her in by contacting her returned, and I tightened my hold on the phone. Hopefully not. Hopefully License 16 was focused on *me.*

The next text thread—from Kelly—distracted me. I scrolled through it, raising an eyebrow. Had she really asked if I'd *died*? What, was she expecting an answer if I had? Knowing her, maybe.

It took two tries before I found my voice. "Can I call or text on this without alerting the whoever? License 16?"

"Not quite yet," Sky murmured. I jolted. While I'd been absorbed in my phone, he'd made his way around the table and now stood at my side. I looked up at him as he explained, "Once we get the scanner up and running. I think it'd be safer to wait until we're moving to try to contact anyone." He paused meaningfully. "If you're willing to wait a bit longer."

A request this time. Not an order. A concession, despite the fact I hadn't earned it.

No wonder I was a goner for this broody alien.

"It'll at least make it harder on the bastards," Bast interjected, "with the encryption and being on the move." I made myself look away from Sky's dark gaze. The other Pladian was tapping away on his makeshift touchscreen. "I should have the scanner calibrated in another few hours. That'll allow us to track Enil movements more reliably, at least, which is the only way it's safe to move anywhere with your glowstick hand." He looked up, glancing at the pile of crap on the table. "I may need to make a run into town for more supplies. I want to try to beef up the cuff's resonance field before we go anywhere, and I don't have the juice for that and running scanners like this." He pivoted to Sky. "How'd your suit do with the last charge?"

I followed his gaze, confused by the question.

"It handled it fine," Sky said, leaning on the table. "Much better than the second fight with the Enil at TWU."

Bast snorted. "Three Enil at once. Yeah, I'm surprised you didn't melt right there."

"Wait. What's that mean?" I asked, glancing between them.

Both aliens looked at me. Bast frowned, while Sky's mouth tightened.

"What's *what* mean?" Bast arched a brow.

"What do you mean, melt?" I shook my head. "I'm not following."

Bast blinked, then smirked. "Oh, you think we're, like, superheroes? This isn't a Marvel movie. The synth-skins don't make us invincible, sweetheart. We can burn out if we use too much energy. Pull too much juice from the synth-skin, and it'll fry us from the inside out," he added cheerfully, like the prospect wasn't *horrifying*.

I whipped my gaze to Sky's. "*What?* Why have you never told me that? And you were close to…to *that* at the university?"

"I didn't want you to worry." He pushed his fingers through his hair and studied me grimly. "But yes, after that second pair of Enil showed up, we almost didn't make it out, Rae. That's why we ran."

The revelation made my legs wobble a bit. I'd known it'd been a close call, but I hadn't realized *how* close.

Bast's snarky remark might have been meant in jest, but he wasn't far off. I *had* thought of the Pladians as larger than life. They were *aliens*, after all. The thought of them burning out by using up energy reserves, that crackling blue lightning being a finite resource, wasn't something I'd considered.

But it made sense. They were organic beings. Not machines like the Enil. That was part of the problem.

"Anyway," Bast said, dropping the device he still held. "Now that I've shattered Biscuit's inflated view of my partner, I'm going to run for supplies."

I blinked, shoving aside my shock and stepping out of the way when he rounded the table.

"Where are you getting all this crap?" I asked, taking in the tangle of cords and equipment.

The grin Bast shot over his shoulder was devilish and completely unapologetic. "You don't want to know."

But I kind of did. It'd be nice to be aware if I was aiding and abetting some kind of black-market alien tech ring in *addition* to stealing cars.

"Once we can track the Enil and see them coming *and* we have a way to ensure your signal is masked," Sky said, drawing my attention back to him, "we'll work on figuring out the rest. The first priority is obviously safety."

"Of course." Theirs *and* mine. Shaken by the synth-skin revelation for reasons I couldn't quite put my finger on, I lifted my phone again.

I wasn't sure if having access to all this made it better or worse. Seeing the messages and not being able to respond was its own kind of torture.

Bracing myself, I tapped the social media icon, and instantly, the feed was flooded with images and posts about One Willow. My pulse stuttered, and I tipped the screen closer.

"Shit," I breathed.

I'd seen it on the news, but it was even *more* real to see it here, being posted by my friends and family.

The first post read: *Can't even pick up groceries without seeing secret agents. WTF.*

Another read, *Town council meeting at the high school gym tonight to answer questions!*

The hundreds of comments beneath were a mixture of confusion and anger.

Understandably. One Willow was an obscure, nowhere Midwestern town. The definition of boring. Big enough to attract new people, but small enough to be quiet. Peaceful. The old military base my father had worked at had closed over a decade ago, and the town had suffered a little as people moved away. That was the last *exciting* thing that'd happened there.

Until now.

"What is it?" Sky asked, shifting closer.

"Why would *One Willow* be the center of anything?" I mused aloud, frowning at my feed. I angled the phone his way, flashing them both the images. "The halix is gone. *I'm* gone and so are you." I glanced at Sky, then at Bast. "It doesn't make sense."

Sky eyed the photos for a long moment before slowly shaking his head. "I really don't know."

"I don't have any guesses, either," Bast said as he shrugged on his leather jacket over his sleeveless shirt. "License 16 usually does a decent job cleaning up any alien messes. For selfish reasons. They don't want people asking questions. Wouldn't think there'd be *that* much clean-up after what Sky had described. Nothing that'd draw all this extra interest." He swirled a hand in the direction of my phone and the pictures of black trucks barricading The Willow University's entrance.

Swallowing hard, I clicked the screen off, unable to stomach looking at it any longer. "I feel like we're missing something."

Sky leaned more heavily on the table, jaw ticking. "We'll know more when we can run some broader scans. See if we spot anything unusual. Have any idea when you'll be back, Bast?"

Bast swiped the dirt bike keys from the counter. "Don't wait up, Dad. It'll be a few hours. I wanna make sure the coast is clear here, too."

Sky rolled his eyes before tapping the wooden surface and straightening. "Just be careful. License 16 can't be far."

"Yeah, yeah. It ain't my first rodeo." Bast strolled toward the door, pausing to shoot me a pointed look over his shoulder. "This time, maybe *actually* stay away from the alien goods." His mouth curled into a slow smirk. "Or...you know, *don't*. Whatever. You're both adults."

My cheeks burned, and I pressed my fingertips to my forehead, closing my eyes briefly. He sure knew how to make an exit.

Beside me, Sky muttered a curse, and I deliberately didn't look his way. Bast merely chuckled as he yanked the door open. The *snick* of it closing behind him was deafening.

Sky and I were alone. Again.

And Bast's parting shot lingered in the air.

"Sorry about that," Sky said, sighing. "He's incapable of subtlety. I'd call it a tragic character flaw, but I think it's a honed skill."

I huffed a laugh, pushing my hair out of my face. "I've noticed."

Silence stretched before Sky rubbed at the back of his neck and pointed toward the bathroom. "You care if I shower? Bast said there's no hot water, but I could use one."

The way my face was still burning, a frigid shower didn't sound too bad. That awareness was back, pinging between us like a trapped pinball. I managed a wobbly smile. "Sure. Go for it. I'll just stay...out here."

I winced. Of course I would. It wasn't like I was going in there. *With him.*

He'd paused in mid-turn and now eyed me. The epiphany I'd had before, on the porch before Bast interrupted, rushed back, that weight of confusing, heavy emotion. Unable to meet his eyes, I gave him my back and set my phone down carefully on the table.

Feelings for Sky. Worry for Sky. All this confusing, unsure ground with Sky.

I was a mess over Sky.

"Rae?" he asked, and I stilled at the strained note in his voice.

"Yeah?" I turned, forcing a smile.

"You okay? That was just Bast being Bast. He didn't mean… I didn't say anything to him, I mean. About us or things between us…"

"No. Yeah. Of *course* not." I blew a raspberry, waving a hand. "He's just ridiculous. I get it. I'm quickly learning."

"Okay." He studied me for another beat. "You sure you're good?"

I nodded emphatically, catching the inside of my cheeks between my molars. Right as rain. *Just internally screaming over realizing I'm drowning in feels over here.*

"All right." Sky didn't sound convinced, but with one final glance, he picked up one of the duffels from near the couch and shut himself in the bathroom.

I scrunched my face up and scrubbed my hands over it before pausing to glare at the pale marks on my palm. The things that'd started all this.

We were decidedly *not* good.

At least, I wasn't. I plopped down in one of the kitchen chairs, slinking lower.

Because I was crazy about Sky, and that wasn't good at all.

Chapter 25

IN CASE OF APOCALYPSE,
BREAK BOUNDARIES.

IT WAS KIND OF CREEPY how quickly it got dark in these soggy woods. I stood at the single-paned window beside the woodstove and eyed our surroundings through the smudged glass. Murky blue twilight, the same color as Sky's eyes, painted the gnarled trees and the draped moss in inky shadows. The pond had turned oil-black. Instead of alligators, I now imagined all sorts of creatures lurking in its depths. Slimy things with too many tentacles and long, jagged teeth waiting for someone to disturb the water.

Which was ironic, considering I now knew the monsters came from the *stars*, not the swamp.

I shivered and dragged my gaze from the mist slinking over the opaque surface. With the falling darkness, the bugs had somehow grown even *louder*, too. I hadn't thought that possible. The droning vibrated the pane I rested my marked palm against.

The strained silence inside the tiny hunting shack was almost as deafening.

I drew back with a sigh and shifted from foot to foot. The trickling shower had stopped running a few moments ago, but Sky hadn't reappeared. Which was probably for the best. I was *hyper*-aware of the fact that we were alone.

Lowering my arm, I spun the cuff on my wrist around and around, needing something to do with my hands.

At least we'd talked. It felt like too much to hope for, that he'd forgiven me so easily for what I'd done. Like I hadn't deserved that.

And maybe he *hadn't*. Maybe that had been understanding he'd given me, but trust was something I'd have to earn back.

That was fair. I could do that. At least I could *try*, for what it was worth. With what little time we had left.

The reminder caused a swift pang, and I nearly groaned aloud. Had I *really* gone and fallen for an alien from outer space? Despite knowing *everything*? Despite him clearly defining boundaries? Talk about a healthy dose of masochism.

To be fair, *everything* was a little confusing right now, considering we'd been mostly naked together less than forty-eight hours ago, on the verge of wrecking any and everything resembling boundaries—

The bathroom door creaked, and I jumped, flushing guiltily. I couldn't help but turn, though.

Head tipped down, Sky paused in the doorway and rubbed a towel over his curls. He'd changed into a pair of black basketball shorts and a white shirt that clung to him in all the right places. He looked…comfortable. Something about seeing him barefoot and dressed down sent a flash of heat through me.

Who'd have thought basketball shorts would do it for me? I sure as hell hadn't.

Or maybe it was just…*Sky*.

I spun back to the window to hide my flush.

"Feel better?" I asked, proud of my easy tone. My stomach was doing backflips like it was auditioning for the Olympic swim team.

"He wasn't lying about the lack of hot water," Sky muttered. Then: "It got dark in here."

I'd been too lost in thought to pay attention. When I twisted away from the night view, I saw he was right. Not only did next to no light make it through the dirty windows, but the lantern was noticeably dimmer. I hadn't the slightest clue what to do about that.

Luckily, it seemed Sky did, because he hung his towel on the bathroom door's hook and headed to the kitchen. I watched him go, biting my tongue.

I'd never seen his calves before. They were sleek and muscled, just like the rest of him. Of course he'd have sexy calves. Life wasn't fair.

"There has to be lantern oil in here somewhere," he said, and I wrenched my attention from his legs. He circled the couch and checked a small shelf near the woodstove, coming up empty-handed.

"I'll help you look," I said, leaving the window. It was either that or continue ogling him.

Besides, there were only so many places lantern fuel could be in the tiny shack. While Sky rummaged in one of the two drawers in the small kitchen, I bent low and opened the cabinet beneath the sink. Spiders, more cans of that butter-yellow paint someone had been trying to use to spruce up the shack's outside, bleach…I didn't see anything labeled, *Use me to make light.*

"Nothing," I said, pushing to my feet and spinning—

I bumped directly into Sky as he turned at the same time.

His hands came down on my hips to steady me. Mine flattened on his chest.

"Sorry," I said, breathing a laugh. In the faint gray light filtering in from outside, his eyes were depthless. "I didn't realize you were there. Here." *This close.*

And close we were. My lower back rested against the counter's edge. Only a hair's breadth separated us.

I watched the surprise melt from Sky's face. For a heartbeat, neither of us said a word. We simply stared at each other.

"About earlier," he said, finally breaking the silence. His fingers were barely-there pressure. Every point of contact tingled anyway. "Outside. Before Bast interrupted, we hadn't quite finished." A line appeared between his brows.

"I'm okay. If—if you're okay, I mean." Realizing I was still fondling his chest muscles, I dropped my hands, gripping the counter behind me instead. It was an echo of before, when he'd grabbed the soup can for me. He was everywhere when I breathed, that night air scent and soap from his shower. I forced a laugh. "I mean, as okay as I can be, right?"

"Right." Sky's touch slipped away. I didn't miss the quick flex he gave his hands before tucking them into his pockets. "It's been a long few days." His dark eyes swept over my face. "How's your head?"

"It's only a headache." A lie. We both knew it at this point, but I was sticking to it because dwelling on the alternative was too daunting—too overwhelming—to consider. "I'm okay. Just a little tired still."

Thankfully, Sky didn't push, though his gaze lingered, a searching glance.

"You should rest while we've got a chance." He eased a step back, widening the gap between us. The air felt cold without his body heat. "We both should." He pushed a hand through his drying hair, messing up the damp curls. I had the most ridiculous urge to smooth them back down. "I slept longer than you, and I'm still beat."

Because I *was* tired and I missed that heat, the words came tumbling out before I could stop them. "The twin bed's big enough for two if you want to..." I froze, mouth open, then backpedaled so hard, I was surprised I didn't glimpse last week. "I mean— That came out wrong. I just meant…if you don't want the couch. It looks worse than the one in my apartment." I gestured weakly at the checkered piece of furniture that appeared to have weathered multiple centuries and possibly a hurricane or two. Maybe a stampede.

"Oh, uh…" Sky smoothed his shirt down his flat stomach and inched back a bit more, like he could escape the prospect of spooning with me again. *Ouch.* "That's okay. I can sleep anywhere."

"Cool." I ambled a step to the side and risked peeking at him as I did. He stood near the couch in question with that pleasant, controlled bartender smile in place. The one that was impossible to read. The one I hated. I hesitated, worrying my bottom lip. "Are you sure?"

"Yeah." He looked so composed and calm. *Pladian.* "If it's too bad, I'll take the loft bed until Bast gets back. Thanks for the offer, though."

Look at us being so *cordial*. Why was it so awkward? We'd spent two whole days alone together. What had changed?

Besides the fact that we were *truly* alone for the first time since nearly having sex in a seedy motel room. Besides the emotional rollercoaster we'd just weathered together—my betrayal, his forgiveness, this delicate dance around whatever this was between us. The charged attraction I could practically *feel* vibrating along my skin.

My belly leapt at the memory of him tugging his shirt off. The slide of his mouth over mine. My face went up in flames again. The rest of me, too.

All these sticky feelings.

Sky was standing there, outlined in faint moonlight like something out of a fantasy novel, those dark eyes tracking my movement, expression unreadable.

Space. I needed space. Because if I stayed, I was going to stop pretending I didn't want this. And God help me, I did.

Retreat!

"I'm…" I backed up too fast, nearly tripping. "Sorry. I'll just… I'm going to…go sleep now. In there." I pointed in the direction of the small bedroom, then made a break for it, shouldering the door open. The hinges wailed in protest. "All alone!"

I thought I heard Sky say something, but I didn't catch it before I shut the door and leaned my forehead against it. My heart raced with adrenaline and shaky awareness. The grime-covered window cast the barest hint of light into the dark room.

I'd just made that weird. I knew I had.

But what was I *supposed* to do, here? What was the move?

Even if we figured this out, if Bast fixed our immediate issues and solved the map-lodged-in-my-brain problem and we somehow dodged the Enil and everyone *else* chasing us… Sky was still leaving.

Right now really *was* all we had.

Which…which begged the question.

Why the hell were we fighting this?

I groaned, shoving my fingers through my hair.

He was leaving. If we fixed this, his mission was back in action and…

And holy shit—what if this was it? What if this was *our* moment?

Bast was an absolute menace, but he'd said one true thing. We *were* both adults. Why *not* embrace the one good thing in all this insanity? It didn't have to be complicated.

Because I wanted Sky, and if Sky wanted me…

We were both adults.

I was going to tell him that. Right now. If he'd have me. If I hadn't damaged this beyond repair. Whatever *this* was.

This felt like leaping off a cliff. Like cliff diving. If cliff diving was the same as propositioning the hottest alien in the entire galaxy.

Breathing fast, I stepped back and wrenched the door open. "Sky—"

He was *right there*, on the other side. Fist raised like he'd been preparing to knock. He stopped short, eyes widening.

I gripped the door's edge and gaped up at him.

"Oh," he said, slowly lowering his arm. "I was just…"

All the air had vacated my lungs. "Me, too."

"Good," he whispered.

I swallowed hard, staring.

He was tall and broad, his face in shadow. I could make out the glimmer of his eyes searching mine. Looking for the same thing I was, the acknowledgement.

Then one of us—maybe both of us—closed the distance between us, and that was that.

Chapter 26

NOT SAFE FOR EARTH CONTENT

THE KISS WAS seamless. Smooth. I flung my arms around his neck, and his circled my waist. He tasted like the rum and soda from earlier and like Sky. *Familiar.* A breathy noise spilled from me and into him as he tilted his head and deepened the kiss, palms skating the length of my back and pulling me in tight.

Like I was going anywhere. I was exactly where I wanted to be.

I plunged my fingers into his hair, into the silky damp mess of it, as much to feel it as to stop my world from spinning away from me. Reveling in the solidness of him against me, the desperate way his grip moved to my waist and dug in as he maneuvered us out of the entrance. I needed that hungry meshing of lips and shared breath. Needed to feel *him*.

I barely heard the thud as he kicked the door shut behind us, spun, and began to back up, pulling me with him. My blood ran hot, searing my veins.

It felt like a release and something more, like that hug from earlier. Like that tether I'd been seeking. Or maybe the opposite, the snapping of one, because I was finally free from the tangled, convoluted mess I'd been struggling with all day. Like it was finally clear.

Just this moment. That was all that mattered.

Only when we ran into the bed and Sky abruptly sat did we separate. I caught myself on his heaving shoulders. I didn't quite trust my legs to hold me up on their own. Exhaling slowly, he reclined onto his palms and tilted his head back to look up at me.

The room was dark, but after a few blinks, I could make out his expression beneath the drying hair falling over his brow. His parted, kiss-swollen mouth, pupils blown wide.

But I could also see, lurking in the tightness of his jaw, the hesitation.

"Raven." His hands came up and encircled my wrists, dodging the cuff and smoothing up my forearms. "You know I can't make promises—"

And before I could talk myself out of it, I cut him off. "Good. Because I'm not asking for promises."

It slipped out and hung in the air between us.

Sky didn't say anything, but his mouth closed and his brow furrowed, like he didn't like that answer—or maybe he didn't *want* to. He let go of my wrists and gripped the edge of the mattress instead. Looked away.

I felt that loss of contact keenly. And maybe *because* I did, I knew what I needed to do.

My legs weren't going to last much longer. This was a risk, but I'd never encountered one so worth taking. *Cliff diving.* Leaving one hand on his shoulder to brace myself, I climbed into his lap.

He stiffened and his surprised gaze flew to mine again. But his palms came to rest on my thighs, curving just above my knees. Safe. Steadying. He didn't push me away.

A good sign.

I licked my lips, tasting him. He watched me in that careful way he did, close enough that I could see the faint shadow of myself reflected back at me. The pull to lean in was strong, but I held back. Not yet. There were still things I needed to say. Things I needed him to know.

"Earlier," I said, searching his face for any hint of what he was thinking. "It meant a lot that you even tried to understand why I did what I did. Why I sent that text."

"Rae—" he started, but I pressed my fingers to his lips.

He blinked like I'd startled him, and then his mouth curved slowly beneath my fingertips. I bit my cheek against an answering smile.

"No. I need to say this." Any trace of humor drained away as my throat tightened. I pushed through it. "What I did today was selfish."

He stared up at me, breathing slow.

"I wasn't thinking," I went on, my voice wobbling. "And I should have been. I wasn't thinking about you—and that was shitty, Sky. Because you *have* been thinking about me. This whole time. Even with everything you're carrying. Your mission." My chest felt too full of all these feelings. Things I wasn't even sure I could put into words. I had to try. "You kept me safe. And even after I made you blow up your whole damn ship, you were still checking in, and…" I swallowed hard. "You *hugged* me. You listened. You got that stupid soup can off the top shelf and—"

"Can I talk yet?" he asked, the words muffled by my fingers.

I jerked my hand back. "Oh. Yes. Sorry. Rambling again. Um, go ahead."

His soft laugh flashed white teeth in the dark. "It's okay. Unfiltered thoughts, remember?"

"Baby chicken," I whispered, a little shaken by how much I'd just spilled.

"Right." He studied me for a beat before shaking his head. "I don't need you to apologize again."

"But—"

"I don't." He squeezed my legs, then frowned when he caught my expression. "What?"

I toyed with the fabric bunched at his shoulder, worrying a loose thread. "Then I don't know what…"

When I didn't finish, he leaned in until I had no choice but to meet his eyes. "Don't know what?"

I shrugged. "What now. Not with the mission. But…"

With us.

I didn't say it out loud. I didn't need to.

"That depends," he said quietly.

Something in his voice made my pulse stutter. I swallowed as he tucked his fingers beneath my chin, tipping my face back to his. His expression was completely serious. "What do *you* want?"

Oh. *That* was a loaded question.

What did I want?

So many things. *Too* many things. Things I didn't even want to let myself think about. I stared at him. The somber slant of his full mouth, the shine of his unearthly blue eyes. He was unfairly beautiful in moonlight.

"Well," I said, sighing. I gripped the collar of his shirt and finally leaned in. "This is kind of embarrassing, but I think I've made it painfully obvious by now. For…a while. In case you haven't noticed." I lowered my voice to a stage-whisper. "There's this bartender at work. And I kind of have a thing for him."

"Is that right…?" His breathless laugh turned into a faint groan as my mouth found his.

The helpless sound unraveled me. I tightened my knees around his waist as his tongue brushed mine.

The kiss became something bigger. Something real. Something that said more than I could put into words at the moment.

And then *more*.

I wrapped tighter, burrowing closer. One of his hands found its way into my hair, and the other gripped my hip, pulling me down onto him. There was no mistaking how hard he was under those thin basketball shorts.

An ache twisted inside me in answer.

I tugged at his shirt, needing skin and, breaking the kiss, he reached back and tore it off in one swift motion. I had the briefest second to admire tanned skin and corded strength before his lips were on mine once more.

Maybe that'd been it. Maybe he'd just needed to hear me say it because the hesitation I'd glimpsed was gone. I lost track of minutes, seconds—possibly my own name—as one kiss bled into another, near-frantic. Like we'd both finally reached that point of no return.

As if he, like me, was ready to leap.

His skin was on fire. So was mine, and I couldn't help but shift in his lap, rubbing myself against the thick length trapped between us. Sky's strangled curse was accompanied by an arch of his hips, and his hand tightened in my hair.

I was *so* ready.

Needing air, I broke away, lifting my face to the shadowy ceiling. His lips found the edge of my jaw, and he cupped the back of my head, angling it to give him access to my throat. The soft drag of his lips raised goosebumps.

There were no Basts to stop us. We were alone and touching, and this was everything I'd needed. I reached for my shirt.

But because he was Sky, he curled his hands over mine and stopped me himself.

"You should know something, too." He pulled away, and I sat back, trying not to focus on the fact that I could feel him throbbing against me. He looked down, thumbs caressing my hands where they gripped the hem of my borrowed shirt.

I didn't say anything, relinquishing my hold. I got the impression he was fighting for the words, and I was right. A second later, his confession came out raspy in the darkness.

"It's been…well, a *while* since I've done this. The lying…" He shook his head. My heart skipped a beat when he raised his face again. He reached up, hooking a strand of hair behind my ear before his eyes skimmed back to mine. "I didn't like lying about who I was. *What* I was. It felt wrong."

I stared at him, mouth parting. Of course. *Of course* he wouldn't. The Sky I knew *wouldn't* feel right about that.

Because Sky might be an alien, but he was also *good*. A good *person*.

God, if I hadn't already been head-over-heels for him, that quiet confession would've tipped me over the edge. Leave it to me to find the universe's biggest green flag—and have him be totally and utterly out of reach.

That seemed like a problem for future Rae.

I took his face in my hands, the roughness of his stubble scraping my palms, and brought us eye-to-eye. "Well, in case you have *any* doubt whatsoever, Sky." His gaze was searching. Open in a way I hadn't seen before. "I want this. I want *you*. All of you. Fully aware of the fact that you're an alien from another world, and that…" And twinge tried to rise. I stuffed it back down. "And that you're going back there, and no promises—and *all* that. All the alien stuff." I couldn't help but laugh, though it wasn't quite steady. His confession had rocked me. Mine, too. "I'm really not sure what all this says about me at this point, but…"

"Good things," Sky murmured. His knuckles traced my cheekbone before his fingers slid to my nape, thumb tipping my chin up. His eyes dropped to my mouth and darkened. "It says really, really good things, Raven."

And then he kissed me again, and I had to agree.

So many good things.

Like the slide of his lips over mine, the way he tasted, the sound of our breathing and the feel of his skin, the impatient way he moved under me. The current between us, electric. Buzzing.

I knew that sensation. Light flared behind my lids. I opened my eyes in time to watch the silver ripple out from where my palm rested over his heart.

Sky's synth-skin melted away beneath the light. The shimmering alien silver bloomed in a patch, sparkling ever-so-slightly in the soft white glow radiating from my palm.

Neither of us spoke. His chest hitched as I drew my hand back. Together, we watched the gleaming handprint fade, melting slowly to tan. I touched him on the stomach, then the bare thigh, transfixed by the glimpses of glinting skin beneath.

It, too, was beautiful. Otherworldly and strange and stunning. Like him.

Raising my eyes to his, I gave a small shrug. As if to say, *see? I told you I didn't care.* Sky shook his head, a smile ghosting over his lips right as they met mine.

There was no awkwardness this time when we worked together to get my shirt and bra off. They disappeared somewhere in the darkness, possibly lost forever. I couldn't bring myself to care. He murmured words I wasn't sure were actual words into my skin as his mouth closed on my nipple.

For being out of practice—and, you know, from a whole other world—he was doing just fine. My fingers found his hair as I arched my spine, shuddering in his lap. My heart pounded everywhere. He cupped both breasts, his tongue hot, teeth nipping.

This was what I'd wanted. Needed. Right now, I didn't care that he was leaving and flying off into the stars—at least not at this very moment. The fact he wasn't even human meant nothing.

I wanted this with *Sky*. Because he was Sky.

Because I'd thought about him—*this*—for so long…and I'd rather have memories than regrets.

The emotion bubbled up. Too much. Too intense. Too complicated. So I pulled his face to mine before I fell too deep. A needy ache settled low in my belly, and I moved against him, over him, chasing friction. More contact.

With a muffled groan, Sky fisted the bunched fabric of my too-baggy sweatpants in both hands and pulled me down onto him harder, thrusting upward with his hips. Grinding his cock into me, and that was it. Enough teasing.

"I can't…" I moaned into his mouth, not even sure what I was trying to say. Luckily, he translated correctly.

"I know." His arms came around me, and in a blink, I was on my back on the small, squeaky bed, under him. His eyes were a dark gleam before he kissed me again.

I lost myself to it. To him. His mouth was everywhere. His hands.

The rest of my clothing vanished with my shirt. I didn't know if it was the shadows or Sky, but for once, the self-consciousness wasn't there as I stretched out on the scratchy comforter, shivering.

"Cold?" Sky murmured, drawing back.

I shook my head and reached for him. "Not at all."

No, I was burning. Especially with the heat of him and his mouth blazing a path down my neck.

He explored me with the thoroughness I decided I both loved and hated. Like he was mapping out every spot that made me shudder and cry out. He swallowed my broken sounds when his fingers slid between my legs. He'd learned me *far* too well already. He watched me in that intense, unbearably sexy way, too, intent and steady and *so* scorching I could barely breathe. Like he was drinking in everything as I came almost embarrassingly quickly.

I drifted back to Earth while he rose from the bed. Anticipation curled deep. I pushed myself onto my elbow to watch, trying to catch my breath and failing. My pulse took off again.

My eyes had adjusted to the gray moonlight fighting through the dirty window. Sky held my gaze as he hooked his thumbs into the waistband of his pants and pushed them down. When he straightened, he raked a hand through his hair, pushing it back from his face. Some things apparently transcended solar systems, because the sliver of a smile he sent me was all male pride.

Understandable. I tried to stop my mouth from dropping open but failed miserably. Naked Sky was…everything I'd hoped he would be. Sculpted, long-limbed, and lithe. I had a new appreciation for the synth-skin.

And, though I'd already surmised as much, I could now confirm he had all the parts.

My body tightened. Nerves, anticipation, impatience—everything knotted together until I couldn't breathe again.

When he settled back against the wall by the window, one leg bent, he lifted his gaze. A wordless question. An invitation.

Yes.

I moved to him before I could overthink it, rising onto my knees and closing the space between us. He tipped his head back, eyes never leaving mine. Outside, insects buzzed in the dark, but inside the room felt suspended. Like everything else had gone quiet.

I hesitated just long enough for the weight of it to hit.

Then his hands were on me.

"Come here," he murmured, bracketing my hips. Before I could even blink, he'd pulled me the rest of the way to him and settled me in his lap, my knees on either side of his thighs. With nothing between us, the hot slide of him against my core made us both suck in a breath. The bedsprings gave the smallest creak of protest, but that was the last thing I cared about. I steadied myself on his shoulders, pulse hammering.

The moonlight illuminated his healing bruises and scrapes, his tousled hair. I gave in and pushed that floppy curl off his forehead like I'd always wanted to.

Sky cupped my nape and gently pulled my face to his. Those brilliant, stars-and-mysteries eyes sought mine. There were *things* I recognized in that stare, things I also felt and hadn't the slightest clue what to do with.

It would've been easier if they weren't there. If this was just scratching an itch. *So* much easier if we were just succumbing to an urge, like I'd tried to claim.

He brushed his lips over mine, then pulled back enough to meet my gaze. That question lingered, one I answered by reaching between us. He hissed through his teeth when I wrapped my fingers around his thick length. His grip tightened on the back of my neck before releasing. His palms settled on my hips instead.

Heart in my throat, I lined us up and sank down.

He watched me through glazed, half-closed eyes, the tendons in his neck cording as he arched from the bed and met me halfway—

And then he was seated deep, and I could feel him everywhere. I couldn't bite back my breathy moan if my life had depended on it, a tremor rocking me at the stretch, the fullness. His rough curse was just as gutted, his fingers flexing and digging in when I fell forward.

"You good?" he ground out, the words guttural. His hands weren't quite steady as they swept over my back and then returned to my waist. Neither were mine when they found his shoulders, seeking leverage so I could draw back to face him.

"Oh yeah," I breathed, swallowing hard. "I'm fantastic." His amused huff broke off when I gave my hips a testing swivel, and with a quiet groan that formed my name at the end, Sky came alive.

He dragged me forward, lighting up nerve-endings in a trail of fire as he lunged for my mouth.

The kiss was messy and searing, full of desperation and ragged breaths as we moved together. Months of pent-up tension finally—*finally*—released. He clamped one hand on my hip, guiding my movements, grinding me down onto him, while the other was everywhere. My hair, my shoulder, my back. I could already feel another orgasm building, fire and pressure winding tighter and tighter.

I planted my palms on his hot chest to anchor myself.

Felt the tingling buzz as my right hand brightened.

Wanting to see, I forced my lids open. Where my palm pressed to his torso, silver rippled out in a wave. I'd shorted his synth-skin again. Except this time…

Gasping, I froze as the gleam spread. Over his chest, his shoulders, down his stomach, smoothing tan into a taut, glittering sheen. And then lower—

Sky went completely still beneath me, heaving in a choked breath. My heart stopped. Not from fear. At least, not entirely, because the rest of Sky was transforming, too, and…

Oh.

"Wait, Raven—" he started.

But it was too late. I squeaked, spine snapping straight as the size of him inside me *changed*. Subtle, but enough to notice. Expanded, the texture—the shape—shifting…

Well. *That* was different.

Sky let out a shocked wheeze, gripping my waist hard enough to leave bruises. *"Fuck."*

Indeed. I blinked once, twice, staring down. Beneath my palm, between my thighs, *under me,* his skin—*all of him*—had altered. Where tanned flesh had stretched over muscle, now glittering silver did.

There were similarities. Enough that this…well, it worked.

But he wasn't human.

I was having sex with an alien.

Slowly, shock stinging, I raised my gaze to his. Sky—*alien* Sky—stared back at me, eyes wide. His whites had darkened to ink against wide, vivid irises in every swirling shade of blue. His dark hair was gone, replaced by smooth, shimmering skin and twin black stripes tracing along the sides of his skull. A flatter nose, sharp ears. *Alien.*

Beautiful. Overwhelming.

I wanted to feel all of it.

In a daze, I lifted my free, non-glowing hand and ran my finger-tips over his angular cheekbone. His skin was textured. Coarser. He leaned his face into my hand, staring up at me in half wonder, half astonishment.

Alien. And yet...I could still see *him*. The emotions were still there. *Sky* was still there.

Hottest alien in the galaxy. In *all* forms.

My heart thumped. The shock was fading, giving way to... excitement.

"Are you okay?" he asked tentatively, the words oddly resonant. Like there were extra vocal cords somewhere inside his graceful throat. He hadn't loosened his death grip on my waist.

"I...I think so." I took stock of my body. He was still inside me, and it felt...different, but not in a bad way.

Actually, in a way that had a dark thrill tingling to life.

Sky drew in a slow breath through his nose, let it out through his mouth. I caught a glimpse of teeth. Similar to mine but with extra canines. Curiosity stirred. That was a tongue, too. Darker. Blue?

This was *so* strange. Forbidden delight had become a pulsing, living thing.

I watched his gleaming silver chest rise and fall under my palm. He hadn't moved beyond breathing. Neither had I.

"If you break the contact," he said softly, that beautiful, melo-dious voice vibrating where I still touched him, "it'll go back to normal. It'll stop."

"Stop?" I trailed the fingers of my free hand down the side of his neck. He was softer there. Like fine-grained sandpaper and silk. He tilted his pointed chin, giving me access. Tiny facets caught the glow in a star-like shimmer. "I don't want it to stop."

I felt his eyes on me, but I couldn't look away from the play of moonlight over his skin.

"Are you sure?" he finally asked. The echo of his human voice peeked through. That hesitation. Wariness. Checking, always check-ing, in his Sky way.

I dragged my attention from the defined tendons sloping down into his broad shoulders and met his black-on-blue eyes instead.

"Yes. Yeah, I think I'm... I don't want to stop, Sky." Blood warmed my cheeks, but I'd already decided. "I want to try this."

Something molten flared in his gaze, that faint blue glow luminescent in the dark. His fingers slackened and slid down, palms rougher than before when they curved around my thighs. *Alien texture.* "You're positive?" he murmured. I watched his lips, a shade shy of navy, form the words.

I suddenly, badly needed to taste them.

"Everything...um, works the same?" I shifted a little in his lap—and bit my cheek against a moan when sensation sparked along my spine.

Sky's fingers sank into the meat of my legs, and his stifled groan with that musical lilt was pure sin. "Yes," he breathed. "It—close enough. God, Rae...that feels..."

Agreed.

His lids lowered, only the barest bit of beautiful, glowing cerulean shining through when he took a deep breath and slowly raised his head again. Searching my face. My heart beat in my throat. In my belly. Lower.

I was really doing this.

"Tell me if we need to stop," Sky said, scraping his fingertips in a featherlight line back to my hips.

I nodded jerkily. Somewhere beneath my palm, his heart hammered. A Pladian heart. *Sky's* heart.

His face may have been different, but this was the same Sky who'd protected me. Who'd kept me safe. Who'd hugged me, even after I'd colossally fucked up.

In answer, I kept one hand on his chest and lifted myself up before sliding back down. And down.

And that, apparently, was all it took.

With a hungry growl, Sky reared up and sealed his mouth over mine. He tasted the same, like Sky, but the feel of his lips was different now, softer and somehow more mobile. He covered the palm pressed to his chest with his own, holding it there as the light poured from it and shorted the synthetic suit.

I had the fleeting thought that he'd been right to worry—this *absolutely* was going to complicate things—but then he moved inside me, meeting every slow roll of my hips with a matching thrust, and thinking became impossible.

His vivid eyes locked onto mine, half-wild and reverent all at once. His free hand guided my hips, urging me faster. The rasp of glittering alien skin against mine was foreign and exquisite, and when I threw my head back, my palm glowed red behind my lids.

"*Sky*," I panted. Heat coiled tighter and tighter in my belly, pressure building so fast it stole my breath.

When it snapped, the tension didn't just break. I *shattered* around him with a broken cry, my forehead falling forward onto his shoulder. He caught me against him, rough alien skin contrasting against my softer human.

Vaguely, I heard him choke out a string of lilting words I didn't understand, and then he rolled us. The movement jostled my palm from his torso, and I opened my eyes in time to watch his alien form shimmer and melt back into the Sky I knew. Messy curls, flushed skin, human eyes with pupils wide and dark. My pulse stuttered wildly.

Holy *shit*.

We were sharing air, skin sticking. He brushed my hair back, his expression awestruck. I tried to collect the pieces of myself, but they didn't seem to fit back together the same way as before.

"That was…" I managed.

"Yeah." He was just as winded. "Yeah, it was."

The laugh that escaped me was more of a gasp and probably had something to do with being high on endorphins. "You didn't…" I couldn't quite form words yet. Couldn't think. Still inside me, still hard, he held himself up with one arm. His free hand traced a path from my rib cage to my hip and back up.

Heat was already starting to build once more.

Why had we waited so long to do this, again?

"No." He reached for my wrist, the one wearing alien metal, and lifted it, looping my arm around his neck. "Not yet." His smile was small and crooked as he lowered over me, balancing on his forearms. "We're just getting started."

I bit my lip against a smile, a warm bubble of…*something* fizzing in my chest at that cocky little grin. The way it faded to intent as he dipped his head, brushing his lips over my cheek, the kiss almost chaste. Sweet.

Then he pulled back and paused to study me. "Are you sure you're okay?"

Way beyond okay. My inner muscles clenched around him, and the way his eyelids fluttered told me he'd felt it. I nodded and slid my knee along his thigh, toying with the ends of his hair. "Are *you*? That was…unexpected."

"There aren't human words to describe how I feel right now," he murmured, with a light laugh against my lips—right before kissing me. Once. Twice. Then deeper, slower, until my toes curled.

That fizzy thing in my chest burst, spreading, and I pulled back. "That's okay. I'll take Pladian ones."

His full smile flashed his dimple. "Deal."

Then he became serious again as he hooked his arm under my knee and raised up enough to brace one hand on the wall over my head. Eyes on mine, he began to move again in smooth, even thrusts. I hung on to his waist, his shoulders, his hair, careful not to let the quick flare of white light and silver skin disrupt the rhythm this time.

He might have spoken Pladian. Hell, there was a chance I did. It was hard to tell.

For a moment, the world outside didn't exist. The Enil, the danger. Tomorrow.

For now, there was only Sky.

Chapter 27

OUT-OF-THIS-WORLD
INTERIOR DESIGN

"***RAVEN***! Wake up. Come on."

I knew that voice.

The urgency, the barely leashed panic, though…that was new.

I groaned. My head…

It hurt. Like my brain was slowly being squeezed through a toothpaste tube. Maybe a black hole. Grimacing, I tried to wet my dry lips, only to find that my tongue was made of sandpaper.

"*What*—" I tried to speak, but my throat was glued shut.

"Come on, Rae," Sky whispered. Hands cupped the sides of my face. "Open your eyes."

He sounded worried. Weird. The last thing I remembered —

We'd had sex. Finally.

I'd had sex with Sky in *alien form*.

My eyes flew open. I no longer cared about my aching head, no longer cared about the fact that I tasted blood—

Wait. *Blood?*

Everything was blurry. I blinked, raising a hand to rub my eyes. I froze in mid-motion.

My hand was covered in yellow. I squinted. Was that paint?

Slowly, I lifted my other arm. Not just one, either. *Both* hands were covered in pale, buttery-yellow paint.

"What the hell?" I whispered. My throat felt raw, ripped up.

The haze cleared enough for reason to creep in. Something was wrong. Fear, a shivery finger of it, traced down my spine.

I wore nothing but Sky's T-shirt, which I'd slipped on before crawling, pleasantly exhausted, into bed beside Sky…

Except I was now lying on the floor, half in his lap instead of beside him. And while he was still shirtless, he looked a lot less sleepy and contented than he had what felt like seconds ago.

Something told me I'd lost more than a few seconds. Probably more than a few moments, actually, judging by the faint blue light bathing the cabin's interior. How was it already dawn?

I had more pressing concerns, though. Like the fact that Sky was staring at me with shock, concern, and something dangerously close to horror.

Not exactly the kind of post-coital snuggles I'd imagined all those times.

That icy fear gave another pulse. So did my head.

"What happened?" I asked, trying and failing to sit up. I winced at the stabbing pain behind my eyeballs, but I forced my lids to stay open.

My body didn't seem to be working right. Luckily, Sky's arm braced between my shoulder blades, holding me upright. His palm cradled the back of my neck.

Why were my hands coated in paint?

When he didn't answer right away, I frowned and looked past him.

Oh. *That* was why.

The entire cramped living and kitchenette area was *covered* in glyphs, symbols, and shapes. Written in yellow paint.

It didn't take a rocket scientist to figure this out. Or, you know. A flying saucer one.

"I did that, didn't I?" I asked, my voice shockingly even.

Probably because my head didn't feel quite connected to my

body. None of this felt real. Waking up here, like this, having done all *that*...

Sky took my chin, turning my face back to his. "We'll get to that in a minute. Raven, *are you okay?*"

He was breathing hard. Shoulders heaving, face pale. He studied me with near-frantic intensity.

Holy shit. Sky was scared.

That was enough to send another surge of trepidation through me. I snapped my mouth closed, swallowing hard. I had no saliva to speak of.

"M-my head hurts," I stammered, blinking fast. "Worse than before. But I think I'm all right. Did it happen again?"

I mean, obviously this was different than the motel-room seizure. After all, I'd apparently *painted freaking alien writing all over the walls and didn't remember a thing.* It took effort, but I didn't look at it.

Sky's mouth pressed into a tight line. "Can you stand?"

I shrugged because I honestly wasn't sure. I couldn't feel my legs. He also still hadn't answered my question.

"Let's try it," he muttered, standing and gently hauling me with him. My knees immediately buckled, and he caught me deftly around the waist.

I gasped when my head took a slow, dizzying spin. My vision fractured. I reached for one of the pair of Skys and missed, my nose smashing into his hard chest. His arms tightened around me.

"Easy," he said, and it reverberated against my face. "I've got you."

I breathed through it, and after a few sluggish heartbeats, I cautiously opened my eyes.

Better. Nothing swirled anymore.

Besides the yellow paint all over the walls and anything standing against them. Even the shelf in the corner hadn't escaped.

"Shit," I breathed. I'd painted this entire freaking room.

"We'll worry about it in a minute." Sky tugged me toward the sink.

In a daze, I stumbled along on baby-deer legs, Sky supporting most of my weight. I didn't look away from all the writing until he hitched me up by the armpits like a toddler and set my butt on the counter.

It was enough to distract me.

"*Sky*," I muttered, pushing away his hands. "What are you doing?"

I was hyper-aware of the fact I wasn't even wearing underwear. Heat crept into my face, and I pulled down the shirt's hem, smearing tacky paint.

I wasn't sure why I was worried about modesty when Sky had just seen me naked.

Or, better yet, why the hell I was worried about anything at all besides the fact that I'd just *painted the entire cabin in*—

"Hey." Sky's voice brought me back to myself.

I let out a shuddery breath and met his eyes.

Some of his color had returned, but he was still pale. A muscle pulsed in his temple as he turned his head and cranked the faucet handle. The pipes gurgled and water spewed out.

Brown water.

We both stared at it.

"Bast did say to let it run," I said.

"Yeah." Sky returned his attention to me. Brow furrowing, he examined my face. "How do you feel now?"

"Confused," I said, chewing on my lip. "What the hell happened?"

He blew out a breath and jammed a hand through his hair, shoulders tight. "I have no idea. I was almost asleep when I felt you get up. I thought you were just going to the bathroom or something, but when you didn't come back, I found you prying open the paint cans."

I gawked at him.

He caught my look and sniffed bitterly. "Yeah, I know. I kept asking what you were doing, but you didn't answer. Your pupils were blown, and you didn't say a word. You just started...painting. I tried to stop you more than once, and you fought me." He broke off with a muttered curse, looking away. "I didn't want to hurt you any more than—"

He stopped himself and swiped a hand down his face, but I heard the words anyway. *Any more than I already had.*

So that was why he was so agitated? Was he blaming *himself*? How was any of this his fault? I mean, besides the alien device that'd started this whole thing—but even that was on his ancestors. Not him.

I didn't have the computing power to process this yet. Not when my eyes kept drifting from him to the strange writing.

It was all Raven-height. None of it was higher than I could reach on my tiptoes. And I'd done it all with absolutely zero aware-ness. Like I'd been asleep.

What if I hadn't woken up?

The skulking thought flitted in. I shoved it away, focusing on the streaks of still-drying paint reflecting the soft light in wet gleams. The eerie, flowing shapes and scrawls looked like a language I almost knew…

The sensation nagged at me, frustrating. Like I'd forgotten something.

"What does it say?" I asked, breathless.

He followed my gaze to the writing, then turned back with a sharp exhalation, like the sight of it was too much.

"It's the full greeting," he said tersely.

"The full greeting, huh?" I opened my marked palm. Under the drying paint, some of the faint shapes looked like a match.

He didn't look at me. Instead, he reached for the pile of dishrags, shook one out, and put it under the now-clear stream of water pouring from the faucet in fitful glugs.

"Hold out your hand," he said.

Only then did I realize why he'd put me up here. He was cleaning my hands.

Despite the shock—and the creeping terror that I'd just sleep-recreated an alien tourism pamphlet—a warm flutter brushed the inside of my chest. Like wings unfurling. I couldn't help it. My smile slipped free, and I rolled my lips inward, trying to hide it.

It didn't work. Sky caught it. "What are you *smiling* about?" he asked, brows drawing into a tight V. "Raven, I just told you that you went into some kind of trance most likely induced by *alien technology* you've been exposed to—"

"I can wash my own hands, Sky," I said. A weak laugh escaped. "You don't have to wash me."

He paused a beat, looked down at the rag he held, then slowly back up. As if that exchange had broken through his tension, a bit of it bled from his shoulders.

"Right." He shook his head, his quick glance chagrined as he extended the towel. "Yeah. Of course. Sorry."

"No." I nudged it back at him. "Don't be sorry. It's kind of nice to have the big bad alien warrior fussing over me."

His gaze flew to mine. He blinked once before his lips curved faintly. Grudgingly. "*Logician.*"

"What?" I asked, frowning.

"Logician. I'm an alien *logician*, technically," he clarified, looking at me from underneath his lashes. "Bast is our technology specialist, and I'm…" He sighed, hint of a smile fading. "I'm the logistics half of the Pair." He braced the heel of his hand holding the rag on the counter. "You'd never guess, given how royally I've fucked this up."

"Sky," I said quietly, curling my fingers against the urge to reach for him. I had a feeling he'd pull away. "It's not your fault."

The muscle jumped in his temple, and he didn't look at me, his deep blue eyes trained out the window behind me. Far away. He looked a little better. Like he'd finally caught up on sleep. He needed a shave again, though. Stubble roughened the graceful planes of his face.

"If you say so." He straightened and reached for me again, avoiding my eyes. "Here, Rae. Let me help. Give me your hand."

If it made him feel better, what could it hurt? I lifted the first paint-covered hand and placed it in his.

My throat felt oddly tight as I watched him gently push the purple-pink cuff down my arm. My skin tingled as he began to run the wet rag over each of my slick fingers, cleaning away the pale-yellow smears. Scrubbing in places where it'd begun to dry and flake.

That errant curl fell over his creased forehead. That urge to smooth it back rose, but I checked it. The ground was shaky where Sky was concerned. Especially now. His lips were drawn once more into that broody line.

It was a distraction, and for a moment, I recalled how they'd felt against mine. How he'd felt against me.

Inside me.

That glitter of silver, the contrast against my softer, human skin. It'd all been… okay, fine. It'd been life-changing. *Sky* had been.

I was screwed—no pun intended—because now that I'd experienced that with him, how was I ever supposed to move on?

How was I not supposed to want it again?

Right now, for example.

Heat rushed up my neck. I shifted on the counter and, despite the pounding in my head, I had to squeeze my thighs together against a shiver.

Sky caught that, too. His motions slowed, and he darted a glance up at me. He was close enough that I could see the shards of silver and black inside his indigo eyes, different from what they'd been before when they'd been black-on-blue and hazed with pleasure.

There was a distinct feeling in my chest when I looked at him. Something I shouldn't be feeling. Something that felt an awful lot like possession. Like he was *mine*—

His stare softened, and he enfolded the hand he was washing in his. I couldn't think straight when he looked at me like that. My breath hitched—was that panic?—and for a second, his attention flicked to my mouth and away. "Raven, I—"

But of course, the door crashed open at that instant, letting in a rush of swampy morning air. I startled and nearly pitched off the counter, grabbing Sky's bare shoulders to catch myself, smearing tacky yellow paint on his skin.

Bast burst through the entrance, plastic bags swinging from both hands. His eyes landed on us, and he stopped short. The sound he made was one of pure disgust.

"Seriously? On the counter?" Then he blinked and slowly took in the rest of the shack. When he looked back, both brows were high. "Gotta say I'm on the fence about the redecorating, too."

I winced, relinquishing my hold on Sky's shoulders to tug the hem of my shirt down again. Sky glanced at me, a dark frown replacing the softness that had been there a second before.

"I'm glad you're back." He pivoted to face Bast. "We need to talk. Something's wrong with Rae."

"*Wrong* with me?" Pulse skipping, I struggled to get off the counter without flashing Bast anything R-rated. Heaven forbid he be a gentleman and give me some privacy. He was still standing in the doorway, holding bags and staring at us. I stretched my toes toward the floor. "I mean, that seems—it's not like that. I'm okay now. I feel better."

"What's it like then?" Sky aimed an arched-brow look my way, belatedly offering me a hand I ignored.

I managed to gain my footing without giving anyone a show. But I couldn't help but glance at the paint-smeared walls.

I didn't have an answer because I didn't know *what* that was. Any of this.

And that scared me.

That sudden shift to standing hadn't helped anything, either. My temples pulsed. I closed my eyes briefly, fighting down a swell of nausea.

When I opened them, Sky was watching me, shoulders tense again like he was ready to snatch me up if I swayed. I avoided his eyes, instead focusing on Bast, who'd moved the rest of the way inside the shack. He pushed the door shut with his elbow and strode for the table.

"Okay…" He dumped the bags next to the tangled mess already atop it and turned to face us. "So I'm assuming Biscuit here is responsible for the charming new motif?" He indicated the dripping walls.

I tugged my shirt's hem lower and tried not to look.

Beside me, Sky nodded grimly. "It was like she was in a fugue state. She was unresponsive but was moving and doing…" He gestured at the drying scrawls, too. "All this. And then there was the seizure she had at the motel."

I winced at the reminder.

"Whoa, whoa. *What?* Seizure at the motel?" Bast threw up his hands. "Did you both forget to mention that?"

That caught me off guard. I frowned at Sky. "You didn't tell him?"

"I hadn't yet, no." He turned to Bast. "But I did tell you we needed to remove the halix information as non-invasively as possible—"

"Yeah, but *damn*, Skaiven. A heads-up that it was possibly melting your girlfriend's brain would've been nice!"

Girlfriend? I blinked, then shook it off. I had more important things to worry about at the moment—like the fact these two aliens were discussing my horrible death like I wasn't sitting *right* here. I lifted my hand in a sarcastic wave. "Hello?"

Sky sent Bast a scowl. "A little tact, maybe?"

"Sorry," the other alien muttered.

Sky sighed. "Rae." When I avoided eye contact, he grasped me by the shoulders and gently turned me toward him, bending down until I had no choice but to meet his gaze. "I think maybe we need to reevaluate. We should consider taking you to a hospital."

To a hospital? The word ripped the air from my lungs.

"What? *No.*" My stomach turned to stone, dropping straight to the floor. I jerked out of his reach and lifted a yellow-smeared hand. "Absolutely not."

"They'd be better equipped. They can make sure you're okay—"

"That's not your decision to make, Sky." The rising flood of anxiety tasted sharp and cold.

Sky took a deep breath, conceding, "No, of course it's not, but—"

"No hospitals," I said, setting my teeth.

His eyes narrowed. "Raven, you didn't see yourself—"

"I said *no.* " I didn't bother dulling the edge of my voice. I started to wrap my arms around myself before remembering the wet paint and settling on balling my hands into fists at my sternum instead. I felt too exposed, standing here with no pants, barefoot, the rough wood scraping the soles of my feet. "I'm not going to a hospital. I'm *fine*. It's just a headache."

And an extraterrestrial art-trance.

But even if I *could* force myself to step inside a hospital, it wasn't feasible. *Realistic*. After all, we were wanted fugitives.

I clung to that rationalization, shaking my head when Sky continued to stare at me.

He apparently saw that I meant it because he turned away with a bitten-off curse, shoving both hands through his hair, every line of him screaming frustration. Guilt wiggled its way in. Twice in the span of a day, I'd broken past that controlled composure of his.

Because he cared.

A confusing rush of emotions clogged my chest. Everything was becoming a tangled, complicated mess. The paint in my periphery mocked me.

A clatter by the table drew my attention. Bast held up one of the strange, handheld devices cobbled together with electrical tape and electronics.

"You're not emitting any signal, at least," he said, eyeing it, then me. He cocked his head. "So I guess whatever happened to cause that," he pointed at the paint, "is over."

For now. I heard the unspoken words. Giving in, I looked at the writing, a chill creeping through me.

Who knew when it'd happen again, though?

First the seizure and now this. I had no memory of doing *any* of that painting. Then there were the dreams. The things I couldn't quite recall.

What exactly was this map doing to me?

When I turned around, both aliens were looking at me like they were wondering the same thing.

And if *they* didn't know…

Just how screwed was I?

Chapter 28

GETTING HANDSY WITH
THE ALIEN GOODS AGAIN

IT **WAS MY TURN** to need space—both to put on pants *and* to process —and our tiny swamp shack offered very little of that. I once again sequestered myself in the small bedroom off the living area.

I lay on my side and watched the shadows cast by the trees outside dance along the paneled walls and ceiling. Through the door, I could make out the Pladians' low voices in the front room, along with Bast's occasional thumping. As day broke outside, the light filtering through the smudged window brightened, and the temperature was already rising.

It didn't chase away my chill.

Sighing, I sat up. The pleasant ache between my thighs— muscles that hadn't been used in a while—made me blush as I perched on the edge.

That reminder wasn't helping anything. I leaned my elbows on my knees, dropping my aching head into my hands.

I hadn't meant to snap at Sky for suggesting a hospital. He had no way of knowing I avoided them like the plague. That I hadn't stepped foot in one since Dad had died. The rational side of me knew that was ridiculous, but it didn't help the cold sweat that broke out at the thought of them. That antiseptic scent and hushed murmuring. I shuddered.

But what if he was right? What *if* this thing in my head was killing me? There was no point in denying the fact that *something* was happening. First the midterm at the university, during which I'd scribbled down words I hadn't even known. The constant headaches. Then the seizure. Now…well, that mess outside.

Something was wrong with me.

And what if they couldn't fix it? The swoop in my stomach felt like I'd stepped off the edge of a steep drop.

A floorboard groaned outside the room's entrance, and I sat up straight as the door creaked open. Sky stuck his head in. When he saw me, he pushed it wider with one hand, the other carrying a plastic water bottle. He'd donned a shirt, though he still wore those silky basketball shorts.

With effort, I looked away from his calves.

"I didn't want to wake you," he murmured. "I thought you might be sleeping."

"No way." I summoned a wobbly smile. "Too much to think about."

He stepped in and closed the door after him. "Understandable. How are you feeling?"

"Okay. My headache's better." Kind of, anyway. He offered me the water, and I took it. "Thanks."

He blew out a breath and crossed the small room, perching beside me. The bed groaned under his weight, and his shoulder brushed mine. I tried really hard not to think about the fact we'd been naked together right here only a handful of hours ago.

I failed.

"How are you feeling besides that?" he asked. The furtive glance he sent my way and the faint red tinge to his cheeks told me I wasn't the only one taking a trip down sexy memory lane.

Awareness sizzled between us, and I set the water on the floor and spun the cuff on my wrist. Shy, for some reason, despite every-thing that'd just happened. "I'm okay. A little…" I bit my lip. "A little sore. It'd, ah, been a while since I'd… Well, it'd been a while for me, too."

I turned my head—at the same time he turned his. His dark eyes swept over my face.

"I hope I wasn't too rough." He was unfairly attractive, gilded by dawn light and shadow. His expression was wary, but there was something else there. Something lurking as he studied me. Soft and poignant.

"What?" I breathed a laugh, shaking my head. "No. Not at all. It was…"

Well, there weren't really words. Sky gazed back at me steadily. My heartbeat picked up until I felt it in my throat. I forced myself not to look at his mouth, instead dropping my attention to my shirt's hem. Yellow paint had dried on its edge, and I picked at it. A beat of silence followed.

"Raven," Sky said quietly, breaking it. "I think we need to talk."

I knew that tone. That was the one he used when he was about to tell me something I didn't want to hear. I dragged my eyes back to his. My stomach dropped.

He pressed his lips into a line but didn't look away. "I…I think what happened to you—the paint, the trance—I think it was related to your hand glowing. To…" He hesitated and exhaled through his nose, mouth tightening. "Related to what we did."

Wait, *what?*

I sat up straighter and stared at him for a solid ten seconds before I found my voice. "You think having sex with you inspired me to scribble Pladian writing all over the walls. Is that what you're saying? *How?*"

"Think about it," he said. He examined his hands in his lap. That muscle in his temple fluttered like it did when he struggled. "The seizure was after we'd…" He clicked his tongue and scrubbed his knuckles under his chin, the scruff there. "After we'd kissed. Then just now…"

My mind reeled as I struggled to make sense of what he was saying. Could he… could that be *right?* No. No way.

"Well, what about," I flailed, searching for words, "before Bast got there, at the second motel? It didn't… I mean, *we* didn't…"

"Your hand didn't glow." The tendon flickered, and he finally turned his head again. "You didn't touch my skin—the synth-skin —with the markings. It also…well, we weren't at it for a long time." He winced a little at the wording. "You know what I mean."

I did. I wished I didn't, though.

I felt sick to my stomach suddenly, and I didn't think it was the protein bar I'd wolfed down before coming in here. "What are you saying, Sky?"

His throat worked, but he held my gaze. "I think maybe it's best that we keep some distance until we figure out what's going on. I mean…physically. Not that…"

He broke off with a disgusted sound, dropping his head back and scrubbing his palms over his face. For a moment, he stared at the ceiling, and when he spoke again, his tone was bleak. "I was worried about this getting complicated, Rae. This is…beyond that." He clenched his teeth, speaking through them. "I can't *protect* you from something I don't fucking understand."

I stared at him, fisting my marked hand on my lap. Arguments —denials—rose, but I couldn't seem to summon words. Sky took a deep breath. Let it out.

When he lowered his chin and looked at me, there was something pained in his dark gaze. "*Especially* if what's hurting you is…is being close to me."

Oh. It hit me square in the chest, plunging deep. The pent-up air in my lungs rushed out. "I… *Sky*…"

He held my stare, his face taut with tumultuous emotion I couldn't quite name.

This shouldn't hurt that badly. That's what I told myself, anyway, as I scrabbled for reason.

It wasn't like we'd changed anything by sleeping together. In fact, we'd specifically talked about the fact that it *couldn't* change things between us. Not really.

No promises. No tomorrows. We'd agreed.

The mission, the map—everything this crazy situation entailed —meant the future was as uncertain as ever.

So then why did it feel like somebody had kicked a hole in my chest?

"Sure. I guess that...um, makes sense." I cleared my throat when my voice came out croaky and eyed the marks barely visible in the darkness, running my thumb over them. "Okay."

"Okay? *Rae.*" Sky shifted on the bed to face me. The springs groaned in response, another fleeting, unwelcome reminder. I didn't look at him, though I felt his attention boring into my profile. "Every time we activate the halix tech, there's a reaction. The hypnosis. The motel. This." He flung a hand toward the door, beyond which my redecorating waited. "Each time, it feels like you're slipping farther away. It's *harder* to bring you back."

His voice grew harsher at the end, sending a shiver down my spine. It was enough that I finally turned my face toward him, and for some reason, a last-ditch effort spilled out. "What about the stairwell of my apartment? We kissed, and my hand glowed—and nothing happened then."

"I don't know." He searched my eyes, his brows drawn together. "I *don't know.* And that scares me even more." His lips flattened, and this time when he spoke, it was low, tight. "You didn't see what I just saw. You didn't see what that was like. I couldn't wake you up. You weren't even *there.*" I flinched at that, and his face was a mask of intensity, nostrils flared. "I was terrified, Raven. We don't know what's going on here. And I know you're trying to hide it, but the headaches aren't letting up, are they?" At my grimace, he swore and jammed a hand through his hair. "That's what I thought. They're getting worse. You don't want to go to a hospital. That's fine. If we still had the ship, we could run scans, but..."

Right. But we couldn't because the ship was gone. Because of me.

The way he was looking at me, with heaviness and regret, made everything ten times worse. It felt like more than just a, "*Hey, we shouldn't touch.*" It felt like a...

Shit, it felt like a break-up.

"I just don't think it's a good idea. Not now. Not until we know..." He shook his head. "At least until we have an idea what is happening," he murmured, wrenching his gaze from mine. "I'm sorry. For what that's worth. I didn't mean for any of this to happen."

Any of *this*. That could mean so many things. This as in *this*—brain-melting, fugue-painting, halix-absorbing craziness? Or *this*, as in the fact that we'd just spent the entire night wrapped in each other and I could still taste him and this entire tangled thing between us was way more complicated than it had any right being?

What a mess.

"It's okay, Sky." I waved a hand and forced a puff of air out that I hoped sounded unbothered, despite the churning in my stomach and how something in the region of my heart seemed to be cracking apart. "It's not that big a deal."

He turned his head, brows raised. "Yes, it is."

Okay. It was. That didn't change the fact that he was right. There did seem to be a correlation. Whether or not it was coincidental wasn't something I could answer.

Which was a problem.

He was right.

That didn't mean I had to like it. Because I didn't.

But because a part of me was still capable of logic, I took that giant knot of feelings and shoved them down. Hid them away in the place I'd always hidden everything when it came to Sky.

This wasn't *that* different. Not really. I'd gotten pretty good at it. It wasn't like Sky hadn't always been there but just out of reach. Now it was a touch *more* star-crossed.

That term had never been more fitting.

I wasn't sure if that made me want to laugh or cry. Probably cry. Because the thought of putting walls back up where he was concerned was *so* much harder now that I knew the real him.

But what choice did I have? I liked my brain intact.

And we had agreed on no promises. *I'd* agreed.

"It's fine," I said again, going back to picking at the dried paint.

Sky said nothing. For a long time. The buzzing insects and Bast's angry swearing in the main room were the only sounds.

When I finally glanced up, Sky was watching me with a faint frown, mouth downturned. Hard to read but there was a heaviness there. The weight of worlds. So much responsibility all on one person, one being.

I couldn't blame him for doing what he needed to do here. For me. For us. For him. For his people. Hell, for his whole damn planet.

Maybe distance wasn't the worst idea. The fact that it hurt like this wasn't a good sign. I was already feeling all mixed up when it came to Sky. One big snarl of emotions.

He wasn't even going to *be* here once we figured out how to fix this. Once we got his map out of my brain and there was no longer a risk of me going all *The Walking Dead* on him.

He was leaving.

And I was going to get my heart broken if I wasn't careful.

More broken?

I blinked and realized Sky had been studying me all the while, like he was trying to read my emotions. I schooled my features and hoped like hell it wasn't as easy as it usually was.

Whatever he saw in my face had him sighing and leaning in. "Rae, I'm not saying—"

"*Guys!*" Bast shouted from the front room.

We jolted apart, exchanging a frown. Sky pushed off the bed as booted footsteps thudded closer.

Bast threw the door open with no regard for privacy. He wore a tense expression, green eyes serious. "Put your pants back on. You'll both want to see this."

And just like that, we were back to alien crises.

"WHY THE HELL would the Roswell ship be in One Willow?" I sat down heavily in one of the kitchen table chairs, staring at the screen Bast had set down. There was no denying the location of the pulsing dot visible on the map overlay. I knew those highways like the back of my hand. "Are you sure this thing's right?"

"It may not be the entire ship, just the mainframe. It's in parts now. Tracking those pieces is what this was calibrated for." Bast sliced a glare my way. "And I just worked an entire day on this and haven't slept. I'm gonna pretend you didn't question my accuracy."

"Okay." I held up my hand. "Sorry."

His scowl didn't lighten as he cracked a beer and took a long swallow. I refrained from commenting on the fact that the sun was barely up. I supposed if he hadn't slept, it really didn't matter, did it?

Sky leaned past me and slid the tablet closer to himself. "I thought you were looking for the Enil signal."

"I *was*," Bast said, after he'd finished chugging. He turned his attention to his partner. "But since I was tracking these energy signatures, I figured what the hell? At first I thought I'd read something wrong, but I've double-checked it." He sent me a pointed look. "Three times."

"I guess that explains the military presence." I leaned back and shook my head. There was a piece of Pladian metal near me, oval-shaped and shining dully in the morning light. I couldn't look away from the play of colors, the way the lantern flame and stifled sunlight made it gleam like oil. "But *why* would they suddenly move whatever's left of the Roswell ship there? Because it wasn't there before, right?"

"I think we'd have noticed if it was under Sky's nose this whole time," Bast said, snorting into his beer. "Sky's not the tech guy, but he's not completely useless."

Sky lifted his gaze from the scanner long enough to send him the Look. I scraped my teeth over my bottom lip. "It doesn't make any sense, though."

"It *is* weird." Sky handed the device to Bast. "Can you narrow down the location? Maybe that would help."

"Nah." The other Pladian chucked the tablet onto the table. It scattered some of the haphazardly stacked computer boards. "Not without getting closer."

"Closer—like, going back to One Willow?" I gripped the table's edge in front of me. Hope flared, bright and sudden, but a surge of anxiety instantly followed. Going home meant facing the police and possibly License 16. Explaining all this to my family and friends. Was that a possibility?

Bast looked up slowly. "No. No way."

"If the ship's there, one of us is going to have to go there. Eventually," Sky murmured, sounding distracted. He stood over my right shoulder, and so far, I'd avoided looking directly at him since we'd come out of the room. The undercurrent of unresolved tension burned strong between us.

"Yeah, but…come on." His partner crossed his arms. "We just finished going over the fact there's been a License 16 invasion back in Mayberry or wherever the hell this is, remember?"

"Let's think about this logically." Sky balanced his fists on the table and took a deep breath. "Cons. License 16 is active there. The Enil have also identified it as a hot spot." He glanced between me and Bast, the latter who scowled. Sky raised his brows. "Pros. What we need from the ship could be there. From a logistical perspective, running like this with whatever's happening to Raven is becoming…" He slid a glance my way, mouth thinning. "Dangerous. If we weren't fugitives, a hospital would be an option."

I swallowed hard, trying not to cringe. Privately, I disagreed, but for the sake of this argument, I'd let him think what he wanted.

Bast, for once, kept his quip to himself, and Sky continued, "If we can come up with a cover story for being gone, involve local law enforcement, that could also prove beneficial." He pushed off the table and paced away, rubbing his chin. "We know License 16, while well-funded, isn't all-powerful. They need deniability, and that's our advantage. If we come back publicly, local law enforcement—and media—become leverage. License 16 can't move quietly with witnesses."

"What do you mean?" I asked, trying not to let myself perk up like I wanted to. Was he truly making an argument in support of going back to One Willow?

He pivoted toward me, and his eyes softened. "I mean that, while License 16 is a concern, they're not going to risk *publicly* hunting down a small-town college girl who, say, gains notoriety by arriving home and going straight to her local police after a nation-wide BOLO was mistakenly publicized with her face on it."

I ignored Bast's scoff and gaped at Sky. "*Seriously?* What, we *weaponize* their BOLO against them?"

"Hide in plain sight. We've gotten good at it." Sky sighed, scrubbing his hand through his curls. "We know they want you for questioning. So we give them what they're after. Talk to the police and clear up any 'misunderstanding'—and we *use* it to throw them off our trail…maybe you wouldn't have to run anymore." He paused and leaned in, expression grave. "But only if that's something you're up for, Rae. I won't lie. Bast's right. It is risky."

I nodded, staring up at him. Barely breathing. Barely daring to hope.

He held my gaze for a heartbeat, then turned to Bast. "This scanner was calibrated for tracking the communication array or the crystal interface specifically, right?"

Bast grunted and picked up his beer. "It's the best lead I've had in a while. The strongest signal. Which leads me to believe it would be one of those two devices, yes." He drank deeply, like he was trying to wash the taste of agreeing to this out of his mouth.

"Exactly." Sky lifted a shoulder. "Locating those alone justifies a trip to One Willow."

"Yeah, but we'd be walking right into License 16's hands," Bast said, throwing up his arms, nearly spilling the beer. "You want to just *offer* them buy-one-get-one-free Pladians for vivisection or what? Personally, I like my insides on the inside, thanks."

"We'll have a *plan,* Bast. Besides, as far as we know, they don't suspect I'm anything other than a *human* who was with Rae at the university and saw what she did," Sky said, turning to me. "They suspect we're traveling together. We can put a spin on that." He gestured at Bast. "And they'll have no clue who you are. You've been careful."

"Right. I *have* been," Bast said, jaw jutting to the side. His gaze was flat. "Previously. Until now."

I spun the cuff. "So we'll just pretend…what, we got scared and ran away?"

Sky released a slow breath. "We have time to figure that part out. We'll come up with a story. Something that makes sense."

"This is a shitty idea," Bast muttered, hefting his beer. "For the record, just because it's our best option doesn't make it less shitty." He used the can to gesture between himself and Sky. "We're great at hiding in plain sight because it's what we trained to do." He shook his head. "Sorry, Biscuit. But you really think you're going to waltz into the police station and lie straight to some cop you've served burgers and beer to?"

I flushed at the accuracy—Officer Sterling liked the Tuesday wing specials—but something about it *also* made me want to prove Bast wrong. "No—no, I can do this. If I go in and...and come up with a story that they believe, play into this, maybe I can help." I planted my palms on the table and started to push to my feet. "If you guys are going to end up in One Willow, anyway, then maybe I could get information—"

Several things happened at once:

My knees wobbled.

The room spun, throwing off my equilibrium.

And when I fell forward, my marked hand brushed against the oval piece of Pladian metal.

White light exploded in a silent *whump* that scalded my retinas. Energy burst free, throwing me back. I'd have fallen if Sky hadn't caught me, his arms locking me against his chest. He spun us, shielding my body with his.

Sparks popped and sizzled. The LCD screen Bast had been using shorted, spewing smoke, and he lurched away with a shouted curse. A series of flashes engulfed the room in blinding light.

I shrieked as brilliance erupted from every piece of Pladian metal on the table. My cuff lit up, too.

But it wasn't done.

Through watering eyes, I watched as the circular piece I'd touched lifted into the air. It hovered there, inches above the table-top. The shining amethyst surface shimmered and writhed. The air hummed with a faint, almost song-like resonance that made my ears pop.

Inside the light, I could've sworn something moved for an instant. Shapes. Voices whispered.

And then everything went dark.

The pieces dropped back to the table in a series of clangs. Tendrils of smoke drifted like ghostly snakes.

I blinked hard, willing away the spots dancing in my vision. Sky was breathing hard, still holding me. I lifted my marked hand. The cuff was inert once more. The white glow radiating from my palm was a less vicious version of the fire that had, seconds ago, lit up the room like a flare.

It took two tries for me to find my voice. "What…?"

"What the *hell* was that?" Bast shouted, waving away fumes. The air smelled like fried electronics. Burning plastic. "What the fuck did you do?"

"What did *I* do?" I transferred my stunned stare to him. "*I* didn't do anything. I just stood up!"

Warmth dripped down my face. Frowning, I swiped the back of my non-shining hand under my nose. It came back smeared with red. A nosebleed.

Sky's hold tightened as his eyes dropped to it and narrowed before rising to mine. His jaw flexed, like he was biting back words. Realizing I was still plastered against him, I stepped out of his arms, turning away.

And found Bast gaping at my glowing palm.

"Holy *shit*. That's what you meant by 'light up', Sky?"

Sniffing, pressing the back of my free hand to my nostrils, I uncurled my fingers and held out my palm for him to see. The glyphs stood out in stark relief, the bones and tendons rendered in shadowy lines beneath. The brilliance formed a halo against the lingering smoke.

"God. That's…" Bast leaned closer and made a face. "That's kind of creepy."

Twisting, he fumbled for one of the smoking devices on the table, mumbling to himself as he adjusted dials. Out of the corner of my eye, I caught Sky watching me carefully. Like he was checking for a reaction, a sign of what he'd seen earlier, that fugue state.

"I'm fine——" I started to say, but Bast swore, interrupting me.

"Shit. *Shit.*"

I whirled to face him as he ripped a device from the table. The handheld one he'd used to scan me when I'd first gotten to his trailer. He raised it, glancing from it to me, the sudden blanching of his tan face sending dread shooting through me.

"Raven," he said, low and tight, "whatever just happened sent a signal big enough to let every single Enil in the solar system know you're here."

I fisted my hand around the marks like I could hide the light. "*What?*"

"We need to go," Sky said. He spun and made for the pile of duffels.

"Yeah." Bast raised his head, mouth set in a grim line. "We need to go *now.*"

But I had a sinking feeling it was too late.

Chapter 29

A WHOLE NEW MEANING
TO HARVEST TIME

EVEN WITH the early morning sunlight breaking through the trees, my hand shone like a star. I fisted it between my stomach and Sky's back as he maneuvered the dirt bike through the swamp underbrush. Not that it would help matters. It wasn't like the Enil were following me by sight.

At least, I didn't think so. They were searching for a signal.

Like the one I'd inadvertently just sent out.

Was the cuff still working? There was no way of knowing. Not right now. Now, we had to focus on getting the hell out of here.

Adrenaline stung my veins. I held tight to Sky's waist as he took a sharp turn, following Bast through a pair of trees. The landscape had grown less marshy, less dense. The trees elongated into spiky cones, and pine needles cushioned the bike tires.

Despite them, my teeth still rattled in my skull when Sky hit a large root, soared for a few inches, and then jolted back down. The bags I carried thumped behind me.

I threw my other arm around Sky, clasping my hands. We couldn't afford to take this slower. The Enil were after us.

The cuff burned against my skin, getting hotter by the second.

It'd done the same thing at the motel, too. When it'd malfunctioned long enough for them to track us.

That couldn't be good. Not at all.

I craned my neck, frantically searching the patches of sky visible overhead for any glowing orbs. Nothing yet, but it was only a matter of time. My heart kicked against my ribs like a horse trying to escape a stall.

We were almost there. Bast had said there was a highway—

I recognized the electric sizzle in the air, the prickling, stinging sensation raising all the hair on my arms. I opened my mouth to cry out in warning—but it was *too late.*

Twin balls of brilliant light shot through the canopy *directly* in front of us.

My scream finally burst free as Sky braked hard, mashing me against his back. Light drenched everything, fractured, chromatic flickering bleaching the trees white and searing red behind my eyelids. Stopped my heart.

The Enil.

Sky gunned it, wrenching the handlebars, and I slid. Like he'd felt it, he snatched my leg with one hand, keeping me firmly on the seat as we veered sideways, fishtailing. Dodging the small sun swooping toward us. I shrieked again, burying my face between his shoulder blades and locking my arms around his waist.

I barely had time to gasp air into my lungs, to make sense of the blinding flashes of color and shapes.

Then the bike's tires caught, and we shot forward.

"Hold on!" Sky shouted, the words nearly lost to the wind and the engine's high-pitched whine as he returned both hands to the bike.

Oh, I was. I was holding on *tight.* To him. To my sanity.

Coral, pink, blue, and green light drenched *everything.* The gnarled trunks flashing by. Spiky branches. The staticky vibration in the air stung my skin.

But when I peeled my face from Sky's back, I caught a glimpse of a road through a gap in the trees. Just ahead. Or miles away. It was hard to tell. The tires hit a huge bump, and my stomach dropped out as we sailed high—

We hit pavement. Our tires chirped, and we bounced once and wobbled before Sky leveled us out. It was a real, asphalt *road*. A narrow, single lane.

We'd made it.

But the Enil were still directly overhead, blinding, flashing lights bearing down. I gritted my teeth at the wave of hot energy, tightening my hold on Sky.

On one side was the woods, the other a sheared-low field of some crop I didn't recognize. That terrible light made writhing shadows of the trees. Through it, I caught a glimpse of dawn-stained sky, puffy, hazy clouds, and a cute gray and white barn before Sky cranked the throttle. The back tire squealed then caught.

We arrowed forward, accelerating, but I knew without looking it wasn't enough. My skin prickled, the hair on my nape rising. The light grew more intense—

"*Rae*—" Sky shouted.

But I'd never know what he was about to say because the static charge building in the air burst, crashing down from above.

Stinging electricity crawled over the bike, snaking over my legs. I yelped and covered my head with one arm, clinging for dear life to Sky with the other as we careened in a terrifying swerve across the road. The screens and dials went dark. The engine died.

Sky swore as he wrestled the bike to the shoulder. His boots scraped asphalt, then gravel, and he managed to slow us enough that the sudden stop didn't send me flying. Ahead of us, Bast threw down his dead bike and kicked it before whirling in place, searching the skies.

Breathing hard, I twisted in the seat and did the same.

Nothing. The Enil were gone. Like they'd never been there. Only empty sky stretched in every direction. *What the hell?*

I leapt off the seat and let the bags slide to the ground. White light pulsed from my palm, and I closed my fingers around it, spinning. "Where did they go? What *was* that?"

Sky didn't answer. Head bent, he toed the clutch and cranked the bike, but it didn't turn over. I watched him shake out his hand, summon sparks, and try again, but nothing happened. "It's dead. They fried the circuits," he muttered, looking up. He was breathing hard, his hair a mess, but his eyes were trained on my shining hand. "We're stuck."

I hadn't seen a single car on this road, either. The only signs of civilization were the power lines strung along the shoulder and that distant farmhouse on the other side of a mowed-down field beside us.

"We've got bigger problems than the bikes," Bast said. He crunched over the small stones and red-tinted dirt to stand by Sky, staring at something over my shoulder.

Apprehension curling in my stomach at his grim tone, I turned to follow his gaze.

The Enil lights had reappeared in the distance. At least one had. It hung over the gray barn. The other was nowhere to be seen.

"What's it doing?" I asked, edging closer to Sky.

It wasn't moving. Just…hovering.

"*Shit*," Bast muttered.

"What…?" What was it waiting for—

A thick green beam shot down from the UFO and slammed into the barn. I gasped and staggered into Sky. His hand closed on my hip, steadying me. I barely felt it because a second later, the structure detonated in an explosion of rubble and smoke. I clapped my hands over my mouth.

The delayed boom reached us, muffled and quiet, like a distant rumble of thunder.

From inside the dust cloud, lights flashed. The same light sequence the ship cycled through. Coral, pink, green, and blue. Overhead, the orb pulsed in time with it.

The green beam vanished. The UFO hung there, soundless and eerily still.

A heartbeat passed.

Then two.

And then, from the depths of that murky, settling debris, something emerged.

A misshapen figure lumbering on two massive tree-stump legs. A pair of too-long arms dragged behind it. Spiky, horrifying, a mash-up of twisted metal. It loped across the field like a gorilla, chewing up the distance between us. The soft dawn light glinted off metal, its details impossible to make out at this distance.

Until it got closer and...

Oh my God.

It was an Enil *made out of a combine.*

They'd created a combine mech-suit. An alien farm-bot with teeth for arms. And it was coming directly for us.

"Sky!" Bast shouted, charging past. "We're gonna have to take it out."

"*Take it out?*" I hissed. "No, we should run—"

"We can't run." Sky grasped my arm and turned me to face him. "Stay here." He gave me a gentle shake, his eyes wide and dark against the morning sun. "Keep out of sight, okay? We'll take care of it."

Out of sight? There were UFOs overhead and a monster charging across the field toward us. They'd clearly already spotted us.

And I, for one, was impossible to miss, what with my spotlight of a hand. Panic bubbled up until I couldn't breathe. The memory of the university, of Sky's limp form crashing through debris, returned. I hadn't realized how close we'd come to *not* making it out then. Now I did.

How was I supposed to just sit by and *watch?*

I reached for his upper arms with shaky fingers. I *wanted* to tell him to be careful. To maybe *not* go confront the farm-equipment robot from hell, but what choice did we have?

"Stay here," he said again, punctuating it with a soft squeeze. "Okay?"

And instead of saying any of the things I wanted to, I forced myself to nod.

With one long, final look, he released me and turned. Bast waited with his eyes on the Enil stirring dust clouds on its way toward them, and together, they shifted to face the oncoming threat.

I clasped my hands together, muffling the glow from my marked palm.

Both Pladians moved with the same smooth determination. Bast had said they weren't superheroes, but watching them fall into step and stalk forward to confront the creature racing across the field, it was hard to picture them as anything else.

And here I was, cowering by the dirt bikes. Practically a blazing neon sign that read: *Hey, Enil. Right here, buddy.*

I made myself breathe in. Back out. It'd be fine. He'd be fine. I'd seen Sky face an Enil before—several times now—and he'd come out unscathed. Relatively.

But Bast was here, too. This time it was two against one. The odds were even better than before.

Even if this one was a farm-equipment demon pulled straight from the depths of Tractor Supply Company–themed horror comic.

I unclenched my jaw and rolled my shoulders. They'd be all right. I'd just stay right here like Sky had told me—

A sleek metal blur shot from the left—from the trees—streaking across the road too quickly for me to track. I opened my mouth to scream, but it was too late. It plowed directly into Bast and Sky, sending them flying.

My belated cry slipped free as they sailed through the air and hit the ground hard enough to send up twin puffs of dirt.

Stomach lurching, I surged forward, hand outstretched. I slammed to a halt when I realized what I was seeing.

It was another Enil. The second ship. It had made another suit.

There were *two.*

This one was six-legged and low to the ground, a multi-jointed, streamlined beast of black-and-silver metal, with a flat head and razor-sharp spikes flaring down its spine.

It rotated in place in a clicking, undulating reset of shining plates. Its glowing green eyes locked directly on me.

Not that I was hard to spot with my blazing palm.

The new Enil skittered forward a step in my direction. Sharp talons dug into the red dirt. Mechanical gears churned and groaned.

Past it, I saw Sky struggling upright, though he stumbled slightly from the blow. Bast wasn't far behind, shaking off dirt. And past him, the combine-creature thundered nearer by the second, lumbering over broken stalks. The closer it got, the more horrifyingly detailed all those spiky appendages became.

It would take *both* Pladians to bring that thing down.

But there were also two Enil now.

And one was coming straight for me. Moving in halting, wavy jolts like some kind of twisted mechanical caterpillar.

I didn't think. I staggered two steps to the left, back the way the thing had come. Away from Bast and Sky.

Those sickly green eyes fixed on my hand, on the muted light radiating from my clenched fist.

"Rae—don't—" I thought that was Sky's voice, far away. Telling me to stay put. To hide.

It was too late for that. For either of those things.

Then the flat-nosed monstrosity charged with terrifying speed. Garbled, mechanical noises tumbled from it. Metal plates clacked and shifted.

All thought drained.

Sky shouted again, but the other Enil was nearly on top of him and Bast. He couldn't help. He had to fight.

I did the only thing *I* could do, considering I was a puny Earthling with no lightning powers or invisibility. Not even a stick to shake. Nothing but a shining hand and, apparently, a death wish.

I ran.

And the vicious caterpillar robot from outer space gave chase.

Chapter 30

THAT'S NOT COMING OFF, IS IT?

I **PUMPED MY ARMS**, my shoes slapping the packed ground along the roadside. Breath scraped from my too-tight lungs. Sweat stung my eyes. The pain in my head pulsed in time with my pounding heart.

The trees flashed by on the lane's other side, their branches ominous and reaching. The forest we'd emerged from. Behind me, metal gears and thudding impacts in rapid succession rent the air. The Enil was gaining on me.

Too slow. I was too slow.

I didn't have a plan. I was just...running.

This was a stupid idea. I wasn't a runner. I was dangerous over short distances—like from the Oasis kitchen to the dining room—and that was about it. I was already slowing.

Mechanical roars and the snap of sizzling electricity shattered the air. Distant, but closer than I'd like. I risked looking over my shoulder.

There, in the center of the sheared-low field, Bast and Sky had engaged the other Enil. I had the briefest glimpse of two figures darting and vanishing, crackling blue bolts, and swinging, vicious arms lined with jagged, combine spikes before I faced forward.

I could only spare a glance. I had to keep going. It wasn't much use, though. I only made it maybe twenty feet before the Enil behind me sprang.

It hit me square between the shoulder blades, the impact driving me forward. The whiplash wrenched my neck hard. My bones shrieked in protest.

I managed a short scream before smashing into the ground, face-first.

Dirt forced its way into my mouth. Rocks dug into my chin, my palms, my shoulders. I rolled onto my back, sucking in a single gulp of air before a sharp-taloned foot stomped down inches from my face.

"*Shit!*" I rolled again, tried to push to all fours and scramble away, but a telltale *whir-thud-whir-thud* sounded behind me. Instead, I instinctively curled into a ball—not a second too soon. Claws gouged the soil where I'd been a second before.

Holy *shit*. This thing wasn't trying to catch me. It was trying to *crush* me.

Desperate, breath ripping out of me as a sob, I sank my fingers into the sandy dirt and dragged myself up the embankment. The Enil's second pounce narrowly missed me. It landed in the road beyond, whirled, and reared up on its hind legs. Its flat head cocked to the side. Sickly green eyes scanned me. Calculating and cold.

I crouched on the embankment's lip and stared back, gasping, sweaty hair sticking to my neck and forehead. My fisted hand blazed brightly enough to rival the sun climbing in the sky. Morning light glanced off the patchwork metal quilt of the alien monster's body. I spotted a rusted car door, a Roomba insignia, maybe a chunk of a security panel, melded and shaped over its midsection.

And claws. Shiny, vicious claws.

There was nowhere to go. It blocked the path to trees. Only open field and road remained.

The Enil dropped back to all six legs and rushed me. Its multi-plated frame shifted in a segmented ripple of blurring metal. Joints whirred and groaned as those shining feet churned over asphalt, sending up sparks. Golden sunlight flashed along the bladed spikes lining its back.

I shrieked and scrambled backward on all fours, crab-walking. Wheeled around. I somehow got my shoes under me—

I made it two steps before I tripped on the uneven ground and went down hard on my knees.

I knew before I looked back I wasn't going to make it. The Enil had already crested the embankment, claws finding easy purchase in the loose dirt. I tried to push up on trembling limbs, but it was no use.

But then, like a shadow made flesh, a dark form wavered and solidified.

Sky, wrapped in lightning, his broad shape crowned in snapping power, appeared between me and the Enil.

"Get down!" he shouted over his shoulder.

Then he smashed his hands together.

Electricity burst outward.

I threw my arms up. The air ripped apart. Burnt ozone stung my nostrils. A seething ball of light *slammed* into the Enil.

The crackling orb of light hit dead-center, throwing the killer robot back into the road like a rag doll.

It hit the blacktop and skidded in a shower of sparks and shuddering metal parts. Electricity popped and writhed across the ground in jagged webs. Power lines along the ditch swayed. The poles groaned, leaning until a cable snapped loose and slithered across the earth, arcing wildly.

It nearly clipped me, and the close call jerked me from my stupor. I screamed again, covering my head as another line broke free, and more sparks dripped down like liquid fire.

A few landed on me, but I didn't feel them.

Because something else was happening.

Shit. My hand.

My hand was *burning*.

Gasping, I splayed my marked, glowing palm. It was growing warmer by the second. Hotter even than the cuff.

A cuff...whose surface churned with lights and colors—like the Pladian equipment did when Bast activated it.

Fear sliced through me. I clutched my wrist in my other hand, frowning down, splitting my attention between it and Sky because he was yelling my name.

"Rae!"

Curled on my side, I raised my head and balled up my hand to block some of the fierce glow. My teeth chattered. Rolling, I sat up as he strode for me.

He was covered in blood, soot, and dirt. But alive. For a moment, the rush of relief I felt overpowered everything else.

"Are you okay?" he shouted over the explosion of sparks spitting from the fallen lines. From him. The nearest pole swayed precariously, and he ducked, lifting an arm and eyeing it warily. Strands of blue rippled off his frame, wafted from his shoulders. Even his eyes glowed faintly. He looked otherworldly, his face tight as he returned his attention to me, giving me a quick scan. Like he was checking for himself when I didn't answer right away.

Was I okay? Loaded question with the pulsating pain, but I nodded anyway, struggling to breathe through it. The heat was intensifying. Gritting my teeth against a groan, I tightened my grip on my wrist like I could contain it.

Something was very wrong.

Before I could speak, though, the awful, warped squeal of moving metal broke through the sizzling electrical storm. Sky stiffened, his gaze flying past me. I twisted to follow it.

The Enil was rising again. Its plating was scorched, joints jerky, but it was staggering to its feet. With a glitched-out roar, it skittered back across the road. It wasn't done yet.

But neither was Sky. He lit up again, electricity wrapping like gauntlets around both wrists. With a grunt, he leapt past me and hit the ground running. Charging forward to meet it.

I shoved to my knees, cradling my burning hand to my chest. Sky and the Enil collided in a burst of blue light and flashing metal.

But I couldn't focus on it. I hissed, doubling over at the waist as the phantom fire intensified. My chest was too tight to even cry out.

My hand hadn't hurt like this before. It shook when I lifted it. I'd lost track of the times it'd glowed, but the pain...this was new. It hadn't *hurt* since I'd first been marked.

And even worse: the burning was spreading, like lava ran beneath my skin instead of blood. Gasping, I extended my trembling arm. The cuff shone bright purple—nearly translucent, like the crystal tablet had been when I'd touched it in the lab. And below it…

Horror froze me in place.

The shapes, the markings…they were *spreading*, crawling up my forearm. I could *see* them appearing. The pearlescent shapes and symbols shimmered to life beneath my skin like etchings from a ghostly tattoo gun. The script crept higher, to my upper arm, my shoulder. A full sleeve of pearlescent alien circuitry, alive and gleaming with inner light.

What the hell?

The pain reached a fever pitch, and nausea surged. My skull squeezed from the inside out. White spots speckled my vision.

I lifted my head, blinking hard. Swaying where I knelt in the dirt.

Through the haze, I could see Sky in the road, fading, flaring, dodging jagged claws and whipping metal. The shapes swam there, too, dancing in and out of view. They'd invaded my vision.

Then whiteness crowded in, eating away the rest of my sight.

Sky was gone. So was the world. Everything.

The heat rose. My neck. My face. My chest.

Pressure bloomed behind my eyes, then popped—

A sharp snap in my sinuses, and liquid ran hot down my face. I tasted copper. Blood. The pain dulled a second later. Not because it stopped.

Because my body was going numb.

Something was *very wrong*.

I fell backward. I knew the dirt was beneath me. Rocks. The broken stalks of the field. The Earth.

But I couldn't feel them.

Above me, the sky vanished.

The incessant, all-encompassing light swallowed it all.

This…this had to be death.

The halix, not the Enil, was going to kill me after all.

Chapter 31

I'M ASSUMING THIS IS
THE SCENIC ROUTE?

I NEARLY DROWNED when I was seven.

I remembered it clearly. Even now, almost two decades later. Dustin and I were playing at Uncle Joe's pool. I'd taken his shark toy, so he'd pushed me in. A real Dustin move.

Only…I couldn't swim.

I recalled the feeling. That moment. Being weightless and somehow weighty, sinking slowly. The sparkle of the summer sun atop the surface, a glittering blur.

The brief flare of panic when I realized none of my thrashing was going to work. The odd, surreal sense of peace that followed.

Of course, Uncle Joe had snatched me out with one arm like a superhero. Dustin had gotten in *so* much trouble. I'd never stopped needling him about it. He hated it, both the reminder that he'd nearly killed me *and* the fact that I wouldn't let it go. Siblings, amirite?

Now, though, no one snatched me back from my slow descent into nothingness.

And it was still…weirdly peaceful.

A *lot* more peaceful than being shredded by claws or stomped to death by taloned toes.

The mayhem had all faded. The war machine roars, the blood in my ears, the crackle of alien electricity.

All I could hear was the sound of my breaths. My lungs working. A simple mechanic I'd never really stopped to appreciate.

Inhale. Exhale.

All I could see was brilliant, shimmering white.

That sparkling sheen reminded me of Sky's skin. His *real* skin. The skin I'd touched last night. If I was going to go the way of the dodo bird, at least I had that memory to cling to. The memory of experiencing something otherworldly. Something weird and beautiful amid all this chaos.

Of experiencing him. Even if only for a fleeting moment.

That twisted something too deep, too soft, so I pushed it aside. Other thoughts crept in.

If this was death, I'd never meet my nephew. Lisa had to be close to having him now. Dustin had better show that boy the Big Dipper. Explain what it meant. More than a collection of stars—it was a reminder of love.

God, I'd never go on my first real dig.

Never tell my mom I was sorry for putting her through this.

Never thank my brother for loving me in the quiet, constant, grudging way he always had, even if he was sometimes the worst.

Never thank Amelia for being the family that chose me.

Never tell Sky…

Well. Anything.

The white churned, swirling like the too much cream I liked in my coffee. Like a hurricane. Like a whirlpool of light, sucking me down.

I descended.

Inhale. Exhale.

And as I moved deeper, something inside me shifted, too. Cracked open. Bent.

Fell apart.

Or maybe…maybe it fell together.

Finally *clicked*.

Light within light. A knowing. There it was.

Like the light was breathing with me. Filling my lungs. Filling my mind and every single cell, the pieces that made me Raven Eloise Barrister.

And something else.

I squeezed my eyes shut, spine bowing. A current crackled through me. I might have moved, might have thrown my arms over my head if I still *had* arms…

Then everything stilled.

I blinked.

Inhale. Exhale.

Stars. There were stars everywhere. Endless, infinite, and beautiful. I floated among them. They dotted the space between nebulas, hazy clouds of space dust, and patches of velvety dark. Pinpricks of ancient light and tiny promises.

I'd never known there were so many. I mean, I'd *known*. I'd watched documentaries. Plenty of them. More than I wanted to admit. But it was *different*, seeing them like this.

Here they were. Everywhere. Everything. I was so small and also…so big. It was all inside me. Somehow.

And there—

There it was. A path. *The* path.

Inhale. Exhale.

A golden thread. It lit up across the dark, weaving between all those infinite suns. All those infinite points of light that held, in themselves, *realms*.

The path led me. So naturally, I followed. Adrift, I trailed after it, through stretches of nothingness. Through voids. Past spherical smears in the blackness. Whole solar systems, trapped in there. Suns and planets flashed like the inside of luminous marbles.

I was following that twisting, snaking line toward a rhombus-shaped constellation. One all-too-familiar. A horse's head. As I got closer, it morphed, flattening, expanding, folding in on itself. Breaking apart to become *stars*.

The thread kept going.

Past twin suns. A glowing cloud of green gas. A blue comet blazing like a fiery fist plowing through the dark.

Copper flooded my mouth, hot and metallic.

Seek us.

Find us.

Inhale. Exhale.

Toward one yellow star. A lot like one I knew.

Then past. Zooming in. Toward a planet. Blue and green and alive in a way that reminded me of being barefoot on grass and swimming in oceans.

God, it was so similar to Earth. And yet it wasn't. It might've *looked* like home but…it was alien.

It was our home.

No. I was confused. It was *theirs*.

We are the Pladians.

The pressure built. Like trapped steam, surging magma, building light behind my eyes. My ears popped. Thick, iron blood coated my tongue. Spilled out. I was *choking* on it.

A planet.

The planet.

And its path.

Holy shit. Holy shit—I'd done it. This was the map.

Inhale.

But the pressure was too much. Building inside my head until I screamed. White fire exploded from my chest, ripping outward.

Through my skin. Through my bones. Through every part of me.

It burned away everything I was—

Until only truth remained.

The map.

I saw the map.

It really had been inside me all along. I'd been trying to remember, trying to recall. It'd been *trying* to get out, but it'd been too big. Too much.

Only now it wasn't.

And as if that was its purpose, as if it'd been summoned from everywhere and nowhere *simply* to impart that understanding…

The white light cleared away.

I was still on my back in the field, staring up at the sky. Not the star-strewn, otherworldly cosmic sea I'd been swimming through. A pale blue one dotted with fluffy clouds.

My own rattling breath sounded loud.

Nothing moved. No mechanical roars. I thought I heard shouting in the distance, but everything was muffled. Like someone had stuffed cotton into my ears.

I smelled burning things. Scorched…earth?

Hell, it could be me. That burning… My body still felt hot and tingly, but I could move now. I turned my head.

Oh.

That was what was burning.

Charred ground radiated out from my body in a perfect disc. I would have chuckled at that if I'd had air in my lungs. Crop circles. Really? Kelly would love this.

But shapes in the field weren't important. The shapes in my brain, however…

I remembered.

Planets. The path. It was hard to make sense of, jumbled numbers and shapes I didn't exactly understand. But the *knowing*…it was there.

Pins and needles prickled my hands. My limbs. I wiggled my toes. Sensation was creeping back.

Just in time. I rolled onto my side and puked into the burned-up dirt, gagging. There was nothing in there, but my stomach twisted and heaved anyway.

I felt the ground vibrate a second before someone fell to their knees beside me. I was too busy throwing all my guts up to look, but I recognized the low curse. Sky's hand flattened on my back. "Are you all right? *Shit*, Raven. Talk to me. Are you okay?"

I could only imagine what he'd just seen. Blood had gushed from my nose, and when I raised a shaky hand to rub it away, it'd dried in streaks. Probably not my best look, either.

Thankfully, my stomach finally decided nothing else was in there, and with one more dry heave, I collapsed onto my bent elbow. Cold, clammy sweat coated my face. I turned my head and blinked through tears. Sky reached for me, his fingers wrapping my forearm. Like he needed to confirm I was still here. Real.

Same. I fumbled for his knee, the closest thing I could reach. He'd taken on the Enil again. He was breathing. Whole. In one piece.

That made one of us, at least. I felt…*shattered.*

"The Enil," I rasped. My throat felt like someone had taken a cheese grater to it. "Bast?"

"The Enil are taken care of," Sky said, glancing up and over me, at something I didn't have the energy to check out. "Bast's fine." Breathing hard, he tilted his head to the side, running those dark blue eyes over my face. His grip on my arm tightened. "Can you stand? We have to go."

Stand. I doubted that. Everything was still swimmy and dull.

But when I caught the distant *whump-whump* of helicopter blades and the wail of far-off sirens, I sat up. Too quickly.

I clutched my head. My heavy, wobbly head. "God."

Sky's fingers tightened for a split second before he let go. "Hang on. I'll get you."

Through tunneling vision, I saw him start to rise. I snatched his wrist, stopping him.

He paused and looked down. "We've got to…"

He trailed off when I lifted my face. His eyes brimmed with the same vast *everything* I'd just drawn inside myself. The same vast everything that'd launched me back out with a suddenness that still had me reeling. It was like I could see him clearly for the first time—even more so than seeing him with silver skin and black-on-blue eyes.

Probably because I'd just seen *Pladia.*

"I remember," I whispered, voice cracking.

Quieter, really, than it needed to be to encompass the massive, swelling balloon of knowledge, convoluted and still too overwhelming to begin to decipher.

He stared, brows twitching downward before he looked away, over his shoulder. He reached for me again, as if he was ready to drag me to my feet as he asked distractedly, "You remember what?"

"The map, Sky. I remember the map."

He froze, and his head turned my way with immeasurable slowness. His wide gaze found mine and searched it. Like he wasn't quite sure he'd heard me right.

"The map. I remember it... I can't." I squeezed my lids shut when the world began to darken. When I forced my eyes open again, clinging to consciousness with pure willpower, Sky was staring. Wonder dawned beneath the scrapes, dirt, and smudges. Like a sun, breaking through clouds. Even beaten up, he was so striking.

Like that void of endless stars had been. Galaxies.

"You remember?" he breathed, leaning in.

The thumping helicopter blades were louder than ever. Or maybe that was my heart beating in my ears.

I let out a shaky breath and forced out words. "I remember how to get you *home*."

And then everything went black.

Chapter 32

SUNFLOWERS, STARBORN, AND A STOLEN CAR 3.0

STEAM ROSE from the water spewing from the dingy gas station's faucet. Crumpling the wet paper towel I held, I leaned my palms on the sink's edge and breathed. It still hurt a little. My lungs felt tight. Raw. But at least the blinding headache had subsided to a muted ache.

My hand wasn't quite steady when I patted down my hair.

I had no idea what state we were in now. Everything had blurred together. I'd come to in yet another stolen car, careening down the highway at about Mach 6, Bast behind the wheel while Sky cradled me in the backseat. The argument over whether or not we'd be detouring to a hospital hadn't been my favorite way to wake up.

Unconsciousness had been a lot more peaceful.

I'd won, but barely.

It helped that the wooziness had faded a bit—though that hadn't stopped Sky from trying to follow me into the bathroom. Back-to-back halix-induced trances, it turned out, cranked his protective tendencies up to eleven.

I'd stood firm, though. A girl needed some alone time.

Besides, I'd survived, hadn't I? We all had.

I was okay.

Ish.

Leaning close to the cracked mirror, I used the wet paper towel to clean the last few rust-colored specks from between my nostrils and upper lip.

How my sinuses had produced that much blood, I had no idea. I'd wiped away the rest of the smears of it, along with the dirt and grime, and my skin was ashen beneath. My hazel eyes were watery and shadowed, bloodshot. And yet…a quiet relief had settled in.

I'd remembered the map. Finally. Sky had been resolute this whole time, but deep down, I'd wondered if it'd really been in there.

There was no disputing it now. Not with what I'd seen in that field. In those stars.

And now we were going home. The rush of relief made my knees weaken, and I gripped the counter harder. It meant seeing my family. Amelia.

Of course, with that came a multitude of other emotions. Complications. Home meant explaining all this. Or at least a redacted version. It meant facing the consequences. Lying even *more*.

It also meant the beginning of the end, too. I was going to help Bast translate the convoluted, confusing mess in my brain. Their way home.

And then we needed to see a man about a spaceship.

After that, Bast and Sky would be gone.

I rolled my lips into my mouth, frowning at my reflection. Tried to ignore the slow, dull pulse of pain that had nothing to do with tablet-induced visions. Maybe a little distance between me and the biggest green flag known to man or alien wouldn't be a bad thing. I was already in too deep with Sky. This could only end one way.

Heart heavy with emotions I wasn't ready to pick at, I left the bathroom and shouldered through the gas station's glass doors, squinting in the warm light. Not the brilliant white that'd taken me on a tour of the Milky Way, but golden. Familiar.

My sun. Not some alien one. The one that had been a constant my entire life.

Like breathing, sunshine was something I'd never really… thought about. I'd never really realized how much I appreciated it.

That didn't stop it from stinging my eyes, though. I started to lift my arm to block it—and stopped in mid-motion.

Speaking of being in too deep.

The sunlight glinted off the graceful glyphs and shapes embedded in my skin, whorls and faint lines tracing up my forearm, past my elbow, and disappearing beneath the sleeve of my *Mind Your Biscuits* shirt—the only anything-close-to-clean one I had left.

I had a full sleeve of alien markings. *Me.* Raven Barrister. Anyone that knew me would know I'd never in a million years have considered anything as permanent as a tattoo. Amelia had once tried to bribe me with a *Star Trek: The Next Generation* marathon in exchange for me getting matching ink with her. It'd been tempting, but I'd turned her down.

This new body art was *also* going to be fun to explain.

I sighed and let my arm fall to my side.

My attention immediately snagged on the tall, lean, dark-haired Pladian leaning against the gas station's side, his face lifted toward the sun. Sky's eyes were closed. He was basking again, enjoying the warm glow of a star he'd only discovered he loved since landing here. The gold light cast hollows beneath his high cheekbones.

Watching him, that quiet ache crept back into my chest, nestling in. Secret and safe, as long as I kept it tucked away.

As if he felt my gaze on him, Sky's lids cracked, and when he saw it was me, they flew wide and he pushed off the wall. His lips tilted into a faint curve in greeting, though I didn't miss the careful way he took me in. Likely double-checking I wasn't going to faint again.

Understandably. I wasn't entirely sure, either. My head felt a little floaty still.

But I managed a return smile. "Ready?"

With a nod, Sky fell into step with me, sliding his hands into the pockets of his sweatpants. The rusty brown van—our newest acquisition—waited in a parking spot in the shade. Bast was nowhere to be seen.

I was ready to sleep in my own bed and wear clean clothing. To hug my mom and deal with the inevitable Amelia rant.

"How's your head?" Sky asked as we walked. There was a hint of that bartender voice there. The Pladian control. Like he was just as uncertain as I was where we stood. Like his guard was up.

I tried not to let it bother me.

"Better," I said as we reached the van's front. Unwilling to give up the warmth quite yet, especially knowing the fall chill would have settled in back home, I leaned on the grille. We were waiting on Bast, anyway. Sky joined me, crossing one long leg over the other and bracing his elbows on the hood.

"That's going to take some getting used to," Sky said quietly, a strange note to the words. I glanced over to find him studying the marks on my arm with a frown. "Seeing you covered in Pladian writing."

I'd prefer to be covered in Pladian.

"Yeah." Fighting a flush at the wayward thought, I lifted them to the light again, pursing my lips. "It's pretty in an…almost-melted-my-brain kind of way."

"Right." His soft sniff held very little amusement. "Are you ready for this?"

I let my arm drop and twisted toward him. "To go home?"

"Yeah." He searched my eyes. "And everything that's going to entail."

There was no easy path out, here. But at least this way, I'd be done running.

And it would be the end of hurry up and wait.

Swallowing hard, I nodded and eyed the markings, turning my arm over to follow the curving shapes. "I'm ready, yeah."

Sky didn't say anything for a moment. Long enough that I raised my head. He was watching me with a faint frown. Worry. I'd come to recognize it.

To hide the swift thud reverberating in the region of my heart, I turned away and tipped my face to the sun, channeling my inner sunflower. Its warmth kissed my cheeks and glowed red behind my lids.

It *was* nice.

Maybe it was okay to just bask in the now. Because things were complicated enough, and dwelling too much on a future that wasn't guaranteed couldn't do anything but bring heartache. *Especially* when it came to the alien beside me.

The silence stretched out, and I could almost hear the unspoken words between us—

"Well, if you two are done meditating or communing with the hood ornament—or whatever the hell is going on here—let's hit the road. Oh, and shotgun."

I opened my eyes to shoot Bast a flat look over my shoulder, one he responded to with a wink before he opened the van's front passenger door and leapt in. The vehicle rocked, and I turned back around with a sigh.

"Looks like it's time," Sky said, pushing off the grille and gesturing at me to go ahead of him. Despite the fact that they had no texture, I rubbed the marks on my arm as I slid past him. He fell into step behind me, his presence tingling along my spine.

The awareness was as strong as ever. Even stronger now that I'd been naked with him. After everything we'd been through.

At least I had plenty to focus on. Distractions.

The Enil were still out there, and so was License 16. I had, like, six midterms to make up, shifts to cover. I'd missed my rent payment to Bob, who was going to be *way* more pissed over the fact that I'd disappeared than that I owed him money.

Couple that with the fact that the police and the government were going to have *so* many questions—and *I* was tasked with throwing them off our trail.

Anxiety churned, and I did my best to push it down.

I stopped short when Sky brushed past me and opened the sliding passenger door for me.

"Here," he said, offering a hand.

"Oh." For some reason, heat crept into my cheeks. "Thanks."

I placed my unmarked hand in his. His fingers closed over mine, and I tried to ignore the flutter in my stomach as I allowed him to help me into the car.

But then he didn't let go of my hand.

When I looked back in surprise, he held my stare. Serious now.

He gave me a brief squeeze, a lingering pressure. Warm. Steady. Just like the sunlight had been. Just like he'd been this whole time. Despite everything.

Then he let go, and he was shutting the door after me, moving toward the driver's side.

Pulse a little unsteady, I settled into the bench seat.

"You should know," Bast said, twisting to look back at me, "I still think this isn't Sky's best plan."

"What isn't?" I focused on buckling in. "Going home?"

Bast huffed, kicking a dirty boot up onto the dash. If this had been our car, I'd have made a comment. But alas…

I was getting far too comfortable with stolen vehicles.

"I just think we've been fine on the road this long." Bast shifted his broad shoulders under his leather jacket. He rubbed his palm over his short hair. In the sunlight, it glinted like burnished gold. "What's a little longer?"

Sky sighed as he started the van. Classic rock blared out of the speakers—also Bast's doing—and Sky turned it down a notch before speaking.

"One of us has to go to One Willow, anyway. We've been over this." He put the van in reverse and backed up. "And besides, running forever isn't feasible. Circumstances have changed."

Circumstances, as in I was here now, the Enil were circling closer, and the Pladians no longer had a spaceship. All of which could be blamed on me. I turned my face toward the window.

"If you say so." Bast twisted again, waiting until I turned my head his way. "And you. You really think your friend Amelia is the best bet when it comes to planning a homecoming?" He leaned an elbow on the armrest, arching a dark brow. "The very same one who sent sixty unanswered text messages? She sounds *real* stable, Biscuit."

I rolled my eyes. "For the last time, she's my best friend, and I disappeared without a trace. She was *worried*. Besides, things were weird the last time we saw each other…" She'd seen me with Sky, and we were arguing over… nothing, really. It'd been right before the Enil had attacked the university.

I could only imagine what her reaction was going to be when she learned the truth about all this. Grimacing, I glanced at Sky in the rearview mirror. His eyes flicked my way, and I gave my attention back to Bast.

"She's someone I trust completely. She'll be able to fill us in on what's going on in One Willow—and she's got connections." I sat back, crossing my arms. "She's our best bet."

"Whatever you say," Bast muttered. "Just as long as she stays out of my way. I don't need another human complicating this mission."

I nearly snorted. He had nothing to worry about there. I eyed his torn jeans and the way he'd turned the classic rock channel back up so he could play air guitar to the hair metal song. Never in a million years. Amelia would eat him for breakfast chased with a mimosa.

I leaned my temple against the headrest and watched the highway fly by. Another road trip, but this one I was okay with. Despite this stolen van and the fact that the now-singing Bast couldn't carry a tune to save his life.

Because I was going home.

And whatever came next, I'd face it. I glanced at Sky in the rearview mirror, the way his dark eyes were trained on the road. Focused. Then, like he sensed me, he blinked, his gaze shifting to seek mine, and I hastily looked away. Back out my window.

Even if that meant facing goodbye.

Chapter 33

...OR SOMETHING.

Amelia

Later that day

WHEN THE REDIAL didn't go through, I jabbed the *end call* button and tossed the phone down on my marble countertop, shoving it away with a disgusted scoff.

Then I picked up the cabernet bottle and dumped the rest of it into my glass, shaking it to get every last drop out. After all, it *was* a 1979 Château Lafleur, room-temperature. I'd swiped it at the last meeting my father liked to pretend was a family dinner.

I needed it.

When the glass was full to the brim, I picked it up and side-eyed the seemingly innocent phone. It was silent now. Screen dark.

"What the *hell*, Rae?" I whispered, tapping the glass with a manicured nail.

I'd spent the better part of this week worried out of my goddamn mind about her. I'd gone full Nancy Drew. Scoured her socials. Talked to all her other friends. Her classmates. Her coworkers. Dustin. Her mom. Mama B had been beside herself, which hadn't made me feel any better.

I'd even made myself deal with *Kelly*, for God's sake. If *that* didn't convey my desperation…

It wasn't enough that the entire town had gone insane. Even my father, who was knee-deep in defense contracts, didn't have answers as to why soldiers in unmarked military vehicles were patrolling One Willow's streets. Or what the hell was going on at the base. Why the university was mysteriously on lockdown. Classes were supposedly starting up again next week, but I had a feeling that was just for show.

And now this cryptic, stilted phone call from my best friend, who'd up and disappeared for *days*.

Days. Without as much as a single text message.

I'd been checking all week. Her last location ping had been that very same university now being patrolled by agents immune to charm *and* my last name. I suspected something very, very weird was going on.

And now? After *that* phone call? I was positive.

Sipping the overfilled glass of wine before I spilled it, I leaned my elbows on my kitchen counter and frowned at the plate-glass windows across the room.

That vague, short conversation hadn't helped anything.

"Meet me at the place Brendon Henderson bought us beer the first time," she'd said. *"Don't tell anybody."*

She'd given a time and that was it. Then a dial tone.

I knew the place. The shitty gas station between Maryville and One Willow. It was in the middle of nowhere. We'd been seventeen when Brendon had gotten us the six-pack, and we'd each taken one mouthful of cheap beer before spitting it out and deciding it was the most disgusting thing we'd ever tasted.

No one else knew that story. It had to be her.

Curiosity gnawed at me, along with a healthy surge of annoyance. She couldn't just come out and tell me what the hell was going on? What, was this some kind of "this line isn't safe" bullshit? I scowled into my wine, glancing at the phone over the top of the glass.

Her call *had* come from a weird number. It hadn't even looked real. My cell wouldn't dial it back.

Something wasn't right.

But that'd been Rae's voice. The gas-station story… It'd been *Rae*. She hadn't *sounded* scared. Weird, yes. Frightened, no.

I also found it too much of a coincidence that hot bartender of hers had *also* missed shifts at Oasis, according to pink-is-my-color-and-cardboard-is-my-personality Kelly. Even if his had been supposedly due to illness and covered by the other bartenders. I pursed my lips and shook my head.

I had suspicions. Especially considering the last time I'd seen my best friend, he'd been with her, and things had been tense. To say the least.

It didn't matter whether Sky Acosta was with her now or not. Either way, I'd be there at the gas station in the morning. I was seeing Rae tomorrow. Getting to the bottom of this mystery.

And I'd have a few choice words for my best friend about vanishing off the face of the planet.

Not *literally*. I snorted into my wine glass, gulping down a healthy amount. At least there was *that*.

At least she hadn't been abducted by aliens or something.

Want more aliens, angst, and adventure?

Sky, Rae, Bast, and Amelia will be back very soon for the last installment of the *It's Definitely Not Aliens* trilogy (though there may or may not be surprises in store). It's projected for late summer/fall of this year!

Make sure to visit www.elledeyesso.com and join the newsletter mailing list to get all the news first. As always follow me on all the socials, too, to stay up-to-date and do all the chatting! I'm way more active on there than I should be.

IF YOU LIKED THIS BOOK, PLEASE CONSIDER LEAVING A REVIEW! I am grateful for each and every one.

Thanks so much for reading, Earthlings! See you soon.

Acknowledgments

Where to start on acknowledgements…!

I'm not going to lie, friends! This book was hard! The whole process! So. Many. Rewrites. Rae, Sky, and Bast went through the wringer, and so did their wrangler. This may be the most difficult book I've ever written, and y'all, I've written a lot of books. The feels in this one. *Whew.*

I need to start by thanking my writer buds:

The CDH gang. You…you are simply the BEST. You keep me laughing every day. Our hypothetical Chipotle dates will live on in infamy. So glad we found one another. I don't know what I would've done without you this last year. You guys have become family. All hail CD.

And, of course, the Mars Needs Writers Discord server. You all keep me either sane or insane, depending on the day or necessity. It's really hit or miss, and I wouldn't have it any other way. It has become a little sanctuary of weirdos. Thank you.

Also to Lauren, my friend on the other side of the world. Still hate the time difference but appreciate you.

Reyna. Pet Poe and Oryx for me. Wish you were closer or we had a portal or a dragon or something.

My indie author crew. All of you. So many different folks in different genres and different paths. Seriously, I lucked out when I started down this road. The connections I've made have been incredible. I am so lucky to have each and every one of you to chat with, seek advice from, or just hang out with while we muddle through this thing.

My "real life" friends. You are all the best. The support, the love, the cheerleading. I have the best people. The way you've rallied around me, even the ones who don't read my books, has meant so much.

Diane. The very best beta reader. Really, you started it all with our Roswell marathons. Max and Liz (really, Michael and Maria because, come on, enemies to lovers?) were the OG. Thank you for being my ride-or-die, but make it an X-wing? And Mom. Since that kitten book. I hope you enjoyed this and skipped **those** parts, Mother.

Also, please thank Dad. I really hope he's not reading this, but without him, I never would've fallen in love with writing *or* sci-fi like I did, and this lore would not have existed.

Danielle Fine. Seriously, you shredded this book to pieces in the most loving way, and I like to think we built it, brick-by-brick, into something so much better. I would be a hot mess without your digital red pen. Thank you for being the very best there is. Sorry about the formatting fiasco.

My ARC and Street Team! You are the MVPs of this indie world, and I don't exaggerate when I say that.

My husband. You are the best parts of me. Thank you for believing in me even when I don't, for dealing with my emotional roller-coaster even when I tried to jump off it, the late-night scrambles, the marathon edits, the frantic self-doubt spirals, the highs, the lows, and the everything in between. You make everything possible. I love you more than I ever thought myself capable of loving another person.

And just so you know. Even if you were silver…*always*. *awkward winky face emoji*

I have to close with this, though:

<u>You, reader</u>.

When I wrote Stardusted, I had NO IDEA what to expect. Maybe a few sales, some friends picking it up out of curiosity, a few people grabbing it because they thought it was funny I wrote about hot aliens. And, you know, me to have a shelf trophy to look at and be proud of. I mainly wrote it because it was fun, and I wanted to tell the story.

I did not expect what happened to happen. For it to actually do something. For people to read it and connect with it and… well, *like* it.

The fact that people out there read my weird, crazy story about hot undercover aliens and now you're back for more humbles me beyond belief. Thank you. I am crying right now as I write this. I wish I had words to express how it feels that you finished this book and are here with me right now, too, in the It's Definitely Not Aliens universe. YOU, reader, are a *dream come true*. Connecting with you has brought me joy I can't begin to describe. Each of you holds a special place in my heart. I love hearing from you, too, so please reach out and talk to me.

Thank you. You make this daydream a reality.

See you next time.

All my weirdo love,

Elle

About the Author

ELLE DEYESSO writes sci-fi and fantasy romance and has a soft spot for sarcasm, slow burns, and complicated characters who banter their way through problems.

Her stories blend romance, action, and out-of-this-world adventure.

An avid lover of all things sci-fi and fantasy, Elle lives in the Midwest with her family and is powered by iced coffee and binge-reading every genre imaginable. When her nose isn't buried in a book, she enjoys video games, cooking, hiking, and convincing herself she can keep a houseplant alive.

It's Definitely Not Aliens is her debut, a romcom series full of spacey swoon, slow-burn to spice, and hot undercover aliens totally worth phoning home about. 👽

You can find her on Instagram, TikTok, and Facebook, and she absolutely wants to hear from readers.

For more sneak peeks, make sure to sign up for the newsletter on her website, *www.elledeyesso.com.*

www.ingramcontent.com/pod-product-compliance
Lightning Source LLC
Chambersburg PA
CBHW071248250626

47163CB00002B/373

* 9 7 9 8 9 9 3 2 5 2 2 1 6 *